**Also ava**

Gone South Series

*Sweet Gone South*
*Scrimmage Gone South*
*Simple Gone South*
*Secrets Gone South*
*Santa Gone South* (novella)
"Slugger Gone South" in *Take Me Out* (short story)

**Nashville Sound Series**

*Face Off: Emile*
*Slap Shot: Bryant*
*High Stick: Jarrett*
*Body Check: Thor*

Stay tuned for the next book in the
Good Southern Women series,
*Smooth As Silk,* from Alicia Hunter
Pace and Carina Press, coming April
2022.

In memory of Justin Provencher.
Rest easy, baby.

# SWEET AS PIE

# Prologue

*Hell on Earth.*

Pro hockey defenseman Jake Champagne understood the meaning of the phrase, but had never lived it until that March day at the end of his second season with the Nashville Sound.

He woke to the sound of pounding and the smell of hockey stench. At first, he thought the pounding was in his head but, as the fog cleared, he realized someone was intent on getting into his hotel room. When he opened his eyes, the first image he saw was a blurry half-empty bottle of Pappy Van Winkle bourbon. No wonder he couldn't see straight. He was usually a beer guy, but special nights called for special liquor and last night had been spectacular—though not in a good way.

Oh, no. Not at all. After hoisting the cup two years in a row, his team had gone four up and four down in the playoffs. Plus, it was cold here in Boston and he hated the cold, hated the snow. You wouldn't catch any snow on the ground in March in the Mississippi Delta—or any other time either. That was just one of the things he missed about home.

The pounding on the door became more intense just as a warm body rolled over next to him.

Hellfire and brimstone. It was all coming back now, and that was where the hockey stench was coming from. She was wearing his nasty jersey, had insisted on wearing it while they made love. He laughed under his breath. *Made love.* Ha.

He pulled on his sweatpants and caught sight of the clock as he crossed the room. Five forty-one freaking a.m.! The team plane didn't leave until ten o'clock. He was going to kill somebody—probably Robbie. His best friend most likely hadn't been to sleep yet. The last time he'd seen him, Robbie'd been doing shots with a red-head, the companion of the blonde in his own bed. He jerked open the door. "What do you want?"

Not Robbie. It was Sound staff member Oliver Kle-packi, who frowned at the tone of Jake's voice. "Sparks." He used Jake's nickname.

Dread washed over Jake. This man was not in the habit of knocking on hotel doors at this hour. In fact, from the looks of him, he had just rolled out himself. "Sorry, Packi. Is something wrong?"

"You need to call your mother."

After closing the door, Jake reached for his phone with shaking hands. He'd turned it off last night, even before coming back to the room with his latest charming companion. Not wanting to talk to anyone who might want to commiserate over the loss to the Colonials or the minutes he'd spent in the penalty box because he'd showed his ass on the ice for no good reason, he'd taken the landline phone off the hook.

But that seemed small now. Something bad had happened. Christine Jacob Champagne was a Mississippi Delta Southern belle who took breakfast in her room every morning at eight o'clock. She spoke to no one before then. In any case, she wasn't the type to hunt down her grown son like a dog who needed his worm medicine.

He didn't call right away. There had to be a clue on his phone, and he couldn't take another breath without knowing if his dad and sister were okay.

Fourteen missed calls, five voice mails, and six text messages later, he knew. His uncle Blake—the man who had put him on skates at four years old—had had a heart attack.

And he was dead. The texts and voice mails hadn't said so. His mother would never leave that in a message, but he had to be. Otherwise she wouldn't have hunted him down in Boston at this hour.

He started to call, but paused and looked down at the woman in his bed. His mother would probably know she was here, would probably be able to smell her through the phone. He went into the bathroom, quietly drawing the door shut behind him before he dialed.

"Darling boy." Christine answered immediately.

"Uncle Blake?" he said.

There were tears in her voice. "I know how you loved him."

*Loved.* Jake hadn't realized that he'd still held out a miniscule bit of hope until his mother spoke in the past tense. He had known before he even made the call, but—at the same time—how was it possible?

"So hard to believe…only forty-seven…" Christine's voice trailed off.

"Forty-six." Jake was very sure of that. Jake had been four and Blake twenty-five—just the age Jake would be come October—when Blake had moved to the Delta to work at Champagne Cotton Brokers. Not long after, he had married Christine's younger sister.

"Forty-six," Christine said. "You're right, of course. Would've been forty-seven in June."

*Would've been.* Cruel words.

There were things he should be saying, questions he should be asking to prove he wasn't an asshole. "Aunt Olivia?" He said the words, but his thoughts were on himself.

In a land where football was king and baseball crown prince, Blake had taught Jake to skate by standing behind him, hands on his waist. Blake claimed trainer walkers that beginning skaters typically used to steady themselves encouraged bad posture and technique.

"She's resting," Christine said. "At least I hope she is."

"I hope so, too." The words were hollow. *Hope* wasn't much of a word right now.

Blake had showed him the movie *Miracle on Ice* and bought him a souvenir 1980 U.S. Olympic Hockey Team puck. At the time Jake didn't understand that the puck had not been in the actual game—or for that matter, that *Miracle on Ice* wasn't actual footage of the famous Soviet/U.S. match, or that the game had been played years before his birth. And later it didn't matter. By then, the puck was his constant companion and good luck charm.

"Adam and Nicole?" Jake asked after his two teenage cousins. Even after Blake and Olivia had children, he had not forsaken his bond with Jake.

"About like you'd expect," Christine said.

But what was that? How did anyone know what to expect?

*Expect.* Things would be *expected* of him by people who seemed to instinctively know the correct behavior for every situation known to man. "Naturally, I'm coming home." For the first time today, his voice sounded sure and strong.

And suddenly, that was what he wanted, all he wanted—to be home in Cottonwood, Mississippi. He wanted to drive down Main Street, past the bakery, the hardware store, and the drugstore that still had a soda fountain. He wanted to go to the house that been home to three generations of Champagnes, sleep in his childhood room, and smell the bacon and coffee that Louella had made for his family every morning for thirty years. He wanted to take his grandmother to lunch at the Country Club and hit a bucket of balls with his dad.

But Christine was talking, interrupting the flow of his thoughts. "No, Jake. No."

"I don't need to wait until morning," he assured her. "I won't be too tired to drive. I'll pack a few things and get on the road as soon as I can. I'll get into Nashville around noon and be home by bedtime—well before." Certainly in time to stop at Fat Joe's and pick up a sack of famous Delta tamales.

"No, Jake! Listen to me." Christine began to speak very clearly as if she were speaking to a child. "Do *not* come home. We're all flying out tonight to Vermont. You need to go there."

"Vermont?" Did they have tamales in Vermont?

"Yes. You *do* remember that Blake is from Vermont, don't you?"

"Well, yes, but…" Of course he remembered. Vermont was the whole reason Blake had played hockey as a kid, the reason he'd taught Jake to love hockey. But it didn't make any sense. Cottonwood had become Blake's home.

Christine seemed to read his mind. "He has—*had* family there. His father is unwell and unable to travel under the best of circumstances. The funeral will be there. You need to go to Vermont. We've reserved a block of rooms."

So, no home. More cold weather. Probably snow. But there would be people from home. That was something.

"Who's going?" he asked. "Besides y'all, Olivia and the kids?"

"About who you would expect—your grandmother, your sister, Anna-Blair and Keith, your aunt—"

"Evie? Is Evie going?" He cut her off. The mention of his godparents, Anna-Blair and Keith Pemberton, naturally led to thoughts of their daughter.

"No," Christine said. "She can't get away from work."

Evie had opened a pie shop in a fancy-pants section of Birmingham, Alabama, a few years back. There had been a time when she would have—pie shop, or no pie shop—crawled over glass to get to him if he needed her. However, that was before he'd let life get in the way and hadn't bothered to take care of their friendship. But he couldn't think about that right now. He had to get to Vermont.

"Okay, Mama. I'll go there from here. Text me the particulars and I'll book a flight. Or rent a car and drive. Yeah. Probably that." It would be faster, and not nearly as annoying as dealing with a commercial airline.

"All right. Text me your ETA when you know. Your dad wants to talk to you. I love you, Jake."

"I love you, too, Mama."

"Son!" Marc Champagne's big booming voice was the next thing he heard. Jake could tell in that one spoken syllable that his dad was driving this heartbreak wagon, bossing everyone around, and making them like it. He couldn't fix it, but by damn, he would make it go as easy as he and his money could. If Marc had his way, he'd probably move Olivia and the kids into the Champagne ancestral home.

"Hello, Dad."

"This is bad business, Jake. Bad."

"As bad as it gets," Jake agreed.

"Listen." Marc always said that before he said something important, even when the person he was speaking to was already listening. "I'll buy you a plane ticket back to Nashville from Vermont."

Jake opened his mouth to remind his dad that he could afford his own ticket. But that wasn't necessary. Marc knew how much the Sound paid him.

"Sure, Dad. Thanks." Jake hung up and walked back out to the bedroom. He needed to get that woman—Meghan, if he recalled correctly—out of here. Good-time girls had no place in bad times.

It was when he put out a hand to shake her awake that he saw it—the glint of gold on the ring finger of her left hand. Just when he thought he couldn't feel any sicker, his stomach bottomed out. Since his divorce two years ago, he'd taken raising hell to a whole new art form, but there was one line he had never crossed: he did not sleep with married women.

"Hey." He poked her shoulder.

"What? Stop!" When she jerked the covers over her head, he saw that the ring was not a wedding band after all, but some kind of little birthstone ring that had turned around on her finger. He didn't feel much relief in that. He hadn't asked, hadn't even thought about it. That was a first. And if he had been willing to cross that line, what was next? His eyes darted to his bedside table. He was relieved to see an open box of condoms there, though it didn't negate the panic and shame coursing through him. But this was no time for self-refection. "Hey, Meghan." He pulled the covers off her head. "You have to wake up."

She opened one mascara-smudged eye, seemed to consider, and decided to smile.

"Hello there, Southern boy. Come back to bed."

"I can't."

She sat up. "Sure you can. I want to see if you speak Southerner as good in the morning as you do at night." She ran a hand up his thigh.

"No. Really. You've got to go." He moved her hand.

"Why? What time is it?" She frowned and picked up her phone. "What the fuck! Do you *know* what time it is?"

"I do. I'm sorry. But you have to go." He was repeating himself, but apparently it was necessary.

She pouted. "I thought you liked me."

"I did. I do. But you still have to go."

She threw her legs over the side of the bed. He thought he had won, but she was relentless. "All right," she said with a sigh. "I'm just going to jump in the shower. Why don't you order breakfast? I've never had room service before."

And he was done trying to trot out his Mississippi Delta Cotillion manners—not that he'd been very successful. "And you aren't going to have it now." She didn't deserve it, but he was out of time, out of patience, out of everything except the raw feelings marching through his head and heart. He reached for his wallet and peeled off two hundred-dollar bills. "Buy yourself some breakfast and an Uber."

Meghan looked at him like he was a snake recently escaped from a leprosy colony. He couldn't blame her. She had signed up for a little uncomplicated fun and had woken up to a complicated man in a complicated situation.

When she didn't say anything, he peeled off another hundred. "Ubers are expensive."

"*You* are an asshole," she said.

He nodded. "I am that."

She snatched the money from his hand, gathered up her clothes and boots from the floor, and stomped to the door. With her hand on the knob she turned and hissed, "I'm keeping this jersey."

He nodded. "Please. I want you to have it." It was a good thing it reached her knees because apparently she couldn't stand him another second, not even long enough to put on her jeans.

Understandable. He couldn't stand himself.

Jake needed concrete evidence there was a time when he didn't drink a six-pack every night and sleep with women who were more interested in his jersey than in him—needed to remember a time before he'd lost so many pieces of himself that he didn't know who he was anymore.

He didn't want to be a man Uncle Blake would have been ashamed of.

But if things didn't change, he was going to become the kind of person that everyone hated as much as he was beginning to hate himself. He loved the Sound, loved his teammates, but it would be easier to start over somewhere else with people who didn't naturally assume he was going to raise hell.

His scalp prickled at the thought.

*Start over. Leave Nashville.*

Leave the Sound? Maybe he ought to. The team had enough heavy-hitting veteran players that he was still the new kid in town. It would be years before he skated first line in Nashville, and who knew if he had years?

Blake certainly hadn't.

Jake picked up his phone again and dialed his agent, Miles Gentry, who answered immediately, despite the early hour. "Jake! I was just—"

"Trade me," he blurted out.

"What?"

"Trade me. Hopefully to somewhere I can skate first line. But it *has* to be a place where I don't have to buy a snow shovel. I don't care where. California. Texas. Florida. Arizona. Just get me the hell out of Nashville."

"Are you sure about this?" Miles asked.

"As sure as the fact that death is coming for us all."

Miles was quiet for a moment. "How do you feel about that new expansion team down in Birmingham? The Alabama Yellowhammers."

Right. He hadn't considered the new Birmingham team. It was still in the South—and Evie lived there. Maybe he could get their friendship back on track. Those were pluses, but the team was an unknown quantity. "Talk to me," Jake said.

"They've asked about you. I was waiting until the playoffs were over to tell you."

"Playoffs aren't over. Just over for the Sound—and me."

"Semantics," Miles said. "So—Alabama. Brand-new state-of-the-art practice facility. Drew Kelty is the head coach." Jake didn't really know him other than by name, but Kelty had plenty of pro hockey experience—as a player and a coach. "From what they said, I would think first line is an excellent bet. Any interest?"

And Jake said something neither he, nor any other Ole Miss fan, had ever said before. "Roll Tide."

# Chapter One

*Five months later*

Evans Pemberton considered the dough on the marble slab in front of her.

What was wrong with pie in this country was the crust. No one made quality crusts anymore or thought about which kind of crust went best with what pie. Butter crusts were wonderful with fruit pies, but too rich for pecan pies. Savory pies needed a sturdy crust, but it was important to get the right balance so as not to produce a soggy mess. A bit of bacon grease gave crusts for meat pies a smoky taste, and Evans liked to add a pinch of sage for chicken pot pies. Crumb crusts had their place, too.

As did Jake Champagne, she thought, as she gave the ball in front of her a vicious knead. And his place was now apparently *here*. He was going to land in town any day, any hour.

He hadn't spoken to her in almost three years. Sure, back in March, he had texted to thank her for the funeral flowers she'd sent when his uncle died and apologized for not making more of an effort to keep in touch. According to her business manager, Neva, he'd also stopped by the shop a month later when he'd come to Laurel Springs to sign a lease on a condo, but Evans had been in New York taking a mini puff pastry course.

She didn't know why she was thinking about him anyway. Who knew if he would even try to contact her again? He had abandoned her once after a lifetime of friendship. There was no reason to think, despite the text and drop-in, that anything would change.

"You're looking at that dough like you don't like it," said a woman behind her.

"I don't." She turned and handed her friend, Ava Grace Fairchild, an apron and chef's hat. Ava Grace was no chef, but Evans had given up on trying to keep her out of the pie shop kitchen, so she'd settled on doing what she could to make Ava Grace acceptable should the health inspector make a surprise visit to Crust. "Though I suppose it's not so much that I don't like it. I don't *know* it."

"I thought you knew every dough." Ava Grace tied the apron over her linen dress and perched the hat on the back of her head so as not to disturb her loose chestnut curls. She looked like a queen dressed as a chef for Halloween.

"I don't know this one." Evans placed her hand on the dough. Normally, she wouldn't think of putting her warm hand on pastry dough, but this was a hot water pastry so it was warm to begin with.

Ava Grace slid onto a stool and crossed her long, perfect legs. "What makes this one different?"

"It's for a handheld meat pie with rutabagas, potato, and onions. The crust has to be sturdy but not tough. That's tricky." She gave the dough another vicious slap. "They're called Upper Peninsula pasties, from Michigan."

"Never heard of them," Ava Grace said.

"Claire has, and she wants to feed them to the new hockey team on their first day of training camp tomorrow."

Ava Grace's mouth twisted into a grin. "For a silent partner, Claire isn't very quiet, is she?"

Evans laughed. Ava Grace would know. Claire was her "silent" partner, too. "Well, she never promised to be quiet."

"That's a promise she couldn't have kept. Why is she so set on these little pies?"

"You know as well as I do that Claire doesn't have to have a reason, but she says most of the team is from up North, so we should give them some Northern comfort food."

Evans had not pointed out to Claire that not all hockey players would associate these pasties with home. She knew of one in particular who would need barbecue pork, hot tamales, and Mississippi mud pie to make him think of home. Claire wasn't an easy woman to say no to, even if Evans had been willing. Saying no had never been Evans's strong suit, which was why she was catering this lunch when she just wanted to make pies.

Evans had thought it would be years before she could fulfill her dream of having her own shop, until Claire had taken her under her wing. Now Crust was thriving.

The old-money heiress had excelled in business, and successfully played the stock market rather than living off her inheritance. A few years ago she had decided to help young women start their own new businesses.

Evans and Ava Grace were two of Claire's girls, along with Hyacinth Dawson, who owned a local bridal shop.

"Claire must really like hockey," Ava Grace said.

"I don't think it's that, so much as she likes a project and loves the chase." Claire was one of several locals who owned a small part of the Yellowhammers. Her uncle and nephew had been the ones to bring the team here, but Claire had quickly formulated a plan to turn Laurel Springs into Yellowhammers Central. "She knows a bunch of rich hockey players are going to live and spend their money somewhere and she wants it to be here." She had convinced the owners to build a state-of-the-art practice rink and workout facility in Laurel Springs, renovated the old mill into upscale condos, lobbied for more fine dining and chic shops, and turned the old Speake Department Store building into a sports bar and named it Hammer Time—all to welcome the new team.

"It looks like she's getting her way," Ava Grace said. "Everywhere you look there's a gang of Lululemon-wearing men in Yellowhammer ball caps."

"We should be thankful for them," Evans said. "Sponsoring our businesses was part of her master plan to make the area appealing to the team. Had to be."

Ava Grace pulled at one of her curls. "I'm sure she knows what she's doing. I've lived here all my life, and I've never known Claire to fail," she said wryly. "At least not yet." Of the three businesses Claire had backed, Ava Grace's antique and gift shop was the only one losing money. Claire insisted that was to be expected in the beginning, but it was still a sore subject. "Anyway." Ava Grace clapped her hands together like she always did when she wanted to change the subject. "Hockey in Birmingham. Hockey people here in our little corner of the world. I've never even been to a hockey game. Have you?"

And here it was. She'd never mentioned Jake to anyone in Laurel Springs, not even Ava Grace and Hyacinth, who were her best friends. And she was loath to do it now. What if he ignored her as he had the last few years?

"I have. A guy I've known all my life is a hockey player." She wasn't about to mention that he'd been the best-looking thing in Cottonwood, Mississippi—plus he had that hockey-mystique thing going for him in a world where most of the other boys played football and baseball. "His parents and mine are best friends, so we went to a lot of his games when I was growing up. After college, he went on to play for the Nashville Sound, but he's going to play for the Yellowhammers now."

Ava Grace widened her eyes. "Really? He's coming here?"

"If nothing has changed since the last time I talked to my mother. I haven't talked to him in a while." Technically not a lie—condolence texts didn't count as talking.

"Is he married?"

"Not anymore." She slammed her fist into the ball of dough.

Ava Grace's eyes lit up and Evans knew what was coming. Ava Grace was all but engaged and was always looking for romance for everyone else. "Is this an old boyfriend?"

"No! Of course not." She hadn't meant to sound so vehement.

Ava Grace narrowed her eyes. "You never went out with him a single time?"

"No. Never entered my mind." If she'd been Pinocchio, her nose would be out the front door. There had been this one time at a holiday party—for just a fraction of a minute—when Evans had thought he'd looked at her differently, when she'd been sure that Jake was finally going to ask her for a date. But they'd been interrupted, and the moment had passed. To this day, she never saw a sprig of holly or heard a Christmas bell without the memory of the humiliating disappointment slamming against her rib cage, driving the breath out of her.

"It's a new day," Ava Grace said. "I grew up with Skip, and look where we are. It could happen for you, too."

"Not likely." Evans floured her rolling pin. "A couple years back, my cousin Channing married and divorced him in the space of about seven months in the messiest way possible."

"Wow." Ava Grace raised her eyebrows. "Your cousin just up and stole your man, easy as you please? Why, you must've been madder than a wet hen!"

Evans shrugged. "He wasn't mine." She clenched her fist and the dough shot up between her fingers. "I doubt he would be open to romance with another Pemberton woman. Not that I would—be open to it, I mean."

The words had barely made their way out of her mouth when one of her assistant bakers ducked into the kitchen.

"Evans, there's a guy here to see you."

She stilled her rolling pin.

"I think I conjured up a man for you." Ava Grace laughed and removed her cap and apron. "See you tonight at Claire's house."

"Right." It was mentor dinner night with Claire, something they did every few weeks where Evans, Ava Grace, and Hyacinth gave reports and swapped advice.

Ava Grace nodded. "I'll just slip out the back."

"Who is it, Ariel?" Please, God, not the rep from Hollingsworth Foods—a regional company that provided frozen foods to grocery stores. According to Claire, they were interested in mass-producing her maple pecan and peanut butter chocolate pies. So far, the rep had only tried to contact her by phone and it had been easy enough to elude his calls, allowing her to tell Claire that she hadn't heard from them.

Ariel shook her head and played with the crystal that hung around her neck. "I don't know."

Evans sighed. Of course she wouldn't have thought to ask. The female hadn't been born who was more suited to her name than Ariel—ethereal, dreamy, not of this world. But she could make a lemon curd that would make you cry.

"All right." Evans reached for a towel and wiped her hands. As tempting as it was to follow Ava Grace out the back door, she supposed it was time to deal with it. "Will you cover these and put them in the refrigerator?" She gestured to the sheet pans of oven-ready meat pies.

Ariel nodded. "I'll just get the plastic wrap." And she floated to the storeroom.

Evans still had a few meat pies, then peach cobblers to make for the Yellowhammer lunch tomorrow, so the quicker she sent him away, the better.

She hurried through the swinging door that led from the kitchen to the storefront—and looked right into the eyes of Jake Champagne.

*Eyes.*

He had eyes all night long and possibly into the next day. Big, cobalt blue eyes with Bambi eyelashes. They weren't eyes a woman was likely to forget even if he turned out to be a man she had to walk away from. Still, Evans had thought the day was done when those eyes would make her forget her own name. *Evans. Evans Blair Pemberton*, she reminded herself.

Jake widened those eyes. That was a willful act. She was sure of it because she'd spent years studying him— so she knew what it meant when Jake Champagne went all wide-eyed on someone. He understood the value of those eyes and the effect they had on people. When he widened them, he was either surprised or angling to get his way. This time he was surprised. If he'd been trying to get his way, he would have cocked his head to the side and smiled. If he wanted his way really bad, and it wasn't going well, he'd bite his bottom lip.

Speaking of what he wanted—what in the ever-loving hell was he doing here? She was pretty sure he had not gone to work for Hollingsworth Foods.

"You look great, Evie." She was suddenly sorry she'd studied him. Knowing he was surprised that she looked great wasn't the best for the ego.

Besides, she didn't look great. Her hair was in a messy ponytail, she was wearing an apron covered in flour, and any makeup she'd applied this morning was a memory. She only looked great compared to the last time he'd seen her—at the Pemberton family Thanksgiving two years ago, when she'd been coming off a bad haircut and sporting a moon crater of a cold sore. That had been five months after his wedding and two months before his divorce. Now, three years later, he could still send her on a one-way trip back to sixteen.

"Hotty Toddy, Jake!" Why had she said that—the Ole Miss football battle cry? Neither of them had gone to Ole Miss, though most of their families had. They were fans, of course, but she didn't normally go around saying *Hotty Toddy*.

"Hotty Toddy, Evie. That's good to hear in Roll Tide country."

She stepped from behind the counter and the awkward hug they shared was softened by his laughter. Though she didn't say so, he really did look great— however, in his plaid shorts and pink polo, he looked more like a fraternity boy on spring break than a professional hockey player. Jake's eyes might be his best feature, but he was gorgeous from head to toe. His caramel blond hair was a little shaggy and his tan face clean-shaven.

They came out of the hug and she looked up at him— way up. He was over six feet tall to her barely five feet four.

"It's good to see you, Evie."

*Evie,* rhymed with *levy.* He'd christened her that— probably because it was easier for a toddler to say than Evans. "Only people from home call me Evie now," she babbled.

He raised one eyebrow and his mouth curved into a half smile. She'd forgotten about that half smile. "I *am* from home."

He had a point.

"Would you like some pie? I have Mississippi mud." His favorite. The meringue pie with a chocolate pastry crust and layers of dense brownie and chocolate custard was one of her most popular. She glanced around to see if one of the round marble tables was available. Though it was after one o'clock, a few people were still lingering over lunch, but there was a vacant table by the window.

"No, I don't think—" He stopped abruptly and narrowed his eyes. "Yes. I would. Can you sit with me? For just a bit?"

Of course she could. She was queen of this castle. She could do whatever she wanted. But did she want to? Ha! What a stupid question, even to herself.

"Sure." She might still be making cobblers at midnight, but that was nobody else's business. "Joy?" She turned to the girl behind the counter. "I'm going to take a break. Can you bring a slice of Mississippi mud and a glass of milk? And a black coffee for me." She met his eyes. "Unless you've started drinking coffee."

He looked a little pained and she wondered why. "No. I still don't."

He held her chair before sitting himself down in the iron ice cream parlor chair opposite her. What had she been thinking when she'd bought these chairs? Apparently, not that hockey players—let alone this hockey player—would be settling in for pie. He looked like a man at a child's tea party. She laughed a little.

And in that instant, with the sun shining in the window turning his caramel hair golden, Jake came across with a smile that lit up the world. Good thing she'd packed up all those old feelings, right and tight, when he'd gotten involved with her cousin. Her stomach turned over—a muscle memory, no doubt.

"What's funny?" he asked.

"I was thinking I didn't choose these chairs with men in mind."

"You don't think it suits me?" He leaned back a bit. "Maybe you could trade them for some La-Z-Boys."

"Not quite the look I was going for."

He looked around. "So this is your shop? All yours?"

"I have an investor, but yes. It's mine."

She loved the wood floors, the happy fruit-stenciled yellow walls, the gleaming glass cases filled with pies, and the huge wreath on the back wall made of antique pie tins of varying sizes. Five minutes ago, she'd loved the ice cream parlor chairs. She probably would again.

"I knew you had a shop." He looked around. "But I had no idea it was like *this*. So nice."

*You might have, if you'd bothered to call me once in a while.* Evans bit her tongue as if she'd actually spoken the words and wanted to call them back. Instead, she packed them up and shoved them to the back of her brain. Jake was here. She was glad to see him. That was all.

"I've had some good luck," she said.

His eyes settled on the table next to them. "You serve lunch, too?"

"Nothing elaborate. A choice of two savory pies with a simple green or fruit salad on the side. I would offer you some, but we sold out of the bacon and goat cheese tart and you wouldn't eat the spanakopita."

He frowned. "Spana-who?"

"Spanakopita. Spinach pie."

He shuddered. "No. Not for me, but I'm meeting my teammate Robbie soon for a late lunch anyway." She knew who Robbie was from *The Face Off Grapevine*, a pro hockey gossip blog she sometimes checked. They called him and Jake the Wild-Ass Twins, though they looked nothing alike. For whatever reason, this Robbie was coming to play for the Yellowhammers, too. Jake went on, "He's been in Scotland since the season ended and just got in this morning. We're going to a place down the street."

*So I'm only a pit stop.* "Hammer Time. Brand-new sports bar for a brand-new team."

He nodded. "I hope Hammer Time is half as nice as your shop. You obviously work really hard."

"I do. But I don't have to do it on skates." She held up her chef clog-clad foot. Why had she said that? Belittled herself?

He laughed like it was the best joke he'd ever heard. Ah, that was why. She'd do anything to make him laugh. She'd forgotten that about herself.

"Here you go, Evans." Joy set down the pie, milk, and a thick, retro mug decorated with cherries like the ones on the wall.

"No pie for you?" Jake picked up his fork.

She sipped her coffee. "No. I taste all day long. The last thing I want is a plateful of pie. Are you sure you want that? Aren't you about to eat lunch?"

"I want this more than I've wanted anything for a long time." He took a bite and closed his eyes. "Other people only think they've had pie."

If she never got another compliment about another thing, this one would do her until death. "Mississippi mud is a hit in Alabama."

"Don't tell her, but this is so much better than the one from your mother's bakery."

No kidding. Anna-Blair Pemberton was all about a shortcut. "If she'd had her way, I'd be back in Cottonwood, making cookies from mixes and icing cakes with buttercream from a five-gallon tub."

Jake laughed a little under his breath. "My mother might have mentioned that a time or six."

"No doubt." Christine Champagne and Evans's mother were best friends. When Evans had deserted her mother's bakery after graduating from the New Orleans Culinary Institute, it must have given them fodder for months.

"I, for one, am glad you're making pie here." Jake took another bite. "There's something about this… something different. And familiar." He wrinkled his brow. "But I can't place it."

Evans knew exactly what he meant, and it pleased her more than it should have that he'd noticed.

"Do you remember the Mississippi mud bars we used to get when we went to Fat Joe's for tamales?"

"Yes! That's it." He took another bite of pie. "We ate a ton of those things, sitting at that old picnic table outside. Didn't Joe's wife make them?"

"She did. I got her secret and her permission to use it. She used milk and dark chocolate, and she added a little instant coffee to the batter."

He stopped with his fork in midair. "Coffee? There's coffee in here?"

Evans laughed. "You've been eating Lola's for years without knowing." She reached for his plate. "But if you don't want it…"

"Leave my pie alone, woman." He pretended to stab at her with his fork. "Those were good times."

"They were. We did a lot of homework at that picnic table."

He grimaced. "Well, it wasn't the homework I was thinking about. I'd have never passed a math class without you."

"Oh, I don't know about that."

"*I* do." He shook his head and let his eyes wander

to the ceiling like he always did when he wanted to change the subject. "What about the beach this summer. How was it?"

The question took Evans aback. Jake hadn't been on the annual Champagne-Pemberton beach trip since Channing came on the scene. She was surprised he even thought about them anymore.

"Sandy. Wet. Salty," she quipped. "Like always."

He grinned. "Must have been a little *too* sandy, wet, and salty for you. I hear you only stayed two days."

"Lots to do around here." She gestured to the shop.

He let his eyes go to a squint and his grin relaxed into that crooked smile. "Too much sorority talk?"

"I swear, it never stops." She slapped her palm against the table. All the women in that beach house—Evans's mother and two older sisters and Jake's mother and younger sister—were proud alumnae of Ole Miss and Omega Beta Gamma, the most revered and exclusive sorority on campus. Addison, Jake's sister, had recently made the ultimate commitment to her Omega sisters by taking a job at the sorority's national headquarters.

Jake took a sip of his milk and chuckled. "I hear you. Especially with rush coming up."

"It's like being in a room full of teachers who won't talk about anything except test scores and discipline problems. You just get tired of it." But it was more than that. Legacy or not, Evans would have never made the Omega cut had she gone to Ole Miss instead of culinary school. She wasn't tall, blond, and sparkly enough. She loved those women—every one of them—but she had always been a little out of step with them. Plus, living with all that sparkle could be hard on the nerves.

Jake laughed. "Well, they have to do their part to keep Omega on top, where it belongs."

"Sorority blood runs deep and thick in Mississippi," Evans said. "Sisters for life."

Jake went from amused to grim. "I don't think Mama and Addison feel very sisterly toward Channing anymore."

Channing had, of course, been the poster child for Omega. "For what it's worth, my mother and sisters don't either." *And I don't feel very cousinly toward her. Not that I ever did.*

He shrugged. "I've moved on—not quite as fast as she did, of course. Miss Mississippi, hockey wife, music producer wife, all in the space of eight months. I suppose you've heard she's pregnant?"

"Yes." The baby would probably have mud-colored eyes like Mr. Music Producer, when it could have had the bluest eyes in the world. Baffling.

"But I'm better off," Jake went on.

She studied his face and decided he meant it. "I'm glad you know it. You're better than that, Jake. You deserve better."

Jake looked at his pie, and back at her again. "You remembered my favorite pie and that I'm not a coffee drinker?"

Thank goodness for the change of subject. "How could I not remember? You always asked for Mississippi mud pie when you came into the bakery at home."

He took a deep breath. "I'm glad to see you, Evie."

"I'm glad to see *you*," she echoed. And she was. But something was niggling deep in her gut. It seemed Glad and Mad were running around inside her, neither one able to get complete control. She beat back Mad and embraced Glad. It was impossible to control most emotions, but mad wasn't one of them. She had always believed that if you didn't want to be mad, you didn't have to be. So what if he'd only come to see her because Crust was near his lunch spot? They had history. That was what was important. And he'd been through a lot: divorce, Blake's death, a new town and team, and— well, she didn't know what else, but wasn't that enough?

"I probably don't deserve for you to be glad to see me, but I appreciate it." Oh, hell. He was going to try to get negative now, just when she'd talked herself into a good place. She would not allow it. The only thing she was better at than turning out a perfect puff pastry was turning a situation around.

"Why wouldn't I be glad to see you?" She smiled like she meant it, and she did. Everybody always said you had to clear the air before you could move on. As far as she was concerned, that was way overrated. Some-times it was better to just let it go. Saying yes when others might say no sometimes made life go smoother.

"Let's not pretend I don't owe you an apology." He cocked his head to the side and widened his eyes. What was the point of that? She'd already forgiven him.

"Jake, there is no need for all of this."

"There is. I haven't been the friend to you I should have been. I guess when I met Channing, I didn't think about anything except her and hockey. I know I texted that to you a few months ago, but I wanted to say it in person." He lifted one corner of his mouth. "I did come by before I took Olivia and the kids to Europe, but you weren't here."

"I was in New York."

"I know. Please say you forgive me."

It would have been easier to downplay the whole thing and say it didn't matter. But no one was going to believe that, so she did the next best thing. "It's in the past. Our friendship goes back far and deep. It can withstand a storm or two." The truth of that lightened her heart.

Jake looked relieved, happy even. Maybe she did matter to him. "I shouldn't have let our friendship slip away—let you slip away."

The hair on the back of her neck stood up. *Slip away?* With that, Mad slammed a boxing glove into Glad's face and a foot on to its fallen body.

Why had he had to go and say that? She hadn't *slipped away.* She had gone kicking and screaming. It was true that she hadn't contacted him for a month after *that Christmas*—the Christmas of Channing—but wasn't she entitled to that, considering how things went down? And he damn sure hadn't bothered with her.

Evans had been home from culinary school for the holidays, and Jake from the University of North Dakota. They hadn't seen each other since summer, so they'd filled their plates with Anna-Blair's fancy canapés and found a corner to catch up—though catching up wasn't really necessary, because back then they talked and messaged each other at least three times a week. But they laughed and talked and she thought she'd finally seen the spark she'd felt for twenty years reflected in his eyes. He almost confirmed it when he said, "You know, Evie, my fraternity spring formal is going to be in New Orleans, and I was thinking that—"

But she'd never know for absolute certain what he had been thinking. Maybe he wasn't going to invite her. Maybe he was only going to ask her for a ride from the airport or advice about where to get the best gumbo.

Channing's family seldom made the trip from Memphis to Cottonwood and never for Christmas—but they had that year. And Channing chose that precise moment to sail in, looking like Vogue and smelling like Chanel. Or maybe it was Joy. Who the hell knew? It damned sure wasn't vanilla extract. Whatever it was, Evans had gotten a good whiff when Channing swooped in and hugged her—something Evans could never recall happening before. Of course, Channing had never walked in on Evans in conversation with someone who looked like Jake before either. "Well, cousin, who do you have here?" Channing had asked. Evans had introduced them, and then it was all over but the crying.

And Evans had cried—for a month. But what purpose would it serve to go into all that with Jake? It was over. It didn't matter—except it did. Strange that it only occurred to her now that if Jake had been planning to ask her to the dance, maybe it was because she was going to school in New Orleans anyway—convenient.

"You know, Jake, I didn't slip away." She took down her ponytail and put it back up again. "I didn't go easily." After that month had passed, she'd batted back the humiliation and put on her big girl panties. Still, no matter how many times she'd called or texted, he never had time for her. Even if he answered, he was somewhere else. The next time she'd seen him had been in New Orleans the morning after that dance, when she'd met him and Channing at Brennan's for breakfast. Channing had brought the nosegay of white roses and succulents that Jake had bought her for the dance and held hands with him under the table. Evans had cursed herself for saying yes to that breakfast invitation, when she should have said no. It wasn't the first time, and it wouldn't be the last. "I fought for our friendship."

The moment the words cleared her mouth, she was sorry. He'd apologized. What more did she want? Jake's face went white and he put his fork down. Understandable. He probably didn't want to eat any more of her pie after what she'd said. Why hadn't she just left it alone?

"I'm sorry. I shouldn't have said that," she said hurriedly.

"Why? It's true." There was real hurt on his face.

"Nonetheless. You apologized, and I wasn't gracious about it. And after all you've been through. It's behind us. Let's move forward."

He looked skeptical, but nodded. "That's all I want. And you've been gracious to forgive me at all." Eyes wide. Head cocked. Lip bite. "I'll make it up to you."

He had never, as far as she could remember, had to get to the lip biting with her before. "There's nothing to make up."

He picked up his fork again. "I disagree, though it may not be possible. But I will say this: for a while there, I forgot what was important. After the divorce, I forgot my raising. But after Blake... It made me stop and think. I won't forget again. I'm going to be a better man—a better friend."

He covered her hand with his, and her heart dropped like a fallen star.

"We're good." What was wrong with being convenient anyway?

Then he nodded and smiled like he was pleased. Pleasing Jake Champagne had once been her life's work.

She supposed she was glad she had finally accomplished it.

## Chapter Two

Jake's phone had been vibrating against his thigh like a jackhammer on concrete for twenty minutes, yet here he was eating Mississippi mud pie like it was his job. Robbie was usually patient and easygoing, though anyone would be annoyed at being kept waiting this long. But the apology was done and the air was clear between him and Evie. They wouldn't have to go there again.

He put the last bite of chocolate heaven into his mouth. He'd ordered this pie in restaurants many times, but he'd never had any that was right—that tasted like home—outside the Delta until now.

"Would you like another piece?" Evie asked.

*No, I really have to go meet Robbie, but I'll see you soon.* That's what he opened his mouth to say.

"No thank you, but I would like some more milk." *What?* Was there some milk-loving demon alien in him—one that didn't care that he had to go?

"Sure." She smiled and her dimples waved at him.

She rose from her chair and sashayed away with his milk glass.

He watched her go.

With her peachy skin, dark shiny hair, and compact little body, Evie was lovely. The thought jolted him.

He'd never used the word *lovely* in his life. He was more of a *hot* or a *babe* guy, but those things seemed a little too aggressive for Evie's quiet kind of beauty. She wasn't his type, of course. He went for tall, blond bombshells, though there hadn't been any lately.

The bow from Evie's apron sat low on the small of her back. That was an interesting look. In his experience, bombshells didn't do a lot of apron-wearing. They might if they knew what a good accessory the bow would be.

Evie was coming toward him again, smiling and speaking to people as she walked. People liked her. And why not? She was nice and she had pie, good pie. Plus she was so smart, way smarter than he was. Now she was laughing at something a teenage girl had said. If she could bottle and sell that laugh, she could get out of the pie business. Though she probably didn't want out. She was happy.

*Happy.* How long had it been since he'd been in the company of a truly happy woman?

It would be good to be around some joy—with someone who wasn't looking for romance, or sex, or a game-worn jersey. His phone vibrated again. He really did have to go.

Jake almost rose to do just that, but then Evie set the milk down in front of him. Right. The milk-loving demon had asked for milk.

"Thank you." He drained it in one gulp and stood up. "I should let you get back to work."

"And you have lunch waiting." She was on to him. She always had been.

"Can't be as good as this pie. I believe I'll take one with me—a whole one." He reached for his wallet.

"No." Evie put a hand on his wrist. "Your money is no good here." She led him to the counter. "Tell Joy to box up whatever you want. I insist. We're family."

"Not anymore," he pointed out.

She half closed her eyes and shook her head. "Of course we are, Jake. Delta family. We were that long before you married my cousin."

*Home. Family.*

"Let's get together soon," he rushed to say when she turned to go.

Evie gave him a smile over her shoulder as she walked toward the kitchen door. "I'll see you tomorrow. I'm catering the team training camp lunch."

He got the feeling he'd landed exactly where he needed to be.

With pumpkins and scarecrows decorating storefronts, the streets of Laurel Springs looked like fall, but felt like summer. His phone vibrated again. Robbie—just as he'd thought. He didn't answer, but hurried his steps. He was forty-five minutes late and, clearly, Robbie was uncharacteristically agitated—and for good reason. If not for Jake, Robbie wouldn't have uprooted himself from Nashville. Jake had been astounded when Robbie had asked for the trade. He claimed that he, too, wanted a chance to skate first line, but Jake knew Robbie had made the change because of the bond between the two of them. They were a couple of guys who'd made it to the major league despite hailing from places that weren't exactly hotbeds of ice hockey—Mississippi and Scotland.

If Robbie's decision hadn't been surprising enough, another Sound family member had made the switch to the Hammers, too. Former center Nickolai Glazov had retired and immediately signed on as an assistant coach with the new team. Jake wondered what had brought that on, but doubted if he'd ever know. If the former Sound captain ever explained his motives, it wouldn't be to anyone he called "wet behind the ears baby dogs" like Jake and Robbie.

Jake quickened his pace as he scanned the buildings for Hammer Time. Ah. There. He saw Robbie's silver Corvette—illegally parked—out front before he saw the restaurant sign. As glad as he was that Robbie had made the move, he was not looking forward to telling his former partner in bad behavior that he was cleaning up his act. Jake had not wavered from his convictions that came on the heels of Blake's death. There would be no drunken partying and no indiscriminate sex.

He stepped from the steamy, hot mid-September afternoon into the dark, cool building. Sure that Robbie already had a table, Jake opened his mouth to tell the hostess he was meeting someone when he saw Robbie sitting on an upholstered bench, aggressively stabbing at the keyboard on his phone—which was odd for the easygoing Scot, Jake's lack of punctuality aside.

"Sorry I'm late, but—" Jake began.

Robbie looked up and jumped to his feet. "Sparks!" He used Jake's nickname. "Where've you been? We've got to go. Glaz wants us."

Ah, hell. When he'd been their captain, they'd said, "How high and how often?" when Glaz had said, "Jump." Now that he was one of their coaches, it was bound to get worse.

"What does he want?"

"Do you think I asked?" Robbie started for the door.

Jake looked down at the bag from Crust he carried. "Do you suppose you can put this in the refrigerator for me?" he asked the hostess. "I'll pick it up later."

On the ride to the Laurel Springs Ice Center, Jake discovered his two dozen texts and missed calls were divided evenly between Robbie and Glaz. None of them gave any clue why the man wanted to see them.

"You talked to him?" Jake asked.

"Aye. Long enough for him to task me with finding you and—I quote—'Get your asses to my office immediately. Try to bring your brains as well.'"

"I'll text him and say we're on our way."

Robbie relaxed a bit. "Maybe he's calling us in to say we'll be skating first line and make us co-captains."

Jake laughed. He really had missed his friend. "Sure. Because first-year assistant coaches always get to decide that."

Robbie echoed Jake's laughter then let it die.

"How was France? Saw you on *The Face Off* running through the airport with your auntie. Stupid eejits captioned it 'Wild-Twin Snares a Cougar?'"

Jake shook his head; that gossip rag wasn't worth worrying about. "Lots of beach time and cheese eating." And shopping. Adam and Nicole had returned home to Cottonwood with enough clothes, shoes, and electronics to open a shop on Main Street. Olivia had urged him to stop buying for them, but eventually gave up.

"Not the off season you had in mind," Robbie said. "I know you wanted to go home."

"Sometimes going home is just doing what you ought to do," Jake said, "no matter where you are." What was important was that when he'd returned Olivia and the kids home, they looked healthier and seemed calmer. Maybe he was, too.

Robbie nodded. "You can go for Christmas." He sounded wistful.

"I will. And you'll come with me." The team wouldn't have enough time off for Robbie to go to Scotland. Maybe Evie would travel with them, though he'd have to rent a vehicle. There was barely room in his Lamborghini for him and a weekend's worth of clothes. Maybe he'd buy another car—some kind of SUV.

Robbie brightened. "That would be grand." He parked and nodded toward the ice center. "If we live that long."

"Relax," Jake said. "He probably only wants to say hello. Besides, we haven't done anything. Lately."

After a few wrong turns and a few inquiries, they found themselves outside a door with Glaz's name and title. The big, dark-haired Russian jerked the door open after Jake's first light tap.

"Ah. The Wild-Ass Twins. You two are late." He held a framed photograph of his wife and child.

*How can we be late when we didn't have an appointment?* Jake wondered but did not ask.

"Sorry," Robbie said.

"Come in." Glaz stepped aside and placed the photograph in an open banker's box on his desk. The office was in a state with boxes against the wall and framed hockey memorabilia and files scattered about. It was hard to tell if he was coming or going. Maybe he was going. Maybe he'd been fired. "Sit." He gestured to two chairs in front of the desk as he went to sit behind it. Glaz waited until they were seated to let himself down in the fancy leather desk chair. Jake had the impression he'd wanted to tower over them for a bit before getting down to business—whatever that business was.

"Something has happened," Glaz said. "Something bad. We must speak of it before the media releases it. Drew Kelty was fired."

"Freaking fuck me!" Robbie burst out.

Glaz gave him a sour look. "Kelty is accused of sexual harassment by former Vultures ice girl. She has video to prove it."

"Well, shit," Jake said after a few seconds, because he couldn't think of anything else.

"It was deserved," Glaz said. "I call you here to tell you I am new head coach and to develop an understanding between us."

*Head coach? At this level? With* no *coaching experience?* How was that possible? The question must have shown on Jake's face and Glaz, for whatever reason, decided it was worth addressing. "Interim head coach," he admitted. "This happened today. They are desperate. I convince the owners I am up for the job—which I am. I will succeed. This team will succeed."

So Glaz was going—but to a bigger office. Robbie and Jake nodded. "Congratulations," Robbie said.

Glaz gave a half nod. "I was your teammate. I am now your coach. You must act appropriately."

"That won't be a problem," Jake said. And it wouldn't. Glaz had always been so far above them in the pecking order, they hadn't been inclined to pal around. Besides, he had earned their respect. "Coach," Jake added for emphasis.

"No problem at all," Robbie agreed. "Coach."

"Good. We understand each other." Glaz rose from his chair and came to sit on the edge of the desk in front of them. Was it possible for a man to look more menacing?

"We are about to have scandal. Is no way to begin a season—a team, but we have that. I will have no more." He leaned forward. "There will be no more Wild-Ass Twins."

*No problem, Glaz. I came here to get away from that. Can't speak for my friend Robbie.*

"You are good players. I am happy to have you here. I intend to keep this job. *Interim.* Bah! I sometimes wondered what I would do when I was finished playing. But this chance came and I knew was right. We will go to playoffs. You will be instrumental in that, but you will behave."

Robbie and Jake looked at each other and nodded.

"There will be no public drunken behavior, no standing on tables and spraying people with beer at parties, no urinating in public—"

Robbie burst out, "We never! My mum—"

Glaz put up a hand. "Silence! If I see your pictures on that silly online gossip rag, you had better be visiting sick children in hospital or raising funds for art museum." Glaz's nostrils flared and he loomed over them a little closer. All he needed was a ring in his nose to look like a bull about to rampage. "And I swear on the head of Sebastian, Patron Saint of Hockey—"

Glaz paused for effect, or maybe to search for a word in English like he sometimes had to do. Robbie gasped and clasped his hand to his chest over the St. Sebastian medal that Jake knew he wore under his shirt. For a Catholic, swearing on the head of a saint was serious business. For a United Methodist, not so much. Still, Jake believed him.

"I swear," Glaz repeated, "if you so much as look at an ice girl with a gleam in your eye, you will not set blade on ice. If we do not make the playoffs, if we win not one game, if I am fired and have to open bingo parlor, I will do it before you see one second of game time. Am I clear?"

Very clear. Despite the reference to urinating in public—which they had not done—Glaz knew their past sins well.

"Yes, Coach," they said simultaneously.

To Jake's surprise, Glaz smiled easily. "Good!" He stood up and clapped his hands together. "I see you here tomorrow. Now, go. I have things to do and we have a storm to weather." He laid a hand on each of their shoulders as he ushered them out.

Once a safe distance down the hall, Robbie said, "He meant that."

"You think?" Jake said.

Robbie grinned. "I guess we're going to have to be a little more clandestine in our activities with our charming companions."

And here they were. "About that, Robbie…"

"Yeah?"

"We need to talk. Let's go back to Hammer Time, get some food, and catch up."

It was time for the Wild-Ass Twin powers to deactivate.

## Chapter Three

Fifteen minutes later, the hostess at Hammer Time ushered Jake and Robbie to a table in the bar and asked for their drink orders.

"Sam Adams, please," Jake said.

"Harviestoun OlaDubh." Like he always did, Robbie asked for his favorite Scottish dark ale. He wasn't going to get it. He almost never got it.

But the hostess—Gretchen, her name tag said—only nodded. "Coming up. And Mr. Champagne, I'll bring your pie out when you're ready to go."

She knew who he was?

"Wait, lass! Hold up!" Robbie said as she started to walk away. "You really have Harviestoun OlaDubh? And you know who Sparks is?"

She nodded. "And you're Robbie McTavish. Forward. Number five. Our owner gave us a roster of the team with pictures and tested us on it. She has made it her business to stock the favorite drinks of the players and coaches." She turned to Jake. "We're carrying Sparkle water, too."

"How does she even know that?" Jake asked. The commercial he'd shot for the sparkling water he endorsed hadn't even been released yet.

"That's a good question," Gretchen said. "Claire knows a lot of things. I'll get your drink order turned in."

"I like it here," Robbie pronounced.

"Of course you do. They know your name and have your beer."

"Ale," Robbie corrected.

"Whatever." Jake looked around at the time-worn marble floor and the wood-paneled, brass-trimmed walls. "This place is old. I heard it used to be a department store."

"Not so old." Robbie looked around. "Couldn't be more than a hundred years. Come to Scotland. I'll show you old."

"You're such a snob." Jake opened the menu. "I'm going to have the double bacon cheeseburger with a baked potato." Despite the pie and milk he'd had earlier, the smell of grilled meat had made him ravenous.

"Sounds good. I'll have the same." Jake had expected that from Robbie. Except for sweets, which he loved, Robbie didn't much care what he ate as long as there was plenty of it. "Maybe some wings, too, though did I hear we have a pie to eat? Where did it come from?"

"*I* have a pie to eat. I might give you some when we get home." He and Robbie both had condos in The Mill, a renovated defunct textile mill, but, except for a piano, Robbie didn't have any furniture yet so he would be sleeping on Jake's couch tonight. Aside from a bed, television, and his gaming systems, a couch was all he had. He planned to do something about that, though. It was time he stopped living like he was camping out. "I have a friend from home who has a pie shop here. Crust. I stopped by to see her and she gave me a pie."

Robbie frowned. "You didn't say you had a friend in town. Her name is *Crust*?"

"I haven't said much of anything to you. We haven't had time. And, no. Her name is not *Crust*, dimwit. That's the name of her shop. Her name is Evie—Evans."

Robbie brightened. "Is she pretty?"

*Yes. Though* lovely *is a more accurate description. I don't know why, exactly, but that's what she is—lovely. And sweet.*

"Doesn't matter if she is or not." *Not to me or you, but especially not to you.* Jake studied the flavors of wings on the menu. "She's off-limits."

"Ah." Robbie nodded. "Then she's like a sister."

Jake's head jerked up in surprise. "No. I wouldn't say that." He took a deep breath. "She's Channing's cousin."

Robbie let out a low whistle. "Freaking fuck me."

"Watch your language," Jake said. "Here come our drinks." Jake—like most hockey players—had a pretty colorful vocabulary himself, but he didn't hold with saying certain words in front of women. His dad and Blake had taught him that.

"If Glaz has his way, bad language is all we've got left."

The waitress set down their drinks and Gretchen appeared behind her. "This is Casey. She'll take your order."

Jake looked at the menu again. "We'll start with two dozen hot wings, half honey barbecue and half maple chipotle. Two double bacon cheeseburgers, medium, with loaded baked potatoes."

"Very good," Casey said. "Anything else?"

"No." Then Jake eyed his beer. "Wait. We need waters. Could you maybe bring us a whole pitcher?"

"What the hell, Sparks?" Robbie asked after the waitress had gone. "I only drink water for hydration purposes. Not recreational." He gestured to the table. "This is recreation. Fish fu—" He looked around. "Have sex in it."

"Then order a Coke," Jake said. "You heard Glaz."

"One beer with lunch does not make for public intoxication," Robbie said.

"And you're having one beer. Ale. Whatever."

Okay. Time to have that talk with Robbie. And he opened his mouth to begin when two tall, leggy blondes entered the bar. Their shorts were short, their hair was long, and—unless Jake missed his guess, and he seldom did—there was glitter powder in their cleavages. They cast their eyes around, barely hesitating upon catching sight of Robbie and Jake. They slid onto bar stools in full view, turned toward each other, and crossed their legs.

Jake had seen this dance a thousand times and today it made him tired.

"Well, well, well," Robbie said. "Our lucky day. A couple of charming companions. And they aren't joining anybody. Do you want to do it or should I?"

Jake and Robbie had a dance of their own. Just as the bartender approached to take the women's order, one of them—usually Robbie—would move toward the bar, lean in, and say, "Run a tab and give it to me." The girls would protest but they would all end up at the same table and, more often than not, leave together.

"Which one do you want?" Robbie asked.

Jake looked them over. "Neither one—but if I did, it wouldn't matter. They look alike."

Robbie let his eyes settle on the women. "They look nothing alike."

"Not interested." Jake sipped his beer.

"Come on, Sparks. I was only kidding about bad language being all we had left. Glaz said no scandal. He didn't say we had to be saints. I know he wasn't much of a player even before he married Noel, but he wouldn't think buying two pretty young ladies a drink was out of line."

"No." Jake sighed and ran his hand through his hair. Was this going to be the end of his friendship with Robbie? Was their relationship based solely on raising hell in and out of the bedroom? "It wouldn't end there. It never does. You do what you want, but I'm done with that. And it has nothing to do with the lecture we just got."

Robbie's expression turned serious. "What's up, Jake?" Robbie almost never called him Jake.

"We talked about why I asked to be traded…" Jake let his voice trail off.

Robbie took a drink of his beer and nodded. "Channing is pregnant and you're tired of seeing her picture plastered all over the society page."

That had been the easiest long-distance explanation at the time, though he didn't much care anymore that his ex-wife had moved on at the speed of light. Casey appeared with their food, and Jake pondered his response as she placed the dishes and Robbie made small talk with her.

"That's what I told you," he said after she'd gone. "And there's some truth to it, but it's more than that. I need to slow down, take stock. I was never that guy— drinking, carousing, with a different girl every night.

That last morning in Boston I woke up with a woman whose last name and marital status I didn't know. Hell, I had to think hard before I remembered her first name. Then I got the call about my uncle."

"That was a bad time," Robbie said quietly.

"I'm better now, but I need to slow down."

"I don't."

"You, in fact, do—that is, if you want to play for this team. But I've made my choices. You make yours."

"Let me get this straight. You don't plan to drink or have sex anymore?"

"Why do you take everything to the extreme? No. I did not say that. I'm drinking now." He held up his beer. "I don't intend to drink a six-pack every night and sleep with someone I've never had a conversation with beyond, 'Nice ass. Want to put it in my lap?'"

Robbie's face relaxed. "That's good to hear. The boozing, you could take or leave alone, but the women—that's a different story. You couldn't make it three months." Robbie brushed his hand against his shirt, leaving a wing sauce stain.

*Couldn't* do it? That didn't set well. "I could. I did it all summer."

"Ah, but trotting around Europe with your auntie and cousins did not lend itself to romance. You're back on the ice again, now. No chaperones." He nodded toward the bar where the shiny blondes sat. "Temptation all around."

Robbie had a point. Plus the exhilaration of playing hockey tended to heighten his senses—*all* his senses. Truth was, he had never intended to swear off sex— only to be more discriminating.

"I could do it, if that's what I decided."

Robbie narrowed his eyes. "Really? Then why don't you? Swear off sex for three months?"

"Maybe I will," Jake said. "You'll be sorry when you don't have a wingman."

Robbie took a drink of his beer. "I don't need you, Sparks Champagne, to help me get a woman. But the fact remains—three months, no sex? There's no way. You will fail, my friend."

Would he? There was a time when he hadn't known the meaning of the word *failure.* He'd had it all—looks, beauty queen wife, great family, amazing hockey career. Then his marriage had failed, and his self-control tanked along with it.

He needed to do this. Maybe just to prove to himself he could.

He turned his phone on and looked at the screen. "It's September thirteenth. I, Jacob Hunt Champagne, hereby declare myself celibate until this time in December."

"Really?" Robbie stopped with a wing in midair and shook his head in disbelief.

Jake did not like being doubted. "Want to make it interesting?"

Robbie laughed. "Sure you don't want to give up gambling too?"

"It's not even a gamble." Jake spread ketchup on his burger. "It's a sure thing. Just me taking your money. What do you say to a thousand?"

Robbie shook his head. "No. If we're going to do this thing, we'll do it right. Money wouldn't make it interesting. You have money; I have money. It needs to be something else—something more important than money." Robbie closed his eyes and wrinkled his brow.

Jake's mouth went dry. Robbie was going to ask him

to bet his puck—*the* puck, the Miracle on Ice puck that Blake had given him. Of course, Robbie didn't know Blake had given it to him. He only knew that it always resided in Jake's hockey bag or locker room stall and that, sometimes between periods when he was having a bad game, Jake took it out and turned it over in his hand three times.

And now Robbie was going to ask him to risk it— something Jake knew in the bedrock of his soul that Robbie would not do if he knew where it came from. But maybe it was fitting. That puck was part of the foundation of the person he'd been and the person he needed to find again.

Sure enough, Robbie crossed his arms, laid them on the table, and leaned forward to say the fateful words. "Your puck."

Jake could have played dumb and tried to pretend it was one of the game pucks that Jake had from various games where he'd scored the winning goal, but what was the use? His mouth had gotten him into this bet and that puck would get him out. Aside from the sentimental value, that puck was his good luck charm. Except maybe baseball players, there wasn't a breed alive more superstitious than hockey players. On the one hand, Jake saw the irrationality in that, but on the other, the puck had brought him this far and he would *not* lose it.

But Robbie was going to have to risk something, too.

Jake nodded. "All right. My puck against your St. Sebastian medal."

Robbie's eyes widened and he clasped his hand to his chest over the medal, as he had done earlier in Glaz's office.

"But it's sacred."

"No more sacred than my puck," Jake said. "Not to me."

"Don't even say such a thing!" Robbie looked around like he was expecting a legion of angels to enter and take Jake away to a dungeon. "I couldn't expect a Protestant to understand. It was blessed by the Holy Father. My aunt—who I might add is a nun—brought it to me from Vatican City."

Jake shrugged. "If you're afraid…"

Robbie's nostrils flared. He hated nothing more than having his courage challenged. He nodded. "All right. There's no risk anyway. There's no way you'll make it three months. Longer, if you count time served this summer. But we must agree on the rules."

"Rules? What rules? It's simple. I'll remain celibate until this time on December thirteenth."

"And just what does *celibate* mean? No kissing? No fooling around? How about hand-holding and dancing? You know how you love to dance."

"None of that has anything to do with celibacy, but we'll let the dictionary decide." Jake whipped out his phone. "Here we go. 'Abstaining from marriage and sexual intercourse.' Doesn't say anything about kissing and dancing."

"Fair enough," Robbie said, "but remember where kissing and dancing leads."

"I'm not fifteen years old. I can control myself."

"We'll see." Robbie bit into his burger.

"I suppose next, you'll want to know how you'll know if I stick to my word."

The amusement left Robbie's face. "I'll know because you'll tell me. We've never lied to each other."

Jake's gut twisted. Maybe he didn't have to worry

about the strength of their friendship, after all. "Right. Sorry. I guess I forgot that for a moment."

Robbie grinned and cast his eyes at the women at the bar. "What you say we forget something that's worth forgetting? Like this bet for now? Have one last go, and let it start tomorrow?"

Jake laughed. "No, I'm all in. You go ahead. But they might be ice girls, and you don't even have a bed."

"No bed? How is a hockey player to get any rest?" Jake heard the voice before he saw the woman. She sounded like private school and country club brunch.

He and Robbie met eyes before they looked up. She appeared to be about the age of his mother. Maybe. It was hard to tell.

She extended her hand. "I'm Claire. Don't get up." Telling them not to get up might have been construed as a reprimand since they had made no move to rise—but Jake didn't think so. She just seemed like the type men always stood up for. Her handshake was firm. "I own this little establishment, and I wanted to welcome you."

"Everything was grand," Robbie said. "Thank you for stocking my ale."

"My pleasure. We want you boys to feel at home here." Jake hadn't noticed that she carried the Crust bag that contained his pie until she set it on the seat beside him. "I see you have been to my girl's shop. You're in for a treat."

*Her* girl? What did that mean? He used to know everybody Evie knew.

"Ah, the pie maker. She's Sparks's childhood friend. She makes a good pie, does she?" Robbie prattled on.

"Indeed, she does," Claire said. "I'm very proud of her. In fact, I have three girls under my tutelage who

I'm very proud of. They all have beautiful shops on Main Street. I'm sure you'll meet them as time goes by."

Oh. This was the investor Evie mentioned.

Gretchen walked up. "Ms. Watkins?" *Watkins?* That rang a bell. "I'm sorry to interrupt, but I needed to catch you before you leave. Chef asked me to tell you he has one more question about tomorrow's lunch."

"Of course, Gretchen." She looked back at them. "Jake. Robbie. Again, welcome. Let me know if we can do anything for you."

"You can put our jerseys on the wall," Robbie said. "The Big Skate in Nashville had our jerseys on the wall."

Claire gave them a steely smile—one that let anyone who was paying attention know just what a force of nature she was. "I intend to do just that—one by one, as you earn it." And she was gone in a swish of silk, leaving behind the scent of something spicy.

"Who *was* that woman?" Robbie asked.

"If I am remembering right, she's our landlord—and one of our bosses. I think she owns a piece of the team."

"I might be a little afraid of her," said the Scot who never admitted to being afraid of anything.

## Chapter Four

"We're out of chocolate caramel and maple pecan."

Evans looked up from the brandy peach cobbler assembly line to meet Neva's eyes. "So early?" Running out of pie wasn't unusual, or especially undesirable, depending on the time of day. Evans never sold products more than twenty-four hours old. But it was highly unusual to run out of top sellers before closing time, and it wasn't even three thirty yet.

Neva sighed as she made her way to the laptop on the table in the corner of the kitchen where she would note the time and the shortage on a spreadsheet. "Afraid so." Neva did not approve of running out of pie or refusing to sell day-old pie. After all, people ate on a pie at home for several days. But then Neva had managed an office supply store and the china department of a jewelry shop. Though she had a fantastic head for business and was super organized, her philosophy didn't always jive with the artisan mindset. "It's been a busy day."

They had been busy, but not much more so than usual. Had Evans not been fooling with meat pies and cobblers all day, she would have been on top of this and replenished midmorning.

"How's the coconut holding out?"

"There's plenty of French coconut, but we're low on coconut cream." She paused. "Your friend took the last Mississippi mud."

Apparently, Neva did not approve of giving away pie either—though, as a rule, neither did Evans. But let's face it. She'd give Jake Champagne a kidney. There certainly was no alternate universe where she wouldn't give him a pie.

She shook her head to clear her mind of Jake thoughts. She would not—could not—go down the Jake road again.

Forgive him? Of course. It was already done. Be his friend? Certainly. She'd meant what she said about their friendship going back far and deep. But she could never again let him dance around her every thought and breath.

"How's it going?"

Evans jumped. She'd been so deep in her musings that she hadn't noticed when Neva had come to stand beside her.

"Done." She covered a peach cobbler. "Everything is ready for the oven. I've got about a dozen meat pies that didn't turn out." Meaning they weren't pretty. Either the staff would bake and eat them or they would end up at the Episcopal Church's soup kitchen like her other failed and day-old products. "If you'll print me a list of what we need tomorrow, I'll get the crusts ready." Thankfully, freezing unbaked crusts had no effect on the quality, so she always had some stockpiled, but it was never enough.

"I've already done that." Neva laid the printout on the work table. "You know, Evans…" And Evans did know; she knew exactly what Neva was going to say.

"Maybe you could let Ariel and Quentin help out with the crusts. You've got a lot on you with this luncheon."

"They make the crumb crusts for the black bottom cherry cream, key lime, and peanut butter banana icebox."

But crumb crusts were one thing. Pastry was another. Evans had tried and tried to explain to Neva that an inferior crust made an inferior pie. "You're exhausted," Neva said. "It's not as if I'm suggesting you buy frozen crusts at Piggly Wiggly. Quentin says he can make a crust. I'm not saying that Joy and Dory should start whipping up lemon meringue, or, God forbid, that I should." Joy and Dory were college students who worked part-time minding the front and cleaning up. "But Ariel and Quentin *are* your assistant bakers and they spend as much time working the front as they do in the kitchen."

Evans began to ferry cobblers to the refrigerator. "I've got it, Neva." Quentin and Ariel could probably learn to make crusts to her standard. She just hadn't had time to work with them enough yet. Eventually, she would.

Neva opened her mouth to speak again, but the doorbell jingled. "I'd better get back out there. After-school crowd."

When Evans went to store the cobblers, she caught sight of the two pear pies she'd made earlier for a special order. Kate Johnson was supposed to pick them up this afternoon. She'd package them and move them to the case out front.

And she wouldn't think of Jake. She would concentrate on lowering Kate's pies into boxes without breaking the fluted pastry edges. Done. Now she'd think

about the logistics of transporting the pasties and cobblers to the ice center tomorrow and keeping it all warm
until serving time.

After all, she wouldn't want Jake to eat cold food or—
even worse—be embarrassed for her that she had served
cold food to his teammates. Or maybe he wouldn't be
embarrassed. Maybe he wouldn't acknowledge her.

He might—

*He might what, Evans? Exactly what is it that Jake
Champagne might or might not do? Be sure and consider every possibility like you would have when you
were sixteen years old. Don't leave anything out and
don't forget to mull over what your various reactions
could be. You certainly want to revert back to those
good times.*

It all slammed down on her, all the things she hadn't
thought of in so long, the pieces of her life that brought
her to a good day that went bad at Christmastime four
years ago—birthday parties, cotillion classes, those
shared family vacations, preschool story time at the li-
brary when she'd held his hand because he was afraid
of the clown puppet.

Her heart raced. She had to stop. And she would—
starting now, by taking these pies out front.

She pushed the swinging door open just in time to
hear Claire Watkins ask Quentin, "Is Evans available?"

Suddenly, Evans felt centered. This was her shop, full
of people having after-school snacks. She was among
her employees and her mentor. She had exited the Jake
Road without incident.

"I'm right here, Claire." She held out the pie boxes to
Quentin. "Would you put these away? They're special

orders." She stepped around the counter. "Would you like to have a seat, Claire? Can I get you anything?"

Claire shook her head, moving away from the counter near the wall. "No time." Evans followed her.

Claire was a good-looking woman for any age, whatever that age might be. Evans didn't know and Claire wasn't telling. From time to time, it was a subject for debate among Claire's girls, and they had deduced that she was somewhere between fifty and fifty-five. She looked younger—especially since her month-long vacation to Aspen last year. She wore her blond hair in a messy, low bun—though there was nothing messy about Claire. Evans imagined that it took a great deal of effort to achieve that devil-may-care look. Today, she wore an amber silk wrap blouse with brown pants, and butter-soft loafers with bows.

Even in the flat shoes, she stood a head and half taller than Evans. If they had been of an age, Claire would have probably appealed to Jake.

Damn. There he was again.

Claire frowned. "Are you all right, Evans?" Now that Evans noticed, Claire looked a little grim. She hoped it wasn't because of something she had done—or not done. She couldn't think of anything, but the Jake Road took up a lot of energy.

"I'm fine. What can I do for you?"

"Two things," Claire said.

*Sure, Claire. Make it three. I'll add that on to making pies and this hockey hell lunch.*

"First, I want to touch base with you about lunch tomorrow. I just left Hammer Time and everything's on track there. Ten of my waitstaff will be there to help. I'm sending over macaroni and cheese, assorted salads, and drinks an hour prior to lunch. The facility has dishes."

They had been over all this before, but this was the cue for Evans to assure Claire that her part of the meal was in order. "My part-time girls are helping me transport the food and they can help with the serving, too. I have the pasties and cobblers ready to be baked in the morning. I had ice cream for the cobbler delivered to the ice center today."

Claire nodded. "Good. Now for the second thing—I need to cancel our little dinner tonight."

"All right." This was a relief. She could make pie crusts tonight.

"I have to go out of town for a few days on Thursday, so I'd like you, Ava Grace, and Hyacinth to get together on your own this weekend to talk about your plans for the fall festival. Then we'll all meet and go over it."

Which meant Claire wanted final approval for their decorations, refreshments, and activities for the Laurel Springs Fall Festival. It was understandable. A lot of people turned out for the street fair that had taken place the Saturday before Halloween for years.

"We can do that," Evans said. "I'll get everyone together."

Claire nodded. "Thank you and I do apologize. My uncle and nephew came into town today and are spending the night with me so they don't have to turn around and drive back tomorrow for the first day of training camp."

That would be Claire's charming, eccentric Uncle Tiptoe and her nephew by marriage, the former Yankee star Polo MacNeal—the principle owners of the

Yellowhammers. They lived about forty-five minutes away in Merritt, Alabama.

"They came this morning because there was an unexpected Yellowhammer meeting," Claire went on.

Did *unexpected* mean *emergency?* And if it did, what did that mean for Jake?

Evans smiled and tried to look nonchalant. "Trading players at this late date?"

Claire steadied her gaze on Evans and narrowed her eyes. "Some of that, yes." She hesitated. "It'll be common knowledge soon anyway, but we fired Coach Kelty. He sexually harassed some ice girls where he coached a few years back. There's no room for that here—or anywhere. Nickolai Glazov is taking over. Everything's fine, but please don't talk about it."

Oh, sure. Fine for the *team.* But what about Jake? What if he'd been traded to Winnipeg where it snowed all the damn time? He would be miserable. Like every other Southern child, he had once loved snow on the rare occasions when they had it, but he'd come to despise it in North Dakota.

"But the players traded—" Evans began.

"I am not at liberty to say who." Claire dropped her eyelids. "But your friend Jake is still with us."

Evans let out a breath of relief. Where *did* that woman get her information? She'd never told her she knew Jake.

"I'll see you tomorrow, then." Claire looked over Evans's shoulder. "Maybe I'll get a pie to serve Uncle Tiptoe and Polo."

"We're out of Mississippi mud, maple pecan, and chocolate caramel." And who the hell knew what else with the onslaught of the after-school crowd?

"It's hard to keep up with all the crusts, isn't it?" Claire asked. "When you insist on doing them all yourself."

Oh, hell. Why did she have to mention they'd run out? Claire would have never known the difference. "It's not that bad," Evans said. "It's just been busy—getting ready for the lunch."

"But now that you want to do some catering…" Claire's voice trailed off and she raised her eyebrows.

*But I don't want to cater!* Evans's inner voice screamed.

"Yes," her outer voice said. "I do hope that can work out. In time."

Claire nodded, with a satisfied expression. "Good. Did you know," she said slowly, "that there is a machine called a pie crust press that can turn out five hundred pie crusts in an hour?"

This was a prime example of why everyone should not be allowed access to the World Wide Web.

"Yes, Claire, I do know about those, but I don't need to produce five hundred crusts per hour." That was four thousand crusts in an eight-hour day. How many if you made crusts around the clock? A lot. Too many.

"But who knows what the future holds?" Claire persisted. "And I know you love to decorate your pies with those pretty cutouts of leaves and flowers and such. That would give you more time to spend on that. The press is quite an investment, but I think it's worth it. I would be willing to front you the money."

Evans sighed inwardly. Claire meant well, but she didn't understand artisan baking. She reached into her gut—*deep* into her gut—and found *no.* "I'm just not good with that, Claire. I know those machines promise handmade results, but it simply is not true." *No* was hard, so hard that she had to add a caveat. "Maybe the quality will improve eventually." That would never happen, but it would buy her some time.

Claire looked at her for a few beats and nodded. "All right, but you must agree that if you're going to grow, you can't continue to insist on personally making every crust by hand yourself."

It was Evans's turn to nod. "I do know that." *But why do I need to grow?* Evans had an inkling that Claire pictured a five-acre pie factory with *Crust, Inc.* painted on the side. "I've been planning to work with Ariel and Quentin."

"So that would free you up to do some random catering—on a case-by-case basis."

"Absolutely." Case-by-case didn't sound so bad. After all, it was a cheap trade-off for not having a godforsaken pastry press inflicted on her.

"One more thing," Claire said.

And wasn't there always? "What's that, Claire?"

"Have you talked to anyone from Hollingsworth Foods yet?"

"No. I haven't." And that was technically true. She swallowed her guilt.

"Hmm." Claire narrowed her eyes. "If you haven't heard from them by the time Yellowhammers camp is over, I'll make a call."

Camp lasted a week. She'd think about that then.

"Now for my pie. I'll just see what's in the case."

*Yeah, Claire. See what's in the case. You won't find a substandard crust.*

# Chapter Five

"We're just concentrating on hockey and the upcoming season." That's what Glaz had said on ESPN last night when the Kelty scandal had broken. That's also what the players had been instructed to say—and nothing else—in the team meeting earlier. Beyond that, it wasn't to be discussed.

That was fine with Jake. There was hockey to play—and the team lunch to eat. That's where they were headed now. After that, they'd hit the ice with their new team for the first time.

"How was your physical?" Jake asked Robbie.

"Not the best," Robbie said. "I gained ten pounds in Scotland. I thought I'd lost it, but I'm still up four pounds. I blame it on the pie."

*Pie. Evie.* She'd said she was catering this lunch. Was she here yet? "Blame it on all the cake frosting you ate over the summer."

Robbie looked around. "Shut up about that." It was common knowledge that Robbie's ancestral home was the premier wedding venue in the Highlands, but he wasn't anxious for his teammates to know he had a knack for cake decorating and still helped his grandmother make wedding cakes in the off season.

"How many icing roses *did* you eat?"

"None." Robbie hissed. "You don't eat flowers you've gone to the trouble to make." He looked chagrined. "But it's hard not to scrape the bowl. The point is, I'm fat and slow." Robbie could whine when he was of a mind to.

"You are," Jake agreed. "You should quit today. Maybe some minor league team will take you on. But don't tell them you're up four pounds. That would be a deal breaker. Then there's nothing for you but the beer league."

"You're a hard man, Sparks."

"If you want to be coddled, call your mother."

"I did. Right after my physical. She said I should weigh after we skate today. Do you think I can skate off half a pie?"

"I don't think you'll be able to skate. I doubt any of your equipment will fit. Probably your feet are so fat, your skates won't fit. Don't even try your pink lace thong."

"You are an ass," Robbie said.

"But not a fat one." The truth was he'd put on some weight, too—too much French cheese—but he wasn't worried. Skating would take care of it.

"Can't complain about the facility," Robbie said.

That was for sure. The Laurel Springs Iceplex had three sheets of ice, great workout equipment, and was brand-new.

"I wish we played where we practice," Robbie said. "Like in juniors and college."

"Maybe your new farm team will play where they practice. I don't know any major league teams that do."

Robbie sighed. "How long does it take to get to the arena downtown?"

"Ten minutes for me because I drive fast. Fifteen minutes for other people. Longer for you, since you're fat and slow." Jake paused before a door. "Meeting room C. This is where we're supposed to be."

"How about we go downtown tonight?" Robbie asked. "You can show me where the arena is."

"No." Jake pushed open the door. "You don't care where the arena is. You just want to go downtown to find some nightlife—the very thing I came here to get away from."

"What's the harm in seeing if we can scare up a little fun?"

"We have a bet. I don't need to scare anything up."

"Not sure I thought it through before making that bet," Robbie said. "It's no fun carousing alone."

"You have a whole new team. Pick a new guy," Jake said. "Or maybe we could join a knitting club."

"You can be celibate, but you're not taking me down with you."

"I'm not trying," Jake said. "I just want to take that pretty little necklace off your hands."

Robbie put his hand over his heart. "Are you going to stand there or go in the room? I'm hungry."

Right. The room where Evie was likely to be.

"Nice," Robbie said as they stepped inside. It was. Thick carpet. Round tables for six set up around the room. They were some of the first to arrive, though there was a tableful of rookies in the corner and a few guys looking around, getting the lay of the land.

No Evie. Maybe she had a meringue emergency, or the bow fell off her apron.

"Let's sit here by the door," Jake said. He liked to be able to make a quick exit.

"Naw," Robbie said. "That's not how it works. Didn't you see the list on the door with seat assignments? We're at table four."

"I did not. What is this with the seat assignments? Kindergarten?"

"Here we are," Robbie said. Sure enough, there was a sign in the middle of the table, with a big 4 and a list of names. Their table was front and center, but there was nothing to do but sit down. Robbie plucked the sign from the holder.

"Who are we eating with?" Jake asked.

"Able Killen," Robbie read off the card.

Jake remembered him. "From Iowa. Defense. He played for the Ice Demons last year. Decent guy. Next."

"Dietrich Wingo."

"Goalie. Fresh out of University of Denver. He's phenomenal. He might need an attitude adjustment. But he won't be the number one—not with Dustin Carmichael on the team." Carmichael, lately of the Ottawa Ice Demons, was a two-time goalie of the year trophy winner and had hoisted the cup once.

Robbie nodded. "We can adjust Wingo's attitude."

"Spoiling for a fight, are you?"

Robbie shrugged. "Not much else to do around here."

"You can practice the piano or maybe open up a cake decorating business. Who else?"

"Logan Jensen," Robbie read the next name. "I met him earlier while waiting to get weighed."

"The Walleyes?"

"Aye. Before that, the University of Minnesota. He's from Minneapolis. Forward. He has a kid. Single dad."

"Who else?" Jake fiddled with his silverware. The table was set with real dishes, but there wasn't any food.

No buffet line either. Maybe they were just having pie—or not. Still no sign of Evie.

"Holy family and all the wise men!" Robbie burst out. "What is Luka Zadorov doing here?"

"No!" Jake snatched the card from Robbie. "Let me see that." But there it was in black and white—the name of the big Russian center.

"That's what it says," Robbie said. "I didn't see him in the team meeting."

"No," Jake agreed. "But we were sitting on the second row. I didn't look around much."

Robbie looked back at the card and shook his head in disbelief. "No way the Colonials would have traded him."

"Maybe he asked for the trade. We did."

"I suppose, but they didn't let us go easy and we weren't even skating first line. I can't believe the Colonials would agree." Robbie glanced at the door. "Here he comes."

Yep. And it looked like the other three were trailing behind him. They must have read the door.

But still no Evie.

They all shook hands and Jake noted the expressions. Wingo was cocky, Killen looked happy and friendly, Jensen was pleasantly neutral, but Luka Zadorov was nothing short of pissed off beyond reasonable understanding. He wasn't even trying to hide it.

Might as well take the bull by the horns. "So, Zodorov," Jake said, as they settled into their seats. "You're the surprise of the table—probably the whole team."

Zodorov reached into his backpack, removed a water bottle, then tossed it back in with a grunt of disgust—

but not before Jake noticed that it was a Boston Colonials water bottle.

*"Da,"* Zodorov said. "Was surprise to me as well. The trade came last night. I flew in a short time ago. I am in hotel. Not even my smoothie maker do I have."

They were all silent for a moment. It happened all the time, traded and gone in a matter of hours. It could happen to any of them.

"They traded you?" Robbie said.

Zodorov gave Robbie the stink eye. "Why else would I be in Alabama? The Colonials need goalie. This new team had Dustin Carmichael. No more."

"What the hell!" Cold washed over Jake. Carmichael was *gone*? Zodorov was good news, but did it balance out the bad news that Carmichael was in Boston? He thought back to the team meeting. Was there anyone else missing who should have been there?

"Seems like they would have told us this in the meeting earlier," Robbie said.

"Bigger fish to fry, I guess," Logan Jensen said. "Kelty, and all…"

"Sounds like they weren't willing to trade me." Wingo spoke for the first time, and the words that flowed from his mouth did not do one damn thing to negate Jake's fear that he needed an attitude adjustment.

Zodorov slowly turned his head and gave Wingo a look that would have frozen a flame, though Wingo didn't seem to notice. For a few seconds the only sound was from the tables around them.

"And you would think that," Zodorov spoke slowly, his Russian accent getting heavier with each word, "the Colonials offered for you *first*? That they would trade me for a rookie? An unknown quality?"

"I think you mean *quantity*." Jensen cleared his throat. "The word is *quantity*."

"Who are you, Logan?" Zodorov said. "Suddenly Mr. Daniel Webster?" There was clearly some camaraderie between those two, but Jake couldn't ferret out why. As far as he knew, they'd never played together.

"Noah," Jensen said. "And I didn't say *no*, as in the opposite of *yes*. It was *No-ah* Webster who wrote the dictionary."

"Shut up, Logan. Is the same."

"It's not," Jensen insisted.

"Then it makes no difference." Zodorov turned back to Wingo. "You think I would be traded for a rookie?"

Wingo grinned. "I won the National Championship at Denver last year."

"*You* won? *You* won alone? That tells me more about you than I want to know." Zodorov shook his head. "But never mind. I am already tired of you, college boy. College sports mean nothing."

As the only Southerner there, Jake supposed it was up to him to break it to Zodorov. "You will find that the good people of Alabama do not agree with you on that last point. In fact, no one in the South would."

"What?" Zodorov narrowed his angry eyes.

"You are in the college football capital of the world." Jake paused to let it sink in. "I'm not saying college football is a religion in the South, but when my little cousin was asked in Sunday school if she could name three of Jesus's disciples, she rattled off two Southeastern Conference coaches and a starting quarterback."

Everyone except Luka laughed. If possible, he looked even more incensed.

"I've got to get out of here." Zodorov looked around

as if there might be a hockey fairy who would whisk him away. "Hockey should be revered."

But then a voice boomed from the sound system. Jake jumped and looked up, and saw Nate Ayers, the Yellowhammers' general manager, at the podium.

"Hello again, gentlemen."

"Is he going to talk?" Robbie whispered. "Are we never going to eat?"

"It was that attitude that got you ten extra pounds," Jake whispered back. "Be quiet."

"I think we're all here," Ayers continued. "We're about to get lunch underway, but I'd like to introduce you to the principle shareholders of Yellowhammer Hockey Team, Inc—Marc 'Polo' MacNeal, former first baseman for the New York Yankees, and Tiptoe Watkins."

The men made the usual speeches—*looking forward to a great season, welcome to the Yellowhammers, blah, blah, blah.*

Jake had heard it all before. He looked around for Evie. Where was she?

When the owners finished, Logan Jensen leaned forward. "I heard that Polo MacNeal put up most of the money. He's related to Mr. Watkins by marriage. Claire, who owns Hammer Time and The Mill, is Mr. Watkins's niece, and she also owns a little piece of the team. Nobody thought they would get an expansion team, but they did. Obviously." He gestured to his surroundings.

"How do you know all this?" Wingo asked.

Logan grinned and Jake decided he liked him. "I come from Hockey Country, USA. Everything worth knowing about hockey is everyday talk in Minnesota."

"Is true," Luka said. "I must get out of this land of

college football and get to a place where hockey is re-spected as it should be."

"Thank you, gentlemen." Glaz now had the mic. "Team, meet me in the locker room after lunch. A fine meal is about to be served, courtesy of Hammer Time and Crust. Thank you to the owners of these fine estab-lishments, Claire Watkins and Evans Pemberton." Jake surveyed the room again. Where was she? Claire and a gang of servers were gathered next to a set of double doors, but no Evie. "I'll see you in an hour," Glaz con-tinued. "We'll get you some equipment and see who can still skate." Laughter floated through the room and Glaz went to sit at a table with all the other important people.

"I can still skate," Wingo said. "I'm in the best shape of my life." Jake shook his head. That boy would be lucky to make it to the season opener.

"Can you skate with broken limbs?" Luka asked. "Because that's where you're headed if you don't stop bragging."

Thankfully a girl—Jake figured her for college-aged—appeared at their table with a tray as big as a bicycle wheel.

"Hello, gentlemen." She made *gentlemen* sound like three separate words. "I have some lunch for you." Jake looked around again. Still no Evie—just this girl in black pants and a white polo with *Crust* embroidered on the left breast. Should he ask her where Evie was? No. Apparently Evie had just sent staff.

He wasn't sure if it was the girl's pretty smile or the smell of the food that distracted his tablemates, but he was grateful for it. For the moment, college football, the loss of a seasoned goalie, and Wingo's self-love seemed forgotten. She leaned over between Wingo and Robbie.

"If you will just excuse me, I'll set this here." Hellfire and brimstone. Robbie sniffed her hair. Jake gave him a dirty look and Robbie shrugged.

She pulled a card from her apron pocket. "We have today traditional Upper Peninsula Michigan pasties with beef, rutabagas, potatoes, and onion." There was a plate of golden brown half-moon pies that looked like fried fruit pies, except twice the size of any Jake had ever seen—plus a bunch of different salads and some little casserole dishes.

Able Killen let out a happy groan. "I played my junior hockey in the Yooper. I love those things. Never thought I'd get them in Alabama."

The girl smiled. "That's great. I'll tell the chef." That would be Evie. *Chef.* Good for her. "We also have Caesar, fruit, and spinach salads, and macaroni and cheese with chicken. Joy is right behind me with a drink cart. Is there anything else I can get for you?"

Jake started to speak, but Zodorov beat him to it. "Thank you so much. You are very kind." He could find his manners when he needed to, and maybe he'd realized he was the alpha at the table.

"Please let me know if you want anything else, but save room for dessert."

After Joy of the drink cart left them with a tableful of Gatorade and water, they passed the food. Though he'd been taught to eat his salad first, Jake was too curious about Evie's meat pie to wait.

Nothing could have prepared him for the party in his mouth. He took another bite. The first one had not been a fluke. He eyed the serving tray and counted. They had each been provided with two pies. He almost reached for his second one right then, and would have if he hadn't been afraid his grandmother would suddenly swing in from the Delta on a flying trapeze and give him an etiquette lesson. You did not take a second helping of something until you had finished the first.

"Just as good as what I had in the UP," Able said.

"Better," Jensen said. "It's got a smoky taste."

"You're in barbecue country now," Robbie said. "Everything tastes smoky."

Jake looked around the table to make sure everyone was eating Evie's pies with the relish she deserved. No one had touched a salad or the macaroni and cheese, though he knew they'd all get around to it.

Jake finished off his pie and reached for another.

"Don't you think you ought to eat some macaroni and cheese before you eat another one of those?" Wingo asked. He had catsup on his mouth.

"I do not." He bit into the pie, though Wingo was probably right. It was practically a law for hockey players to eat pasta before an important skate—and the first skate of the season was almost as important as a game.

"You should carb up before you skate," Wingo persisted.

Jake pointed at the pie. "Plenty of carbs here. Potatoes, crust, maybe rutabagas. Do they have carbs?" He'd never had a rutabaga that he knew of.

"But pasta—"

Able cut Wingo off. "Wonder who that is. She's a cute one."

Jake immediately knew who *she* was. Slowly, he raised his head and followed Able's gaze. There she was, walking from table to table, smiling and making small talk. Just then, Miklos Novak, the forward from the

Czech Republic, said something to her and she laughed, patting his shoulder lightly as she walked away.

It was lightly, wasn't it?

"She looks nice," Logan said without much commitment and went back to eating. Jake was somewhat annoyed that he hadn't been more emphatic.

"That's the look I like," Able said. No one could have argued with his enthusiasm, though Jake didn't like that either—though he saw Able's point.

Unlike yesterday, Evie's dark hair was down, shiny and swinging around her face. She wasn't wearing clogs and chef's pants today, but a black skirt with a scalloped hem that hit right above her knee, and a white cotton blouse with a collar and a pocket over her left breast.

And on that pocket was a tiny bow, which made him think of the apron bow. Her shoes had enough of a heel to make you look at her legs without making you think she might break her neck.

She continued to work the room, but she wasn't getting any closer to their table. She didn't look his way.

"Do you suppose she'll come over here?" Able was half out of his chair.

"Whoa there, Killen." Jake had been silent as long as he could. "I know that woman. She's not a puck bunny." *She's a Delta-born cotillion graduate who minds her manners, kneels for communion, says hotty toddy, and loves her mama. She is not for you.*

Able looked incensed. "I never thought she was. I lost interest in puck bunnies in juniors. I like real relationships. She's my type. That's all."

"How do you know? Have you had a conversation with her?" Jake asked.

"What's wrong with you?" Able asked. "And why

do you care? Are you seeing her? Because if you are, just say—"

"I'm not. But you need to stay away from her," Jake said.

"She's Sparks's childhood friend. Cousin of his ex."
*Thanks for the help, Robbie.*

Able nodded and his good-natured manner returned. "I understand. So she's like a sister to you?"

*No.* "Yes." A lie, but you don't date your teammates' sisters. That was part of the Bro Code. Everybody knew that. It was a lie well spent.

"Good. She's single, then, and fair game."

Jake nodded before he realized what Able had said. Then the words sunk in.

Jake took a deep breath to clear his head. "What? No." Apparently Able did not understand the Bro Code. "I don't think you under—"

The eyes that had been on him suddenly shifted above his head and Jake smelled cinnamon.

"How is everything?" The voice behind him had the cadence and sound of the Delta. "Is your lunch to your liking? Do you have enough of everything?"

Everyone sounded off at once, like a bunch of puppies trying to get attention.

*"Fantastic, Wonderful. Never had anything like this, but it's great. Really good. Better than in the UP,"* all tumbled out of their mouths at once. Not surprising. Hockey players worshipped those who fed them. He looked around. Able was the only one who appeared to be smitten in a way that had nothing to do with pie. He was looking at Evie, while the others looked back and forth between her and their plates.

"How about you, Jake?" She laid a hand on his shoulder. He caught himself before he reached up to cover her hand with his. "Did you like the pasty?" It wasn't lost on her that he hadn't joined in the Greek chorus of pie praise.

He turned and met her eyes—happy eyes. Really, her whole face was happy. That made him smile. "It was delicious. I ate two."

She raised an eyebrow. "As good as Mississippi mud?" Outstanding. Let them know he'd had her pie before.

"That's a hard question. I guess I'd just have to say it's a whole different part of my mouth. There's room for all pies."

She opened her mouth to reply but, damn it all to hell, Killen jumped to his feet.

"I'm Able Killen. Defense. I really enjoyed the pasty. I played in the Yooper and you could teach them a thing or two."

"That's very kind, Able." She looked pleased, but there didn't appear to be any sparks flying. That was important. He owed it to her parents to see to it that she didn't get involved with the wrong guy. The Delta Queens, as he thought of Evie's mother and his own, would have plenty to say if he let Evie get involved with an unsavory sort. Able seemed like a good guy, but that's what the neighbors always said about serial killers.

And things were just getting better and better. Robbie was either trying to help him out or didn't want to be outdone because he was on his feet, giving Evie that smile he mostly used in bars.

"I'm Robbie McTavish." He leaned forward, just a little. Jake knew that move, too. He was going to have to kill his best friend. "Of Kennamara. Near Inverness. In the Highlands." He gestured to the table. "These are our other teammates: Logan Jensen, Luka Zadorov, and Dietrich Wingo."

They all stood and made polite greetings—and a damned good thing.

Jake was about to bring this little meeting to a close and help Evie move on, but Robbie wasn't done.

"Really good pie that Sparks brought home last night."

"Are you two living together?" Evie asked.

"No!" Robbie and Jake said at the same time.

"No," Robbie repeated. "We're across the hall from each other at The Mill, but I'm staying with Sparks until I get a bed. We ate all the pie."

She looked amused and cut her eyes at Jake. Her dimples deepened. "Oh, you did? All? I hope it didn't make you sick."

"Could nectar of the gods make a man sick?" Robbie asked.

She laughed. "Is that what it was? I thought it was Mississippi mud. Maybe I'll change the name to nectar of the gods."

"I've never heard of it," Wingo piped up. And why not? It had been a while since he'd heard the sound of his own voice.

"It's a chocolate pie," Evie said. "Some say it originated in our home—the Mississippi Delta." *Their* home. A warm feeling came over Jake. "Some say not. I like to think it did."

"My nana says it did, and that's good enough for me," Jake said.

Evie laughed, so joyful sounding, and put her hand

on his shoulder again. "If Miss Althea says so, that's good enough for me, too. No one would dare argue with her."

"Is her pie as good as Evans's?" Able asked.

Jake and Evans looked at each other and burst out laughing. No one else joined in. Why would they? Only he and Evie knew how ludicrous the very thought was.

"Nana doesn't make pie," Jake said. "She *directs* someone else to make pie."

Evans brushed her hair back. "She has more important things to do—like take her hats to the florist to have them decorated with fresh flowers before every bridge club, luncheon, and church service."

Jake hadn't exactly forgotten that about Nana, but he hadn't thought about it in a long time either. He suspected that he and Evie were visualizing something very similar right now: Nana's Lincoln parked in front of the Flower Cart—the same shop that had provided flowers for every dance, wedding, and funeral in Cottonwood all their lives and before.

"Well." Evie closed her eyes and shook her head. "If I can't get you anything else, I'll move along. I want to make sure your peach cobbler gets served while it's still warm. It was nice to meet y'all."

With the exception of Luka and Jake, everyone at the table made noises like baby birds who were about to be fed.

"Will there be ice cream?" Wingo asked.

"Is there any other way to serve peach cobbler? I hope you'll all stop by Crust and see me," she said as she walked away.

"Aye," Robbie said. "Pie makes every day better."

"For sure," Wingo said.

"Absolutely," Logan said.

"Of course," Luka said, though he didn't sound sincere.

"You can depend on it." Able sounded exceedingly sincere.

Jake didn't say anything. He just watched her go.

The cobbler had been served and Evans's feet were beginning to ache from her heels. Noting that Claire, who had been sitting beside her uncle, had disappeared, Evans surveyed the table where the brass was sitting, but didn't interrupt. They didn't appear to need anything and were in deep, intense conversation.

It was over. There was nothing left to do but clean up, and Claire had said the Hammer Time staff would do that. She'd see about things in the prep kitchen, get her purse, and head home to change before going back to Crust.

She reached in her skirt pocket for her phone to check the time just as it vibrated. There was a text message from Ariel.

Sarah Jane Cathcart wants ten apple pies because the PTA is having Apple of My Eye Day tomorrow at the high school for the teachers. She needs to pick them up at 7:30 am because they are serving pie and coffee in three shifts starting at 8. What should I tell her?

*How about that, as pie makers, we don't advocate serving pie at that time of morning?*

Did no one think ahead? But what else was she going to say, but yes? They were in the pie business. It was reasonable that Sarah Jane should expect to be able to

buy pies from them—no matter what time she wanted
to serve them. It wasn't Sarah Jane's fault that Evans
had used her time unwisely this week.

Evans quickly typed: Tell her we'll have them ready.
I'm on my way and I'll get them knocked out.

In the interest of optimum freshness, she debated on
getting the pies oven ready and baking them early in the
morning, but they might be too warm to cut. She'd have
to go for fresh enough and pies that wouldn't fall apart.

Ariel replied: Should I measure out the flour for you
and grate the cheese for the pastry?

Evans considered. It would be nice to be a step ahead
before she got there, but Ariel had said *measure* the
flour and Evans baked by weight. And what if she didn't
use the small holes of the grater for the cheese? There
was no time for mistakes today.

Evans texted back:

That's okay, but you can peel and slice the apples.

Ariel knew she liked the apples almost paper thin
and would put them in lemon water to keep them from
discoloring.

But she didn't answer—maybe because she was disappointed, maybe because her brain had moved into a
different universe.

Evans stepped quickly toward the kitchen, intent on
asking Joy and Dory to pack up their equipment and
meet her back at Crust. But Claire popped out of the
kitchen before Evans could pop in.

"That went well, wouldn't you say?" Claire looked
pleased.

"I would say that," Evans agreed. Jake had eaten two

pasties and the last time she'd sneaked a peep at him, he'd been wolfing down peach cobbler.

"I have some excellent news for you."

Oh, hell. Evans got the feeling that the news was not going to be excellent at all.

"What's that?"

"Nate was really impressed with your food."

"Nate?"

"Nathan Ayers. The general manager," Claire said with exaggerated patience, like she did when Evans suspected she really wanted to add, "Keep up!"

"They have a team chef, but Nate would like for us to do some catering for special events."

Not excellent. Not even good. Just plain bad. She lifted her shoulders. She needed to say so. She'd had a half dozen pissed-off customers yesterday because they couldn't have the pie they wanted and now there were ten apple pies breathing down her neck.

"That sounds…amazing. And—to be honest—a little overwhelming."

"I have faith in you," Claire said. "It's a great opportunity. And you wouldn't be doing it for free in the future."

But at what cost?

Evans knew she ought to flat-out tell her she didn't want to cater, but she didn't have the time or energy. *Or gumption.* Couldn't leave that out.

She put on a bright smile. "That's amazing!"

Claire nodded. "It's certainly a start." She paused a beat. "Still nothing from Hollingsworth, I take it?"

"No."

Claire nodded. "Well. Have a good afternoon," she said as she walked away, leaving Evans with her guilt over the half-truth, anxiety over impending catering jobs, and dread of producing ten apple pies because of everything she'd let slide today for this lunch.

But even with all that on her mind, she didn't forget to glance back at Jake before she left. To her surprise, his gaze was on her. They didn't wave, but their smiles met in the middle.

# Chapter Six

Jake took off his helmet and stored it on the shelf of his new stall. He knew the stall was his because it had a flat-screen TV mounted above, complete with the training camp schedule and scrolling messages.

*Welcome, #8 Jake Champagne!*
*Yellowhammers, Hustle and Heart!*
*Skate Hard, Win Big!*

The locker room was sweet. The lounge, hydration bar, weight room, and team meeting room were pretty standard, but there was nothing standard about the stalls—at least none Jake had ever had. His own personal TV aside, he'd never had one that hadn't been defiled by some former player's hockey stink—and that was just the beginning. There were USB ports, a ventilation system, and fans for drying skates, gloves, and helmets. Jake found the compartment with a keypad lock a little sad. He'd never use that. Teammates wouldn't steal from each other.

But then again…

He opened the compartment and put his lucky puck

inside. Teammates might not steal from each other, but they would jerk the hell out of your chain.

"Locking up my puck, are you?" Beside him, Robbie sat down and began to unlace his skates.

"It's not your puck." Jake stripped his upper body down to his sweaty Under Armour, sat, and began to unlace his own skates.

"It will be." Robbie shucked his jersey and pads.

Jake opened his mouth to reply, but was stopped.

"Silence!" Glaz belted out. The noise in the locker room ceased and those who were still shedding their newly sweat-christened gear stilled. "That was somewhat acceptable, though you look like hill of ants in rainstorm. Is expected. You know nothing of each other. Soon you will dance together as one. In ten days is first preseason game. It will *not* end in a loss to the Northern Lights. Understood?"

"Understood!" rang out.

"Good." Coach nodded. "Team meeting first thing in the morning." Yep. At eight o'clock. It said so on Able Killen's TV, which was right across from Jake. "That's all." And Glaz disappeared through the door.

"I'm starving." That came from Miklos Novak, the Czech defenseman seated on the other side of Robbie.

"Me, too," Robbie said.

They all were. No matter how much they ate before, everyone came off the ice ravenous.

"Anyone want to go to Hammer Time?" Logan wandered up.

*"Ne,"* Novak said. "I would like more of what we had earlier. I am going to that pie shop."

The hair on the back of Jake's neck stood on end. Novak had made Evie laugh at the lunch. What was that about? So far, Jake hadn't noticed anything funny about him.

Able sauntered across the room, careful not to step on the logo. "I'll go with you, Magic Man," Able said.

Magic man? That was his nickname? Why? It couldn't be because his given name—Miklos—sounded like it. Ought to be milkman.

Ryan Bell called out. "I'll go, too. The pie was okay, but did you see the tits on the pie maker? Wouldn't mind getting my hands on those."

Jakes insides turned to concrete and his mouth went dry. He opened his mouth to speak, but no words would come.

Able, however, didn't have any trouble speaking. "Hands off."

"You will not—" Jake was surprised that his voice didn't come out louder.

"Sparks." Robbie laid a hand on his arm and stopped him. "Not cool, Bell. The lass is Sparks's pal from childhood."

"Oh," Ryan said. "Sorry, man. It's just talk."

Jake forced himself to dial it back. What Bell had said, they'd all said—and much worse. He wasn't going to tell him it was all right, but he did nod in his direction.

Robbie cut his eyes at Jake and grinned. "Let's all go to Hammer Time. You know. Decent steak, maybe some decent cleavage."

"To hell with steak and tits," Novak said stubbornly. "I will have that meat pie."

"See you there." Able took off for the shower.

Jake finished undressing as quickly as a fifteen-year-old virgin who'd just been offered a roll in the hay. He needed to get to Crust first.

"Champagne!" Jake turned toward the sound of his name to see the equipment manager, Leland Puckett. "Come by my office before you shower." And he was gone.

Damn.

A few minutes before closing time, Evans slid the apple pies into the oven and set the timer. Neva stuck her head in the kitchen.

"Evans, there's a man here to see you."

*Déja vu.* Jake? "Who is it?"

Neva shook her head. "I don't know. He has an accent, but I don't know what kind." That would not be Jake. Neva spoke Mississippi Delta. "He wants—I quote—'that little pie with meat and other stuffs inside such as I have before.'"

It was a hockey player wanting a pasty.

"I can tell him you're busy," Neva said. "I was about to lock the front door."

But she was curious. "I'll talk to him." She wiped her hands. "Go ahead and leave. I'll lock up."

The guy at the counter was all decked in Yellowhammer gear and looked familiar. He smoothed his straight brown hair behind his ears and produced a smile that he had probably practiced in the mirror.

"Hi, Evans." He smiled wider, leaned on the counter, and inclined his head in her direction.

"Hi." There was no point in pretending she remembered his name, if she'd ever heard it.

"I am Miklos Novak. Thirty-nine." Then he laughed

a little. "Not in years. That is my sweater number. In years, I am twenty-seven."

She nodded. "How are you?"

"Good," he said, "but hungry. I just come from practice. Whole time I'm on ice, all I think of is the little pies you bring us."

Did he really think she would believe a professional hockey player thought about anything except hockey when he was on the ice? "I'm glad you enjoyed them."

"I was hoping to purchase some, but I do not read them on your menu." He gestured to the chalkboard wall.

"The pasties were something I did especially for the Yellowhammer lunch. They're not a usual menu item."

He sighed and looked crestfallen, like maybe his village had been burned, all the hockey sticks in the world with it.

"You have none? My new favorite food?" He was a drama king, all right.

She did, in fact, have some—the imperfect ones that had a bit of filling leaking out or uneven crimping. "I do," she said slowly, "but they aren't as pretty as they should be."

He brightened. "But the taste? It would be same?"

"Yes, but I don't sell things I'm not proud of."

He nodded and reached for his wallet. "Is the taste you should be proud of. I do not care about the pretty." He put a little devil in his smile and let his hair fall in his eyes. "Except for pie bakers."

She laughed. He was probably the kind who flirted with everyone, but it lifted her spirits after such a hard day. "You really want those pies, don't you?"

"More than you know," he said with mock earnestness.

"I couldn't sell them. It's a matter of integrity, but I'll give them to you."

"I respect your integrity, and I will take the pies any way I can get them. Is a favor you do for me. I will do same. I endorse Nike. They give me shoes. I will get some for you. Would you like that?"

"Why not? Size seven." He would probably never think of it again, but that was okay. She had shoes.

"Good. I call tomorrow." He placed his hands on the counter. "Now. I like the American beer Budweiser." He said *Budweiser* like it was two words—a man's name. "And I will have that."

Oh, good cow. "We don't sell beer, Miklos. We're more of a coffee, tea, and milk place. And besides—"

He interrupted her. "Ah, well. Then I will have tea—not the cold tea that you like here, but hot."

"Hold up." She put her hands in the air. "Here's the thing. It's closing time." She gestured to the empty shop. "I'm going to give you the pies. You can have all I've got—about a dozen. But you're going to need to take them home and bake them yourself."

Miklos wrinkled his brow. "In microwave?"

"No. They will need to be baked in a regular oven."

His mouth formed an O and he looked perplexed. "Cook? No. I cannot do that thing. Impossible."

Ridiculous. Anybody who had enough sense to make millions of dollars playing hockey could certainly use the oven.

"I'll tell you how. It's easy. All you have to do is preheat the oven to 375°, put the pasties on a parchment-lined pan, and bake for forty-five minutes." With every word she spoke, he looked more puzzled. She took her tone to a bright new level. "And you can have a beer with it at home."

"These words you speak—" He waved his hands. "I hear them, but they make no sense."

She ran what she'd said back through her mind and tried to discern what—if anything—could have been remotely unclear.

"You don't have parchment?" she asked.

He looked at the ceiling and shook his head. "I don't have *pan*." He looked pitiful. It was contrived, but Evans was somewhat amused that he was going to the trouble. "Could you do for me? You say is easy."

She hesitated. Why not? She could throw the pasties in the oven and tell him to pick them up in forty-five minutes. She'd be here anyway, minding the apple pies. Unlike a lot of things she agreed to, she actually wanted him to have the pies. She wasn't attracted to him any more than he was attracted to her, but he was cute and he amused her.

"All right."

But before she could tell him to come back later, before she could cross the shop to lock the door, before she could even take a breath, that door opened and in came two of the guys from Jake's table—Dietrich Wingo and Able Killen. And there were two more guys behind them.

Miklos turned. "Able! Wings! Christophe and Mick, whose name has the sound of my own! My teammates. Come in!"

*No. The shop is closed, even if I haven't managed to lock the door. Baking a few pasties for cutie pie here is one thing, but a hockey party is another. So, don't come in.*

But they did. "Hi, Evans." Able gave her a sweet little smile, let his eyes rest on the display cases and come back to meet hers. "This is the best place I've ever been. And I've been to Disney World, the Grand Canyon, and Niagara Falls."

"Thank you. Disney, you say? High praise." Especially since the cases were almost empty.

Miklos piped up. "She give me meat pies. I give her shoes. Nike Air Max, I think."

"Yeah? I just signed endorsement deals with Campbell's soup and Gillette," Able rushed on. "I can get you some soup and razors." He looked like an eager puppy.

Soup? Razors? Her gut told her that Able might produce what he promised. The thought of opening her door to find cases of chicken noodle soup and plastic razors was not appealing.

"Thank you, but—"

"I've got a deal with Visa and Under Armour," Dietrich Wingo said. "I doubt I can get you a free credit card, but I can get you some shorts."

"Uh…no. I'm good."

"Wings, Able!" Miklos burst out. "The pies are *mine*. She give to *me*, though I will share. But she has no beer. Christophe, Mick, go get us some beer while Evans bakes pies. Budweiser."

"No!" Damn. She had forgotten about the other two—Christophe and Mick, apparently, who either had no endorsements or weren't willing to barter for pie. But they were already leaving. One of them said, "I'll call Davis and Dempsey."

Wingo and Able were pushing tables together. They were about to turn Crust into a potluck, beer-swilling free-for-all!

Evans knew when she'd been beat; she always had. Practice made perfect, and she'd had plenty of practice. But what the hell? There was leftover pie in the cases. They could eat what they wanted of that, too. There would still be some for St. Ann's soup kitchen.

She laughed and shook her head. Maybe a little free-for-all would do her good.

"I'm going to put the pasties in the oven," she said. "Someone lock the door."

## Chapter Seven

That was an hour of his life that Jake would never get back.

Leland Puckett considered himself the god of skate sharpening. He hadn't liked how Jake's skates had looked on the ice, so he'd insisted on sharpening them at a different angle and watching Jake skate a few laps. Jake had never been as particular about his skate blades as some guys, so that had been all well and good, but after the third time Leland insisted on going through the resharpening and skating routine, Jake had had enough.

He had to admit that his skates did perform better in the end, but he knew for sure that by now Crust was closed, and Evie would have had to deal with Miklos and Able on her own. Evie wasn't helpless, but she was a little sheltered. She would have no idea how hungry hockey players were when they came off the ice—for food and sex. Maybe he'd go see her after he ate. He didn't know where she lived, but he could text and ask.

He climbed into his bright green Lamborghini—the consolation prize he'd bought for himself the day his divorce was final—and drove down Main Street toward home, considering food. He could stop at Hammer Time. Some of the guys might still be there. Or he could head out toward the interstate where the fast food places were. He should buy groceries—should have already. Maybe tomorrow.

Most of the businesses on Main Street were dark, but—what was that? Were there lights on at Crust? He slammed on his brakes and backed up.

Hellfire and brimstone! It looked like there was a hockey player party going on in there. And there was Evie—waltzing around with a water pitcher in her hand, filling their glasses. Who the hell did they think they were, letting her wait on them like they were little kings and she was a servant?

Jake did a U-turn in the middle of street and parked the Lamborghini in the Employee of the Month space in front of the bank. He threw open the door and tried to get out without unbuckling his seat belt. It didn't work. Finally, his feet hit the pavement and he stomped down the street, seething as he went. He was spoiling for a fight, but breaking up a party would have to do.

When he went to jerk open the door of Crust, it didn't budge. Locked. He rattled the knob. No one looked his way.

Oh, hell no. Pretty boy Christophe Bachet got out of his chair, took Evie by the arm, and led her to the pie case. He pointed to a pie and Evie said something. Then he pointed to another, another, and another. They laughed together like pie was funny. Evie went behind the counter and Wingo, Davis, and Able rushed up like catfish in a pond at feeding time—all pointing at pies.

He did a quick inventory. No Ryan Bell. That was something. Still, he had to get in there. Rattling the knob again did no good, so he pounded on the glass. They were all laughing and partying so hard they didn't hear that either. Evie sliced a pie—*his* Mississippi mud, if he wasn't mistaken—and handed it to Bachet.

He started banging on the glass again, and this time he didn't stop until Evie saw him. She looked surprised, but then she smiled. Good. She would come let him in and he would get control of this situation, explain to her what letches hockey players could be. At best, they were taking advantage of her good nature by making her stay late and pour them water and cut them pie. At worst, they were trying to get in her pants—or her bra, as Bell had so eloquently put it. He would tolerate neither. As soon as she opened the door, he would pull her outside and explain things in no uncertain terms.

But she didn't come to open the door. Instead, she said something to Miklos Novak, pointed toward the door, and kept cutting pie.

Miklos turned and looked at Jake through the door, gave a wave, and got to his feet—he took his sweet time doing it, too. After an eternity, Miklos unlocked the door.

"*Ahoj*, Sparks," Miklos said.

"Hmm." More like *annoy*.

"There are no more little meat pies. We ate them all, but Evans has promised to put them on her menu, and we have promised to buy them. Now Evans is giving out sweet pie. Perhaps she will serve some to you."

Perhaps? *Perhaps?* He was tempted to tell Miklos that yesterday Evie had not only served him a piece of pie, she had *given* him a whole pie. Even if she was doing them a favor by allowing them in her shop after hours, she was *selling* them pie. So there.

"She is not taking money."

She was *giving* them pie? Didn't she know they were multimillionaires? She had a living to make.

"She say the sweet pies will be stale in the morning after sitting out whole night. A church picks them up to feed people who are poor."

"You are not poor," Jake growled.

"No," he said happily. "I was once poor, but no more."

"See to it that you leave her a tip—a very generous tip. And see to it that the other guys do, too."

Miklos narrowed his eyes, and they turned mean. "She is very nice to me. I know what to do in return. I do not need lessons from you, Sparks."

Jake didn't reply, but brushed past Miklos and headed straight for Evie. Apparently, she had been dishing out pie for a while because there was lots of pie eating going on. His teammates called out to him. He gave a general wave in their direction, but didn't slow down. They looked like a bunch of idiots sitting on those fancy little iron chairs with the heart-shaped backs that were meant to hold women drinking tea and eating little cakes. Never mind that he had logged some time in one of those chairs.

"Hello, Jake," Evie said. "Here you go, Dietrich." She handed Wingo a plate. "Apple cranberry walnut. I hope you enjoy it."

"Hey, Sparks." Able was the only one who hadn't gotten his pie. "What do you recommend?"

*Oh, brother, you don't want to know.*

"Jake likes Mississippi mud," Evie said, "but I just gave Christophe and Mick the last two pieces."

She was on a first-name basis with them? Jake didn't

even know all their first names. And they'd had the last of his pie. Damn them.

Evie went on, "But the cherry is very popular. I macerate the fruit in brandy before I make the filling. It adds a little something extra. There're some ground almonds in the crust. You aren't allergic to nuts, are you?"

"No allergies. I don't know what macerate means." Able tried to give her a flirty look. He wasn't good at it. "But if you say it's good, I'll have that. Any chance you'll come sit down and have some, too?"

"She doesn't eat pie," Jake said.

Evie frowned at him. "That's not exactly true. I taste pie all day long. I just don't usually eat a whole piece." She took the pie out of the case. It had a crisscross top crust made up of little sparkly cherries.

"That looks nice," Able said.

She smiled like she meant it. "Thank you. I try to make them pretty."

Jake let his eyes wander to the case. There were only partial pies left, but he could see that she had taken pains with them, putting little leaves, flowers, acorns, and such on the edges and making fancy tops with braids, strips, and cutouts. He hadn't noticed if his Mississippi mud yesterday had been decorated.

"Not pretty," Jake said. "They're beautiful. You're an artist."

"Why, thank you, Jake." She put her hand over her heart for a second. "Not everybody notices the extra touches. Sometimes the decorations give a hint to what's inside."

He pointed to a pie with bees around the edge. "Are there bees in that pie?" He gave her a little wink.

She laughed that laugh that reminded the world she

was a happy person. "No. No bees, but it's honey pear, one of the fall specials." She handed the cherry pie to Able. "Here's your pie, Able."

"Please come sit with me?" Able asked.

*Not if I have anything to say about it.* Which, Jake realized to his horror, he did not.

"Thank you," she said, "but I need to clean up and box some pies for early pickup tomorrow."

Able stood there a moment, like he didn't know what to say—which he obviously did not. "Sparks, get some pie and come have a seat. We've got some beer left."

Jake just looked at him.

"Beer? Really?" Jake asked once Able had gone back to his little chair of torture.

She closed her eyes and shook her head. "They brought it. Don't ask."

"What are they doing here anyway? You're supposed to be closed." He suddenly felt like he was the grown-up in charge of a bunch of wild eighth graders. Maybe he had it coming. He and Robbie had certainly given some of the more senior Sound players some headaches.

"Long story." She wiped her hands and returned the cherry pie to the case. "Would you like pie?"

"No, thank you." The thought made him a little queasy.

"Too full from dinner?" she asked. "I can wrap up some for later."

"I haven't had dinner. I'm starving, but—"

"Sugar on an empty stomach. I get it. Come with me," she said. "I have some good sourdough bread, and I can make you a hot ham-and-cheese sandwich."

His mouth watered and his stomach twisted in anticipation. "Can I have two?"

"If you're good." Her apron bow danced up and down as she walked away.

Damn that bow—not that he didn't enjoy the sight, but his barbarian teammates were probably enjoying it, too.

He followed her though the employees-only door into the industrial kitchen. *Take that, guys. See where I'm getting to go and you're not.*

With its stainless steel appliances and stark white walls, the room should have felt cold and sterile, but there was something about it that felt homey. Maybe it was the smell of cinnamon or the black-and-white checked floor that reminded him of Anna-Blair's shop in Cottonwood. Maybe it was Evie herself.

She opened the big refrigerator and began to pull things off the bottom shelf—ham, cheese, mayonnaise, and a dish with a partial stick of butter. He opened his mouth to tell her he didn't like mustard, but she left it where it was. She remembered. Over the years, their families had grilled hundreds of hamburgers together. There had always been two kinds of potato salad—one with mustard and one without.

She walked toward the counter with her arms full. "Would you mind closing the refrigerator door for me?"

"Sure." He was about to do that when he caught sight of something interesting behind the cartons of yogurt—a half-eaten pie that looked like one of his favorite things in the whole world.

"Is this chicken pot pie?" He held it up. It had to be. The chunks of chicken, potatoes, peas, and carrots were suspended in rich, yellow gravy. The crust was brown, flakey, and had been oddly embellished with what looked like Santa's sleigh and half his team of reindeer—the other half gone by the way of someone's fork.

Evie looked up from the bread she was opening. "Oh. That. Yes. I had some leftover dough, and I made it for the staff's lunch a couple of days ago. I wanted to practice for some Christmas pie decorations."

"Can I have this? Instead of the sandwiches?"

She had been about to slice the bread, but stopped. "Are you sure? It's not what I would call fresh. This bread was just baked this afternoon, and it's fabulous. I trade savory pies for bread from Kirstin's Bakery."

She sure worried a lot about how old stuff was.

"My rule is if there's no green growing, it's good."

She shuddered—actually shuddered. "You're welcome to it."

"Chicken pot pie is my favorite food."

She looked surprised. "I didn't know that. I thought tamales were."

"It's my non-Delta favorite food. There was a diner in North Dakota that made chicken pot pie. I got in the habit of eating it the night before a game."

"I'll warm this. How much do you want?" She held up the pie.

"I can eat it all—save it from getting a day older. That ought to make you happy."

"There is that." She removed the plastic wrap and covered it with aluminum foil.

"Hey, you can't put aluminum foil in the microwave. Even I know that."

"It's not going in the microwave. It would come out soggy." She walked over to a contraption with glass doors and racks underneath. "A convection oven is almost as fast."

He gathered up the sandwich makings and returned them to the refrigerator. "I usually eat the frozen kind."

"Here. Sit." She gestured to a small round table for four in the corner that held a laptop, a mug of pens, a notebook, some cookbooks, salt and pepper shakers, and a stack of napkins. He sat down. Thankfully, these chairs were real—wood with high backs and seats that would hold a hockey player.

"Do you still eat chicken pot pie the night before a game?"

"I try to. It doesn't always work out when I'm on the road."

"Is that for luck?" Evie opened the refrigerator and poured a glass of milk from a gallon jug.

"I don't worry about luck like I used to." That was true, though it didn't mean he didn't worry at all. "I eat the pie because it's high carb, and I like it."

She set the milk in front of him. "Even the frozen kind? You must be easy to please."

*Not that easy.* But just then she smiled all the way to her eyes until they sparkled and he realized, easy to please or not, she pleased him. She wasn't wearing a lot of makeup and no jewelry except for some small silver earrings shaped like leaves.

"I would only consider frozen chicken pot pie emergency food." She wrinkled her nose. So cute, so flirtatious. He smiled back at her—and then made himself stop.

There were about a hundred reasons he couldn't be attracted to Evie—good reasons, even aside from the bet. One: she was his ex-wife's cousin. Two: she was his childhood friend. Three: she was the daughter of his parents' best friends and his godparents. Four: he had just gotten his friend back and found a piece of home. He couldn't ruin it.

That might have seemed like only four reasons, but the last one counted for at least ninety-six times. Maybe he needed to say something to remind himself—and possibly her—that there could be no flirtation or anything else beyond friendship between them.

"It *is* a chicken pot pie emergency if you don't have anyone to make it for you, and you don't know how yourself." He took a drink of his milk. "Your cousin used to make it for me." With those words, he placed an elephant in the room, to remind himself of reason number one.

Evie nodded but she didn't change her facial expression at all. He'd been wrong. She hadn't been trying to flirt with him. She was just a happy person, spreading smiles and joy for those who would take it. "I could teach you to make it."

He laughed. "I don't see that happening. Maybe you could just make them for me."

"You play how many games? Eighty-something? I don't see *that* happening."

"Not all of them are home games. I wouldn't need a whole pie for every game. One per series would do me." He sipped his milk.

Evie closed her eyes, and her face went sad. "I should have said this yesterday, but I'm sorry about all that happened with Channing. Do you miss her?"

The question caught him off guard. He did not miss Channing. He missed who he'd thought she was and what he'd expected them to have together. There didn't seem to be a right answer.

"It's hard to miss a woman who put you out of your

house on game day because 'it wasn't like she thought it would be.'" Time to lighten the mood. "I for sure don't miss the house. It was like Pinterest threw up in there. Lots of jars with candles, and chalkboards with sayings on them."

Evie smiled. "Pinterest can lead you astray if you let it."

"She got her chicken pot pie recipe from Pinterest, too. It had canned mixed vegetables, chicken, and soup. She used those frozen crusts."

"Nothing wrong with that." But from the purse of Evie's lips and the tone of her voice, it was clear just how little she thought of that.

He laughed. "You're such a pie snob."

"Nothing wrong with *that*," she repeated and raised an eyebrow—just one. "Stick around. I'll turn you into a pie snob, too. I'll ruin you for all other pies."

Their eyes locked and a moment of pure, light amusement passed between them. How long had it been since he'd felt that? Just the joy of being with another person, with no complications? No one was trying to get into anyone's pants. No one was trying to get a game-worn jersey. No one was trying to get a giant diamond ring and a mansion in which to hang lying chalkboard signs that spouted philosophy about forever. It was just a fall night, a glass of milk, and a girl who felt like home.

A little ding sounded and broke the spell. Evie snapped her fingers. "Your food is warm."

He closed his eyes to keep from watching her walk away. He was in a good place now, and he wasn't about to let a bow do him in.

"Here you go." She set the pie plate on the table and

hurried across the kitchen. "I'll be right back with a plate and fork."

"Just a fork," he called after her. "No need in dirtying up a plate."

"As you like." She handed him a fork, closed the laptop, and pushed it to the side. "Let me get this out of the way."

"Is this your office?" he asked.

"Yes." She sat down across from him, opened a bottle of water, and drank deeply. "And our lunch table. Sometimes our dinner table if we have to stay late."

"Like tonight?"

He took a bite of the food—and immediately knew food was too generic a description for the morsels in his mouth. The parade of flaky pastry, rich gravy, and tender chicken might have brought him to his knees if he'd had a little less pride. It was pure buttery and creamy comfort.

"Like tonight? What do you mean?" Evie spoke and broke the food spell.

He swallowed and got his brain out of his mouth. "Tonight?"

She gave him a puzzled look. "Yes. Like tonight. It's a dinner table tonight because I stayed late. Have you been hit in the head too many times?"

"Probably." He took another bite. "But I was distracted by this manna from heaven."

"Ha! That's not manna from heaven. The Israelites complained about the manna."

He laughed. "You're pretty cocky about your talents, aren't you?" It struck him that Evie displayed more confidence here in her shop than he remembered her ever showing anywhere else.

Suddenly, some things made sense. She was prettier, funnier, happier, and more charismatic than he'd ever seen her—and it was all because she'd found the place where she was entirely comfortable in her own skin. That was what drew his eye to the bow on her apron and made him want to bask in her laughter.

She shrugged. "Why shouldn't I be cocky? You're the one who was so distracted by that pie you couldn't remember what we'd been talking about."

"About that…"

"About what?" He liked how she leaned forward a little when she asked a question, like she cared about what his answer would be.

"That you're here late."

"What about it?" She leaned in a little more.

He pointed toward the door that led to the shop. "You shouldn't let them run over you. You should have made them leave."

"It wasn't any big deal. I had to stay anyway. I had things to do." She gestured to some pies on the counter and sat back again. "Besides, it was sort of fun."

Fun? "They were taking advantage of you."

Her smile faded a bit. "No. Miklos came in first, wanting pasties. He thought they were a regular menu item. They aren't, but I had some left and was glad for him to have them. We had a little bit of language barrier, and the next thing you know, I had a shopful of hockey players—and a case of beer."

"I don't think you understand how hockey players can be. They can have ulterior motives."

A storm cloud descended over her face. "Ulterior motives? Are you implying that they praised my pie in hopes I would have sex with them? One at a time, Jake?

Or all at once? Either way, I can take care of myself, but I'm just wondering what imaginary tale you have racing around in your head."

Fuck. This was going all wrong. "No. That's not what I meant. They didn't even pay you!"

"It was my food to give away—food that I wasn't going to sell anyway. You must not think much of me if you think they were just being nice to me to get *free* pie."

"I think the world of you. That's why—"

Evie didn't seem to hear him, but plowed ahead. "Though I'd like to point out that they don't need free pie. I suspect there's not a person on your team who couldn't buy and sell this shop ten times over—land included."

Worse and worse.

She stood and put her hands on her hips. There were probably more disagreeable things than a woman looming over you with her arms akimbo, but he couldn't think of much right now. "Do you think I'm so hungry for attention that I have to buy it with pie?"

*No, Evie, I don't think that. I've passed enough time with enough puck bunnies to know what a woman hungry for attention is like.* "That wasn't what I meant," he repeated.

"Then, tell me: what did you mean?"

He took a deep breath. "It's just that hockey players are unpredictable. You can't trust them. They say one thing and then forget it in a flash. And they can be a little wild."

She nodded. "Oh yes, they bought a whole case of Budweiser. Beer and pie today and what next? Driving through cotton fields? Rolling yards? Setting up dogfights?"

"I never knew you had such a sarcastic mouth on you. You've always been so nice." He knew the minute it came out, he'd said the wrong thing.

"I'm plenty sarcastic in my head. I just don't usually get mad enough to let it out. And I never knew you could be so insulting."

That wasn't fair. He had not insulted her. It was time to take this situation in hand, and he was going to do it on his feet. He did not, however, put his hands on his hips.

"I did *not* insult you. I was trying to look out for you."

How could such a sweet face suddenly look so huffy? "I think I'm a better judge than you whether or not *I* have been insulted."

"No." He crossed his arms. "You are a better judge of whether you feel insulted. I am a better—no, the *only*—judge of whether I meant to insult you. And I did not. That's not the guy I am."

She looked a little uncertain or at least a little less huffy.

Time to go in for the kill. "I know hockey players. They're used to getting their way. They think every woman they run across wants to sleep with them."

*I know because I have been that guy, and I'm trying to not be anymore.* But she didn't need to know that.

"There's been a lot of…virtue surrendered to a lot of hockey players." He made sure his voice was soft. She wrinkled her forehead, which he took to mean she was considering what he'd said. Placing his hand on her arm hadn't been a conscious act, but there it was. There was warmth there and a little slow burn sparkle. She

felt it, too. It was evident in the way she briefly looked down where he held her arm. He ought to remove his hand. "I can't let you be a casualty at the hands of one of my teammates."

She jerked her arm away from his hand. "A casualty? If you think I can't take care of myself, you know less about me than I know about hockey players. Furthermore, you're not the boss of me." Her eyes blazed.

There was no pure, light amusement and fun between them now. No slow-burn sparkle either—not a bit. She had some hellcat in her and he'd brought it out. And somehow that was very appealing.

"I—" he began, but his mouth went dry and images that were wrong, wrong, wrong moved in. He should not be thinking about backing Evie up against that big stainless steel refrigerator and lifting her against that part of him that had a mind of its own.

He began to sweat. He didn't really want Evie. It had been a long dry spell and he had that fresh-off-the-ice horny adrenaline going. Combine all that with the knowledge that women were forbidden fruit right now, with Evie the *most* forbidden—the apple that would doom all of mankind—and you had yourself some impure thoughts.

Hellfire and brimstone, times a hundred.

Maybe he should apologize, even if he had meant well—get things back on a friendly even keel. Maybe if he explained himself a little better, she would get it.

He hurried to add, "There was a time when you would have listened to me when I tried to warn you about something, when I was trying to help you."

She nodded. "I agree. But that was back before you abandoned our friendship."

His gut bottomed out and he suddenly felt hollow

inside. "You said you forgave me." At least his impure thoughts took a hike. "You said it was behind us."

She nodded. "I did forgive you. I do. I meant what I said. But it happened, Jake. We can go on from here, but we have to deal with the new reality, where we didn't talk three times a week and share everything that went on in our lives. There are things that are off-limits that wouldn't have been before."

*Before.* Before was exactly what he wanted—before Channing.

And what if there had been *instead* of Channing? His mind wandered back to that Christmas party when he'd almost asked Evie to the Sigma Chi formal. Funny thing. He hadn't been planning to invite her, wouldn't have thought someone so smart and focused would have been interested in going out with a guy who had a pro hockey pipe dream and no backup plan. Besides, the dance had still been a long way off and his head firmly in hockey season. But he and Evie had been laughing about something and she had pushed her hair out of her eyes and looked at him a certain way and it suddenly just seemed right that he should ask her. He would have if Channing hadn't appeared and he hadn't gone out of his mind over her. What would have happened if Channing had arrived five minutes later?

Well, that ship had sailed. Probably for the best. But he wanted—needed—this friendship back. He didn't want anything to be off-limits. He needed to apologize. Again. More. Better.

"Evie—" But before he could finish and just when he thought things couldn't get any worse, who should come through the kitchen door but the clean-shaven, Midwestern picture of morality and integrity, wholesome Able Killen? And he was carrying a stack of dirty plates.

"Evans, I told the other guys to go home and that I'd make sure everything was cleaned up."

*I'll just bet you did.*

Evie turned to sunshine again. "Oh, Able. How nice. But you didn't have to do that."

"No way I'd leave you with this mess." Would Jake have cleaned up after himself? Maybe. He wasn't exactly known for it, but he had put the sandwich stuff back in the refrigerator. "If you'll show me the way to the sink, I'll just wash these dishes up."

"No need to do that. We'll put them in the Hobart." Evie turned her back to Jake. "This way."

Jake stepped away from the table. "I'll help. I know how to run a Hobart." And he was almost sure that was true. The church back at home had one. He'd never actually done it, but he'd hung around and seen it done.

"Sit back down and eat your chicken pot pie, Jake. We've got this." Her flat tone said it all. *Don't you dare follow me.*

"This was really nice, Evans," Able said as they walked away. "I'd like to take you to dinner to say thank you."

"Oh, Able, you're sweet! No thanks are necessary." But, again, her tone said it all. *That would be just grand!*

The bow bounced when she walked.

He ate another bite of chicken pot pie.

It tasted like glue.

It was lucky that Evans had driven to work today because it was raining when she left Crust—which matched her mood.

Challenging anyone wasn't like her; challenging Jake was unheard of.

Even when he'd joked about her making chicken pot

pies for his pregame meals, her first inclination had been to say yes, that she would absolutely do that—just tell her how many and how often. But then she'd seen that little glint in his eye that indicated he was teasing. She'd been down that road before—before she'd understood what that glint meant. He would ask for something ridiculous—clean his room or gas up his car—and yes girl would answer the call. Then he'd have to admit he was kidding, and she'd get red-faced, aware that she'd just shown how eager she was to please him.

Awkward, but that would have been preferable to the clash of the decade.

She wasn't even sure who had been more wrong—Jake for acting like a caveman in charge of all other cave people or her for throwing the past in his face. After ordering him to eat his food while she and Able loaded the dishwasher, she'd returned to find him gone—the pie with him. Their relationship might be lost again, and this time permanently. Maybe she ought to call him.

As if it knew she was thinking of it, Evans's phone rang as she pulled her Honda CRV into the entrance of Bungalow Circle. Maybe it was Jake! Maybe he wanted to settle things between them, too. But no. Her mother. She let it go to voice mail. She wasn't avoiding Anna-Blair, but it could wait until she changed from her rain-splattered clothes and made a cup of tea. Once settled on the sofa under a throw, she made the call.

"Hello, Mama. Sorry I didn't pick up. I was driving."

"That's good. Don't drive and talk. Were you out doing something fun?"

"Just getting home from the shop."

"It's late to be working."

"Early pickup order tomorrow." Evans chose not to mention the hockey player pie-eating convention.

"Have you seen Jake yet?" Anna-Blair had said *yet* because she couldn't fathom a world where Jake and Evans would be in the same town and not get together. Her family must have known that she and Jake had not had as much contact during the last few years as they once had, but they probably marked it up to his marriage, their careers, the end of his marriage, and a hundred other things. She'd never discussed it with them and had been evasive when Jake was mentioned.

"Yes. I've seen him a couple of times." *Three in fact. The first time for pie and apologies. The second, for pie and some Delta reminiscing. The third, for pie and ruining our friendship—again.*

"I called because I wanted to tell you I just talked to Christine."

Great. Jake's mother. What fresh hell was about to be visited on her? Had he called and reported in about their dustup tonight?

"You talk to Christine every day. She's your best friend."

"True. But I wanted to tell you that we're coming with her and Marc for Jake's first home game—the pre-season game with Vancouver." *No. No. Jake and I may or may not be speaking. At best, it will be awkward. At worst, humiliating—for me.* "So, put it on your calendar so we can all go together. In ten days. You can do that, can't you?"

*Not a chance. I'll be in Boston making lobster pot pie for Harvard's rowing team.*

"Of course I can. It'll be good to see you."

"Great. Christine and Marc are staying with Jake,

but I made a reservation for your father and me at the Laurel Springs Inn."

"You could have stayed with me." Though she was grateful that wasn't going to happen. She loved her 1940s bungalow, but it was small.

Jake, on the other hand, probably had lots of room. She'd heard those condos were sweet—not that she expected to see it.

"No," Anna-Blair said. "We don't want you to have to sleep on the sofa. We're looking forward to a great weekend with all of us together—like we used to have."

"You bet!"

*Damn it all to hell.*

## Chapter Eight

"We have a grilled salmon with Greek spices and feta cheese," the Hammer Time host said. It was Saturday night and Evans, Hyacinth, and Ava Grace had met for dinner to go over their fall fest plans. "The drink special is spiced apple margaritas. Stacy is your server and she'll be right with you."

"He didn't offer to bring us that drink," Hyacinth said after he left. "I could use one after shoehorning Chloe Harper into her wedding dress. I swear, she's gained ten pounds since her last fitting."

"Soup Carter isn't old enough to serve alcohol. That's why he's a host." Ava Grace knew everything that was worth knowing about everybody in Laurel Springs—and a whole lot that wasn't worth diddly-squat.

Evans drew her wrap around her. The heat had broken, leaving a whisper of fall in the air, but the cold weather that Jake hated was still a long way off.

*"I'm freezing my Southern ass off."* That's what he had said nearly every time they'd talked when he was at the University of North Dakota and she was in culinary school. She would complain that it was muggy in New Orleans because it always was. Then they would laugh and spend the next hour expounding on the par-

ticulars of their lives—his sore ankle, her soufflé class, what they would eat when they were next together in the Delta. Tamales. Always tamales from Fat Joe's—with Cokes in bottles when they were teenagers, and later, Abita beer—eaten at that outside picnic table that hadn't seen new paint since 1987.

And now she was never going to get that picnic table back. During the argument she'd felt that her reaction was valid, but she wasn't so sure anymore. And even if it had been, had it been worth it?

She still hadn't heard from him.

In the three days that had passed, she'd picked up the phone to call him more than once, but hadn't followed through. She'd thought he might be here tonight, but there wasn't a hockey player in sight. Maybe Claire's plans for this to be the Yellowhammer hangout wasn't working out. It was just as well. What would she say to him if she saw him?

"Are you looking for someone?" Hyacinth interrupted her thoughts.

"The waitress," Evans lied. "And here she comes."

Once they had a whole pitcher of apple margaritas and had ordered food, Evans took a notebook from her bag. "Should we go ahead and get this done?"

"I have something first." Ava Grace pulled two envelopes from her bag and handed one to Hyacinth and one to Evans. "Claire came by my shop before she left town and asked me to give y'all these."

"What is it?" Hyacinth asked, already ripping the envelope open.

"Yellowhammer season tickets. She gave us each two for all the regular season home games," Ava Grace said.

This meant Claire expected them to go to these

games. Evans wasn't sure how she felt about that. If
she and Jake were no longer on speaking terms, did she
really want to go see him play?

"The preseason games are not included," Ava Grace
went on, "but she wanted us to have these so we could
go ahead and get the games on our calendars."

Hyacinth leafed through hers. "Mother of Pearl! How
many games do these people play?"

"A lot," Ava Grace said with a sigh. "It took me thirty
minutes just to write them on my calendar."

Hyacinth tossed the envelope on the table and took
a sip of her drink. "It won't take me that long. In fact,
it will take me *no* time."

Evans was afraid of that.

"What do you mean, Hyacinth?" Ava Grace asked.

"I mean I don't need to put them on my calendar
because I'm not going to any stinking hockey games."

"Now, Hyacinth." Ava Grace was the blue blood of
the group and spent a great deal of energy trying to
keep Hyacinth from causing herself trouble. "Claire
was kind enough to give us the tickets and the seats are
good. You know she wants the community to support
the team. She's been so supportive of us, the least we
can do is go to *some* of these games."

Hyacinth rolled her eyes. "I guess. But you can believe it now or believe it later. I'm going to as few as I
can get by with."

"Oh, come on," Ava Grace coaxed. "You might have
fun."

"How would you know?" Hyacinth said. "You've
never been to a hockey game in your life. None of us
have." She gestured to the table with her glass.

Oh, hell. *Here it comes.* Evans could feel it bearing down like a rickety wooden wagon on a country road.

"Evans has," Ava Grace said like she was delivering good news. "One of those Yellowhammers—Jake Champagne—is her friend from the Delta. She'll want to go see him play. If nothing else, we should keep her company."

Hyacinth sat back, crashed her eyes into Evans's, and smiled an evil little grin. "Are you, now?" She had the look of a vampire who smelled blood. "Why didn't I know this?"

Evans shrugged. "I don't know. I didn't think much about it."

Hyacinth put her elbow on the table, made a fist, and leaned her cheek on it. "Is that right? All anybody has talked about for months is hockey, hockey, hockey, Yellowhammers, Yellowhammers, Yellowhammers. And you *never* thought to mention that your friend was on the team. I wonder why."

Evans didn't have an answer for that and it didn't matter because Hyacinth plowed on.

"Could it be that he's an old boyfriend? Are you rekindling a romance?"

"Give it up, Hyacinth. I can't be your hookup for *All Dressed in White*."

Hyacinth's fondest wish was to get on the reality show that went to bridal salons and filmed brides picking dresses. She had hounded the producers until they told her if she could come up with a high-profile customer, they would consider it.

"Are you sure?" Hyacinth said. "A pro athlete ought to be famous enough."

"Of all the things I'm unsure of in life, I can promise you I won't be buying a dress from you to marry Jake Champagne in."

"Too bad." Hyacinth looked unconvinced.

"If Jake gets engaged, I'll pass that information right along to you." That caused a little pang to radiate through Evans's gut, but not nearly like the one she'd felt when he'd publicly proposed to Channing at her college graduation party. She supposed it would get easier and easier. By Jake's fifth engagement, she probably wouldn't feel anything at all.

"That's something." Hyacinth brought her back from her mean thoughts.

Evans opened her notebook. "Why don't you tell us what you're doing for fall fest?" It was time—past time—for a change of subject.

"Sure. I'm having a photo booth with a graveyard theme." Hyacinth was clearly pleased with herself. "I've pulled some shop-worn wedding dresses and bought some used tuxes from Goodwill. The idea is for people to do dead bride and groom pictures. Not everybody will go to all that trouble, but they can still use the photo booth in their regular clothes. Anybody who tweets a picture gets a chance to win a wedding dress—no expiration date."

Ava Grace looked a little panicked, and Evans got the idea she hadn't planned much.

"I'd like to have some live wedding background music," Hyacinth went on. "I'm still working on that."

Evans was officially impressed. She hadn't thought of music.

"What are your refreshments?" Ava Grace asked.

Hyacinth rubbed her hands together. "I'm having a

wedding cake that looks like a haunted house with spiders, cobwebs, and a dead bride and groom topper."

Ava Grace's eyes got wider with every word Hyacinth spoke. "Claire will love it—especially the tweeting part."

"You've gone all out," Evans said. "My plans aren't nearly that elaborate. I'm serving miniature pies, coffee, and hot chocolate. For my activity, I'm having cornhole. I ordered two boards last summer, one with a ghost and one with a pumpkin. At the end of the night I'll give away a pie a month to the people with the three highest scores."

"That's smart," Hyacinth said. "A prize will get them back in the shop."

"I wish I had thought of something that smart," Ava Grace said forlornly. "Oh. Here comes our waitress."

Once they were settled with their food, Evans got back on task. "Ava Grace, it's your turn. What are you thinking of for fall fest?"

Ava Grace frowned. "I don't have everything worked out yet, but I thought maybe for refreshments doughnuts and cold spiced cider, since a lot of people will be serving hot drinks."

Evans nodded. "That sounds good. I've got a witch's caldron punch bowl from last year if you want to borrow it."

Ava Grace brightened. "I would love that."

Hyacinth said, "You can use some dry ice to make it look spooky."

Ava Grace looked a little happier. "For large orders, Krispy Kreme will deliver, but I don't know how many I need to plan on feeding since I've never done this before." Heirloom had only been open since last December.

"I can help you with that," Evans said. "I'll look back at how much food I served last year and we'll figure it out."

"Thank you," Ava Grace said.

"What about your activity?" Hyacinth asked.

"I was going to have a gallon jar of candy corn and let people guess how many pieces. Whoever wins gets a silver-plated vanity set." She swallowed. "And the candy. They get the candy, too."

No one said anything for a moment.

Then, Evans cleared her throat. "That's a good start, but you really need something to get some attention for your shop—give people something to remember." And doughnuts and candy corn weren't going to do it.

Ava Grace nodded. "I know. Y'all have such good ideas, but I couldn't think of anything."

"An antique store is hard," Hyacinth said kindly, "but we'll figure something out. How about some kind of demonstration? Like how to cane a chair or refinish a table?"

Ava Grace shook her head. "Those things take a lot of time. I don't think people would want to stay in one spot long enough—especially people with children."

"And this is a family event, but there must be something," Evans said. "How about someone who can appraise pieces that people bring in, like on *Antiques Roadshow*?"

"No," Hyacinth said. "We want people to buy Ava Grace's merchandise, not try to sell their own."

And in that moment, Evans had an epiphany. "Ghost stories! We can find someone to tell ghost stories."

The two other women looked at her, interested.

"Damn skippy!" Hyacinth said. "People love ghost stories. The ones where a ghost is haunting an object? That's perfect for an antique store."

Ava Grace clapped her hands. "I would have never thought of it. I can get some books with regional stories to sell. And I have a costume from when I was a hostess for the historical homes Christmas tour my debutante year."

"Maybe we can pour fake blood all over you and give you some slash marks, like someone cut your throat!" Hyacinth's eyes glowed with excitement, but Evans and Ava Grace were taken aback.

"Uh, no," Ava Grace said. "Too scary for the kids."

Evans nodded in agreement.

"I guess you're right," Hyacinth admitted.

"Now all we have to do is find someone who can tell ghost stories," Evans said. "Do y'all know anyone?"

"I do. I can do it."

The voice behind Evans might as well have been coming from a ghost for the start it gave her. But there was no doubt who it was. Nothing like a Delta accent.

She slowly turned and looked, just to make sure.

Jake Champagne stood there with a chapped face, five o'clock shadow, and messy hair, his hands in the front pocket of his gold and black Alabama Yellowhammers hoodie. Despite the cooler temperatures, he wore shorts and Adidas slides.

He'd never looked better—not at their junior-senior prom, not at Addison's deb ball, not at his wedding, not ever—maybe because on those occasions, his smile hadn't been for her. Was that smile an indication that he wasn't mad at her, after all? Or was it window dress-ing for the tableful of women?

Behind him, other hockey players filed past with Soup in the lead carrying a stack of menus. A couple of them waved to her. She waved back, but didn't note their identities.

Jake widened his eyes and let them go soft. "I know lots of ghost stories."

"What?" Evans had to ask because she could not have heard him correctly.

"I know ghost stories aplenty." *Aplenty*? Who used words like *aplenty*? Jake winked at her. "Evie, intro-duce me to your friends."

There was nothing else to do.

"This is Jake Champagne. A Yellowhammers' for-ward and my friend from back home. Jake, these are my friends Hyacinth Dawson and Ava Grace Fairchild."

"Ladies." He smiled and let his eyes sparkle. Damn him.

He pranced up and down the table shaking hands and making eyes like both acts would get him into heaven, laughing that charming laugh that made people want to fetch him a drink, lend him their beach house, and put him in their will.

Evans jumped back in before Hyacinth could become too charmed by him. Hyacinth was a tough nut to crack, but if she decided she wanted Jake Champagne, she wouldn't stop until she was standing at the altar beside him in one of her own dresses or they were both dead.

"Hyacinth owns a bridal shop and Ava Grace has a wonderful antique store. Remember them when you do your Christmas shopping."

"Sounds great. Wedding dresses and sideboards for everybody."

They all laughed, but Evans found herself less and less charmed, maybe because that smile wasn't just for her anymore. He was sharing it *aplenty* with her friends.

"Hyacinth sells more than wedding dresses. She has lovely accessories."

"Can't have too many of those." He winked at Hyacinth. "Now." He smiled up and down the table. "Who needs ghost stories?"

"I do," Ava Grace said. "For the Laurel Springs Fall Festival."

"I'm your guy." He smiled at Ava Grace like she was the last woman on earth—and she *was* his type. Tall, beautiful, poised. She wasn't blond like most of his previous girls, but her long, chestnut curls were worthy of a shampoo commercial.

*Dial it down, Sparky. Ava Grace is all but engaged.*

"You don't even know when the festival is," Evans said. This was not happening. It was bad enough that he was standing here letting his big eyes do their magic. He was not getting involved with her friends. "You might be playing hockey in Canada."

"I do so know, and I will not. I've already gotten word from above that I'll be helping out and glad-handing there, so this is perfect. This can be my volunteer gig."

Ava Grace snapped her fingers. "Right. When she brought the tickets by, Claire told me the team was going to volunteer. I guess I forgot to tell you."

"I guess you did," Evans said.

Jake continued to make friends and influence people. "I'll be glad to do it. And if I do say so myself, I'm not half bad."

"Really?" Ava Grace said. "I can't thank you enough." And wasn't it just like Ava Grace to believe everything she was told?

Evans met Jake's eyes. "You don't even know any ghost stories." *You just want to get in good with Ava Grace.*

His mouth fell open and he had the audacity to look shocked. "I do, too!"

Evans took a sip of her drink. "Name one."

He closed his eyes for the barest second—just long enough to confirm that he was flying by the seat of his pants. She knew that look. When he opened his eyes again, he looked very sure. "I can name more than one. There's 'The Atchafalaya Swamp Witch,' and 'The Haunted Doll of Maple Leaf Plantation.' She comes to life and digs her way out of a grave." He curled his hands into claws and made a digging motion.

He paused when Ava Grace and Hyacinth made shivery little sounds of glee. Evans wanted to scream at them not to encourage him.

"Those two are from the Delta. There's also the dead goalie who haunts Scotiabank Saddledome in Calgary. He took a skate to the carotid artery. It happened fast." He closed his eyes, lowered his face, and shook his head, as if he were questioning how such an awful thing could happen. "They say he doesn't know he's dead. He still comes back to defend his net and leaves blood on the ice. You won't find anything about it online; they don't talk about it. But one of my college teammates plays for the Express. He's seen him—the blood, too."

*You won't find it online because it didn't happen.*

Evans gave her friends a sidelong glance. They were mesmerized—even Hyacinth, and mesmerizing her was a tall order. Was Evans the only one who had any sense here?

"I was born and raised in the Delta, same as you," Evans said, "and I've never heard of any swamp witch or haunted doll."

He smiled that heartbreak smile and laid a hand on her head. "You were a sensitive child, Evie. We didn't talk about things like that in front of you." The hair on the back of her neck stood up—certainly from frustration because he was patronizing her, and not because he was moving his fingers against her hair.

*Moving his fingers against her hair.* He was ruffling her hair like she was a toddler! She moved her head away.

"*Me* sensitive?" Evans said. "I wasn't the one who ran screaming from the room when the clown showed up at Rusty Kane's eighth birthday party."

"It was his fifth. And I think it was pretty smart of me. Have you ever seen the demonic look in those balloon animals' eyes?"

Everyone laughed, never mind that balloon animals didn't have eyes.

"I can't thank you enough for this," Ava Grace said.

"My pleasure." Yep. There was pleasure on his face for sure.

"Hey, Sparks!" a dark-headed man called from around the corner. "Are you coming? The waitress is taking drink orders."

*Good. Go, Jake. Shoo. Order a big manly drink. Play with your friends and leave mine alone.*

"No, Ryan. I'm good. I think I'll join these ladies."

He met Evans's eyes and jerked his head, indicating that he wanted her to move over.

*Don't you jerk your head at me!* "There's not enough room," Evans said before she remembered it was a table for four.

He opened his mouth to speak, probably to point that out, when Hyacinth's text notification chimed. It was Mendelssohn's "Wedding March." She looked at the screen then let out a cry of frustration and started gathering her things.

"Let me out, Evans. I have to go."

"What's wrong?" Ava Grace asked, alarmed.

As Hyacinth slid over, Jake took Evans's arm to help her up.

"Nothing that requires a doctor—or the undertaker." Hyacinth stood up. "Chloe made it through the ceremony, but had a seam burst during pictures. I've got to get over there and sew her back into that dress so she can go to the reception."

"Will you be back?" Evans asked.

"No." Hyacinth laid some money on the table. "I can only imagine what's going to happen when the dancing starts."

"Do you want to take your food?" Ava Grace asked. "We can get them to pack it up for you real quick."

"No time." She gave them a backward glance. "Jake? Why don't you eat it? I just finished my salad. I haven't touched the rest of it."

He let his eyes drift to the plate of Monterey jack chicken, baked potato, and asparagus.

"I believe I will." He steered Evans back to her seat. "Evie, if you'll just slide over and pass me Hyacinth's plate...yes. That's it."

Evans found herself sitting between Jake and Ava Grace with Jake on the outside—in *her* place. How did that happen?

"Thanks," he said. "I like to sit on the outside. More leg room." As he dug into the chicken, his knee knocked heavily into Evans's.

Oh, no he wasn't. Was—was he actually *manspreading*? Evie picked up her knife and stabbed it directly into the heart of her bloody steak.

Jake couldn't believe his luck at running into Evie so soon. He'd just gotten back from a surprise team-bonding trip to Atlanta and had intended to hunt her down after he ate to set things right between them.

After the argument at Crust, he'd felt fairly defeated, but he wasn't going to take it lying down. It was nothing short of divine intervention that he had happened upon the perfect vehicle for getting back in her good graces: helping out her friend. And all he had to do was tell ghost stories. It was true that he didn't know any ghost stories, but who was he to walk away from divine intervention? Besides, how hard could it be? He'd have said he could knit a sweater if that's what they'd been talking about. That had to be way harder than telling a ghost story. You had to have equipment to knit a sweater. All you needed for a ghost story was your own mouth.

And he'd never had any trouble running that.

Ava Grace held up a pitcher. "Would you like some of this, Jake?"

He did not. He did not like froufrou drinks that might have tequila hiding in them. He opened his mouth to decline but Evie jumped in.

"He doesn't want that. Jake can't drink tequila." Evans cut her eyes at him. "He got drunk on it when he was a teenager and has never been the same since." She hacked off a hunk of her giant steak and shoved it in her mouth.

Ava Grace laughed. "That's adorable."

"It was," Evans said. "I especially liked the part where he was sick in my car when he called me to come get him and hide him until he sobered up."

"I paid to have your car detailed." He took another bite of his chicken. It wasn't what he would have ordered. He would have preferred a steak like Evie had—rare and as big as a hubcap. But the chicken had cheese and bacon—never a bad thing. Maybe Evie wouldn't be able to eat all that steak and she'd give it to him.

"I hear you've been in Atlanta, Jake?" Ava Grace asked.

Word sure did get around in this little corner of the world—sort of like Cottonwood. "Yeah. We didn't know we were going until we were herded onto a bus first thing, day before yesterday. It was a team-bonding trip."

"How did you know that, Ava Grace?" Evie asked. "Sometimes it seems like you have a crystal ball."

"One of the players—Logan—" Ava Grace searched for his last name.

"Jensen," Jake said.

"Jensen rents a house on Bungalow Circle. He called Adele and asked her to go over and let the cable people in." She turned to Jake. "My friend Adele's family owns the development. That makes him Evans's new neighbor. Hyacinth's, too."

So noted. This was the first time in their lives that

he hadn't known where she lived and that didn't seem natural.

"What did you do on this surprise team-bonding expedition?" Evie asked. "Play paintball? Tie yourselves together and climb Stone Mountain?"

"Nothing that exciting. We mostly checked into a hotel, had meals together, and skated." It sounded lame even to him.

"But you had to leave without even packing a bag?" Ava Grace picked at her pasta. "I wouldn't like that. What did you do for toiletries and clothes?"

Oh, hell. Now he had to tell them how things worked for major league pro players. "We had bags packed for us, so we had everything we needed." Everything— toiletries, phone chargers, underwear, and Yellowhammer apparel—had been packed in Yellowhammer duffel bags.

Evie frowned. "Do they always do that for you when you travel?"

"Just our hockey gear. We're responsible for our personal items. But not this time because we didn't know."

Evie peppered her potato. "I'm sure your roommate was relieved you didn't have to sleep naked and go all weekend without deodorant."

He almost didn't respond to that, but he'd already lied about the ghost stories. He didn't want to lie by omission.

He swallowed a bite of chicken. "I didn't have a roommate. We don't have roommates. It's in our contracts."

"And where did you stay?" Evie said it like she already knew.

"Ritz-Carlton." There was no reason to feel bad

about any of this. He worked hard—even if it was fun—and the teams made lots of money. "The point of the whole trip was to see how we deal with the unexpected—hotels and unfamiliar ice." Though to be honest, the Ritz was no hardship for anybody and the ice they'd used in Atlanta had been no more unfamiliar than their practice ice at this point. "We ate together and got to know each other better. That's important for a team sport."

"What else did you do?" Ava Grace asked. "Anything fun? Maybe go to a Braves game?"

"We went to Six Flags Over Georgia."

There was silence for a few seconds. "Seems like a Braves game would have been more suited to a bunch of hockey players," Ava Grace said.

"Maybe, but it wasn't about us. They bused some kids over from this area who haven't had the chance to go to an amusement park. They paired up team members and gave us four kids to show around. Robbie and I had six-year-olds."

Ava Grace cooed, and maybe teared up a little. Evie did not. She was hard to impress—not that he was trying.

He went on, "Your pal Claire Watkins arranged it. Turns out she's going to do some PR work for the team."

Evie nodded and her eyes were a little softer. "Even so, that was a nice thing for you to do."

"Thank you." He took the compliment. While it might be true that he hadn't had a choice, he hadn't been required to buy them T-shirts, stuffed animals, and all the funnel cake and cotton candy they wanted—which had been a mistake. Jeremy had thrown up, which had necessitated a whole new set of clothes—and clothes did not come cheap at Six Flags Over Georgia. He could have gone to Vegas for what that little outing had cost. "Major league teams give back to the community."

"Like participating in the fall fest," Ava Grace said. "I can't wait."

Evie's head jerked up from that half a cow she'd almost polished off. She had the look of someone who'd just remembered something important.

"Ava Grace," Evie said, "I know it was my idea, but maybe we should rethink these ghost stories."

"But why?" Ava Grace asked. "It's a great idea. And having a pro hockey player tell the stories is icing on the cake."

"But here's the thing," Evie said slowly. "I'm not sure Jake knows the right kinds of stories." She cut her eyes at him. "This is a family event. Don't you think it will scare the children to hear about dolls that come to life and a dead hockey player who bleeds all over the ice?"

"Oh." Ava Grace looked disappointed. "I guess you're right. I should have thought of that. The stories sounded so good and I got carried away."

Jake felt a little relief—the best kind. Where he would get credit for offering to do a thing without having to actually do it.

"Don't worry." Evie patted Ava Grace's hand. "We'll think of something else. Something *better*." She gave him a nasty little look as she uttered the last word.

Hell, no! He would not be outdone. And also—the new and improved Jake ought to do what he'd said he would, even if there was an easy out.

"Here's how we can fix it," he said. "I'll just get on the internet and find some ghost stories for kids—maybe even order a book. Yeah. That's it. Don't you worry about a thing." He gave Evie a *so there* look and reached across her to pat Ava Grace's hand.

"Oh!" Ava Grace clapped her hands together. "Jake, you would do that?"

"I'll get right on it."

Ava Grace was happy again, even if Evie wasn't. Jake couldn't figure why she was upset. He'd made the offer to help her friend just to please her.

He'd just have to figure out another way to please her. God help him if it involved a clown and demon balloon animals.

## Chapter Nine

"You are such a liar, Jake Champagne," Evans said after she let Jake help her into the passenger seat of his car—a car that looked like it belonged on some European racetrack instead of the streets of Laurel Springs, Alabama. The doors opened the wrong way, making the car look like a giant green insect with its wings spread. She hated to think about what it must have cost. She wouldn't have agreed to let him drive her home if she hadn't wanted to take up this ghost story business with him—probably. "You totally made up those ghost stories."

"Are you sure about that?" He slid into the driver's seat and started the car.

"Of course I'm sure." Kind of sure. Ok, so she'd never really paid much mind to ghost stories. "You made that whole thing up. Invented it on the spot."

"Where is this Bungalow Circle?" he asked.

Damn. She'd already let him go past the turn. They'd have to backtrack, but he wouldn't know the difference. "Turn right at the next traffic light. Go two blocks, turn right again and we're there."

"Seems like," he said as he made the turn, "we should have turned a block sooner."

So he had a good sense of direction. "Seems like we should do a lot of things—like tell the truth."

"Here?" he asked. "Is this the turn?"

"Yes. Mine is the gray house with the white trim."

He parked in front. "Is that your Honda CRV in the driveway?"

That rattled her a little. She had an agenda and he was making small talk. "Yes. Why?"

"No reason. There doesn't have to be a reason for everything. Why did you pick blue?"

"I didn't pick blue. It was the one on the lot with the other features I wanted."

"Hmm." She knew what that sound meant—that it wasn't what he would have done. "I picked green. You should never settle, Evie."

She could have pointed out that if she had paid as much as he must have for a car, she would have chosen the color, but this was a pointless conversation. She had an agenda to get back to.

"I didn't settle. I like blue just fine."

"Never settle for 'just fine.' Get things you love."

"Have you always done that?" *Did you do that when you picked Channing?* She would never have said that part, but he knew what she meant and the question hung between them just the same.

He shrugged. "I've done my damnedest. I've taken a wrong road or six, but I have never settled—even when my choice wasn't the best. But I own that I need to make better choices. I'm trying to do that."

She took a deep breath. Enough of that. She intended to have this fall fest business out with him here and now. "Look, Jake. Implying that you're an experienced storyteller, when we both know you are not, might be fun for you, but Ava Grace is trying to establish a business. She hasn't been open a year yet." She would not tell him that Ava Grace was struggling. That wasn't hers to tell. "She can't have a lame fall fest activity."

He didn't answer her right then. He hopped out, ran around the front of the car, and opened the insect wing door. So much for the here and now. "Who said it would be lame?"

Evans made no move to unbuckle her seatbelt. "You know what I mean."

"No." He shook his head. "I really don't."

"You were just kidding around tonight. I'm not going to let you jerk Ava Grace around."

A frown set in between his eyes. "Can we discuss this inside? I'm cold. The team didn't pack us any long pants and I haven't been home." She hesitated, but then he did it—widened his eyes, cocked his head to the side, and bit his bottom lip. "Come on, Evie. Don't be tired of me."

"That's a tall order. You're about as tiresome as an all-night infomercial, and going all wide-eyed on me won't change that." She climbed out of the car.

He laughed out loud. "That's my Evie."

And it was. As a teenager, she'd always thrown that kind of banter at him when her feelings started marching toward her, intent on eating her alive. Not that she felt that now. Old habits die hard—or, in her case, maybe not at all. She turned on the lamps.

"Nice," he said. "Cozy."

"My mother did it," she admitted. Though she seldom thought of it, Evans picked up the remote from the mantel, pressed the button, and the logs in the fireplace came to life. "I'm not very good at decorating."

He stepped in front of the fire and rubbed his hands together. "But you're great at building a fire."

She laughed despite her annoyance. "This kind anyway. Putting furniture and rugs together, not so much."

"That's not always a bad thing. Do what you're good at. Let somebody else do what you're not. I don't recommend that you take up hockey and I damn sure have no business taking up pie baking."

"Two totally different things. I could teach you to bake a pie," she said. "You'd have good chicken pot pie for the rest of your life. But, as you well know, I can't even ice skate."

When she was twelve, he'd tried to teach her. It had been a disaster.

"I wasn't much of a teacher back then. I'd do better now."

Evans folded her wrap over the back of a wing chair. "Sit down, Jake. We need to talk about the fall festival." She sat on the wing chair and gestured to the club chair across from her. He ignored her and sat on the end of the sofa, close enough to her that their knees almost touched.

"I don't intend to jerk Ava Grace around." He let his eyes bore into hers. "Evie, I don't jerk people around." His lips were chapped.

"But this is a lark for you. The Laurel Springs Fall Festival is a tradition. People expect a quality event. Sure, it's a little hokey, but that's part of the charm. Ava Grace is going to spend a lot of money on decorations and refreshments. She'll advertise that she's having ghost stories told by Yellowhammer player Jake Champagne. You can't flop in there, flying by the seat of your pants, flashing your pretty eyes and counting on your good looks to keep people from realizing you're making it up as you go."

He smiled when she mentioned his pretty eyes and good looks. If she could have, she would have jerked those words back like a catfish on a cane pole, but it was too late. She wondered if he had lip balm.

"I'm not going to do that, Evie." He drew a cross over his heart. "I know I'm not as smart as you are, but—"

Not *that* again. It was true he wasn't a quick study or an A student like she'd been, but his grades had always been good enough to keep him hockey eligible. "Don't start that. You did well enough when you wanted to." She'd assured him enough over the years. Besides, she'd never really bought that he felt inferior to her intellectually, or any other way.

"Well, whatever." He shrugged. "But it's not like I don't have any communication skills. I've been taught how to speak to the press, and let's not forget Miss Violet's instructions."

Miss Violet had been the teacher at the cotillion classes Anna-Blair and Christine had made Evans and Jake attend. Did he know about the warm feelings that encased her heart when he brought up a shared memory? Probably.

"I know storytelling is different," he went on, "but I promise. I'll get online, find some books." He reached for her hand and squeezed. The warmth in her heart raced down her arm to where their fingers met. "I promise I'll study up. It's not like I think I can skim a couple of stories and skate through." He gave her a crooked smile. "Though I am a better than the average skater."

He withdrew his hand and ran it through his hair. Her hand felt lonely.

"You are that." She had to laugh. "I know it seems like I don't trust you..."

"You don't." He widened his eyes, but not in that come-hither way. "I've earned that. But I'll earn my way back into your trust. I know I've had a weird few years, but I used to be a man people could count on. I'm trying to be that man again."

It hurt her heart to see him so raw. "Seems like you were a man Olivia and the kids could count on this past summer." It was only fair.

"I tried." Pleasure crossed his face and it gladdened her to know she'd been the cause of it.

"Okay. I won't question you any more about fall fest." But there was another sticky wicket. "There's something else you should know. Ava Grace isn't available."

He frowned and picked at his chapped lower lip. "Available for what?"

"Available—as in single. She's been dating the same guy since she was a teenager. Everyone says they'll get engaged at the Christmas Gala in December. So if you're doing this for her because..." She let her voice trail off.

"No." He shook his head. "That never occurred to me. I'm not interested in Ava Grace. If you'll remember, I said I could tell ghost stories before I knew who wanted them, or why."

That was true—which brought up an interesting question. "Why *did* you offer to do it?"

He closed his eyes for a moment. "I wanted to please you."

*"Me?"* Her heart turned over.

"Yes. You were talking about ghost stories. I said I could do it to get in the conversation. Then when I found out your friend needed ghost stories for the fall fest, I said I'd do it to please you—win points."

She was baffled—struck dumb. *He* wanted to please *her*? Once she found her voice, she said, "This has nothing to do with me."

"It must, or we wouldn't be talking about it now. I acted like an ass that night at Crust. You were madder than I've ever seen you."

"I was mad? You picked up on that?" She smiled to take some of the sting out of the sarcasm.

"Yeah. I'm perceptive that way. It came to me when you wouldn't let me run the Hobart."

"You don't know how to run a Hobart."

"The church had one when we were growing up."

"That doesn't mean you knew how to run it." She leaned back and crossed her legs.

"I *am* sorry—not for my ineptness with a Hobart, but for trying to throw my weight around with you. I had no right."

She rubbed the back of her neck. "Well. I'm not lily-white in that little altercation. It wasn't fair for me to bring up the past after I had said it was behind us. I accept your apology. I'm sorry, too."

He smiled. "I guess we can start over from here—again."

*Again* was a comforting word.

"I guess you've heard our parents are coming for your first game," Evans said.

He nodded. "Mine are staying with me. I've got to buy a bed this week."

"That should make things more pleasant for them. And it'll definitely be more pleasant for everyone if they don't show up to find us sniping at each other."

"No kidding." He shook his head. "I can hear my dad now. 'Boy, where are your manners? I didn't raise you to act like this.'"

They laughed quietly together for a moment and his laugh trailed off in a yawn.

"Someone's tired."

"Yeah." He stood. "I'd better go. Early on the ice tomorrow."

"And I start making pies at five a.m." She walked him to the door.

"Ouch." He gave her a one-armed hug—the kind meant to be a friendly exchange of affection between pals. But it didn't feel friendly—not to her. The tingle started in her gut and worked its way through her body, leaving her knees weak and her heart pounding. She jerked her head up in surprise and found herself looking into those all-night-long blue eyes. Was it her imagination or did he look as surprised as she felt? If so, was he having the same reaction? Or could it be that he wasn't, but sensed what she felt? Either way, he rotated his body and turned the hug into a full-on frontal embrace.

This must be what it felt like to rest in a warm cloud. She worked to keep her breath even, but let her arms slip around to hug him back.

"Evie, Evie, Evie." He sighed into her neck, and she would surely turn into warm butterscotch syrup and melt all over the floor. "It's good to be with you, even if you do know I'm afraid of clowns. Or maybe that's *why* it's good to be with you."

That long-ago birthday party where Jake had gone screaming from the room reminded Evans of another birthday party—Hollis Allen's fifteenth. Jake had refused to go because Evans hadn't been invited. The sweetness of that memory flowed through her, and she relaxed against him a bit more.

And then, abruptly, the embrace was over. She wasn't butterscotch syrup and she'd made too much of it.

"Get some rest." She opened the door for him.

"Good night, Evie." He was almost out when he turned back. "Let's just suppose—for the sake of argument—that I took you up on your offer to teach me to make chicken pot pie—"

*What?* "Uh...yeah?"

"Could we start with bought crusts?"

Evans's mouth flew open. He couldn't have surprised her more if he'd produced a doll who had dug her way out of a grave.

"I know it goes against your pie-in-the-sky ideals, but a man has to start somewhere."

"I..." She had no doubt he would forget this had even crossed his mind by the time he stepped off her porch. She ought to brush him off, say no. "Well, yes. We could do that."

He nodded and winked. "Good. In return, I won't expect you to stand up on your own on your first skating lesson." He strolled out on the porch.

Holy hell. "Hey! Who said anything about skating lessons?"

He turned back and sparkled at her. "Me. I said it. I'll call you."

And he got into his insect car and drove away.

She watched him go and tried not to think of the promised call that might not come.

## Chapter Ten

Jake squirmed in his seat. Team meetings had never been his favorite thing, especially after practice when he was tired, sore, and in bad need of a hamburger. But it was nearly over. Coach was winding down.

And it was a good thing. He had a pie-making date with Evie in an hour—give or take. He'd told her he'd come over as soon as the meeting was over.

*Pie making.* He still couldn't believe he'd done that to himself. Why hadn't he just asked her to watch Kevin Smith movies? She never said no to Jay and Silent Bob. But pie! He didn't want to make pie, didn't have time to make pie. Honestly, he wasn't going to make pie if he could get away with it. What had he been thinking?

He hadn't been. That was the point.

It was that doorstep goodbye hug. He'd only meant to hug her in a see-you-later friendly way but, though he wasn't sure she'd noticed, it had turned into something else. One brush against her and he was a thirteen-year-old with his first girlie magazine. Evie had been seconds away from learning his little secret when he practically shoved her away from him. The next thing he knew, he'd been babbling about chicken pot pie and ice skating lessons.

He blamed the bet. Forbidden fruit, and all that.

But was it more than that? He wanted to be the friend
Evie deserved, and she didn't deserve his lusty inclina-
tions. From the minute he'd walked into her little house,
which would have almost fit into the living room of
his new condo, he'd wanted to curl up in front of the
fireplace and stay there all night. The whole place felt
like home, even before he'd noticed the few pieces of
that Delta-made pottery on the mantel that everyone
was so crazy about. But it hadn't been about the pottery. Maybe it was because Anna-Blair Pemberton had
decorated the place and he knew her house as well as
he knew his own. And come to think of it, Anna-Blair
and his mother saw things pretty much the same way
when it came to colors and rugs and all.

So now he was making pie—but he was hoping
he would be more of an observer than a participant.
Though he had talked to her on the phone a couple of
times to set up the pie making party, Jake hadn't seen
Evie since Saturday night and today was Wednesday.
He'd considered stopping by Crust, but what with scrim-
mages, arranging for furniture for his condo, and reading a book called *Shiver Stories*, he'd hardly had time
to breathe.

Plus, he'd needed a little time to get his head straight
before seeing her again. His reaction to a perfectly in-
nocent hug was proof of that. He knew the long dry
spell was to blame, and his response would have been
the same to anyone. But Evie wasn't just anyone. She
was his friend, and he wasn't going to mess that up.

That irritating, teeth-on-edge microphone sound went
through the room. Good. He needed the distraction.

"I trust everyone is settled and ready to face the

Northern Lights in two days," Glaz said. "If you have concerns, come see me." His tone dared them to do that. What he really meant was, "If you have concerns, work it out."

Not that Jake had issues. Apart from having to listen to Wingo love himself, things were going okay. And despite his bragging, Jake had to admit that Wingo hadn't been writing checks with his mouth that his hockey stick couldn't cash. He could keep the puck out of the net and that was all Jake wanted from him.

Glaz went on, "I will address now what I know is on your minds: captain."

It hadn't been on Jake's mind. It wasn't going to be him. He didn't even want it to be. Who needed that kind of pressure? But now that he thought about it, he wondered how the selection would be made. With some teams, the players voted. With others, management decided.

"I cannot speak for how we operate in future, but this year the administration and coaches will make this decision," Coach said. "For the preseason games, we will designate captains—different for each game." That would be a reasonably good indication of who the brass was considering.

Five captains for five preseason games. After playing the Northern Lights at home this Saturday, they would travel to Winnipeg to play the Polars Sunday, then on to Minnesota on Tuesday and Buffalo on Thursday. Finally, they'd be at home Friday to play Boston.

"After Colonials game, we'll announce final decision. For first game, it will be Able Killen, with Luka Zadorov and Logan Jensen as assistants."

Well, hell. Maybe being an expert on Upper Wherever meat pies made for captain material. Jake might not want to be captain, but he didn't want to be beat out by Able Killen either.

"Are there questions?" Coach asked, but did not give anyone time to respond. "Good. I know many of you have family and friends coming for the game with Vancouver this weekend. Claire Watkins has information that will be of use to you and them."

Oh, damn. More talk, and from Claire of the iron fist. She might own only a small piece of the team, but she had to be obeyed. Before they'd gone to Six Flags, she'd lectured them for over an hour on the care and feeding of children—most of which had been common sense. At first, her silky clothes and put-up hair might fool a man into thinking she was soft, but she had a plan and, by damn, you had better get with her program. He wouldn't put it past her to pull a throwing star out of that hair and send it in the direction of anyone who argued with her. Even now, she was approaching the podium on shoes with high heels that were an accident waiting to happen. Did her health insurance know about them? If so, they'd cancel for sure.

She spread out her papers on the lectern and adjusted the microphone.

"Good day, gentlemen." She scanned the room, meeting eyes. Probably someone in a public speaking class had told her to do that. Jake closed his eyes. If there was one fewer pair for her to meet, this would be over quicker and he could get out of this torture chair and on with getting Evie to make chicken pot pie with no input from him.

But when he opened his eyes again, she was staring

pointedly at him. Only after he acknowledged her did she give a little nod and get on with it.

"The team building event went well. There was an article in the *Atlanta Journal* about the trip to Six Flags and it was picked up by several other outlets."

*Blah, blah, blah.* So what? Did this woman really think that somebody in New York was going to say, "Hot damn! Those Yellowhammers went to Six Flags with some kids. I think I'll abandon my Big Apples and become a Yellowhammer fan."

Claire turned her paper over. "As Coach Glazov mentioned, I've put together some information that might be useful to family and friends traveling here for the game this weekend. You should have received it last week. In addition to a directory of dining and lodging establishments, I have included a list of events in the surrounding areas that might be of interest. I need to know how many tickets you will need for your guests for the game and for the breakfast we're hosting on Sunday morning here at nine a.m." Breakfast? He'd missed that part of the email.

A groan went through the room and with good reason.

Claire rapped on the podium. "I know. I know it's early, but I expect an RSVP from every single one of you by tomorrow." She did that thing where she scanned the room meeting eyes again. "The breakfast is a mandatory event for you whether you have family coming or not."

It would be. This breakfast was just the kind of thing that his mother and Evie's would chomp at the bit to attend. The only thing they liked better than a social situation was one they could go to together. Scrutinizing other people's outfits and manners wasn't as fun alone. But what about Evie? She was planning to go to the game, but did she know about the breakfast? He'd tell her tonight.

"Ms. Watkins?" Killen was waving his hand in the air. Of course he was.

"Yes, Able? But call me Claire."

"Is Evans catering the breakfast?"

*Was she?*

"No. We thought of asking her to make quiches, but her parents will be in town"—she nodded in Jake's direction—"to see Jake play, so we thought that was a lot to ask."

*Ha! Take that, Killen. Her parents are coming to see me play.*

There were a few catcalls and whistles that Jake answered with a wave.

"One last thing." Claire turned another page. "The Laurel Springs Fall Festival. It's in four weeks. The date is October twenty-fifth. Make sure you note it on your calendar. As we've mentioned, you will be expected to volunteer in some capacity. Two of you have already made arrangements for your volunteer opportunity. That's commendable."

Jake felt good about that. He'd already emailed Claire about his ghost stories.

Claire went on. "You don't have to line up your own activity, of course. I'll be happy to assign you. But if you'd like to, it would be an excellent opportunity for you to get out and meet people in the community. You have a list in your email of the merchants and organizations participating. If you do secure a spot, let me know so you don't get double booked." She looked around the room meeting eyes again. Her eyes looked mean—the color of steel. Shouldn't a woman her age need reading glasses? She must have had some kind of surgery. Or maybe she was a robot. "Any questions?"

*"Oui."* That was Tremblay, speaking French like he was wont to do. There was one in every crowd. "What kind of things will we be doing at this fall festival?"

"You'll pose for photographs, sign autographs, and pass out Yellowhammer schedules and pucks. Apart from that, you'll help with serving refreshments, and activities like pumpkin carving, a hayride, and games. Molly, from the toy store, needs someone to do face painting. It would be good if you would tweet a few times during the event."

Another groan went through the room.

"Oh, come on," Claire said. "It could be worse. Look at the list I sent you. Pick out what you want to do, and contact the appropriate person. Then let me know so I don't assign you to the dunking booth at Clark's Hardware. Two of your teammates have already guaranteed that they'll stay dry." Claire shuffled through her papers. "Jake Champagne is telling ghost stories at Heirloom Antiques."

Good-natured laughter and applause went through the room. *Yeah, baby. I'm on it.* Jake stood up and took a little bow.

"And," Claire went on, "Able Killen is supervising the cornhole game at Crust."

*Hellfire and brimstone!* Jake fell back in his seat.

He'd made a mistake. Why had he not considered that something would be going on at Crust?

Oh, right. Because when he'd said he knew ghost stories, he hadn't known he was volunteering for a fall festival. Now, Killen was going to be hanging out with Evie, eating free pie, handing out beanbags, and—well, he didn't know what else. He didn't know much about cornhole, starting with why it was called cornhole.

The meeting was over. Claire had left the podium and everyone was milling around—everyone except Jake. He was glued to the chair he had so badly wanted out of a short while ago.

"You're going to do *what*?" Robbie stood over him.

"Tell ghost stories at an antique store." Jake got up.

Robbie laughed. "You don't know any ghost stories."

Why did everybody assume he didn't know any ghost stories? It might be true, but there was no evidence of it.

"You probably don't even believe in ghosts," Robbie said.

"Of course I don't. Don't tell me you do."

"It's not a matter of believing." Robbie tapped his temple with his index finger. "It's knowing. I know what I've seen in my own home. Scotland is crawling with spirits of all kinds—witches, too. Fairies, selkies, kelpies. *I* should be the one telling ghost stories."

"Hey, stay off my turf. If you want to find someone to let you hold forth on the Loch Ness Monster, be my guest, but do it far away from my antique store." He needed to find out where this store was, how far it was from Crust. Was there any chance he could tell his stories and keep an eye on Killen?

"Why would I do that? There's no such thing as a Loch Ness Monster. Whole thing was a hoax."

"I'll never understand you," Jake said.

"I'm not meant to be understood." Robbie took a long

drink of Gatorade. "What I want to know is how you got yourself into this and why."

"It seemed like a good idea at the time." *Sort of like the celibacy bet.*

"It has something to do with a woman. It has to."
*True, but not like you think.*

Robbie squinted and suddenly looked very interested. "You haven't already lost the bet, have you?"

"No. And I'm not going to."

"We'll see," Robbie said. "Are you hungry? I'm going with Logan, Luca, and some of the others to poke around downtown Birmingham. It won't be a late night. We just want to get some food and see what's up."

Late or not didn't matter. It was that seeing *what was up* that led to problems—problems that led to losing your lucky puck and landing right back on Debauchery Road.

"No, thanks, but why don't you take Able Killen with you?" He could use a little finding out what was up—somewhere other than in Laurel Springs Village.

Robbie laughed. "Captain Killen? I asked him. He said he was planning to track down someone he'd been wanting to talk to."

Jake's scalp prickled. "Is that right?" If it was Evie, too bad for him. She had important pie business tonight.

"That's what he said. Come on. Go with us."

Jake shook his head. "I really can't. I have plans."

"Are you sure it doesn't involve a lovely lassie?"

*Yes.* No way was he admitting he was getting a cooking lesson. "Just Evie. She's making me a chicken pot pie."

Shame suddenly washed over him. He shouldn't have said she was *just* Evie. She was something special.

Robbie shook his head. "Nursery food with a lass you've known since the nursery. And you say you don't understand *me*."

"You're really something special." Jake leaned in and made use of his eyes like Evans had never seen him do before—and that was saying a lot. Then he smiled. She couldn't help but lean forward a little, too. "You're so special that I think you deserve a little something extra, don't you?"

Then he raised the cobalt blue bottle of sparkling water to his lips, drank, and closed his eyes as if he were savoring the water. Next he treated the world to a glimpse of his eyes again—eyes that matched the bottle perfectly. He held the water up. "Cool, clean, refreshing, with nothing to feel guilty about." He took another sip and held the bottle up again. "Sparkle—the champagne of sparkling water. And I know about sparkle."

And he sparkled—with his eyes, his smile, a wink, and a toss of his head.

Before he turned and walked away from the camera, Evans reached for the remote and turned off the television.

It was understandable that someone would pause to watch if they happened to catch a commercial featuring an acquaintance—especially one who looked like Jake. But she hadn't just happened to catch it. She had recorded it when it hit the airwaves two days ago. And she had watched it over and over again, so many times that she'd found herself reaching for a twelve-pack of Sparkle when she'd gone to Piggly Wiggly to buy chicken pot pie ingredients. And that wasn't the only idiotic thing she'd done this week. She'd also spent a ridiculous amount of time searching online for the perfect eyeshadow before settling on the Urban Decay Naked Smoky Palette—fifty-four dollars plus extra for emergency delivery—and stressing over the correct attire for teaching a hockey player how to make chicken pot pie.

And tonight was the night. She ought to be sleepy, probably would be if she wasn't so keyed up. She'd stayed late at Crust last night and gone in at four this morning in order to get everything done so she could take off this afternoon. She'd needed that time, too. She'd been busy, busy, busy watching YouTube videos of how to achieve the perfect smoky eye and commercials for outrageously priced water—not to mention acquiring said water and prepackaged pie crusts at the Pig.

She had to get a grip.

Ever since Jake had left her tingling at the door three nights ago, she hadn't been herself. It had been one thing to have a teenage crush on him, but here she was again—only this time she wasn't dreaming of moonlight dances, sweet kisses, a bouquet of flowers, and a hundred other childish romantic things that were never going to happen. Now, she wanted mouth on mouth, skin on skin, and a hundred other steamy things that were never going to happen.

Might as well face it. She was traveling full speed on the Jake Road without an off-ramp in sight. All she could do was prepare for the crash and hope to God the airbags worked.

She should erase the Sparkle commercial. It was the right thing to do for her sanity. Besides, Jake was due any minute for his pie-making lesson. If he caught her watching his commercial, she would have to leave town, possibly the country.

She would erase it. Now.

But instead of hitting delete, she found herself playing it again—just one more time. This time she watched it through to the end when, with a glance over his shoulder, he walked away from the camera so that anyone who was in doubt about his identity would see Champagne plastered across the back of his Yellowhammer jersey—the jersey that had, no doubt, been willfully and strategically placed to ride up just enough to show his butt to its very best advantage.

Her heart rate increased and heat gathered low in her belly.

Why, why, why had he come to town? There were thirty-one pro teams in the United States and Canada—some of them in warm climates. Surely, one of them would have wanted him. She'd been just fine baking pies and not thinking about him.

Maybe she ought to go out with Able Killen. He'd called and asked if she'd go to Hammer Time with him and his family after the Vancouver game on Saturday. That—the family part—had seemed a little weird and she'd been relieved to tell him no, that her own parents would be in town. He had taken no for an answer, but been persistent about getting together another time. He'd like to take her out once the training camp and preseason games were over. She hadn't told him yes, but she hadn't told him no either. Big surprise there, but maybe this time it was for the best.

It had been more than two years since her only long-term relationship had ended. She'd been content for almost a year with Chase Hamilton, but that might have been more about the romance of being in New Orleans than anything else. They'd idly talked about getting jobs in the same city, maybe even the same bakery. But in the end, after graduating culinary school, they'd been more excited about their new opportunities—hers in Laurel Springs and his in San Francisco—than each other. Apart from going to last year's Christmas Gala with a friend of Ava Grace and Skip's and having dinner a handful of times with Allan Clark from the hardware store, she hadn't dated since coming to Laurel Springs. Maybe it was time.

She considered Able. He wasn't model perfect like Jake, but he *was* good looking with a big, open smile, and she liked the way his hair lay in big, loose, messy curls all over his head, like he just ran his hands through it and called it a day. Plus, he could run a Hobart and he had that soup and razor endorsement thing going for him. She wasn't a fan of canned soup, but she had to shave every day. Some free razors wouldn't be amiss. She wondered idly where he was from and what position he played—hopefully not goalie. Jake had always said goalies were strange. Maybe she'd google him.

When she picked up her phone to do that, it rang. She jumped a foot off the sofa, and dropped the phone. Probably Jake, saying he was late or wasn't coming, after all. *Aloha, Evie. I am retiring from ghost stories, pie, and you.* Panicked, she turned off the TV and hid the remote under the sofa cushion. After all, she couldn't talk to Jake with the remote in her hand. The phone would transmit her dirty little secret for sure.

Feeling like a bigger fool than the jester at Henry VIII's court, she grabbed her phone from the floor and looked at the caller ID.

*Christine Champagne.*

Why was Jake's mother calling her? She always saw

Jake's parents when she went back to Cottonwood, but she couldn't remember the last time she and Christine had spoken on the phone. Probably when Anna-Blair had her gallbladder out last year.

Maybe Jake was dead. Or Addison. Or it could be that Christine was calling to have her say about Channing and blame Evans for being related to her. Or worse, maybe she had some kind of maternal sixth sense that let her know when her baby was too much on a woman's mind and she intended to shut it down. That wasn't really worse than Jake and Addison being dead, though they probably weren't—at least not both of them.

The phone rang again. She took a deep breath and answered.

"Hello."

"Evie, dear. This is Christine. How are you, precious?"

*Well, Christine, since you ask—not myself at all. Could you have a word with your son and ask him to stop smelling and looking so good? He has me discombobulated.*

"I'm fine, thanks. And you?"

"Just looking forward to seeing you this weekend and excited to see Jake play."

*Enough with the small talk, Christine. Let's get on with it.*

"Jake told me he'd been by your shop."

"Yes. I've seen him a few times."

"A few times?"

Oh, hell. She shouldn't have said that. Now Christine would want details. She loved a detail. How could that have slipped her mind? Evans had spent half her childhood and teen years trying to avoid discussing Jake with

Christine. The trouble was, the more details Christine got, the more she wanted, and she wasn't one to let up. "That's really nice. Where have you seen him?"

"Oh, the usual." Evans tried to sound vague. "I catered a meal for the team. I ran into him in passing at a restaurant."

"There are no friends like old friends." Christine was clearly hoping for more information about the doings of Jake.

"I agree," Evans said, though she did not. Good friendships didn't have to have history.

There was a brief silence, but Evans volunteered nothing further. It was time for Christine to say what was on her mind.

"I suppose Anna-Blair told you that the four of us are traveling over together on Friday."

"Yes."

"We're coming in our SUV since it seats six. We thought, that way, if the six of us want to go somewhere together, there'll be room. Certainly, Jake's car is no good for practical matters. He had such a sensible vehicle before."

"Yes." Evans didn't know what Jake had been driving previous to the bugmobile, but probably not the ten-year-old Honda Pilot he'd had in high school and college. But she knew what *before* meant. *Before your cousin jerked him around, gutted him, and left him for dead in Nashville—causing him to buy an outrageously overpriced automobile with backwards doors that looks like an insect.* Realizing she needed to say something other than *yes*, Evans said, "That's a good idea," though she couldn't imagine where the six of them would go. Then again, maybe they could take off for Six Flags

Over Georgia after the hockey game. There wouldn't be much time, but Jake knew his way around.

"Anyway, what I called for—"

Thank the Lord. She was getting to the point.

"I was wondering if I could prevail on you to make a chicken pot pie for Jake?"

That was *all?*

"Of course. I would be more than happy to."

"He always eats that the night before a game. He started that in college. I think it's as much about his superstitions as anything. I wanted to make it for him, but we'll get in late afternoon on Friday. I was trying to work out the logistics—should I make it and bring it over or try to shop and make it after I got to Jake's? And then there was the question of did he even have any kitchen equipment. At one time, they had the best of… but never mind that. Anyway, Anna-Blair said, 'Why don't you just ask Evie to do it?' That was the best idea. Of course, it goes without saying that I'll pay you. After all, that's your business."

"Well, we'll talk about that."

They both knew that Christine would try to insist on paying. Evans would refuse payment until Christine relinquished. Then Christine would show her thanks later in the weekend with a scented candle or a tea towel printed with "I was raised on sweet tea and Jesus" or "If I have to stir, it's homemade."

Really, it would be less trouble to both of them if Evans would just accept the $14.95 and be done with it.

But that's not how things were done—not in their world. It wasn't the Delta way.

"You can count on me, Christine." *This ain't my first rodeo with a chicken pot pie.*

"One more thing. Jake doesn't like mushrooms."

*I know.* "That's good to know."

"I knew I could count on you, Evie. You always were good to Jake."

What a weird thing to say—in fact, the whole conversation was weird. Was it possible that Christine was playing matchmaker? Surely not, but there was one way to find out.

"Would you like me to deliver the pie to him?"

"No, thank you." Christine sounded surprised. So she wasn't trying to arrange for them to see each other. Of course not. Evans was transferring her feelings to Christine. "I'll pick it up on the way to his condo. I'll text you when I get to town."

"I'll have it ready."

And just then, the doorbell rang.

"I look forward to seeing you, Christine. Be safe, but I have to go. There's someone at my door."

"Oh! See you soon, sweetheart. Bye, now."

Evans did not expound on who was ringing the bell. Maybe he wouldn't smell good. Maybe he wouldn't look good.

She would do well to remember that she'd been raised on sweet tea and Jesus.

## Chapter Eleven

Evie answered the door wearing knee-length khaki shorts and a long-sleeved navy blue T-shirt. Something about her face was different, but he couldn't tell what—didn't care.

"You look good, Evie."

"I do?" She brushed her finger against the corner of her eye. "Thank you."

She had put some little pumpkins and leaves on her mantel beside that pottery. "You've decorated for fall."

She nodded. "Yeah. Mama sent those things. I thought I'd better put them out before she gets here. How was practice today?"

"I've had worse. I've had better. Everybody's tired. Most are out of shape because they were lazy over the summer."

"How about you?" She sat on the edge of one of the chairs that flanked the fireplace, crossed her legs, and began to bounce her topsider-clad foot up and down. She'd always done that. Her daddy once said if she'd been on a bicycle, she'd be to state line in an hour. "Were you lazy over the summer?"

"I could have been better if I hadn't—" He plopped down on the couch and, all of a sudden, the television blared way louder than was healthy for the human ear and there was his face—bigger than life, swigging fancy water with that dopey music in the background. "How?" He jumped like a jack-in-the-box and shook his head like a wet dog trying to get dry. "What the fuck?" He said one of those words he didn't usually say in front of women, but his brain and ears were on fire.

Evie made a sound not unlike a dying animal as she lunged toward him, her mouth agape, eyes blazing.

"No! I just have to—" And she was on her knees in front of him, one hand on his bare thigh, the other digging beneath the cushion under his butt.

"Evie, what the hell?" He could feel her searching around under him while Endorsement Jake was talking about how he knew all about sparkling.

"Raise up!" she demanded.

The words did not compute. Raise up what? Himself? And if so, to where? If he got up, he'd knock her over into the coffee table, where she would hit her head and probably die.

"Hellfire and brimstone! What's going on here?" He raised his voice to drown out his television self, who was waxing eloquent about that ridiculous water.

"Never mind." She pulled her arm out from under him and came up with a remote, which she pointed at the TV, and—after several stabs and a bit of cursing under her breath—made Endorsement Jake go away.

She stared at him looking for all the world like a not very bright mouth breather.

"Sorry," she finally said.

"What the hell?" As the shock of the whole thing dissipated, Jake became aware of her hand—still on his thigh. In fact, it might have slipped a little farther up his shorts leg. She must have noticed at about the same time because—if possible—she looked even more horrified than before and let her eyes drop to the spot in question.

"I swear." It came out with a breathy sigh and she jerked her hand away. "Sorry. So, so *sorry*!"

He pushed his hair out of his eyes. "What happened here?"

"You sat on the remote." She was still half lying and half kneeling at his feet, and her shirt had dipped to show the barest bit of cleavage. The sight of that and the memory of her hand on his thigh sent a shudder through him.

He reluctantly took her hands, raised her up, and eased her onto the couch beside him. "I didn't mean to sit on it."

"I know." She rubbed what looked like a rug burn on her knee.

He began to laugh. She smiled a little and then joined in—though she didn't seem to be feeling it. Boy, she really did not like her TV being turned on by some-one's ass.

"That was bizarre," he said. "What are the odds? My commercial on at the exact minute it happened."

Her eyes went moon-shaped, but then she shrugged. "Yeah. What are the odds?"

She stood up, crossed the room, and put the remote in the drawer of a little table. "Are you ready to make pie?"

"Sure. Let's get to it. How long do you think it's going to take?"

Her face clouded over. "Do you have to be some-where else?"

"No, but I was hoping to eat soon."

She brightened up a little. "Since we're using those pie crusts in a box, probably no more than an hour."

An hour? He'd be dead in an hour. "Well, let's get to it." Maybe she'd give him a snack.

"I've got everything we need ready to go. Just let me get it, and we'll be on our way."

On their way? "Where are we going?"

"Crust." Her voice had an *of course* sound to it.

That made no sense. "You said to meet you here. I thought we were cooking here."

She shook her head. "Since I didn't know when you'd be finished, it seemed easier to have you come here first."

He didn't want to go to Crust, the scene of Armageddon. He was hoping they could watch *Clerks* or *Chasing Amy* while they ate chicken pot pie. Maybe it would be cool enough to turn on the fire.

"Can't we do it here?"

She laughed. "Have you seen my kitchen?"

"No, though I thought I'd be seeing it tonight."

She pointed to the door. "Have a look."

He expected her to follow but he soon saw why she didn't. It wasn't much bigger than a closet—and he wasn't talking about a walk-in closet either. There was barely enough room for one person to stand in front of the counter, with the sink and a microwave to the right. To the left there was a stove like you might find in a camper and a refrigerator the size of the one in the wet bar of his new condo.

When he turned around, Evans was leaning on the doorframe. "Do you see why we can't have a cooking lesson here? I can put together something simple, but that's about all."

"Why would they do this?" he asked. "It's such a nice little house."

"The houses on this street were built in the 1940s for the textile mill management, who only lived in Laurel Springs during the week. I guess the men who lived here didn't need much of a kitchen. This suits me fine. After all, who has a better kitchen than Crust?"

*I do.*

No way was he going to Crust. Unless he missed his guess, Able was on the hunt for Evie tonight and Crust was the first place he'd look. Jake didn't need him busting up in there, delaying when he was going to get to eat. Of course he'd do the dishes. He'd proven that.

"Why don't we go to my place?" he asked. "I've got plenty of room." She looked interested. "I want you to see it anyway."

She smiled. "Well, sure. We can do that. Hand me that bag by the sink and get the one from the refrigerator."

Evans was still shaking inside when Jake punched in the code for his keypad lock. What a nightmare. She was deleting that recording as soon as she got home. If she had the need to watch that commercial again, she'd just have to watch it on YouTube.

"I don't have any furniture yet," he said as the door swung open. "Glaz put me in touch with an interior designer friend of his wife's. Supposedly, everything is on schedule to get it all fixed up on Friday before my parents get here."

"You're cutting it close."

He nodded and led her through a little foyer into the almost empty living room. It was nice—wood floors, built-in bookcases, marble fireplace, and multi-paned windows.

"It's beautiful. Do you want to show me the rest, or get started?" she asked.

"I'd rather show you once I have something more than a couch and TV. Besides, I'm starving."

"You mentioned that. Where's the kitchen?"

"This way." He led her to a central hallway and through what she supposed would be a dining nook into the kitchen.

He was right about one thing. There was plenty of room. Claire had outdone herself—custom cabinets, upscale appliances, quartz countertops that looked like they'd been set with jewels. She had to smile at the built-in wine refrigerator. Maybe he could store his beer in it.

Or the wine he would keep for his girlfriends. There hadn't been anything on *The Face Off Grapevine* lately, but it was just a matter of time.

"Are you all right?" Jake looked at her oddly. "Don't you like the kitchen?"

*Snap out of it, Evans!* "I do! It's great. I was just considering where to set up."

"Whatever you think's best. You know more about that than I do." He opened a stainless steel door under the cabinet. "This is the best part. I've got one of those icemakers that makes that good ice like Sonic has. Do you want some?"

"No, thanks. Not right now." She took the recipe out her bag and handed it to him. "Read over that while I unpack the ingredients." She set the bag she carried on the island and lined up everything in the order they would need it. "Okay. Let's get started. To begin with,

I need a knife and cutting board. Go ahead and get me a skillet."

"Oh, no," he said. His head was cocked to the side, but not in that "surrender to my will" kind of way. It wasn't a look she remembered seeing before. "I don't have a skillet."

"No skillet? What about a saucepan?" That would do, if push came to shove.

He shook his head. "I thought you said you had everything we needed."

"I have the *ingredients.* I thought we were going to Crust, where there is plenty of equipment. Do you have *any* equipment?"

"I have a can opener. A Keurig. My mother bought that. And a corkscrew."

Evie closed her eyes and massaged her forehead. Of course he would have a corkscrew. Couldn't serve screw-top wine to his women.

"Maybe we need to go out and get me a skillet and a knife?" There was a hopeful tone to his voice.

"Jake…" She didn't even know what to suggest. "The hardware store is closed. There's a Williams-Sonoma and a Sur Le Table at the Summit, but that's twenty minutes away—if the traffic is light. You're hungry. I just don't see how… We need to go to Crust."

"Tell you what." Head cock. Smile. "Let's forget this cooking lesson tonight. Let's go to the Summit. We'll get dinner. Then you can help me buy what I need."

Looked like they were going to the Summit. This time she didn't even want to say no.

## Chapter Twelve

Most men claimed to hate shopping, but Jake didn't believe it. All you had to do was consider the amount of money spent every minute that ticked away in every first world country on the map to know that wasn't true. Women weren't the only ones spending all that money. To be fair he didn't know exactly—or remotely—what that amount was, but he was sure if he looked it up, the data would support his presumption. So no. It was just a matter of the merchandise in question. While he would rather eat rocks than spend one second in a store dedicated to smelly candles, fruity bath products, and wine charms, a car dealership or electronics emporium was a different matter entirely.

He expected this kitchen store to be a necessary evil, but he wasn't feeling too bad about it since he now had a full belly, having just eaten eggrolls, Cajun jambalaya pasta, and tiramisu cheesecake. That's what he liked about the Cheesecake Factory. You could eat from all the countries.

As they entered Williams-Sonoma, Evie was listing off the things he would need. "A saucepan, a skillet, a couple of knives. A pie pan, of course. You're going to want to buy those here because you need quality prod-

ucts. Things like measuring cups and whisks, you can
get cheaper at Target."

"But we aren't at Target," he pointed out.

"No," she agreed. "But—"

"If they have that stuff here, let's just get it."

"Are you sure?" She frowned.

"I'm sure. Just imagine you're making chicken pot
pie in your head. Get everything you would use. While
you're at it, pretend to scramble some eggs." He could
scramble eggs. Not having a skillet, he hadn't in a while,
but he was sure nothing had changed about the process.
"Let's get a toaster and a microwave bacon pan, too."
Before he knew it, he'd be able to cook a whole meal.

"All right. I'm also going to insist on a rolling pin. I
haven't given up on your learning to make pastry." The
door closed behind them.

"Whatever it takes to get you through the day," he
said. "I guess stranger things have happened."

"It's really not that hard. If you can run around the
rink balanced on what amounts to a knife blade you
can—" She stopped short, focused on something behind him, and her eyes glazed over. "Oh." She sounded
in awe.

Clearly, she forgot all about him, walked right away
from him like a recently dead soul going toward the
light—only, in this case, the light was a giant display
of copper pots. By the time he caught up with her, she
was caressing a little round pan the same way Addison
had caressed that high-priced pocketbook he'd bought
her last Christmas.

"So gorgeous," she muttered under her breath, and—
as pots went—he supposed it was. This cookware was
a damn sight better looking than that pocketbook with

somebody else's initials plastered all over it. There must have been twenty pieces, not counting the lids. Each one had brass handles and knobs decorated with different things—acorns, lemons, leaves, pumpkins, and little birds. There were even a couple of pieces with turkeys that were probably meant to get you in the spirit of Thanksgiving.

In all the years he'd known Evie, he'd never seen her so taken with anything.

A sales clerk approached. "Hi. I'm Millicent. Can I help you folks?"

His first inclination was to buy it for Evie. Then he remembered the size of her kitchen.

"No," Evie said. "We're just looking."

Looking? They had not come to *look*. Looking was a waste of time. Maybe that was the difference in the male and female versions of shopping.

"We'll take this." He gestured to the display.

"What?" Evie said, clearly surprised. "No." She emphatically shook her head.

"Really?" Millicent looked gleeful. Maybe she got commission. "Which pieces?"

"All of it," he said. At least Evie could look at it at his house—maybe even cook with it. He made a mental note to buy her a set when she got married.

At that thought, his mouth went dry and, suddenly, a movie of the future materialized in his head. Evie was taking that big ass pan with the turkey on top out of the oven. Oddly, the movie was set in his kitchen. Then, none other than Able Killen materialized beside her, took the heavy pan, and set it on the counter. "I'll wash the dishes," he said, leaning in to kiss her.

Jake did not like that movie; he quickly deleted it

from his brain before the kiss could happen. Evie didn't have to be married to get a gift. Most of this didn't seem to have much to do with pie making, or he'd buy it for her now. Maybe later when she got a proper kitchen. He tried to visualize her in her future kitchen, but couldn't come up with what it would look like.

"Jake, no," Evie said. "This isn't necessary."

"What do you mean? You said we needed some pots." *And these make you happy.*

"I did, but I was thinking of some high-quality stainless steel. Look." She turned over the piece she held and showed him the price.

Wow, he didn't know pots cost so much. Still, not that bad. There was a lot of it. Surely, that wasn't for one pan. But the clerk had asked *which* pieces.

"Do you get it all for that price?" Millicent bit her lip and looked at the floor, but Evie just went ahead and laughed out loud.

"No," Evie said. "You get *this* piece for that price."

"The lid is included," Millicent said, hopefully.

That was a lot of money. He was about to say *lead on to the stainless steel*, but when Evie set the pan back on the display, she ran her finger over the little leaves on the handle and sighed happily.

That did it. What the hell? He'd spent a lot more than this at a certain jewelry store in Paris on his honeymoon.

"Wrap it up," he said to the clerk. "We'll take it all."

Evie's eyes widened. "Jake, I can't let you do this. It's insane! It won't even fit in your car. The turkey roaster alone…" Her voice trailed off and she let her eyes rest on the pan from his movie. It was big enough to bathe a Labrador retriever.

She had a point. The Lamborghini had been built for speed, power, and style—not for hauling cookware or much of anything else. Then the solution came to him. "No problem. Lucy Kincaid has a crew coming in Friday to set up the condo. I'll ask her to pick it up. Millicent, you can have it ready for her then, can't you?" He reached into his wallet and gave her Lucy's business card. "That's who'll be picking it up."

She nodded so fast that he was surprised her head didn't fly off. "Absolutely. Shall I ring it up or will there be anything else?"

"Wait." Evie clasped his wrist. "If you really want a piece of this..." She picked up a round pan with apples on the handle. "Get this pie plate."

"We'll take two of those, Millicent." Maybe he could get Evie to make him a Mississippi mud pie, too. "And the rest of it. We also need—what was it, Evie? A pancake turner and some spoons? What else?"

"Yes," Evie said quietly. "I know my way around. I'll find the other things we need."

Once the happy clerk left, Evie hissed at him, "You've lost your mind. You do not need all that. You just bought a four-hundred-dollar paella pan and a fondue pot for God only knows how much."

He smiled at her. "Not only God. I guarantee you Millicent knows. How else would she ring it up?"

"You're not going to cook paella."

"I might. Or maybe I'll have company—someone who wants to cook paella." He wasn't sure what paella was, but Evie would know. He winked at her.

"Ah." Her tone was flat and her cheeks went pink. "I see." What did she see? Was she mad? Was he being an asshole, assuming she would cook paella for him?

"I would help. I can chop, and I'd wash all the dishes."

She ran her hand over her face and came up with a smile. Okay, not mad. "It's your money. Do you want to pick out your other things?"

"No. You're the expert. If it's all the same to you, I'll let you pick." Off she went. "Don't forget the toaster," he called after her. She waved her hand in the air without looking back. He was fairly sure that meant *shut up*, not goodbye.

He wandered around until he found something interesting—a display of all manner of neat little machines that he had never heard of. He didn't want an electric pasta maker, but its existence made the world better.

Then he saw it—the combination coffee/espresso maker. He fell for it immediately. Who wouldn't? With all its nozzles, knobs, and gauges, it looked a like a toy spaceship—probably for time travel.

"Please tell me you're not thinking of buying that thing," said the voice behind him. He felt the smile coming on before he turned around.

"Got to have it, Evie." After all, he'd bought those pots with the fancy handles for her. He deserved this.

"You don't even drink coffee."

"My parents do." *You do.*

"You have a Keurig."

"It's not nearly as cool as this."

"This costs two thousand dollars." Did it? He smiled. She went on, "You don't care, do you?"

"Not at all." He'd spent a lot of money, mostly on other people. He'd been happy to do it, but it was his turn. Though it made no sense, this was the first thing he'd truly wanted since the Lamborghini. And he was going to have it.

"I suppose you want to be able to show it off to your paella-making company."

"Exactly." He winked at her again. "That's the spirit."

She shook her head. "I was going to ask you to come look over the other things I picked out before I spend your money, but I can see it doesn't matter to you that a whisk costs twenty dollars."

It did not.

After Millicent presented him with the staggering bill and ran his credit card, she said, "I hope y'all will be as happy with your purchases as you are with each other."

Happy with each other? He didn't know what to say to that, and Evie looked a little taken aback, too.

He found his voice. "Thank you for your service, Millicent." As soon as it came out of his mouth, he realized it was the wrong thing.

"Uh, right," she said. "You're very welcome. We'll have everything ready for your interior designer."

Once they were out of the store, he started laughing like he was at the circus. It took her a second, but Evie joined in. "Why did I just say that like she was a Navy SEAL? 'Thank you for your service, ma'am!'" He saluted. "I guess I was surprised she thought we were married. I could have told her you were in my wedding, all right. You just weren't the bride."

And in a split second, the laughter died on Evie's face. "Jake, I wasn't."

She hadn't been in that Cecil B. Demille production of a wedding? At least fourteen women had marched down that aisle wearing dresses the color of Bazooka bubble gum; surely Evie had been one of them.

"You weren't? I could have sworn…" How could he have missed that?

Evie smiled a sad little smile. "To be fair there was a lot of pink tulle and ruffles going on with those dresses. It was hard to see who was under all that."

"That's the truth. But you're Channing's cousin."

She shrugged. "Yes, but that doesn't mean I was in the wedding. My sisters were. Your sister was. But it was an all Omega Beta Gamma cast. I didn't make the cut."

She began to walk toward the car and he fell into step with her.

"I guess I had a lot going on—getting ready to move to Nashville, the honeymoon, getting enough groomsmen lined up for all those pink women. But I swear, Evie. I thought you were one of them. I can't believe it."

"Oh, you can believe it, all right. If you don't, ask my mother. I didn't care, but she did. She said if it weren't for you and your parents, she would have refused to go to the wedding."

He sighed and ran his hand through his hair. "I guess I wasn't paying attention. Channing was always accusing me of that. Maybe that's why I'm divorced."

When they reached the car, Evie stopped and met his eyes. "I'll tell you why you're divorced. You're divorced because Channing is a spoiled brat who got distracted." As soon as she'd spoken, her face went pink and she put her hand over her mouth. "I'm sorry. I shouldn't have said that."

He liked that she'd said it. He was over the whole thing, but that didn't mean he didn't appreciate a little righteous indignation on his behalf. "Hey, close or not, she's your blood, not mine. If you can't say it, who can?"

Evie got this prissy little look on her face. "Nevertheless, one shouldn't speak disparagingly about the love of someone's life."

"*One* shouldn't, should *one*?" Jake said.

Evie shook her head. "Me. I. *I* shouldn't have said it."

"Oh, who cares? She wasn't the love of my life anyway. I just thought she was."

"Isn't that the same thing? People are always saying, 'I just *thought* I was in love. I never was.' It's the same thing. If you think you're in love, you are."

"I guess so." He reached to open the passenger door for her, but stopped. An image of Evie at the wedding came rushing back.

"You served the cake at the reception, didn't you?"

"Yes. And what a cake it was—what with the bridges, satellite cakes, and edible glitter." She sounded amused, cheerful. But she couldn't be. Even he knew that though people acted like it was an honor to be asked to serve the bride's cake, the job really went to someone who wasn't quite good enough to stand at the altar with the bride.

It must have been humiliating for her.

He was as much to blame for the oversight as Channing—more. Evie was one of his best friends—maybe his best friend. If he'd known Channing hadn't included her, he would have insisted.

Wouldn't he?

*No.*

He wouldn't have given it another thought. Jake wasn't proud of it, but there it was. As long as Channing was getting what she wanted, he was happy. He had never considered another thing—even making Evie feel like she meant less than nothing to him. But hadn't he already done that—long before the wedding? With the calls he didn't return, the texts he barely answered, the forgotten birthdays?

He had been the biggest dick in Dick Land. Still was. Oh, he'd been sorry before, but not sorry enough. He might have meant it when he apologized, but it was the timing that was the problem—that and the motive. He may as well have said, *"I know I treated you like shit, Evie, but now that I'm going to be living where you are, could you pretty please forgive me? And while you're at it, forget it happened and make me a pie."*

He closed his eyes—from shame and because he didn't deserve to even look at her. "Evie, I am so, so sorry."

"We've been through this."

"No. Not by half, we haven't." He opened his eyes and placed his hands on her shoulders. She was trembling—or was it him? "There's no excuse for how I turned my back on you. I put you in a box, stored you on a shelf, and thought you'd be there when I got ready to let you out again." He moved his hands against her. It felt good.

She put up a hand and started to shake her head.

"No. Don't tell me it was all right."

He locked eyes with her and they were quiet for a moment.

"At the very least, I should have come to my senses after the divorce. I should have thrown myself on your doorstep and begged you to forgive me." But, no. He'd used all his energy chasing ass and drinking. "It never hit me until now—how it must have made you feel, how it would have made me feel."

She didn't blink and then she nodded. "Our relationship was always like a magic carpet ride for me," she said quietly. "Sometimes we flew high and fast, sometimes steady and slow. But it was always there. We were always on that carpet together. I guess the hardest part was that I thought we had just entered a steady, slow phase, but I looked up one day and had to face that I was on the ground—alone. There was no carpet and there was no Jake."

*Broken heart.* People said it all the time. He'd never understood it, not even the day Channing had thrown him out of the house. He'd come closer when Blake died, but even that didn't equal this, and he understood why.

A heart could only be really broken when you were to blame.

Evie let out a ragged breath, closed her eyes, and swallowed. He realized she was swallowing tears and he wondered how many times she'd cried because of him.

His heart went from jagged pieces to crushed into powder.

He folded her against him and cradled her head against his neck. "I'd give anything—*anything*—if I'd never let you go."

She startled and then went still for a beat before pulling away enough to look up at him, her eyes wide and questioning. "What…what is it that you mean, Jake?"

What *did* he mean?

He let his eyes drop to her mouth—the mouth that always smiled at him, but wasn't smiling now. He could answer her question by bringing her mouth to his. He knew instinctively that she would welcome it—and he almost did it. He opened his lips and dropped his face toward her.

But he stopped. How could he answer her with a gesture when he didn't have the answer in words?

"I mean I should have returned your calls. Hell, I shouldn't have waited for you to call. I should have treated your friendship like the fine thing it was—is."

She nodded and slowly pulled out of his arms, leaving a cold void where she'd been.

"Thank you for saying that, Jake."

He still wanted to kiss her, but that wouldn't do. *"Hey, Evie, I really am sorry I treated you so bad, but how about we suck face?"* That would be a real princely move.

Time to lighten the mood. "But at least you didn't have to wear that pink parade float of a dress." He opened the car door for her.

She smiled as she climbed. "One good thing about serving the cake—I got to pick my own dress. It was *not* Pepto Bismol pink."

He laughed. "Tell you what—you can be in my next wedding *and* you can pick the dress." He tried and failed to conjure up an image of what that would look like. No wonder. Another marriage wasn't at the top of his list. At least that exorbitant amount of alimony he'd paid Channing had come to an end when she'd remarried. He might not be as lucky next time.

"I won't hold you to it."

"Well, I figure I've had my last wedding anyway. But, Evie"—he put a hand on her arm—"there's not a woman in a veil you wouldn't outshine."

His *next* wedding?

This wasn't the first time Evans had let herself dance into blissful hope, only to get slammed to the ground in the most humiliating way possible—but, with God as her witness, it would be the last time. When he'd inclined his face toward hers, she'd been so sure that he was—finally—going to kiss her that she had almost put her hands on his cheeks to guide him there. But his expression had suddenly changed and she stopped. That was something, at least. Then he'd started babbling about taking her calls—*that* was what he'd meant by not letting her get away.

And then he'd thrown her that bone about outshining some specter bride.

Would she never learn? She'd gone without sleep, worked late, worked early, took the afternoon off, all so she could do a favor for Jake Champagne—and there still hadn't been a pie-making lesson, nor would there be in the foreseeable future. He was leaving Sunday for a week on the road.

"When you get home, freeze the chicken," she said absently as Jake veered onto the highway that would take them back to Laurel Springs.

She was an idiot of the first degree. With all her silent whining about "not getting back on the Jake Road," she'd missed the truth. She'd never left it, not really. She had just buried it when he had started seeing Channing, and there it had stayed until he'd walked into Crust that day. But now that she was clear about her locale, she was certain about her destination: the next exit ramp. It might take a bit to get there and that was okay. She just had to go straight and keep it between the lines.

Furthermore, what she felt for Jake wasn't a teenage crush, never had been. She knew that now. She was in love with him, just like she'd *thought* she'd been at fifteen, but she was calling a halt to it here and now.

"Do what?" Jake glanced at her. "Freeze what chicken?"

What chicken, indeed. "The chicken in your refrigerator that I bought when I thought we were going to cook tonight. Put it in the freezer. It'll go bad before you get back." *That is, of course, unless your anticipated company is going to come over and cook it up for you. But if that's the case, be sure and let her know that she needs to bring a skillet. The equipment that I spent a great deal of effort choosing for you—and her—won't arrive until Friday.*

"I will. We can have my cooking lesson when I get back from the road games."

"Mmm," she said. Would they? Right now, she wanted to tell him they most certainly would not, but she recognized that she was tired and shell shocked over her realization—not to mention raw that he had bought the most beautiful cookware she'd ever seen in hopes of impressing some woman who might or might not know how to boil water without destroying a four-hundred-dollar Swiss-made copper saucepan.

"I'll need a couple of days to recover from the travel, but then I'll be ready." Apparently, he'd taken her *Mmm* for a yes. Understandable. That's what it had always meant before. "You know what would be good? Some ice cream. Why don't you google us up a place to get some?"

"Actually, I'm kind of tired. Please take me home." The sum of it was he had been everything to her while she wasn't much more than a blip on his radar. She'd been doing just fine the last few years, hadn't even thought of him—at least not much. Then he'd waltzed in, smiled, and she was right back where she'd been. But no more.

"Oh, come on, Evie. Butter pecan. It's your favorite."

Hell, hell, hell. Butter pecan was not her favorite! It was his.

"No." He might as well get used to sound of it right now. "I said I want to go home."

"Okay. Okay. Sorry." He sounded pouty. Well, let him pout. It wouldn't do him any good this time.

Just when she thought they would make the rest of the drive in silence he asked abruptly, "What's your shoe size?"

"Seven." She could hear the weariness in her voice. If he noticed it, he would assume she just needed some sleep—which she did, but that was the least of her fatigue. It was her heart that was exhausted. "Why?"

"I'm going to buy you some ice skates while I'm on the road. Better selection up North." He paused. "You *don't* have any, do you?"

"No, Jake. I don't have any. What's more, I don't need any."

"How are you going to learn to skate without skates?"

"Hmm." Let him make of that what he would. She didn't want to argue, didn't want to tell him there would be no skating lessons. He probably wouldn't buy the skates anyway, wouldn't think about it again—even though he was rattling on about when they would go and how she needed skate socks, so he would pick those up, too. She barely listened and didn't bother to respond. What were skate socks anyway?

They were almost home. She reached for her purse and searched out her keys. She wanted to be ready to bolt out of the car and into her house, wanted away from Jake and his talk about socks, skates, and Dietrich Wingo, who was apparently too big for his britches.

"In case you've been wondering, I've been reading

that ghost story book, so I'll be ready. I'll take it on the road with me and read some more on the plane."

"I'm sure you'll be the star of the fall festival," she said flatly. And he probably would be.

"Hey!" He snapped his fingers like he did when he remembered something. "I need to let Claire know how many guests I'll have for this breakfast thing they're having Sunday morning. I can count you in, can't I?"

She opened her mouth to say, *"Sure, great, yes, yes, yes, and I am so grateful that you considered me! Maybe there will be a cake I can serve."* Then she swallowed the words and batted away the feeling she'd always felt when Jake threw her a bone—elation and hope. How many times had he asked to do something similar, whether it was getting tamales, seeing a movie, or shopping for thousands of dollars' worth of cookware? In the end, she always had to face that it was just tamales, movies, and copper pots.

As children, they done everything together, but it became less and less as they got older when his hockey became more demanding and he'd started to have girlfriends. He might call her for a movie when the girl of the moment was at cheerleader camp or he wanted late-night tamales after the cheerleader's curfew, but—by far—they spent most of their time together during those years when he was between girls. Every time, she had hoped maybe she was the next girl, but she never had been—yet she'd never given up hope until Channing came along and there was no in between.

And the hell of it was he hadn't done one thing wrong. She was his friend, his buddy, his pal. He'd brought her balloons and sat with her for hours when she'd been sick on Valentine's Day the year she was fifteen. Of course, he'd left in time to take the girl of the moment to the sweetheart dance. It was entirely reasonable that he would want to hang out with her when he wasn't otherwise romantically occupied. But no more.

She had to start saying *no* to Jake, and now was as good a time as any. She would go to the game. It was expected of her—by her parents and his. There would probably be some shared meals, but this breakfast wasn't going to be one of them.

"No, Jake. I don't think so. But thank you for asking."

"What?" Wide-eyed, he whipped his head around and had to jerk the car back onto the road. Of course he was surprised. Why wouldn't he be? She fought off the inclination to turn into yes girl, set on pleasing Jake, but she couldn't stop herself from offering an excuse.

"It's not a good time for me. It's going to be a busy weekend. I want to sleep late on Sunday. It's the only day Crust is closed."

He looked baffled. "But my parents are going. And yours. I called my mom earlier and she said so. They'll want to see you before they leave town."

She nodded. "And they can—after they've gone to the breakfast and after I've slept late." *After you're on that plane reading ghost stories, headed to Winnipeg.*

He gave half a nod. "All right." She wasn't sure she'd ever heard him speak so quietly—and he remained quiet for a while before he broke the silence. "Are you sure?" He looked at her out of the corner of his eye and smiled a little, but he didn't cock his head to the side and bite his lip. "It would be fun to have you there."

"I'm sure."

"Okay."

The silence in the car was heavy and tense. She

should have been proud of herself—and maybe she was, at least a bit—but she was also miserable. She might have been able to say no, but she hadn't liked it. Maybe she never would.

At last, he turned down her street. More than ready to escape the uncomfortable atmosphere of the insect mobile, she went through the keys on her ring until she found her house key. If she was quick, she could escape inside before he had time to get out and open her door.

Then, suddenly, a quarter of a block from her house, Jake slammed on the brakes and pulled to the curb. "Hellfire and brimstone! There's someone sitting on your porch!"

Curious, she turned and looked. Sure enough, there was. Even though the moon was bright and the streetlights lit, it was impossible to make out who. Then she noticed that parked behind her car was the biggest, bluest pickup truck she had ever seen.

"I wonder who it could be," she said idly. "I don't recognize the truck."

"Truck?" Jake turned his head and focused. He didn't say anything, but barely changed his expression—enough that she got the idea he knew who it was. "Idaho plates," he muttered under his breath.

"Idaho?" She didn't know anyone from Idaho.

"You stay here," Jake commanded, unbuckling his seatbelt. "I'll take care of this."

For a second, she was grateful that he was willing to investigate why a random stranger was sitting on her steps, but then the person in question rose and the light hit him just right—Able Killen. Having spotted them, he waved and walked toward the insect mobile.

"This shouldn't take long." Jake opened his door.

"Simmer down, Jake," she said. "It's Able. I didn't know he knew where I live."

"He's stalking you. I'll take care of this," he said again.

"There's nothing to take care of, Jake," she said a little more forcefully. "It's Able."

"He's got no business skulking around your house."

"He's not skulking. He was sitting on the steps in the full light of the moon. Stalkers don't do that. They hide in the bushes." Able was almost to the car.

"What do you know about stalkers?" Jake sounded like a huffy child who'd been denied dessert. "I'll find out what he wants."

*Well, Jake, apparently he wants to see me—not you. Otherwise, he'd be waiting on your doorstep, not mine. He went to some trouble to see me and that feels pretty good. So you run on.*

But she didn't answer. She just got out of the car. "Hello, Able."

He stepped in front of her and smiled. "Hi, Evans. Sorry for showing up like this, but I don't have your cell number, and when I called Crust, they said you were off." He looked past her. "Hey, Sparks."

Evans turned and looked. Jake was out of the car—of course he was.

"Killjoy." He nodded toward Able.

Able broke into laughter. It was a nice sound. "Killjoy," he repeated. "I like it. I thought I might be the last living hockey player without a nickname. They used to call me Lincoln, but it died out after juniors."

"Lincoln?" Jake said.

"Yeah. First it was Abe, then Honest Abe, then…

well, you know." He grinned. "I never liked it much. Killjoy sounds much meaner."

"Right." Jake seemed to have only one-word responses in him.

Able turned to Evans. "I don't want to interrupt. I just had something I needed to ask you."

"No problem. You're not interrupting a thing. I went with Jake to help him buy some things for his kitchen, but we're done. Good night, Jake."

"I'll walk you to your door," Jake said grimly.

"Don't be ridiculous," she said. "Able will keep me *company.*" Even with the emphasis on the word, Jake didn't seem to get the reference. He just gave her a blank look, mumbled good night, and drove away.

"Sparks didn't seem too pleased," Able said. "Are you sure I didn't cut your evening short?"

"I'm sure." She turned, walked toward the house, and Able fell into step beside her. "It had already gone on too long." They reached the porch. "Would you like to come inside?"

He hesitated—clearly torn. "I would, but I'd better not. Early skate tomorrow."

"Sure." She got the impression he really regretted turning her down—though she was glad he had. She felt like a tin can full of marbles rolling down a hill. Despite her polite and expected invitation, she wanted to be alone and quiet.

"I hope you won't hold it against me."

"Of course not. You said you needed to ask me something?"

"Yes. Are you coming to the game Saturday night?" He laughed a little. "Though that wasn't really the question I came to ask."

"I'll answer it anyway." He truly was charming, though it seemed random and accidental. Maybe that was the best kind of charm. "I am. My parents are coming, and Jake's. You know, we grew up together."

He nodded. "I've been appointed captain that night."

"Congratulations, Able. That's great."

He grinned. "It's not that big a deal. There's going to be different captains for the preseason games. It doesn't mean I'll be permanent."

"It must mean you're in the running."

"Maybe. I don't think they know yet." He took a deep breath. "But about what I wanted to ask you—there's a breakfast Sunday morning for the team and guests. I'd like you to come with me."

She hesitated. That darn breakfast again. Wait. Did that mean she'd be meeting his family, like she would have if she'd agreed to go with him to Hammer Time after the game?

He might have read her mind, or he might have gotten lucky. Either way, he said, "My family has to fly out early Sunday morning, before the breakfast."

"Sure," she said. "I'd like that." Jake could make of that what he would.

They exchanged cell numbers and he gave her a brief wave before getting in his truck, a vehicle that could have accommodated every turkey roaster known to man—and Williams-Sonoma.

Once inside, Evie sighed and sagged against the door for a full minute. *What a night.* Then, she picked up her remote, cued up the DVR, and watched the Sparkle commercial one last time before erasing it forever.

## *Chapter Thirteen*

Jake paused outside the door of his condo Friday when his phone signaled that he had a message.

His mother. We should be there within an hour. Can't wait to see you!

He answered with a thumbs-up emoji. She hated that, but it was all he had in him right now. She responded with a frowny face. He didn't respond at all. She hated that more than the thumbs-up, but she let it go—which was unusual for her.

It was game day eve for the Yellowhammers and he had just had the worst practice, if not in his life, certainly in recent memory. Back when they'd played together, Glaz had always been encouraging when someone had a bad practice. "Suck it up, Sparks," he would have said. "Bad practice means good game."

That was not what he'd said today. There had been a lot of yelling and cursing—mostly in Russian, but Jake knew cursing when he heard it, whatever the language. Then, before skating off, he'd said, "Go to your house and think of this!"

Well, he was at his house, but he didn't know if he was going to have time to think about the Glaz lecture—or much of anything else.

The interior designer—Lucy Kincaid—was supposed to be in there with her crew making magic. After discerning that he had no sense about furniture or any preconceived ideas about how his surroundings should look, Lucy had given him a book, had him point to pictures of rooms he liked, and told him she'd take care of it.

Given his luck lately, Lucy probably hadn't shown up. All he needed was for his mother to say that she had told him so, that he ought to have let her come to Laurel Springs and square things away while he was in Europe. And maybe he should have. Knowing what he ought to do—and ought not to do—wasn't always easy.

Evidently, he'd pissed Evie off Wednesday night— and he didn't know if it was something he'd done or not done. He could never remember her getting mad at him before he moved here. She had certainly never practically banished him from her presence, forcing him to leave her standing on the side of the street with Able Killen—who, by the way, had skated like an Olympic champion today to the point that everyone was banging their sticks on the ice chanting, "Killjoy, Killjoy, Killjoy!" How had he got the word out that he had a new nickname—which, by the way, Jake had meant as an insult—anyway? Probably Twitter. He'd probably announced it there and changed his handle to something like Killjoy23412.

Jake had tried to call Evie yesterday, but she hadn't picked up or returned his call. That had never happened before.

The whole thing made his head hurt. He needed to get his mind on hockey. Anybody who'd seen practice today could attest to that.

A crash behind the condo door startled him. How long had he been standing there? And a better question: what had Lucy Kincaid broken—if it was, in fact, Lucy who was inside? It could be a burglar in there, but burglars were supposed to steal stuff, not break it. He punched the code into the keypad, swung the door open, and moved through the foyer to the living room.

It was startling to see a house that looked like someone lived there. Lucy looked up from where she was arranging pillows on a leather couch.

"Jake! Hello." She folded a blanket over the back of a chair and came toward him. "What do you think?"

"Looks good." There were rugs, lots of big furniture, and lamps. The sound of a vacuum cleaner emitted from another room. He wondered if he owned that vacuum cleaner now. If not, he'd probably have to buy one and hire somebody to run it.

"We're just finishing up," Lucy said. "Everything is clean. The beds are made. The dishes are washed and put away." She gestured to the door that led to the rest of the house and took a half step in that direction. "Are you ready to do a walk-through with me?"

He was not. He wanted to have a beer and decompress—maybe even take a short nap—before Christine blew in with big ideas and lots of opinions. But the nap would have to wait until after he called Blake. He needed to talk to him about the bad practice and maybe about pissing Evie off.

*Blake.* His stomach went cold and his scalp prickled. He wasn't going to call Blake, could never call him again. How had he forgotten that, even for a split second? He must be losing his mind. Then a new realization came to him, something he was amazed he hadn't thought of before. This would be the first hockey game of his life where he wouldn't at least text with Blake on game day. More than likely, he would have been there.

He felt Lucy's stare on him and snapped back to the matter at hand. She wanted to do a walk-through.

"Are you all right, Jake?" she asked.

"Fine. I heard a crash. Is everything okay?"

"I knocked over the metal coat rack in the foyer. No harm done." He hadn't noticed a coat rack, but he'd take her word for it.

"A coat rack is a good idea. At my place in Nashville, my couch was also the coat rack," he answered on autopilot.

He hadn't needed a coat here yet, but he'd damn sure needed one in Vermont. He'd been cold in North Dakota. He'd been cold in Canada. He'd even been cold in the Delta when the weather took a notion to be contrary. But he had never known cold like that Vermont cemetery with the gravestones that were so old they were illegible. Would Blake's headstone one day be illegible? How long did something like that last? Maybe he'd see a lawyer, make a will that stipulated it be replaced every hundred years or so. Or maybe not. Maybe it was best to let time and weather erase the pain of the past.

Lucy Kincaid was laughing. Apparently he was funny when he was on autopilot. "Which would make sitting tricky. We moved your sofa into the den, along with the television and gaming systems. It's a nice piece."

He took a deep breath, then another, and another. It was like he'd been in a different dimension, but was phasing back in. He was here having a conversation with Lucy, who mistakenly thought his surroundings were important.

"Come and let me show you. I think you'll like the bar and the media storage system."

This woman was determined to make him look at his new stuff. "I'll take a look later. I'm sure it's great."

She frowned. "You don't want to make sure everything's to your liking?"

He gestured to the living room. "Does it all look like that?"

"Not exactly—but I was going for a masculine English country look, and that theme is carried throughout."

"Thanks. Do you have a bill for me?" He reached for his wallet.

"No. I'll send it once you decide you're satisfied."

"Sounds good." If his mother had a place to lay her head, he'd be satisfied—which did bring a question to mind. "Which room did you fix up for my parents?" He would have bet dollars to doughnuts that she would try to make him look at it, but it seemed like she'd gotten the message.

"The yellow room down the hall from the master suite. It's the second largest and has a full bath."

"Good."

Lucy looked hesitant. "I hope they'll be happy with it. I hope *you're* happy."

"What I've seen is great."

She seemed as happy as a decorator who wasn't getting to do a walk-through with her client could. "Fine. I'll be going now. Call me if there's something that you want to change."

"I will." He wouldn't. "Send me that bill."

After closing the door behind Lucy and her army, Jake went to the kitchen for a beer, but thought better of it. Maybe he would lay off the beer until the pre-season games were over. It wasn't as if what little he was drinking would affect his game, but it was a good exercise in discipline.

All that fancy cookware he and Evie had bought was suspended on racks from the ceiling, and there was other stuff scattered around, including his outstanding new coffee maker. The place looked like someone was going to come in and cook any minute.

He had thought that would be Evie.

Jake was reaching in the refrigerator for a bottle of water when his phone buzzed.

His mother, no doubt. Yep. Maybe they would go to dinner as soon as they got here. He could pick up a frozen chicken pot pie to have before bedtime. He wasn't superstitious about that but, after practice today, he wasn't taking any chances.

He opened the text.

We're downstairs. You didn't tell us we needed a code to take the elevator. That would have been a more productive text than the thumb.

He laughed a little and sent a thumbs-up, followed by the number sequences for the elevator and the key pad to his door. Minutes later, his parents sailed through the door, his father loaded down with luggage and his mother carrying only her purse and a white bakery box—probably something from Anna-Blair's shop.

"Well, if it's not Christine and Marc Champagne, the Ole Miss Homecoming Queen and her escort, 1923."

His dad laughed and set down the three bags he carried. "I feel that old after that drive."

Christine closed her eyes and shook her head. She was slicked up and powdered, looking every bit like the credit to Omega Beta Gamma Ole Miss Royalty that she was. "I've a mind to turn right around and take myself back to the Delta this instant." She set her little purse and the box down on a table by the door that he hadn't noticed before.

"Don't lie to me, Christine," Jake said. "Sherman's army couldn't blast you out of here. You're all shined up and ready to meet your public."

"It's *your* public, and don't call me Christine. Do you want your teammates and coaches to see me looking like I just rolled out of bed?"

"You don't look like you just rolled out of bed even when you have."

"Oh, you *are* sweet." She beamed at him and they landed in a group hug.

Christine said, "Let's see where you live." It looked like he was going to do that walk-through, after all. Lucy Kincaid was one thing, but Christine Champagne was another.

He picked up two of the bags his father had carried in and led them to the living room. Christine gasped. "Jake, this is beautiful."

"You like it? I've been doing a little decorating— picked up a few things at Walmart."

"Sure you did." *Damn, Christine. You're on to me.*

Walking through his house was like a trip to a foreign land. There was stuff everywhere—benches and tables in the hallway, lamps, globes, clocks, crystal liquor decanters on silver trays. By the time they got to his parents' room, he was worn out just from looking at it all.

"So tasteful," his mother said. "Very English country."

"Yeah." Jake opened the door to their room. "That's what I was going for. I looked at some books and said, 'That's just my style.' *Masculine* English country, you understand. Then I called Walmart and had them round up everything in their masculine English country section. They'll do that for you at Walmart, if you're Jake Champagne."

She ignored him completely. "I don't know who did this, but it's wonderful." She walked around the bedroom, touching things as she went—the bed with the red checked covers and four hundred pillows, chest with a big pitcher and bowl, and rocking chair by the window.

Jake hauled one of the suitcases onto one of the luggage racks, as his father did the same. "I guess we can put the other one on the chest at the end of the bed." He needed more luggage racks if his mother was going to be visiting regularly. It wasn't Lucy's fault that she didn't know Christine Champagne did not travel light.

"Oh, flowers!" Christine bent to smell the yellow roses on the bedside table. He owed Lucy big for that.

"Uh, yeah. Did you know they have yellow roses right at Walmart—in the *feminine* English country section."

Christine laughed. "Do you think I fell off a turnip truck yesterday? You didn't get these flowers." She frowned a little. "Evie didn't get them, did she?"

Had he heard her right? "No, why would you think that?"

"No reason." She opened her train case, pulled out a brush, and drew it through her perfectly smooth hair.

"The decorator put them there. She brought a crew with her."

Christine nodded with approval. "Nice job. Are you hungry? I brought you a chicken pot pie." That was good news. His mother could make a decent chicken pot pie. She retrieved the bakery box from the foyer and headed toward the kitchen. "I assume the kitchen is through here. Do you have the makings for a salad?"

He should have bought some groceries. "If you can make salad from beer, yogurt, popcorn, CLIF Bars, and cheese. I think there's cheese."

Christine laughed as she entered the kitchen. "This is gorgeous." She set the pie on the counter.

"Nice," Marc said, walking straight to the espresso/coffee maker. "Did this come with the place?"

"No. I bought it so you'd have coffee when you're here. We can make some, but we'll have to figure out how to work it." Except he didn't have any coffee…unless… Maybe decorating a living space included buying groceries. He opened the pantry. No such luck.

"I have to say your interior designer has exquisite taste." When Jake looked up, Christine had taken down one of those fancy pots and was inspecting the little acorns on the handle.

"Oh. Evie picked those out—or at least she put me on to them. She said they were too expensive, but I bought them anyway. They look good in here, don't you think?"

"Did she now?" Christine said. She shifted her eyes toward Marc and set her mouth in a line—not like she was mad, but like she was considering. Finally, she spoke. "Marc, will you go to the supermarket and get some salad makings? And don't forget the dressing."

"Sure." Marc reached into his pocket for his keys.

"No, Dad," Jake said. "Let me. You just got off the road. I should have bought some groceries anyway."

"No, Jake," Christine said. "I want to visit a little with you." Hellfire and brimstone. He knew what that meant. She was about to lay down the law to him about something. That hadn't happened in a while. She slid onto one of the stools at the eating counter, met Jake's eyes, and pointed to the seat next to her. "Get a bottle of pinot grigio, too, Marc."

"Anything else?" Marc asked.

"Uh, better get some coffee," Jake said. "And cream and sugar."

Once Marc was gone, Christine pointed to the bakery box on the counter. "We picked this up when we dropped Anna-Blair and Keith off at Evie's shop."

Evie had made him a chicken pot pie. Maybe this meant she wasn't mad at him, after all. Maybe she was tired and he had misread the whole thing. He pulled the box toward him and opened the lid.

No Santa and his sleigh this time, but what he saw made him laugh. She'd decorated the top with crossed hockey sticks, stars, and the stylized yellowhammer bird that was the team mascot. There were words, too: Go, Sparks, #8!

"This is great!" he said. "I'll have to thank her."

"Do that," Christine said. "She wouldn't take any money, though I tried to insist on paying her when I ordered it. I'll pick up a little gift for her."

Disappointing. Evie hadn't just made it on her own.

"She went to a lot of trouble to decorate it," Christine said.

"She does that," Jake said. "Bees, if there's honey in it; peaches, if it's a peach pie; scenes for different seasons. She really is an artist."

Christine smiled. "Evie looked wonderful, better than I've ever seen her. She's let her hair grow, and her makeup was beautiful."

"She does look good," Jake agreed.

Christine put an elbow on the counter and leaned forward. She was going in for the kill. "Jake, you aren't thinking of getting involved with Evie, are you?"

He hadn't known what to expect, but not that. "No. Of course, not." *And what if I was?* But he wasn't. "You know how it is with Evie and me. We're friends. And it's nice to have someone from home here."

Christine nodded. "I'm glad to hear it. Because you know that wouldn't be wise."

"No." *But why? There are reasons. I just can't think of them right now.*

"First of all, she's Channing's cousin." Right. That was one of the reasons. He didn't need to worry about remembering the rest of them because his mother was going to name them. "It would be a little strange, don't you think?" She didn't wait for him to answer. "Second, she's Keith and Anna-Blair's daughter. They're our best friends—your godparents."

Like he didn't know that. "And their land adjoins ours. In medieval times, you'd have married us off as toddlers."

He laughed, but Christine did not.

"Don't even joke about that, son. You think I don't

know how you've been acting since Channing. I probably don't know the extent of it, but I know enough."

That shouldn't have surprised him. She read *The Face Off Grapevine*. At a loss, he shrugged. He certainly wasn't going to tell her he'd made a bet that he wouldn't have sex for three months. He would prefer his mother think he had never had sex and never would.

She shook her head. "But I don't want to talk about that."

*Thank you, Jesus.*

"It's been a hard time for you. At least you didn't rebound and run off to Vegas. That happens sometimes."

"You didn't need to worry about that."

"Well, I did worry," Christine said. "So did Marc and your grandmother. Olivia. Addison. We all worried. Blake maybe more than anyone." She closed her eyes and bowed her head.

Yes, he would have worried about that, like he worried about everything that concerned Jake. Blake liked Evie, always had. Jake covered Christine's hand with his own. "But it didn't happen."

"No. But, when you get tired of running the streets with a different girl every night, you probably *will* rebound. You will almost certainly get involved with someone who will get you from point A to point C. Jake"—she placed her other hand on top of his—"that can't be with Evie. You can't hurt her."

"How do you know it wouldn't be Evie who hurts *me*?" It was a valid question.

"Surely you're not that dense," Christine said and let her eyes rest on the chicken pie.

"Well, I never was at the top of my class."

Christine frowned and looked like she was going to

say something else, but Marc came through the door with his arms full of groceries. "I got eggs, bacon, and the stuff for pancakes. I'll make breakfast in the morning," he said.

"Good." Christine popped up from her seat. "I didn't think of that, but Jake will need breakfast." She wouldn't have, given that she took her breakfast in bed—breakfast prepared by someone else. "Jake, do you have a salad bowl?"

"Let me look and see." If he didn't, he was sure there was a copper pot that would do. "How do you feel about eating your breakfast off a paella pan?" He was reasonably sure he didn't have a tray.

## Chapter Fourteen

The dining room of the historic Laurel Springs Inn had an old-fashioned, elegant, country-club feel to it, though the food was better than any country club Evans knew. Those places always worried too much about golf and liquor and not enough about food. She'd dropped her parents off here earlier, gone home to change, and was now back to meet them for dinner.

It was filled to the brim with hockey players eating with their families. At least she didn't have to worry about seeing Jake here. By now, Christine was probably spoon-feeding him chicken pot pie.

Her gut tightened at the thought of that pie. She hadn't intended to decorate it, hadn't intended to go one extra inch, let alone an extra mile, for the man she was so mad at. But then it had looked plain compared to the other pies. It was professional integrity that made her add the crossed hockey sticks. Then, it needed a little something more, so she'd tried her hand at cutting out the Yellowhammer logo freehand. That had taken three tries, and during the process, she'd begun to think about why she was angry at Jake. She'd already faced that he hadn't done anything wrong or behaved any differently than he always had.

She sometimes forgot that he'd been a good friend to her in a thousand ways—like the time their cotillion class had gone to a fancy Chinese restaurant and he'd quietly moved to sit beside her and help her when she couldn't get the hang of using chopsticks.

He had simply failed to meet her expectations—and she was the only one responsible for her expectations. And she only had herself to thank for letting him push her into going to his condo to cook instead of Crust. If it had been Ava Grace or Hyacinth who'd behaved as he had, she wouldn't have given it a thought. They were her friends—and so was Jake. That was all he would ever be.

Usually, when she talked herself out of her anger, she felt relieved and happy, but this time she was left feeling flat, empty, and sad. So she had kept embellishing the pie with his name, number, and stars, until it was decorated up like a Victorian side table.

Needing some distance before she talked to him again, she'd let Jake's calls go to voice mail yesterday and she had not called him back. Too bad she couldn't lock herself in her house until the team left on Sunday.

Keith Pemberton stood when she approached. Her father had been to Miss Violet's cotillion classes, too. Then he smiled at her, like he always did, and he hadn't learned that from Miss Violet. It came straight from the heart. Though no one had ever admitted it, Evans knew that, after two girls, she was the child who was supposed to be a boy—the one more try. They never acted like they regretted her, but she wondered how much they would have celebrated a boy.

He held her chair. "You look nice, Evie."

"Thank you, Daddy." She'd changed into a simple

amber linen shift and even gone to the trouble of digging out a topaz bracelet. "You think this is an improvement over my chef's jacket with flour all over it?" It had been splattered with chocolate, too.

"I'm proud of you for getting your hands dirty. I just wish you'd do it closer to home."

*Here we go.* But she didn't panic at the subject the way she used to. It had become a ritual for them to have the same conversation every time they saw each other.

Right on cue, her mother pitched in with, "There's always room for you at the bakery," but without any real conviction. If she'd had conviction, she would have brought it up the moment she'd entered Crust. That had happened before. The discussion had eventually taken on a lighthearted tone as her parents became more accepting of her decision to not return home. It had been a while since Anna-Blair had reminded her that they had sent her to culinary school with the expectation that she would go to work in the family bakery.

"Room for me—not so much for my way of doing things." Evans looked around. She spotted Wingo with an incredibly attractive couple who looked too young to be his parents. Luka Zodorov strolled in and joined Logan Jensen and his family.

No Able. That was good. She was prepared to like him—*did* like him. But he was coming on entirely too strong. He'd called once yesterday and texted her twice today.

She had told him she'd go to that breakfast because she was angry with Jake, though she *wanted* to go. Of course she did. And there was no reason Jake should care. Therefore, there should be no awkwardness.

"I know." Anna-Blair brought Evans back to the

table. She put one hand out, palm forward, and took a sip of her wine. "You want to specialize—to make artisan pies, not cookies from a mix, plain old birthday cakes, and a thousand of my other sins."

"Not a thousand." Evans grinned at her mother. "More like a hundred."

Keith laughed. "To be fair, Anna-Blair, you don't sin as much as you direct the sinning."

Anna-Blair grimaced. "That's not true. I made brownies and thumbprint cookies when Carabeth had that stomach virus."

"That must have been a real emergency," Evans said, looking at the menu.

Anna-Blair's voice took a serious turn. "If you ever decided you wanted to come home, I'd let you have it—run it like you wanted." She swallowed. "Maybe. Mostly."

"You've never done anything *mostly* in your life." Evans laughed and tried to change the subject. "I might have the shrimp and grits."

"You never know," Anna-Blair said breezily. "I might be tired of the bakery business. I think I'll have the shrimp and grits, too."

"You'll never be tired of having something to run. Since you've aged out of Junior League, the church flower guild can't keep you busy enough. And rush only happens once a year."

"Tell you what, baby girl. You just come on home." Keith winked at her. He was a winker, always had been. "There's a building down the street from the bakery. I'll buy it for you. You and your mama can fight it out."

"We'd be the talk of the Delta for sure," Evans said.

"Might be good for business," Anna-Blair said. "People would come from miles around to see it."

"People would come from miles around to eat my pies," Evans said.

"That's my girl," Keith said.

Just then, the server set a glass of wine down in front of Evans. "Merlot," he said.

"I ordered that for you," Keith said. "I thought you'd want steak. Would you rather have something white?"

She took a sip of her wine. "I'm secure enough to drink red wine with shrimp." And she was, but right now, that seemed like the only thing she was secure about.

Keith nodded and addressed the waiter. "Shrimp and grits for the ladies, and I'll have the filet, rare, with the blue cheese-stuffed baked potato. Caesar salads all around?" He looked from Evans to Anna-Blair.

"Sounds good," Evans said, "and I'd like a side of the mushrooms with garlic and sherry." If Jake had been here, she would have never ordered mushrooms. Though he'd never said so, his dislike for them was so intense she could tell it was hard for him to watch people eat them.

Keith brightened. "Good idea. I'll have some of those, too. Anna-Blair, how about you?"

"No. I'll just have a bite of yours."

"Not likely." He addressed the waiter. "Three orders of the mushrooms."

She should have known better than to fall for a man who didn't like mushrooms. Her daddy loved them. She ought to look for someone more like him.

Might as well take care of some housekeeping. "I

thought that after dinner, you could take me home so you can use my car while you're here."

"Are you sure?" Keith asked. "I don't want to leave you without a car."

"I'm sure. I usually walk to work anyway."

"Christine and I are going shopping tomorrow for some things Jake needs. I still can't believe Channing threw him out with the clothes on his back."

*And I can't believe, after all we bought at Williams-Sonoma, that there's a thing left that Jake needs.*

"Now, Anna-Blair," Keith said. "I think it was Jake's choice to leave without his things and Channing sent a truckload of stuff to Christine and Marc's. So it wasn't quite like that."

"Close enough. Anyway, Evans, don't you want to go shopping with us?"

*Yes, Mama, that's absolutely what I want to do—go shopping for Jake Champagne. That would really cheer me up.*

"I can't. Crust is open."

"So is Anna-Blair's, but I'm here. Don't you trust your employees?"

"I do, but I have to work," she said firmly. She wasn't going to have this discussion and she wasn't going shopping. "Since y'all are going shopping, all the more reason to leave Daddy my car—so he and Marc won't be stranded. You can pick me up for the hockey game."

"Of course," Anna-Blair said. "Christine is already planning for us to all go together. Then, we're meeting Jake and Robbie afterward at some sports bar. Hammer Down?"

"Hammer Time," Evans corrected.

"Christine tells me you aren't going to the Yellow-hammer breakfast Sunday morning," Anna-Blair said.

*Oh, hell.* Was it any wonder she didn't want to live in Cottonwood where those two conferred on every single detail of the lives of everyone in their own private universe?

"We thought you would. Your daddy and I can opt out and have breakfast with you," Anna-Blair carried on.

"Actually, turns out, I *am* going," Evans said.

Anna-Blair nodded. "I thought Jake must have misunderstood when he said you wanted to sleep late. The only time you've ever slept past six in your life was when you had the flu. Did you tell him in time to get you added to his guest list?" Evans had long suspected that her mother communed weekly with the late great Emily Post via Ouija board.

"No." She gulped her wine and mumbled the rest into her glass. "Someone else invited me. I'm on his list."

Keith, who had not seemed to be particularly interested in what was unfolding around him, whipped his head around to meet Evans's eyes.

"Well, that's nice," Anna-Blair said. Did she have to sound so surprised? Though to be fair, Evans hadn't set the dating scene on fire lately.

"Is he a hockey player?" Keith demanded. "What's his name?"

"Yes. Able Killen." *And I don't know who his people are, so don't ask.*

Keith nodded, and his eyes started to move rapidly from side to side. It was a bizarre sight for someone who hadn't seen it before, but Evans knew what was happening. Keith had total recall for everything he read, and he had called something up from his brain and was reading it. "Able Killen. Number twenty-five. Defense. Birthday January second. Six feet, four inches. Two hundred twelve pounds. Born in Idaho Falls."

Apparently, Keith had read the Yellowhammer roster. He knew more about Able than Evans did. She never had gotten around to googling him.

"Is he a nice boy? Tell us about him." Anna-Blair gave her a little conspiratorial smile. "Have you been out with him before or will this be the first date? Is he cute?"

Hell. She was in hell. And it would get worse. The Cottonwood Mississippi Inquisition was in session. The Spanish had nothing on them.

"He's nice. I don't really have anything to tell. I don't know him very well. I haven't been out with him, and I'm not sure this breakfast counts as a date, so much as just 'come have some eggs.'"

"It counts," Anna-Blair said.

"Jake asked me and that wouldn't have been a date."

"That's different." Anna-Blair flipped her hand. Of course it was. It always had been. Evans had just fully realized it. Did fully realizing something always equate to giving up hope? "Who are his people? I knew a girl from Idaho at Ole Miss. Karen Chastaine."

*What a coincidence, Mama. That's Able's mother!* If she'd said that out loud, she'd have been sent to stand in the corner. Anna-Blair did not like sarcasm unless she was the one dishing it out.

"I don't know who his people are," Evans said. "For all I know, he may not have any."

"Everybody's got people," Anna-Blair said. "Even if they're dead."

"Is this guy a friend of Jake's?" Keith asked.

It was hard to keep a neutral face. *No, Daddy. Jake seems to have somewhat of a case of the ass for him—though not as much so as for Wingo.*

"I'm not sure Jake has been here long enough to establish who his friends are—apart from Robbie, of course."

"Hmm." Keith finished his bourbon and signaled the waiter for another. "I suppose I'll meet him soon enough and form my own opinion." Not if Evans could help it. "Is his father a potato farmer?"

"I don't know, but everyone in Idaho isn't a potato farmer any more than everyone in the Delta is a cotton farmer and a duck hunter."

"I'm a cotton farmer and a duck hunter," he said, like she didn't know. "What do you know about Idaho?"

She thought for a moment. "They raise a lot of potatoes there?"

They laughed together and she got the sense that Keith had stopped mentally loading his duck- and hockey-player-killing gun.

"Speaking of Jake," Anna-Blair said.

*Oh, Mama, let's not!*

"There's going to be a baby shower for Channing next Sunday. It's in the afternoon."

"What's that got to do with Jake?" Evans asked. "More to the point, what's it got to do with me?" But she knew.

"I'd like you to go and represent the family."

"Mama!"

"I know," Anna-Blair said. "It's a lot to ask, but it's the same weekend as Cassandra's dance recital." She named Evans's six-year-old niece. "Obviously Layne, Ellis, and I can't go."

"It's obvious that Layne can't go, given that Cassandra is her child. It isn't so obvious why you and Ellis can't go."

Anna-Blair closed her eyes and shook her head. "Be fair. We need to go and support Cassandra. I am her mimi." As far as Evans could recall, Anna-Blair had never referred to herself as *grandmother.* "Layne always goes to Ellis's boys' baseball games. It would be great if you could come to the recital, but I understand that, given the distance and your work schedule, it's not a reasonable expectation. On the other hand, Nashville is a short drive for you."

"Not that short," Evans grumbled. "Besides, I wasn't invited."

"Shorter for you than for us, by a lot. And you *were* invited. They sent the invitation to our house."

"Because clearly, I still live there." Wasn't that just like Channing? Far be it from her to go to the trouble to get a current mailing address.

"It'll always be your home," Keith spoke up, "whether or not you ever spend another night there." He leveled his gaze on her. "Evie, you don't have to go, of course, but I hope you'll consider it."

So, that was that. "All right, all right," she surrendered. "I'll go."

"Good," Anna-Blair said. "I brought gifts for you to take. They're wrapped and ready to go."

Of course they were.

*No need to ask good old Evie before wrapping them and schlepping them over. She'll do it.*

## Chapter Fifteen

A losing locker room was no place to be, and this one felt worse than any Jake had ever been in—probably because he had never felt so personally responsible before. He reminded himself that it was only one period and they hadn't lost yet, but it didn't make him feel any better.

He put his gloves and helmet on the drying rack, stripped off his jersey, and collapsed onto the seat in his stall.

Robbie sat down beside him and began to loosen his skates, like he did between every period. "We got what we wanted," Robbie said with an edge to his voice. "Skating first line."

"For now." Jake accepted a bottle of water from the locker room attendant, opened it, and swallowed half of it in one gulp.

Blake had always said skating first line would come eventually, and it had. Too bad it probably wouldn't last. At least Blake hadn't had to see it.

Having redeemed himself at today's morning skate after his lackluster performance at yesterday's practice, Jake had expected to be one of the first line defensemen.

Likewise, he had expected Luka to skate center, with Robbie and Logan as the other two forwards. Wingo in goal was a given. What he had not expected was for Killen to be the other defenseman. He'd thought it would be Miklos Novak—or maybe that's what he'd hoped, because he'd felt that Miklos complimented him more than any of the other defensemen.

Jake had played hard, but that didn't mean he'd played well. The score was 4–2. He would love to blame the opposing team's points on the goalie, but there was no way that was true. If not for Wingo, the score would have been even worse. He was doing his job.

It was Jake who wasn't doing his.

"It's only the first period," Robbie said.

Jake let out a bark of a laugh. Leave it to Robbie to be positive.

"Holy family and all the wise men," Robbie muttered under his breath. "Don't kill him, Sparks. Please."

Jake looked up to see Wingo headed for them like a man on a mission. He had his helmet under his arm and a don't-fuck-with-me attitude. Still in his full goalie pads, he looked like an abominable snowman lumbering through the snow. Jake expected him to start yelling as he closed the distance, but he didn't.

Instead, he stopped in front of Jake and leaned in to say in a low voice, "I don't know what's wrong with you, Sparks. You know defensemen have to work together, and you aren't working with Killjoy. He's doing all he can to communicate with you, but you're in another world. You're better than that."

"Hold on there, Wings," Robbie said. "We're a team. We win together and we lose together. It's not the fault of one man."

"Yeah?" Wingo said. "We haven't won anything yet and if things don't change, we aren't going to."

Robbie rose, clearly intending to keep up his defense of Jake, but Jake stood and laid a hand on Robbie's arm.

"No, Robbie. He's right." A goalie could see it all—the good, the bad, and the ugly. All he'd seen out of Jake tonight was bad and ugly—missed blocks, a disaster in front of the net, and two—*two*—trips to the penalty box because he'd been sloppy.

Wingo looked taken aback. He glanced from Robbie to Jake, gave a half nod, and then walked away.

Robbie and Jake settled back into their seats.

"The nerve..." the ever-loyal Robbie began.

"No. Stop," Jake said. "I'm a disgrace to this team tonight, and you know it. He was right to say so."

Robbie paused and took a deep breath. "Not a disgrace, but you *are* off your game. What's going on, man? I know it's harder to mesh with someone you don't like, though I don't really understand what it is that has made you dislike Killen so much."

*Because I don't have a good reason.*

"Or maybe it's not that," Robbie suggested. "You've got to be thinking about your uncle."

That was true, but it was only part of it.

Game day had gone smoothly enough—until it hadn't. He'd had breakfast with his dad, a good morning skate, his signature pregame meal of chicken Alfredo, and another short nap. He'd woken feeling rested and eager for puck drop.

Then it had happened again. He'd reached for his phone to call Blake—like he always did on game day.

Shaken, he'd gone to dress for the rink and was

greeted by the five brand-new bespoke suits Olivia had talked him into buying in London. At the time, he hadn't seen the point in the expense and trouble, but she'd been sad and it had distracted her to spend hour after hour helping him choose designs and fabric.

He'd dressed in one of those suits and tied a Windsor knot in one of the dozen ties in Yellowhammer colors that Olivia had insisted he needed.

Then, just as he was about to leave for the arena, things got worse. His mother and Anna-Blair Pemberton had stormed in from their shopping with a wagonload of stuff that he hadn't known he needed—fancy towels, candles, a giant wooden salad bowl, and a few things he could not discern the purpose of.

And they started talking—and asking questions. It seemed that Evie wasn't going to sleep late Sunday morning, after all. She was going to that breakfast with Killen. The mothers were giddy with delight, and they wanted to know all about him.

That had rattled him further. His rational self said that Evie could date who she liked with no input from him. He had certainly never worried about it before. He had no right to expect her to remain unattached so she could pal around with him.

But what he felt and what he knew were different things.

"I don't have a good reason," he admitted to Robbie. "He's interested in Evie and I don't like it, but he hasn't done anything."

Robbie wrinkled his forehead. "Do you have a yen for the lass yourself?"

"No!" Feeling some attraction for her did not equal

having a "yen" for her. "No. It's not like that. She's my friend. I don't have anyone and I want her free and clear to pay attention to me. I'm just a selfish asshole."

Robbie nodded. "Honesty counts for something." He leaned in. "Listen, Sparks. It's that stupid bet. You wouldn't feel as such if you didn't feel imprisoned by it. Let's call it off."

"No." It wasn't the bet. It was everything else. "You know what Glaz said."

"You don't need a bet to be discreet. Come on, man. It's affecting your play."

"It doesn't have to. I was rattled, but I'm better now. I'll get it together."

Robbie looked at him for a long moment. "Okay. But you know this isn't all on you. A lot of us could have played better."

"I'm the only one I'm responsible for." Blake had said that to him a thousand times—more. "You'll see a different me next period."

He knew what to do to make that happen. He unlocked the compartment of his stall, reached for his puck, and turned it over in his hand three times, recalling Blake's wise words.

*You have a special talent, but never think you're so special you don't have to work hard.*

*Skate every play like it's the last one of your life, even if you're winning ten to nothing with five seconds left to play.*

*Don't let your ego get in the way of excellence.*

*Leave your troubles off the ice. You owe that to your fans, your teammates, and yourself.*

Jake stroked the hard rubber of the puck, and felt

calmer and more centered. Then he remembered something else Blake had told him, when he was playing juniors. He must have been about sixteen.

*Woman trouble can ruin a career.*

Woman trouble was woman trouble, he supposed—even when the woman in question was just a friend.

"Sparks?" Luka's Russian accent was unmistakable.

Jake opened his eyes. "Yes?"

"Coach wants to see you in his office."

"I'll bet he does." He rose, ready for whatever Glaz was going to dish out—and ready for the rest of the game. He started to lock the puck up again, but decided to hold on to it a little longer.


"He should have stayed in Nashville," Christine pronounced in a whisper. She was truly out of sorts. Christine, not wanting to deprive anyone in earshot of her wisdom, didn't whisper. "I've never seen him play like this—at least not in his adult life."

Evans failed to see how his locale had anything to do with his performance, but she knew better than to say so. Anna-Blair reached across Evans to clasp Christine's hand.

The first period was over and the people around them got up to help themselves to the buffet and bar at the back of the friends and family suite. Keith and Marc rose, but Evans, Christine, and Anna-Blair kept their seats.

"We're going to get a beer," Marc said. "Join us?"

"No, thank you," Christine said tightly.

Anna-Blair declined with a shake of her head. In truth, Evans would have liked to move around, but getting up when Christine was so clearly distressed seemed a little too much like breaking into a foxtrot at a funeral. Which brought up an interesting point—*why* was Christine so upset? While she had always been supportive of her son, she had never lived and died by his performance.

"Can we bring you anything?" Keith offered.

Could they? Evans had started her period today, and she could really use a glass of red wine and one of those brownies she'd seen on the buffet. She looked at Christine for guidance. After all, she was the mother. Christine looked down and shook her head.

"No, thank you," Evans and Anna-Blair said at the same time. So, no moving around, no chocolate, no booze.

When the men had gone, Christine turned to meet Evans's eyes. "What's wrong with him, Evie?"

"He's having a bad game?" The penalties and missed shots alone spelled that.

"But *why* is he having a bad game?" Christine asked. "When he was younger, this happened when he was upset, but by the time he left for North Dakota, he'd learned to leave his feelings off the ice. Even after the divorce, he didn't play like this." Christine ran her hand through her hair—another indication of the level of her distress. She did not like her hair messed up. "You've spent time with him. Has he said anything?"

"No," Evans said. "Not to me. He's seemed fine."

Anna-Blair leaned in. "Maybe he's just having a bad day, Christine. There have been a lot of changes—the move, new team, different coach than he expected. Besides, was it really that bad?" Even after all these years, Anna-Blair had never grasped hockey beyond the final score.

"It was that bad," Christine said emphatically. "When Jake goes to the boards to fight for the puck, he almost always comes away with it. I don't think he has a single time tonight."

"Twice." Evans hadn't intended to say that out loud. Christine and Anna-Blair gave her almost identical questioning looks. "What? He got the puck twice at the boards."

"But out of how many times?" Christine asked.

"I don't know," Evans said. "I didn't count."

Christine shrugged. "I guess I shouldn't be surprised. Blake's death on top of the divorce has been hard on him. But he came back from Europe in a much better state of mind. I was so relieved. He was in such bad shape when we were in Vermont for the funeral."

*Was* Jake in a bad place? Had she been so preoccupied with her own feelings that she hadn't noticed? She knew how close he'd been to Blake. How could she have ignored that?

"The condo is beautiful," Christine added out of the blue.

"It certainly is. Just lovely," Anna-Blair agreed.

What? They had gone from the state of Jake's mind to the state of his home?

"I took that he seems to care about his surroundings to be a sign that he was in a good place," Christine went on.

Ah. That made sense, but it didn't make it true. Jake having his condo decorated had nothing to do with anything except not wanting to hear Christine complain that he was living like an animal. He didn't care about his surroundings as long as he had a TV, gaming system, some beer, and a towel that hadn't gone too far into the mildew zone.

"Evie, has he talked to you about any of this?" Christine asked.

"No. Not a word." Wasn't that telling in itself? And it was telling that she hadn't asked, hadn't considered. She'd sent the flowers, said so sorry, and moved on. She'd been too busy hoping he would love her to be much of a friend. That was a hard truth to face.

"Maybe he just needs time," Anna-Blair suggested.

Christine nodded. "I suppose." She smiled and turned to Evans, signaling the discussion was over. "Evie, I've been so preoccupied with watching Jake, I haven't noticed much of anything else. How is your young man doing?"

"Good question!" Anna-Blair piled on. "Is he playing well?"

*Her young man?* For a moment, Evans was confused, but then it all snapped into place. *Able.* They were talking about Able. Had he played well? Evans didn't have an answer. She hadn't noticed Able or anyone else. She'd been too busy counting how many times Jake had come away from the boards with the puck—and, if she were to be honest, watching him sit on the bench between his shifts.

"Well, you know," she said evasively. "Fine."

"Why don't you ask him to join us at Hammer Time after the game?" Christine said, then added, "His family, too, if they're here."

How had that happened? How had Christine gone from concerned mother to procurer of information in such a short time?

"Yes, Evie," Anna-Blair chimed in. She looked around. "Do you see his parents? I'll just go invite his mother."

Holy hell. Was there a convent in Birmingham and did they accept Methodists? Because anything was better than this. She loved these women—her mother in particular, of course, but Christine, too. But they exhausted her.

"I, uh…" she began, having no idea where she was going.

"Look!" Christine interrupted her. "Isn't that Noel Glazov? Over there, in the ice suite across from us."

There was a petite woman with sandy blond hair standing against the glass, a baby on her hip. She spoke into the child's ear as she pointed to the Yellowhammer mascot, who was skating around with the ice girls.

Evans had no idea if that was the coach's wife and child or not, but she was grateful to her for distracting the women from hunting down Able's family. She could be Lucrezia Borgia for all Evans cared; she'd swear fealty to her right now.

Anna-Blair leaned forward. "I believe it is. Do you know her, Evie?"

"No, but it could be. They've bought a second house here, and she's opening a new quilt shop in Laurel Springs."

"She's a famous quilter," Christine said. "She makes every one of her quilts completely by hand. The wait list is horrendous."

Now, there was a woman who would appreciate a handmade pie. Maybe she'd take her one when her shop opened.

"Just where have you come by all this information?" Evans wanted to keep them going, so they'd forget about Able.

"There was an article about her in *Garden & Gun*," Anna-Blair said.

"I hope we get to meet her at the breakfast," Christine said. "The article made her sound really nice. Let's hope her husband is, too, and will show Jake some mercy."

As the buzzer sounded, signaling the beginning of the second period, Marc and Keith rejoined them.

"It'll be interesting to see if Jake is still playing first line," Evans heard Marc say to Keith in a low voice.

But he was. Not only that, in the first ten seconds of play, he took the puck, skated to the other end of the rink, and handed it off to Robbie, who put it in the goal. The crowd went wild and the tension lifted in their little corner of the world.

From there, everything got better. Jake was a different player and the Yellowhammers a different team. Evans was riveted—and relieved.

She didn't hope for victory. That would have been too much to ask for; it was enough that it was better. Then, in the last thirty seconds, Able fed the puck to Jake, who scored to tie the score. That meant overtime. Evans hated overtime—but she loved that Jake got a goal.

In the end, there was no overtime. For his second assist of the night, Jake sent the puck down the ice, to Luka for another goal and the win.

The Yellowhammers pulled it off. Technically, it might have been a struggle win, but it felt like the victory of the century. In addition to his goal and two assists, Jake had shown the world and himself that he was still king of the boards.

"Well," Christine said as they were leaving, "I guess he was just off his game."

"It happens," Anna-Blair agreed.

"Just nerves."

Evans hoped it was true.

## Chapter Sixteen

Jake pulled into a parking spot down the street from Hammer Time.

Beside him, Robbie said, not for the first time during the drive from the arena downtown back to Laurel Springs, "I still can't believe we won. I thought we had lost it for sure."

They'd had their showers, massages, and closing speech from Glaz. Now they were headed for food with the parents and the Pembertons—which he assumed would include Evie, but who knew? She might be off with Killjoy, the senior Killjoys, little sister Killjoy, and little brother Killjoy.

"I don't think Glaz could believe it either. I think he was happier than he let on," Jake said.

"What did he say to you when he sent for you after first period?"

"It was strange," Jake said. "I went in there expecting to get the ass-chewing of my life, but he was scary calm. He wanted to know if I was okay. He said it wasn't always possible to leave your troubles off the ice, but I had to try."

"Whatever he said, it worked," Robbie said.

*Not really. I had worked it out before he sent for*

*me*. But he didn't say that, didn't want to think about it anymore. He'd already had a gut load of thinking—not to mention talking—about his feelings. Who did that? Right now, he wanted to enjoy the victory and eat pizza.

Jake opened his car door. "Let's go get some food." It was only then that he noticed he'd parked right in front of Crust.

"Are we going to break in and eat pie?" Robbie joked.

"I figured we wouldn't get much closer to Hammer Time."

"Do us good to walk a little," Robbie said, getting out of the car. "Get the kinks out."

Jake paused and looked in the window of Crust. If Evie had decided to entertain the Killjoy family in there, she was doing it in the dark.

"Are you coming?" Robbie was halfway down the block. How had that happened?

A cheer went up when Jake and Robbie entered Hammer Time. "Maybe we do deserve to skate first line," Robbie said.

"Don't believe your own press," Jake said. "Right now, they'd cheer for anybody."

His folks should be here by now. They'd had plenty of time. "We're meeting someone," he told the hostess. "We'll just walk around until we see them."

"Your party left word, Mr. Champagne." She fiddled with the book on the hostess podium. "Yes. They're at the twelve-top in the back left-hand corner."

"Twelve-top?" That couldn't be. Christine and Anna-Blair had been known to insist on a bigger table than they needed because they didn't like to be crowded, but not that much bigger. "There are only seven of us. Are you sure?"

The girl referred to her book. "Yes. *Champagne.* Evans Pemberton was with them. Does that sound right?"

"Yes. I guess so." Maybe Christine wanted to lie down—Anna-Blair, too. Maybe they wanted to have a slumber party right here at Hammer Time. That's all he could think of—because it would never have occurred to him that he would find what he did.

Hellfire and brimstone. Save for two seats, the table was filled. Killjoy and who Jake could only assume were the Killjoyettes were seated with his people, who had traveled from the Delta to see *him* play—on an Ole Miss home game weekend no less. Good thing there weren't more Killjoys, else he and Robbie would be sitting at the bar.

Maybe he could run. They hadn't seen him yet. But no, hell no. He'd been noticed, and by none other than the—temporary—captain himself.

Jake had done what he'd needed to on the ice, but he had avoided Killen in the locker room. He wouldn't always be able to do that, but couldn't a man catch a break? Couldn't he have a little time to work up to it? But there was no avoiding him now, because he was on his feet—out of his chair, which was next to Evie's, of course.

"Sparks, Scotty. Great game, guys."

And the noise level went up in the room. His parents were hugging and congratulating him, his mother kissing Robbie and inviting him for Thanksgiving, Anna-Blair and Keith getting in on the act, Killjoy introducing his family.

Jake couldn't breathe. Finally, he'd been hustled into his waiting throne, next to Robbie and across from

Evie—who had not hugged, cooed, congratulated, or said a word up until now.

"Hello, Robbie," she said warmly.

"Hello, lass. You look beautiful as always. That's a nice sweater, but you need a Yellowhammer jersey. I'll take care of that."

"I'll see that she gets one," Killjoy said.

*Over my dead body.* The thought went through Jake's mind, but that was fifteen-year-old talk. What had happened to his earlier resolve? There wasn't a thing he could or should do about Evie being with Killjoy.

"My, my, who knew I had so many fashion consultants?" She took a sip of her wine and it left her lips all purple and rosy at the same time. Then she turned to Jake. "I was beginning to doubt the power of my chicken pot pie, but eventually it did its magic."

To his own surprise, Jake laughed. She was the only one tonight who'd called it like it was. Though there would be some film watching and a reckoning coming from Glaz, even he'd glossed over that disastrous first period tonight. Luckily people would forgive your sins if you gave them what they wanted in the end.

"Next time, could you make your magic a little faster acting?"

"Next time? Who said anything about next time?" she said.

"There's always next time," he said.

"Sometimes." She nodded. "Unless there's been no time."

"What?" Robbie said. "I didn't understand a word of that."

Frankly, neither did Jake, but it had felt private, intimate. He glanced at Killen. He might have looked confused, or maybe that was just his usual expression.

"Don't pay any attention to them," Christine said. "They were in the cradle together and have a language all their own."

Technically, that wasn't true. When Evie was born Jake had already been too big for the cradle, but he'd learned at a young age not to correct Christine in public, or really anywhere.

"Son, we ordered you a pizza," Marc said, "and two cheeseburgers and double fries for Robbie. Do y'all want anything else?"

"No, Dad. That's great."

"Thank you, perfect," Robbie said.

"We had enough post-game meals with Robbie when they played in Nashville that we know what he likes." Christine addressed Able's parents, bringing the new people into the conversation.

"Able likes lasagna," Mrs. Killjoy said. "I used to make it ahead and freeze it, so he could have it quickly after the game. You know how hungry they get."

Evie winced a little as she took a gulp of her wine— not to be confused with a sip. Maybe she hated frozen lasagna even more than frozen chicken pot pie. She had to if it was driving her to drink.

Killjoy leaned in a little closer to Evie—not so much that she noticed, but Jake noticed.

He eyed the sister. She looked at least twenty, not too young to be flirted with. That would get under Killjoy's skin. Not that he would. He understood the Bro Code. *Thou shalt not date, flirt with, or trifle with thy teammate's sister, girlfriend, wife, ex-girlfriend, or ex-wife.* He wouldn't break the Bro Code. Besides, did he re-

ally want to open himself up to the possibility of a lifetime of freezer meals? He could see it now—Christmas
morning with the Killjoys, Evie serving quiche, Mrs.
Killjoy and the sister doling out frozen waffles.

"Are you in pain?" Evie asked him quietly.

"No."

She shrugged. "You had a painful look on your face."

Mrs. Killjoy and Christine were yammering on about
living through the youth and junior hockey years. Was
Able leaning in even closer to Evie? And if so, what
did he hope to accomplish? The Bro Code needed to be
amended to include all women who might have alleg-
edly been in the cradle with your teammate. He would
propose that to the Bro Code Council, as soon as he
found out who the members were.

"Melba." Anna-Blair was speaking now. Mrs. Killjoy must be named Melba. "We went to Ole Miss with
a girl from Idaho. I know it's a stretch, but might you
know her? Karen Chastaine. She was a Phi Mu."

"No. I'm sorry, I don't."

"Jim," Keith Pemberton said, "what do you do?"
Melba and Jim Killjoy. They were a pair. Yes. Killjoy
was definitely leaning in toward Evie, inch by inch. She
must have sensed it, because she shifted away. Good.
*Don't let him in your personal space, Evie. You don't
know where he's been.*

"I'm an attorney," Jim said. "Private practice. Mostly
real estate."

So, Jim Killjoy, esquire.

"Ah," Keith said.

"Ah," Marc said.

Jake did not know what those *ahs* meant.

"Awww!" Robbie leaned in to hiss, quietly, but ear-splitting all the same time. That meant nothing good.

"What?" Jake looked around. No one was listening to them, with the possible exception of Evie, and that was a slim maybe. All the parents were exchanging career information, and little sister and brother were playing on their phones. Occasionally someone would stop to look at one of the giant televisions where Auburn and Arkansas were playing.

"Holy family and all the wise men." Robbie looked past Jake and gave out a tight little smile.

Jake turned his head and his mouth went dry.

Sashaying toward them were Delilah and Dawn—the two Nashville Sound ice girls who were not twins, but looked so much alike that people thought they were. They played it up by dressing alike and wearing their long blond hair the same way. Tonight, they were wearing Yellowhammer jerseys.

And that's not all. Delilah's—or was it Dawn's—had Jake's number on it. The other one had Robbie's.

*Fuck me and kill me now.*

"Just who we're looking for!" said Dawn. Or was it Delilah?

Jake slowly turned his head and looked at Evie, but she didn't meet his eyes. She wasn't avoiding him, but she was totally taken up with the jersey-clad bookends in front of her. She was all wide eyes, agape mouth, and clenched hands. That said it all. He didn't know exactly *what* it said, but something.

He felt a hand on his shoulder and was compelled to turn his face back toward the mini cloud of perfume that was hovering around him. It was Dawn—Dawn, for sure. She was the one he had kept company with on occasion.

Robbie jumped to his feet. "Well, we certainly wouldn't have expected to see two loyal Sound cheerleaders here tonight, especially not in Yellowhammer sweaters!"

"The Sound is on the road," Delilah said. "You didn't think we would miss the debut game of our two favorite Sound players, did you?"

*Well, honestly, Delilah, we didn't think about it at all. Or I didn't. I can't speak for Robbie but, from the look on his face, I'd say he hadn't pondered it overmuch either.*

"Would you two young ladies like to join us? We can get some more chairs."

Oh, hell. Hell, hell, hell. That had come from Evie's daddy. Keith Pemberton was known for his perfect manners. He would have eaten a blowfish to keep from offending his hostess. *Yes, ma'am, I'd be delighted. Just let me call my attorney first and get my affairs in order. Maybe Jim Killjoy can handle it for me. He's a real estate man, but how hard is a will?*

Delilah and Dawn looked at each other, carrying on a conversation with their eyes.

It was Dawn who spoke. "We won't intrude, but we do need some help. We had a flat tire."

*Is that all? Killjoy will fix you right up. He's a cracker jack at tire changing.*

"My car is downtown at the arena," Dawn carried on. "We took an Uber here, but we can't very well take an Uber back to Nashville—or leave my car in Birmingham."

No doubt someone—probably Killjoy—had tweeted

about hanging out at Hammer Time and these girls were resourceful.

Robbie looked from Jake to the girls and back again. "I could take them back downtown and change the tire if I had a different car." Robbie's Corvette, like the Lamborghini, was a two-seater.

"I have a truck," Killjoy piped up. "A Ford F350. It'll hold five people, six if they're friendly." He smiled at Evie way *too* friendly. "That's not counting the truck bed."

"Are you volunteering?" Jake asked. Because that would be just fine.

"I can't," Killen said. "You know. Family here, and all." *And all* probably meant Evie.

"Excuse us," Jake said to the table, though he didn't look at his mother. "Robbie and I are going to go figure this out." He looked back at the girls. "We'll be right back. Why don't you…have a seat and introduce yourselves?"

It wasn't the best idea, but he couldn't think of what else.

"This is a fucking nightmare!" Robbie said as soon as they were out of earshot.

"I'm glad you at least realize that."

"Don't act like this is my fault. I didn't invite them. You heard what Glaz said about ice girls. I would take an Uber, go back downtown, and change their tire, but I can't be alone with them. They'll take selfies with me and put them on social media that hasn't even been invented yet."

"You idiot," Jake said. "They don't have a flat tire. They're trying to get us out of here to have sex with us. They probably think we *want* out of here."

Robbie cocked his head to the side. "Well…"

"Stop it," Jake commanded.

"You're right. We've got to get rid of them."

"Okay. This is the plan. We're going to *say* we're both driving our cars to take them back downtown, where we'll change the tire. This is what we're really going to do: if their car *is* at the arena—which I doubt—we're going to put them in an Uber and tell them good-bye. If it's parked on the street right outside—and I guarantee it is—we're going to put them on the road."

Robbie looked wistful. "We had some good times with those girls."

"We had a good time on the ice tonight. I would like to keep having that good time."

"Yeah," Robbie reluctantly agreed.

Jake turned to go back to the table.

"Sparks," Robbie said, "what if they really do have a flat tire?"

"Trust me. They don't."

"You haven't even eaten," Christine said with a frown after Jake shared the plan.

No kidding, but he had bigger problems than his growling stomach. "Take my pizza home. I'll see you back there later."

The one silver lining in the whole thing was he was getting out of Killjoy Land.

# Chapter Seventeen

Evans stepped out of the shower, dried off, and pulled on a pair of sleep pants and a tank top. She had never been so glad to be alone. Had it always been so stressful being with her parents and the Champagnes? All through her childhood and teen years? She didn't remember it that way, but maybe that's all she'd known at the time and considered it the norm.

Chocolate was what she needed; she always did when her hormones were raging, but never more than tonight. Plus, she was hungry. Somewhere along the way, she'd lost her appetite at Hammer Time and she'd given most of her quesadilla to Able. Maybe she should have brought it home, but that wasn't what she wanted anyway. It had to be chocolate. Since she didn't usually eat dessert besides taste testing at Crust, she hardly ever had sweets in the house. It was a good thing she'd filched one of those brownies from the buffet as she was leaving the ice suite.

She needed that brownie.

She sat on the sofa and reached for her purse, but got distracted by the gift basket from Christine. It was so big, she'd dropped her purse when Christine handed it to her as she was getting out of their SUV. The card said, "Thank you for making the pie for Jake! We love you, Christine."

They did love her. Even Jake—just not how she wanted to be loved. The basket, which had come from the Gift Emporium around the block from Crust, was all done up in fall colors. Lisa made a nice basket, and it would have cost three times the price of a chicken pot pie. Maybe there was some chocolate in there. She untied the orange ribbon and began to paw through the things nestled in the autumn-leaf-colored tissue paper. There was a cinnamon-scented candle, apple bodywash, some hand soap in a pumpkin-shaped decanter, an Ole Miss coffee mug, a package of toasted pecans, a tin of cheese straws, and some linen tea towels. No chocolate. She picked up one of the oatmeal-colored towels. It had a band of embroidered bees with the words Y'all Bee Sweet depicted above. The other towel was identical, except it said Y'all Bee Kind. A wave of guilt washed over her. She folded the towels with the words to the inside and put them back in the basket.

Nothing like tea towel conviction.

She wasn't being sweet or kind to Able. He clearly liked her. All through dinner he'd kept inching closer and closer to her, and she'd declined his offer of a ride home, knowing he would want to kiss her—and she could not kiss him. No matter how many times she'd told herself otherwise, she was never going to be able to return his interest. He was a decent man who had been nothing but nice to her, and he didn't deserve to be used as a vehicle to help her get over Jake.

She *would* get over Jake, but she wasn't going to do it on Able's time. That was going to stop right now, starting with canceling on the breakfast in the morning. It would be easier to go and leave the hard stuff until later but—at this particular moment anyway—she was more committed to right than easy. And canceling was the right thing. She'd already been seen eating dinner with him by half the team. If she waltzed into that breakfast on his arm, they would be put on the matrimony watch list. Hyacinth would show up at her door with fabric swatches, a sketchpad, and maybe a TV producer.

Unfortunately, the reason for canceling wasn't the easiest thing either. If she made some feeble excuse like she wasn't feeling well, he'd probably believe it and send flowers. That wouldn't help anything. No. She would tell him the truth—up to a point.

She reached into her purse for her phone, but ran across the brownie first. She took a bite as she pondered what she would say to him. It was easy to let the brownie distract her; it was fudgy and studded with pecans. Best of all, it was big—about four inches square. Who cared if it was a little linty? She set it aside. No more until the chore at hand was done.

She'd tell Able that she was emotionally attached to someone else, even though there was no relationship—that she'd thought maybe exploring things with him could help her move on, but she knew now that wasn't true. It wasn't fair to him. She needed to truly get over this and become emotionally healthy, not just distract herself.

That sounded good—yet awful at the same time. If this wasn't a clear case of "it's not you, it's me," she didn't know what was. Telling herself it was for courage, she took another bite of brownie and searched her bag for her phone, but came up empty.

It *had* to be there.

She emptied her purse on the sofa—wallet, keys, smoky eyeshadow palette, dirty napkin from the brownie, linen monogrammed handkerchief that she always forgot she had, pack of tissues that she used instead, four pens, a lipstick, numerous cash register receipts, a little cosmetic bag with extra tampons.

No phone. She must have lost it when she spilled her purse in the floorboard of the Champagnes' SUV.

No matter. Her daddy would bring it to her. He had her car. She'd just call him—

Except she couldn't. No phone. And no landline. She couldn't call anybody.

Hell, hell, hell.

Jake let himself into the condo and listened. Empty. He wasn't surprised that he'd beat his parents back. It hadn't taken long to get Delilah and Dawn on the road. As he'd predicted, there had been no flat tire and their car was parked just up the street from Hammer Time. Robbie had been charming but firm, and blamed the whole thing on Glaz. The girls were disappointed but, all in all, good sports.

"There they go," Robbie had said a little wistfully as their taillights disappeared. Robbie had wanted to go back to Hammer Time and eat, but Jake had nixed that. He was hungry, too, but he'd had all of this day he wanted. He was tired of Killjoys and neckties. More than that, he didn't want to watch Able Killen load Evie into his giant truck and drive off into the night. He knew now that eventually he would have to see it or something similar. Clearly, she was as interested in Able as he was in her, or else she wouldn't be going to the team breakfast with him and allowing their families to mix. That was big business.

He threw his necktie, along with his suit and shirt, in the basket marked *dry cleaning* and pulled on a pair of shorts and an old college T-shirt.

Had he made a mistake? He had to face that his jealousy over Able was irrational. Was there more to it than just wanting Evie to be free to pal around with him? His mind wandered back to that Christmas party where he'd met Channing, but he wasn't thinking of Channing. He was remembering how Evie had looked that night, how she'd smiled a certain way and how he was about to ask her to the spring dance.

She still smiled that way. What if he'd never made the bet with Robbie? What if, after coming to Laurel Springs, he'd picked up where he left off before Channing blew into his life? Of all the reasons why he couldn't be attracted to Evie, the only one that really mattered was the risk to their friendship. But some risks were worth taking. What if this was one of them?

But it was a moot point. Killjoy was probably with her right now, had probably already rounded up a jersey with his name and number on it for her. Jake had to find a way not to be mad about it. Maybe he should have been more proactive before Killjoy came on the scene. *He* sure hadn't been scared to take action.

His stomach growled. His parents would be home soon with his pizza but, in the meantime, he supposed he might as well pack for the road trip. He needed to remember his coat. It would be cold in Winnipeg, maybe in Minnesota, too.

He began to make a mental packing list. Suits first. He'd need two, but when he went to retrieve them, some were missing. That's when he found his suitcase and garment bag sitting by his bedroom door, all ready to go. His mother had packed for him. Wanting to be sure he'd have what he needed, Jake unzipped the garment bag—two of the London suits and his overcoat were inside. She'd even put his gloves in the pockets of his coat. His heart warmed a little. His suitcase was meticulously packed with his shoes in bags, dress shirts wrapped in tissue paper, ties rolled so they wouldn't wrinkle, and plenty of underwear. Looked like she'd thought of everything, even a phone charger and spare shirts and ties. The only fly in the ointment was the toiletries. She had packed them, and he'd need them in the morning.

But when he started to unpack the Dopp kit, he found new duplicates of everything, right down to an electric razor. He shouldn't have been surprised. Christine advocated duplicate toiletries for everyone who traveled more than a few times a year. She'd provided that for him until he graduated from college and he'd kept up the habit, but he'd left his extra kit when he moved out of the McMansion and had never duplicated it.

A chime sounded, signaling that the door had been opened. Christine was setting the pizza box on the bar when Jake entered the kitchen.

"Hi," he said behind her.

She jumped and whirled around. "Jake! You scared me. I didn't expect you this soon."

"I didn't expect to be here this soon either." He slid onto a bar stool and opened the box. Not hot, but not stone cold. It would do. "Thanks for packing for me."

"You're welcome. I know I'm not what you'd call maternal in the kitchen, but I do what I can in other areas. I'm an excellent packer."

"None better," Jake agreed. "Where's Dad?" Maybe it wasn't too much to hope for that she wouldn't question how he'd gotten downtown, changed a tire, and gotten back so fast.

"Parking the car. He let me out at the door." She went to the refrigerator and took out a partial bottle of wine. "Do you want a beer to go with your pizza?"

"No. I'm not drinking much these days and not at all until the preseason games are over, but I'll let you hand me a bottle of water."

"Here you go." She gave him the water and opened a cabinet. "Do you want a glass?" She knew he didn't, but this was her way of reminding him that she didn't hold with drinking out of bottles.

"This is fine." He removed the top and took a long drink.

She brought her wine—in a glass—and sat down beside him. "How did you get home so fast?"

He sighed. "I don't suppose you'd buy that I'm really Superman and took care of that flat tire in thirty seconds?"

She laughed. "No—though you did play like Superman tonight, at least the last two periods."

He took a bite of pizza, and his stomach cheered. "Can Superman skate? I've never known him to skate. It's not a given that everyone can skate, you know." Evie couldn't. He should have been more patient with her when they were young. He'd promised her skates, and he would deliver, but he was through giving her grief about Able—even in his head. He'd buy the skates, but if she wanted Able to teach her, he would be all right with it. Mostly.

"I would bet Superman can skate—if he wants to. So, about the flat tire?"

That woman definitely had the need to know. He'd been trying to distract her for years, and it never worked.

"There was no flat tire. The girls were parked down the street. They thought they were doing us a favor to get us out of what they considered a boring family situation for—shall we say—some more exciting times. We sent them on their way. That's all there was to it."

"Why didn't you come back in and eat?"

*Because I was tired of seeing Able Killen moving into Evie's personal space.*

"I was tired. I wanted out of my suit and tie. I didn't want to come in and admit to everyone that Delilah and Dawn had told a big lie."

Christine shook her head. "Jake…those girls—"

"Mama, stop right there," he said. "They aren't like you and your friends, but they're sweet and well intentioned. Nothing mean about them. We aren't going to disparage them."

She frowned. "I wasn't. I was only going to say that it isn't right for you and Robbie to take advantage of someone you might have power over."

That was a surprise. Christine liked things a certain way, and Delilah and Dawn were not her flavor. "We don't have any power over them," Jake said. *Unless you count my ability to deliver rapid-fire multiple orgasms, and we aren't going to discuss that.* "They're living their lives—at least right now—like they want to. They like hockey players and they're having fun. That's their business. But they won't be having fun with me anymore. I am…reevaluating."

"That's good to hear." She looked relieved. "Let's leave this subject. I'm not entirely comfortable with it."

"Thank God!" he burst out and they laughed together.

Christine's laugh settled into a smile, and she leaned toward him and let her eyes sparkle. It was a good trick. He could do it, too—had learned it from her.

"Tell me about Able Killen. Is he nice?"

Any residual amusement that had been hanging around inside of Jake died on the vine. He ate some more pizza to buy time. "Yes," he was forced to say. "I don't know him well, but he has a reputation for being a stand-up guy."

"Good. Evie deserves it."

That was true, too. Before he had to voice that, the door tone sounded.

"There's Marc," Christine said.

A minute later, he came into the kitchen. "Do either of you know who this belongs to? I found it on the floorboard." He held up a cell phone with a green leather case. Evie's, but how had it ended up in the SUV?

"It's not Anna-Blair's," Christine said.

"It looks like Evie's," Jake said.

Christine snapped her fingers. "That's right. She spilled her purse when we took her home."

That was interesting. "Killjoy didn't take her home?"

"No." Christine shook her head. "I don't know why."

"I don't guess she has a landline?" Marc looked at Jake. "Nobody your age does."

"No," Jake confirmed. Had Able not offered to take her home? Or had she refused him? Or maybe he was going home to change clothes and go over to her house later. Maybe he was there now.

"I guess I should take it to her," Marc said. "I don't like the idea of her alone with no way to get in touch with anybody."

Jake rose, took one more bite of pizza, and reached for the phone. "I'll take it." He moved toward the foyer where his keys were.

"Jake?" Christine called.

Oh, what now?

"Yes?" He turned and met her eyes.

"Aren't you going to get your shoes?"

## Chapter Eighteen

There were ninety-three reasons Evans needed her phone and the first ninety-two didn't count. If she didn't shut this breakfast date down, Able would be here at 8:30 in the morning to pick her up. She would have no choice but to go or be that person who canceled on the front porch—which meant she'd go.

Maybe Jake and Robbie would be there with those twins. They could all sit together and debate the best way to create a smoky eye look. No doubt those women knew their way around an eyeshadow palette and could share some tips. Robbie would call everyone *lass*, and Able would herd everyone into the parking lot to see how many he could fit in his truck.

She was going out of her mind. Maybe it was the emotional overload of the day or the three glasses of wine she'd had—two more than usual. She was willing to call Able up until midnight, but no later, and that time was fast approaching. No phone, no car, no carrier pigeon. She looked out the window to see if Hyacinth's lights were on. Of course not. So no awake Hyacinth either. She might as well be on a one-person island in the middle of the ocean. Pacific, Atlantic. Any ocean would do. The Isle of Evans. That's what she'd call her island.

But wait. There was a phone at Crust—though she couldn't walk there in her pajamas. Feeling like the idiot of the century, she started toward her bedroom to change.

Then, the doorbell rang.

Oh, happy, happy day! She wouldn't have to dress and walk to Crust, after all. They had found her phone. That would be her daddy bringing it to her. She ran across the room and jerked open the door.

"Hey, Evie."

Her whole world stopped.

There stood Jake, blue eyes wide, blond hair a mess, wearing shorts and a T-shirt that had seen some wear and hot water. He looked like he'd been to the gym a few times since its acquisition, too. Then it occurred to her that her tank top was none too loose fitting either—and she wasn't wearing a bra.

Was it her imagination or were his eyes sliding up and down her body?

He held up her phone. "I brought this."

Right. Of course.

She had, for a fraction of moment, forgotten about her phone. She'd thought he had come to see her. Some things never changed. She looked past him to see if Robbie and the twins were waiting outside for him to get his little errand done so they could all get on with the good times.

But no. Just the bugmobile, and it was empty.

"I thought you'd be with Jezebel and Jolene," she said.

He laughed the barest bit. "Delilah and Dawn. I'm not." He stepped inside and closed the door with his foot without turning around. "I thought you'd be with Killjoy."

"I'm not."

He took a deep breath and narrowed his eyes. She couldn't read his expression. That almost never happened, but this look was one she'd never seen before.

Electricity bloomed around them, gradually at first, until the room was alive with full-blown lightning—at least for her. Maybe it was the feeling that she was about to be torn apart by a thunderbolt that made her brave enough to ask, "Do you want to be? With them, I mean?" She immediately regretted the question and braced herself for hearing that he was on his way to catch up with them now. She took the phone and stepped away from him, away from the electricity and the door he would, no doubt, exit in the next five seconds.

"No. If I wanted to be, I would be."

He closed the space between them, placed one hand on her shoulder and the other on her cheek. And there was the lightning—in his hands. The electricity started on her scalp and worked its way down her body, crackling as it went.

"Do you want to be with Killjoy?" He slid his thumb down her neck.

"No. If I wanted to be, I would be," she echoed his answer.

"I'm glad to hear it." He looked deep into her eyes and let his own go soft. "So damned glad."

Her heart lifted and reached for a gold ring engraved with the word *hope*—the same gold ring it had tried to catch so many times.

After years of hiding her heart, swallowing the words she wanted to say, and pretending like her feelings didn't matter, she found her backbone and went for broke. "Jake, don't look at me like that if you're not going to do anything about it." She closed her eyes and waited for the answer.

"What do you want me to do? This?" And he pulled her completely into his arms. "Or this?" He let his hand drift over her collarbone and down—almost grazing her breast—to stroke her side.

Her breath caught, her nipples went on high alert—and she dropped her phone with a thud.

He laughed a little into her ear. "I guess you didn't want your phone, after all. But I'm glad you lost it."

And with that, he lifted her hips and molded her to him, pelvis to pelvis, letting his arousal come to full bloom against her. She felt hot, cold, and impossibly desirable. His desire might be left over from an ice girl or even a faceless fantasy, but—in this moment—she felt like it was for her.

He boldly moved against her, it seemed, just to show her this was not an accident. She went limp and shivered in his arms.

"Is that what you wanted me to do?" he said against her ear. "Or was it this?"

After all these years, and all the longing that the world could hold, his mouth was finally on hers.

This was not a kiss. This was The Kiss.

It wasn't the sloppy kiss of a boy who didn't know what he was doing, but it wasn't a kiss of pure lust either. It wasn't the practiced, perfected kiss that would have made it seem like he'd been to kiss camp. This was the ultimate kiss—a little sloppy, a little lusty, and a whole lot of proof that he knew what he was doing.

But there was something more—a little of *I ought*

*not to be doing this, but I can't help myself.* That made
it better, because there wasn't a woman alive who didn't
dream of making a man—a *particular* man—lose himself.

And she was lost herself.

It was the most romantic moment of her life.

After a time, he lifted his mouth from hers, but his
face didn't go far. Their noses were no more than an
inch apart and his eyes looked all the more blue because, being so close, they were blurry. He cradled her
head in the crook of his arm and she clutched fistfuls
of his T-shirt.

Then he lifted his face a little more, enough so that
she could see his smile. She smiled back—and in one
smooth swoop, they were on the sofa, and he was kissing her again. He might have been to get-her-on-the-
sofa-in-a-reclining-position camp. She laughed a little,
deep in her throat, partly at her funny thought and partly
from pure joy. Every cell in her body was singing, singing a song they had been waiting to sing only for this
man.

"You wouldn't be making fun of me, would you,
Evans Arlene?" he whispered near her ear.

She gave him a playful punch in the shoulder and
laughed, even as chill bumps covered her from his
mouth on her ear.

"Don't call me that!" she said like she had every time
he'd ever called her by her full name—though it had
been a long time. She so hated her middle name—in
part because she had no love for the stern, judgmental
great aunt she'd been named for—that no one in her
present life even knew it.

"Oh, Evie." He rolled over on his back, bringing her

along until she lay on top of him. "I've been fighting this but, deep down, I knew it was coming. I think I've known from the first day I hit town." And he kissed her again.

*I didn't know, but I hoped. I've always hoped. And please, please, God, don't let this be nothing, don't let it mean nothing, because that would be too cruel.*

"Kiss me here." He guided her face to his neck and her mouth to the place above his collarbone. When she opened her mouth and let her tongue trail there, he let out a low moan and shifted their bodies until their hips were pressed perfectly together.

She moved against him, let out a moan of her own, and opened her mouth wider against the spot on his neck.

"Here...let me..." He turned her slightly and ran his hand lightly and briefly over her breasts before reaching under her tank top to cup and squeeze.

It was going to happen. Finally, she wasn't the between-girlfriends gal pal. She was the one he was holding, the one he was going to make love to. Was she wearing pretty panties? What had she put on after her shower?

Then the razor-sharp realization ripped through her. Fuck, hell, damn, and every other curse word that had ever been invented. Granny panties. The ones she always wore when she had her period.

Wasn't that just the way of it for her? *Finally* ending up to be *not happening, after all.* Because she could not have sex. Sure, more adventurous women did, but she wasn't adventurous. And even if she had been, having sex with Jake for the first time during her period was out of the question.

Jake must have sensed the change in her because he stilled his hand on her breast.

"Evie, is something wrong?"

She rolled off him and sat up. "Jake, I'm sorry. I can't do this."

He swung around to sit beside her, confusion on his face. "Okay?" He widened his eyes, questioning.

"It's not that I don't want to," she hurried to say. "I do. Very much." She felt her face go hot. "It's not the right *time*." He had a sister, had had girlfriends, a wife. Surely he knew what she was alluding to. "Do you understand what I mean? What I'm saying?"

After a moment, he nodded. "I do, Evie. Thank you for saying so."

And to her joy, he reached for her hand.

"I'm glad you get it." She stuck out her bottom lip to show him she really was sorry about it. "I nearly forgot and got carried away there…"

He laughed a little. "I know." He reached for a pillow and covered his lap. "I might need to sit here a little while until I simmer down." He smiled and bit his lip. "And I might need to kiss you a little bit, while I do—only kiss you."

"I don't know if that would help the matter at hand, but I might need to let you." And she went back into his arms. They did just kiss—as if there was anything *just* about kissing Jake Champagne—for a long while. Then his hand began to snake up her shirt again. She caught her breath. Should she stop him? Probably, but she didn't want to. Maybe in a bit.

But he stopped abruptly and sat back.

"I said only kissing, and I was about to break that promise." He pushed her hair off her face. "Lord, girl, what you do to me. How is it we missed this when we were teenagers?"

*I didn't miss it, but that doesn't matter.*

She just smiled. His stomach let out a long, loud growl and they laughed.

"Are you hungry?" she asked.

"Since coming off the ice I have had one orange, a CLIF Bar, and about three bites of pizza." His eyes drifted to the coffee table and her abandoned brownie. "You've got a brownie. Can I have a bite?"

She couldn't snatch it up and hold it out to him fast enough. "Have it all. I don't want it."

He shook his head and laughed. "Why do you always do that?"

"What?"

"Say yes, even when you don't want to."

"I don't want it," she insisted.

"You do." He ruffled her hair. "Don't lie to me. You've been eating it. You were eating it when I came to the door, weren't you?"

*Not exactly, but close enough.* "Maybe I just want you to have it. You're hungry. Can you accept that?"

He looked from her face to the brownie and back again. "I can." He took the brownie and ate half in one bite. "But only because my stomach is digesting itself."

"Do you want some milk?"

"More than I've ever wanted anything in my life." Then he grinned and looked at her like she'd always hoped he would. "Well, almost anything."

The brownie was gone when she returned, and he'd opened the tin of cheese straws from the gift basket. She liked that he'd assumed he could have something that was hers; she wanted to give him everything she owned.

"Sorry." He held up a cheese straw. "I'll buy you some more."

"Not necessary. Your mother bought those anyway." She set his milk on the coffee table and handed him a plate with a blueberry muffin and two containers of yogurt. "Provisions are slim. I haven't shopped lately, and I'm out of everything except breakfast food. Maybe that'll hold you until you can get back to your pizza."

He accepted the plate. "Breakfast food. Hmmm." He took bite of the muffin. "I guess I don't have to worry that you'll need this in the morning since you'll be fed courtesy of the Alabama Yellowhammers and Mr. Killjoy."

He sounded jealous. Had he been all along? Could that be why he didn't like Able?

"How did you know I was going to the breakfast with Able?"

He opened the yogurt. "How do you think? The Delta Queens." He spooned yogurt into his mouth. "Peach. My favorite."

"Delta Queens," she repeated. "How appropriate. I think of them as the Information Power Pair."

"That fits, too." He paused. "I don't call them that to their faces."

"Oh, no. Hell, no. Me neither," Evans answered.

They looked at each other for a long moment, sharing moments of their lives and their history that didn't have to be voiced or explained. She had never been able to make clear her relationship with Anna-Blair to anyone without sounding like an ungrateful bitch who didn't love her mother—but Jake knew.

"Do you want to know something they don't know?" Evans asked.

Jake grinned. "I think I already do." He placed his hand on the spot on his neck that she had so recently kissed.

She rolled her eyes. "Besides that."

"I can't wait."

"I'm not going to the breakfast with Able."

Jake cocked his head to the side. "Oh, yeah?"

It wouldn't do to let him think it was because of what had just transpired between them. She didn't want to look like she was making assumptions about a relationship that might not develop.

"I was going to call him before you got here. That's how I discovered I didn't have my phone."

"What made you decide?"

*I'm in love with you, Jake. I always have been. I didn't want to be with him.*

"It just wasn't right. I guess I wanted to head it off before everyone on the team thought we were a couple."

"But you asked his family to eat with us tonight."

She shook her head. "I did not. That was all the work of the Information Power Delta Queens."

He nodded and took a drink of his milk. "I love them, Evie. I swear I do. I even enjoy their company but, Lord have mercy, they wear me out like no skate-'til-you-drop practice ever could."

"I could write the book on *that*."

"So, I won't see you tomorrow." It was a statement, not a question.

"No. I guess it's gotten too late to call Able tonight, but I'll do it in the morning."

He nodded and took her hand. "About the Delta Queens."

"Yes?"

"I don't know what's happening here." He gestured from himself to her. "But something. Can we keep it to ourselves?"

"Oh, yes. The biggest *yes* in the world. Nobody needs that conversation."

"That's for sure."

She hesitated. "There *is* a conversation I want to have—about something I realized at the game."

He looked at the ceiling. "Hockey pointers? I was a mess there for a while."

She nodded. "You got over it. No. About Blake..."

Clouds moved over his face. "What about him?"

"I realized we haven't really talked about it since you came to town. I haven't even asked how you're doing. I know how it was between you two."

His bright eyes darkened, but he smiled a little heart-break smile. "You do." He squeezed her hand. "You saw it."

"How *are* you?"

He closed his eyes and sighed before meeting her gaze again. "I thought I was okay. The whole summer, that's all I thought about with Olivia and the kids—all any of us thought about. But keeping them moving and trying to keep them distracted was a distraction for me, too. Then, I got here, and was so busy, I didn't think about it." He wrinkled his forehead. "But the last few days, a couple of times, I've forgotten he's dead. I've started to call him twice. And I think, how could I forget? I don't know if I'm crazy or a total asshole."

Evans had heard of people who wished they could take someone's pain on themselves, but she'd never felt that way until now. She couldn't do that, but she fought to find some comforting words.

"I don't think you're either. I think you're grieving appropriately. It shows how strong your relationship was that you want to talk to him so much that you let yourself forget he's gone."

He looked at her long and deep. "Thank you. I needed to hear that."

"I'm right here."

They shared a silent moment. "I'm going to count on that."

"See that you do." She stood up and held her hand out to him. "You should go home and rest. Big day tomorrow."

He rose and stretched. "You're right. Christine will have a search party organized if I don't get back soon." He picked up his dirty dishes. "I'll just wash these first."

That was weird. "Jake, you don't need to do that."

"Trust me, I do." And he headed to the kitchen.

When he kissed her goodbye at the door, he tasted like chocolate, peaches, and blueberries.

"I'll call you from the road," he said.

She hugged herself as she watched the insectmobile drive away. Then she ran her hands over her neck, lips, breasts—everywhere he'd touched her—not quite believing it had happened, but praying it would happen again.

## Chapter Nineteen

The plane was almost full by the time Jake boarded.

He slid into the seat beside Robbie and fastened his seatbelt. It wasn't quite time to take off, but he liked to settle in.

"The plane's right posh," Robbie said.

"Did you think it wouldn't be?" Jake pulled his iPad and noise-canceling headphones out of his backpack.

"I don't know. We're used to a team with its own plane. I wasn't sure how a chartered plane would be."

"I don't care, as long as I've got a little leg room and some decent snacks," Jake said. "But I did want the window seat."

"So did I," Robbie said, "and I got here first. There are a few left."

There were. Three to be exact, but Able hadn't boarded yet and Jake didn't want to risk having to sit by him. Oddly—or maybe not so oddly, considering what all had happened—the animosity Jake had felt for Able had dissipated, but he still didn't want to sit by him. True to her word, Evie had not shown up at the team breakfast. Anna-Blair had said that Evie had a headache, and they were going by to tell her good-bye before heading back to the Delta. Jake didn't know what she'd told Able, but that was one conversation he was not going to have.

"One less window seat," Robbie said. "Wingo just took the one up there on the right. He's a rookie. You could make him move."

"Nah." Jake stored his bag under the seat. "I wouldn't want to start any rumors that you and I have broken up."

"Guess I'm the only girlfriend you're likely to have for a while," Robbie deadpanned.

*Maybe not.*

He'd never wanted anyone as much as he'd wanted Evie last night—and it wasn't just because he'd had a long dry spell. It was *her*—the way she smelled, the way she tasted, the way she felt against him. Oh, yes, that last part especially. She had come into his arms so willingly and seemed to know exactly when he wanted her to open her mouth a little more and how he wanted her to move against him. It was like falling down a well, but without fear because he knew what was at the bottom: Evie—Evie, who knew everything about him and liked him anyway. Evie, who had given him, in just a few words, comfort about Blake without insisting that he talk about it until he was hoarse.

Maybe this was it—the meant-to-be that he had ceased to believe in.

He had almost ruined it, almost stripped her naked and made love to her right there on her couch. But it would have been the wrong thing to do. Even with their history, it was too soon. She deserved to be courted and wooed—old-fashioned words, sure, but nice words. Although he hadn't been thinking about that when they were entangled, her mouth on his neck. He would have done it without so much as buying her a taco if she hadn't stopped him.

His lucky puck would have been gone.

Of course, the puck wasn't the point, never had been. It didn't bother him in the least that he hadn't thought about it when Evie was in his arms.

However, it did bother him that he'd forgotten his resolve to be a better man. A better man would not show up on a woman's doorstep—especially if that woman was his friend—and take her to bed with no more forethought than buying a Snickers bar at a convenience store.

But Evie had saved him—saved him with her good sense and wise ways. *It wasn't the right time*, she'd said. She knew it was too soon, despite their history. They needed to get to know each other in a whole different way, on a whole different level.

It might not work out with them, but he was going to find out. Maybe they would always save each other. He would see the bet through, too. He looked forward to the time between now and December for shared meals, skating lessons, watching movies, and just being together. She would come to his hockey games. He would hang out at Crust and wait for her to close. He wanted to wave to her in the stands when he skated out and hold her hand when they walked down the street.

Of course, that wasn't all he wanted to do, but he could wait—should wait, though it wouldn't be that long. If things worked out like he hoped, he would make love to her properly on a cold December day. At Christmas, they would be solid.

He wasn't worried about the Delta Queens. Once they saw that things were working out, they'd be thrilled.

"What are you smiling about?" Robbie broke into his thoughts.

"Was I smiling?" he asked, but he wasn't surprised. Jake felt something he hadn't felt in a very long time—happy anticipation.

"Like Mona Lisa with the Cheshire cat on her lap."

"I was thinking about what we're going to do to Winnipeg tonight."

Robbie nodded. "That's what I like to hear." He yawned and pulled his headphones from his bag. "I'm checking out for a while."

Jake put on his headphones, too, and plugged into his iPad, but he didn't turn anything on yet. He wanted to text Evie.

Hi. On the plane. How is your head?

She answered immediately.

Still attached. Yours?

Anna-Blair said you had a headache.

Yeah, well. Always got to tell Anna-Blair something. How was the breakfast?

The usual: Eggs Benedict, bananas Foster, Champagne with papaya chunks floating in it, lattes made to order. Ordinary stuff.

That was a lie. She knew it. They'd had breakfast casseroles, fruit, grits, cinnamon rolls, and plain coffee and orange juice.

Sounds fancy. I had a piece of stale bread with some

peanut butter because you ate the last of my breakfast food.

That was a lie. She knew he knew it.

I owe you breakfast when I get back.

I'll hold you to that.

I hope you do.

*And I'll hold you, too, if you'll let me.*
The flight attendant was working her way down the aisle asking people to turn their phones off. He figured he had time to fire off one more text.

About to put my phone in airplane mode. I'll call you tonight after the game.

Be safe. Play hard. Win big.

*I plan on it, Evie, and not just this game.*
He turned off his phone and picked up his tablet. Maybe he'd watch *Chasing Amy*.

## Chapter Twenty

It had been twenty-four hours since Jake had kissed Evans at her front door and he still hadn't said it was a mistake—though he still could, if he called tonight like he'd promised. And it was possible that he wouldn't call. She didn't know which would be worse.

She'd find out soon. The game with Winnipeg had ended an hour ago. If he was going to call, it would be soon. Probably. Maybe—depending on what he had to do after the game. Maybe Jezebel and Jolene or their counterparts had flown up and...well. No use thinking about that.

It seemed like a week since she'd called Able to tell him she wasn't going to the breakfast. She had given an abbreviated version of what she'd originally intended, saying only that due to some past history she was emotionally unavailable and it wasn't fair to go out with him. He'd tried to make light of it and laughed a little when he said he was a big, strong hockey player and was willing to risk it. If not for Jake and Saturday night, she might have caved, but Jake and Saturday night had happened, and she'd been firm. Able had accepted it with good grace and had pressed her no further.

She got the sense that she'd hurt his feelings, but

what was she supposed to do? Marry him, have five babies, and freeze lasagna?

Ridiculous thoughts. Asking her to breakfast did not equal wanting to marry her.

The phone rang. Jake. She made herself take five deep breaths before answering.

"Hello."

"Hi, yourself." She could hear the smile in his voice. "How's Winnipeg?"

"Cold. I'd had enough of that so I didn't go out to eat with the guys. I'm back in my room."

"Did someone at least leave a mint on your pillow?"

"I ordered room service. It'll be here soon."

He'd called her before eating. That was a good sign. Wasn't it? "Post-game pizza?"

He laughed. "You sure know me. But no. Too bad for me. I had to talk them into making me something since it's past room service time. I have to take what I can get."

"You should have played the *I'm a famous pro hockey player* card."

"No, ma'am. We had just beaten the home team. I like my food spit-free."

They'd won—only 2–1, but a win was a win.

"Good game," she said.

"Not *that* good. Did you see it?"

"No. I didn't have any way to, but I kept up with it on my iPad."

"We'll have to subscribe to some hockey channels for you so you can watch me play when I'm away."

Did that mean he was thinking of the future?

"You're mighty sure of yourself, aren't you?" she said.

"You *did* keep up with it. Actually watching it is bound to be more exciting."

"Fair enough."

"Tell me about your day."

"Let's see." She lay on the sofa and pulled a throw over her. "I had coffee with the parents before they headed back to the Delta. Claire called and I met her at Crust to go over my books."

"And?"

"I'm doing fine. We talked about my fall fest plans. Ava Grace's mother wants to order pies for the Christmas Gala."

"Sounds like a big party and a lot of work," Jake said.

"It is, but big orders mean good business." And, unlike catering, it was work she loved. She had not told Claire she didn't want to cater for the Yellowhammers like she'd planned. She'd had enough emotional upheaval for one day. "And other than that, Hyacinth and I took a walk." She chose not to go into how Hyacinth had given her the third degree after seeing Jake's car at her house Saturday night. Evans had been evasive and focused on telling Hyacinth that normal people didn't look out the window every time they got up in the middle of the night to pee. "Hyacinth said Robbie's going to play the piano at Trousseau at the fall fest, that Claire arranged it."

"He didn't mention it, but it sounds like him. I hope you'll—" Then his voice trailed off. "Evie, someone's at the door. Probably room service. Can you hang on?"

"You should go and eat—"

"No. Please… I'll be back. I have something to tell you."

Anxiety set in. People hardly ever said they had

something to tell you unless it was bad. If it was good, they just told you.

After about half a minute and a decade, Jake came back on the phone.

"Evie?"

"Still me."

He took a deep breath—further evidence that this was going nowhere good.

"About Saturday night."

*And here it comes, the part where he says it was a mistake and we should just forget it.*

"I don't want you to think that happened because I was drunk and stupid."

"I didn't think you were drunk. I know you weren't. I've seen you drunk."

He laughed a little. "Just stupid?"

"No. Not that either. I've never seen you stupid. Don't start that with me again. You're successful. End of story."

"I guess. But I wanted to tell you that I didn't come to your house planning to put a move on you."

"No, no, of course not." She was going to make it easy for him because that was the best way for her to save face. "You don't have to—"

He cut her off. "But it didn't surprise me."

Really? "It didn't?"

"No. There has been some…attraction—at least on my part. But I've resisted because I didn't want to risk our friendship."

Was it possible that it was going to be all right, after all?

"Here's the thing, Evie. There are lots of reasons not to pursue this. I've thought about them all. I don't need to spell them out. You know what they are. But I think there are more reasons—better reasons—to see where this might go."

Relief washed over her like cool rain on a scorching hot day. "Go on," she said because she couldn't think what else. If she showed the true state of her heart, it would send him running.

"I was about to say that I hoped you would go to our game against the Colonials on Friday, that I can arrange to leave you a ticket. I won't have time to see you before the game, but after, I want to take you out for a proper meal and spend time with you." He hesitated. "I *miss* you, Evie."

He missed her—just like she'd missed him all her life. Was it possible that the missing could be coming to an end?

"I'm not asking for any promises," he said.

*But you could, Jake, you really could. I would promise you anything because I've had a lifetime of wishing I could give you everything.*

"I can't know or promise where we'll end up, but there are things I want," he went on. "I want real dates. What happened between us Saturday night felt right, and I want to give us a chance. I want to teach you to skate—and I won't let you fall. And I do promise this— I will not jerk you around."

She wanted to cry. She wanted to run into the street and shout that life was good. She wanted to kiss babies and hug old people, feed cats and find a home for every stray dog.

If this were a romantic movie, the credits would roll.

"Evie?" Jake said. "Are you there? Can you please

say *something*? Even if it's not what I want to hear, because I'm dying over here."

She laughed a little. She hadn't realized she hadn't said anything. "Yes. I'll be at the game. And afterward, you'd better order your own steak because you aren't getting any of mine."

His laugh had a quality she recognized all too well—relief. How about that? After all these years, Jake Champagne *relieved* that *she* wanted to be with *him*.

Yes, the credits were definitely rolling. There would be a border of hearts, ivy, and roses and the music would be happy.

"I would never try to eat your steak."

"Don't lie to me. But speaking of eating—you should go eat now before your food gets cold." She wanted to hang up before she said something stupid that would make him want to take it back.

"Yeah." He sighed. "I should. I'll call you tomorrow."

"I'll hold you to that," she said.

"And I'll hold *you*—if you'll let me."

*Oh, yes. I will.*

Fade to black on the movie screen.

And they lived happily ever after. Exploding fireworks and hearts and stars tap dancing across the screen.

## Chapter Twenty-One

Jake took the silver dome off his food. Like he'd told Evie, he'd had to take what he could get, which was some pasta with grilled chicken.

Never had he been so nervous about asking a woman for a date. Upon reflection, he couldn't remember ever being nervous at all. Hell, he hadn't even been nervous when he'd proposed to Channing. There had been no reason to be. She'd picked out the ring and planned the whole thing, which was done at her Ole Miss graduation party in the company of about a hundred people. She'd given her bridesmaids invitations on the spot. Shame washed over him again for not realizing—or even caring—that Evie had not been one of them.

But he cared now—enough to make him nervous.

Though tonight, he hadn't started out particularly nervous. After all, they had been on the same page on her couch last night—of that much he was sure. But people reflected and changed their minds all the time, and when she'd gotten so quiet, he'd begun to think that was the case—that she was going to tell him *thanks, but no thanks.*

He'd felt like he was in a rowboat without an oar and no way to get one.

That was the thing with talking on the phone—no facial expressions or body language to give you a clue what was going on in the other person's head. He'd never been one to want to FaceTime. Calling was easier, but maybe he'd rethink it. After all, he was going to be on the road a lot.

Whatever the reason for her hesitation, it had turned out fine. Maybe Evie had just been mulling over what he was asking, considering the drawbacks. Maybe she had some doubts but, in the end, she'd laughed that sweet laugh and said *yes*. And that was all he needed—one yes at a time.

He dug into his meal. The pasta wasn't much to write home about, the chicken either. Hotel food. He should have ordered from Grubhub. It might have been hard to get chicken pot pie, but he could have had pizza. Did they have Grubhub in Canada? Surely they did, or something equivalent, but you never could tell about a place that sold its milk in plastic bags.

There was a soft knock on the door.

Who the hell had come calling this time of night? Since tomorrow was only a travel day and they didn't play until Tuesday, there was no curfew tonight so it was early for anyone to be back from dinner. Certainly not Robbie.

He still had his fork in his hand when he threw open the door—to find Able Killen on the other side.

Hellfire and brimstone.

"I was afraid you might be asleep already." Able was still dressed in his suit and tie, though he looked rumpled.

*Then why did you knock on my door?* Though, to be fair, he hadn't knocked loud.

"No." Jake stepped aside in case Able wanted to come in, which he figured he did. Why else would he be here? "I was just having some bad room service food."

"I guess you don't need this then." He held up a pizza box. "I read that they stopped room service at nine o'clock. I guess that's not true."

"It is true," Jake said, "unless you throw yourself on their mercy, though I don't recommend it."

"Well, then. I don't know how warm this is but you're welcome to it. Pepperoni and sausage. That's what your mother ordered for you at Hammer Time."

"Come on in," Jake said. "Sit. Cold pizza is the story of my life." He wanted the pizza and he might as well find out what Able had on his mind, though he suspected he knew.

Able sat at the round table and loosened his tie. "Another struggle win, but I'll take it."

"Me, too. We're still learning each other. It's better than no win at all." Jake pushed the remains of the pasta aside and opened the pizza box. He had assumed Able had brought him leftovers, but it was a whole pizza. "Thanks for this. It was really nice of you."

Able took off his tie, rolled it, and put it in his pocket. "We're line partners. It's to my advantage to keep you fed."

"We got off to a rough start last night," Jake said, "and it was my fault."

Able shook his head. "Wasn't anyone's fault. Like you said, we're still getting used to each other. Besides, it came together, and I thought we were reading each other pretty well tonight."

Jake swallowed his guilt and chased it with a bite of pizza. *No, Killjoy. I brought my jealousy and woman trouble onto the ice, like my uncle and every coach I've ever had has warned me not to do.*

"By the end of the week, it'll be like we've been playing together forever."

"I'm sure it threw you for a loop when Coach put me on first line," Able said. "It surprised me; that's for sure. And who knows if by the end of the week I'll keep my place."

"I know and you will. You deserve it." That was fair. "I think I'm more of a question than you are." Maybe Able just wanted to talk hockey. "After all, you didn't have a shit first period last night."

"You earned your keep after that. I don't think you have anything to worry about."

Jake relaxed and took another piece of pizza. "You want some of this?" he asked. "After all, you bought it."

"No, thanks. I had lasagna."

Right. His go-to postgame food. Had that debacle of a meal at Hammer Time really only been last night? That had been a lot of miles ago—literally and figuratively.

Able closed his eyes and took a deep breath and Jake's stomach knotted. That's what people did before they were about to say something they were dreading.

"I wanted to ask you something."

*And here it comes.*

"Ask away. I'll tell you if I know." But would he? How could he say that when he didn't know what the fuck Killen was going to ask?

"You're friends with Evans, aren't you?"

That was easy enough, but Able knew the answer, so this wasn't really the question. It was the pre-question.

"Yes. Way, *way* back. Our parents are best friends. We're a year and a day apart."

"I guess you know her pretty well."

That was technically a statement, but it required a response.

"I would say so."

"Well, she dumped me."

Jake's hackles went up. "*Dumped* you? Were you in a relationship for her to dump you *from*?" He was not going to put up with Killjoy implying that there had been more going on with them than there had been.

Able closed his eyes again and shook his head. "No, no. Poor choice of words. It would be more correct to say that I asked her out, she accepted, and then canceled. And it wasn't like she canceled because something else came up. She made it clear that she was not open to being asked again."

Jake nodded. It would be hypocritical to say he was sorry, but he had to give some sort of answer. "If you haven't even been on a date, it's not like you could have that much at stake. Right?"

"I guess. But I did like her."

"I understand." He knew he shouldn't, but he couldn't stop himself from asking, "What did she say?"

Able looked at the ceiling and let out a frustrated sound. "I don't even know. Something about not being emotionally available. Like I know what that means. It sounded like she was reading me a self-help book."

"You read a lot of self-help books, do you, Killjoy?" That was the first time Jake had called him that without malice or sarcasm.

"I have read *no* self-help books, but I figure that's what they would sound like. I didn't understand half of what she said, but I did come away with the bottom line. She's not interested in me."

He couldn't help it and he wasn't proud of it, but there was a happy dance going on in Jake's head.

"Maybe the bottom line was all you were supposed to understand." If they had been talking about some random woman or, maybe any woman who wasn't Evie, Jake would have said something in man-speak about women being impossible to understand. But it was Evie and he was not inclined to lump her in with the rest of womankind like she was some kind of paper doll.

"Maybe." Able sighed. He looked miserable, and dread started to niggle at Jake.

"What was it that you wanted to ask me?"

"Hell if I know," Able said. "I guess nothing. I just wondered if you might be able to shed a little light on this."

"I really can't, Able." That was almost true. Evie had made the decision to cancel the date before he'd gone to her house last night. "I don't know why she decided not to go with you."

Able sat forward in his chair like people did when they were about to leave. Thank God.

"Thanks anyway. As you said, it wasn't like anything had gone on between us. I just liked her and I hoped something might."

*Right there with you, buddy.*

"I guess I just wanted to talk about it to someone who knows her." He looked more and more miserable.

"Sorry I couldn't be more help."

"That's okay." Able got to his feet and stretched. "Guess I'll go get some sleep."

"I hear you." Jake walked him to the door.

"See you in the morning," Able said.

"Thanks again for the pizza."

Jake leaned his head on the door after closing it behind Able.

Had he broken the Bro Code? He'd been so sure that Killen was breaking it that he'd never asked himself that question but, now that he had to think about it, the answer might be yes.

Though unwritten, the Bro Code was pretty clear. Everyone knew the rules and they had evolved for a reason: to maintain team harmony. It boiled down to this: Stay away from your teammates' women—past, present, and future. That included relatives. A team at odds with each other was not a team that could win.

Top players had been traded in the wake of trouble that ensued as a result of dating sisters and ex-wives.

This was hardly comparable, but if there was trouble, it wouldn't matter that Evie and Able had never even been out. Able had stated his intent, loud and clear from the first moment he laid eyes on her. If Jake turned up holding hands with her at Hammer Time, it would, without a doubt, create disharmony. And not just on their line, between Able and himself—it would affect the whole team.

If it had been another woman, gray area or not, Jake would have resisted getting involved. But it wasn't another woman. It was Evie and she was worth it. There was too much at stake.

Then it hit him like a puck to the helmet. It hadn't occurred to him that he was breaking the Bro Code because—fair or not, and it wasn't—he'd always thought of Evie as his.

Maybe he should have told Able that and let the chips

fall. Or maybe not. Hard to know, but it didn't matter. It was too late now.

One thing for sure, though. Since he hadn't told, it had to be kept under wraps. They might be able to have a meal together, but there could be no hand-holding, slow dancing, or any other public displays of affection. The chemistry between them was too strong. The dimmest person on the team would know it in half a second—and that wasn't Able.

In a few months, it wouldn't matter. By then, Able would probably have noticed someone else and, even if he hadn't, enough time would have passed that he wouldn't be embarrassed.

He'd tell Evie tomorrow. She would understand.

*"And I'll hold you, if you'll let me."*

That was the last thing Jake had said to her last night and every time Evans thought of it, her stomach went into a tailspin. Every time she'd woken last night—and it had been often—she recalled those words and they took her to a rich, happy place with all the possibilities in the world. Except sleep; sleep hadn't been a possibility.

Finally, she'd just gotten up. That's why she had already been at Crust for a full hour at 4:30, when she usually came in at five. The blackberries, cherries, and blueberries were macerating for the fruit pies on today's menu and she was well on her way to finishing all the crusts they'd need for the day. In spite of her lack of sleep, she was full of energy, ready for the day and everything good it would bring.

Because there wasn't going to be any bad. She wouldn't allow it.

She still couldn't take it all in. Jake Champagne wanted her—or at least wanted to explore the possibility. Evans had always been good with possibilities. Look what she'd done with a rolling pin and Crust.

And one of the best things—second only to being with him—he wanted to take her out in front of people where everyone would know they were together. It might be shallow for that to be so important to her, but how could it not be when she'd wanted it so much when she was younger? When she'd so wistfully watched him with other girls? Maybe the heart always remembered what the teenage heart had longed for—and she'd longed so much for him to take her hand when they were eating tamales or put his arm around her at the movies.

And it was finally going to happen.

She put the tenth pie crust in the tenth pan and lined them up like little soldiers on the counter. She was about to check the fruits for sweetness when her phone signaled that she had a text.

Puzzled, she wiped her hands and reached for the phone. No one texted her at this hour. Then she smiled. At least no one used to. Jake.

Are you at work yet?

She answered. Affirmative. Making pie.

Are you too busy to take my call?

*Not if I was about to serve pie to a conclave with the Pope, all the leaders of the free world, and the ghost of Queen Elizabeth I.*

Let me pour a cup of coffee and I'll call you.

She settled in at the round table and made the call.

"You're out early," was the first thing he said. He sounded sleepy.

"Got to earn a living. How about you? What are you doing up this early?"

"I'm not." There were some sounds of shifting and she imagined him turning over. "Still in bed." He yawned.

It was the yawn that did it. She suddenly wished more than anything that she was there with him—and she wished she had the courage to tell him that. Someday she would.

"What kinds of pies are you making today?"

"Right now, blackberry, cherry, and blueberry."

"No Mississippi mud?"

"Not today. Maybe Friday." She mentally added that to Friday's list.

"Hell, yeah!" he said.

"When do you fly out today?" she asked.

"Bus leaves for the airport at ten."

"You're awake in plenty of time."

"I've got some skate shopping to do before I leave."

Maybe those skating lessons would be fun, after all.

"Oh? I would think the team would keep you in skates," she said, tongue in cheek.

He laughed. "Good point. Maybe I can shove some old rags in a pair of mine to make them fit you."

"I'm sure that would work just great."

"Uh, Evie." His tone changed and her stomach went into a different kind of tailspin—this one not so happy.

*Surely he isn't calling to say he changed his mind.*

*But he could be.* She lined up the evidence that he wasn't about to say something bad. *He called. He's still talking about ice skates for me. He wants Mississippi mud pie.*

"Yes?"

"Able came to see me last night."

Oh, hell.

"Brought me a pizza."

"That was good of him."

"Yeah, well. He's a good guy."

"I know that, but since when do you think it?"

"Look, I was jealous."

She would have taken pleasure in that if she hadn't felt such trepidation.

"What did Able want?" she asked. "Beyond delivering pizza?"

"He wanted to talk about you canceling your date with him."

"Was he mad?"

"No, no. Nothing like that. More confused than anything. A little sad."

"I'm sorry about that."

"Here's the thing…" He trailed off.

And here it came—the bad thing that wasn't supposed to happen today, and there wasn't one damn thing she could do about it.

"Able and I are line partners."

"I know that."

"Our dynamic is important."

Her eyes filled. She would say it before he had to. "And you seeing me could really mess that up. I get it. This is your job. It would be better if we didn't see each other." There. It was out. She'd said it and it hadn't killed her.

"What?" he exploded. "No, Evie. Hellfire and brim-stone, no! That wasn't what I meant at all."

"It wasn't?" She wiped her eyes. She still might have to cry, but she was going to put it on hold for the moment.

"No. That would be ridiculous. But we might need to keep it quiet for a while."

"What do you mean?" Was he asking her to wait for him? Until when? Next week? Next year? Until he retired from hockey? Well, why not? She'd been wait-ing all her life, so far. Might as well wait the rest of it.

"I want us to see each other. Of course I do. I can't *wait* to see you."

"But?" she asked and braced herself for him to say, *"Just not now."*

But he didn't. "Let's just keep that we're seeing each other between us for a while."

From everyone? She hadn't wanted their mothers to know right now any more than he had, but she'd been looking forward to telling Ava Grace and Hyacinth. But she supposed if Able wasn't to know, there was no way around it. She trusted her friends. They wouldn't tell if she asked them not to, but did she really want to tell them it had to be secret? Would that seem like Jake was ashamed to be seen with her, maybe holding out for someone better?

"Do you still want me to come to the game Friday night?"

"Yes. Absolutely. I'll be disappointed if you don't."

This was sounding better.

"I want to take you out, show you a good time. I just think some of that should wait. It's not like we can't go anywhere together or do anything. I just wouldn't want to embarrass Able."

So, no hand-holding, no arm around her in movies, no walking down the street with him and being proud that everyone knew they were together. But that was okay—a little disappointing, sure, but not that bad. Could be far worse—*had* been far worse.

"That's absolutely fine, Jake," she said. "I understand completely."

"Really?" He sounded relieved. "I'm sorry. It won't be forever."

"Don't give it another thought. I don't want to hurt Able's feelings either, any more than I already have."

"You're the best, Evie. You know that, right?"

"I don't know about that. But don't worry. It'll be fine."

And she hoped that was true.

## Chapter Twenty-Two

After arranging the freshly made pies in the display case, Evans made a dozen crusts for the freezer. Then she called Ariel and Quentin back to the marble counter where she'd been working.

She'd put this off too long.

"I want you to make some crusts today," Evans said.

Quentin frowned. "Are you sure? I know it's still hot, but there's a cold front coming in later today. Are you sure you want to do ice box pies, Evans? According to James Spann, fall really is coming to stay today."

Of course he would think she meant they were going to make crumb crusts. That's all she'd ever allowed.

"We aren't going to make ice box pies." She took a deep breath. "I want you to make the crusts for tomorrow—pastry crusts."

Ariel, who'd been checking her reflection in the glass door of the convection oven, zoned in and widened her eyes in surprise.

"Hot damn!" Quentin clapped his hands and looked around like he was going to grab a rolling pin before she changed her mind.

But she wouldn't. She didn't know what was going to happen with Jake tonight beyond his vague "I'll see you after the game," but she had no reason to think they wouldn't finish what they started Saturday night. In her perfect world, they would spend the whole night together. If that happened, maybe she would want to be late for work tomorrow or take off altogether.

All this had her head spinning, but it had also made her stop and think. She had painted herself into a corner where she *couldn't* take off. You couldn't have pie without crusts and you couldn't have a pie shop without pie. Tomorrow notwithstanding, what about the future? What if things really did work out with her and Jake? She might want to take time off to be with him or travel to an away game. What if she broke her arm? It could happen, especially if Jake was really going to teach her to ice skate.

Quentin and Ariel were entirely capable. Probably. And if their crusts weren't up to her standards, there were some in the freezer.

She pulled a folded printout from the pocket of her chef's pants. "Here's Saturday's menu." There was no need to tell them she wanted all-butter crusts for the fruit pies, cream cheese pastry for the honey walnut, coconut oil for the French coconut, and butter/shortening mix for the rest. She'd harped on it enough that it was impossible for it to be lost on them—even Ariel.

They perused the list.

"You're going to let *us* make the crusts for tomorrow? Quentin and me? Now?" Ariel asked.

"Yes. Now. Chill them, but wait until morning to blind bake them."

"She wants to give us plenty of time in case we screw up," Quentin said.

"That's right." Might as well admit it. Besides, she

might be here at the regular time in the morning. Nothing was sure about what would happen with Jake.

"How about the decorations?" Ariel asked. "Can we do that?"

Evans hesitated. "Sure. No free handing. Keep it simple—leaves and fruit cutouts." There were cutters for those things. "Maybe some braids around the edges."

Ariel gave a little squeal of delight.

"I'll cut out the decorations and make the braids," Quentin said. "You can do the decorating."

"Get the crusts made first," Evans said. "I'm going out front to help Neva open. Weigh out your ingredients and I'll check in with you in a bit."

Neva was checking tickets against the boxed pies in the vertical case for special orders.

"Where are Quentin and Ariel? It's almost time to unlock the door."

"Making pie crusts." Evans replenished the cups next to the coffee maker.

Neva slowly turned her head and met Evans's eyes. "You're kidding. I didn't think you'd ever do it."

Evans laughed. "If you thought that, why did you keep harassing me about it?"

"Sometimes, you just have to have your say—which reminds me." She reached under the counter and handed Evans a business card. "The guy from Hollingsworth came by."

So, he'd given up trying to reach her by phone. "Toss it," Evans said.

Neva looked toward the door. "Looks like we've got some eager customers." A couple of people were now waiting to be let in.

"I'll open the door," Evans said, but just then her

phone vibrated. *Jake.* "Uh, Neva? Could you get the door, after all? I need to take a call. I promise I'll be right back."

"Hello." She hurried through the kitchen, past where Ariel and Quentin were weighing out flour, and closed herself in the supply closet.

"I don't have much time," he said. "About to board."

"Neither do I. We're just opening."

"You're coming tonight?"

"That's the plan." *I'm ready, Jake. I'm shaved, plucked, and polished. I've had a pedicure, a facial, and I think I have mastered the perfect smoky eye. I have a new nightgown, just in case. It's pretty, but not sexy. I've washed it five times so you won't know it's new. I've never been more ready in my life.*

"The box office will have your ticket. Do you need more than one? Want to bring someone?"

"I think I'll come alone. You know. Secrets."

"Right. Probably best. About after—"

Her heart went into anxiety rhythm. "If you need to go out with your teammates, it's fine."

"Are you trying to get rid of me?" There was a smile in his voice.

"No! I just thought—" *maybe you had changed your mind.*

"Don't think. I'm in teammate overload. I thought I'd just come to your house when I get back."

"Bad plan. Hyacinth will see your car. She's already grilled me about why you were there Saturday night."

"Really?"

"It's not as if you drive a Ford Focus. But to be fair, if you did, she would have grilled me about that, too."

"So what? It's not like we're married to other people. It's just Able we're hiding from."

"Jake. Think. Gossip."

"Right. You're right. This is so stupid."

"Text me, and I'll come to your condo." But if she did that, what about the nightgown? She couldn't just pack a bag like she took for granted she was staying over, but she didn't want to be caught without a toothbrush either. Why did this have to be so hard?

"Bad plan. Killjoy lives in the building."

"I didn't know that." It had never occurred to her to wonder where he lived.

Jake was silent for a moment. "Okay. New plan. I'll ride to the game with Robbie and ride back to Laurel Springs with you."

"What will you tell Robbie?"

"That you came to the game and I'm riding home with you."

"Won't he think that's odd?" Or maybe Jake had told him about them. She hoped he had. That would make it more real.

"No. He has seven sisters and doesn't think women ought to be on the lam late at night alone."

He hadn't told him—but that was good. It was just their secret.

"Okay. I'll wait for you at the arena. Text me when you're done and tell me where to pick you up."

"Perfect. I need to go."

"Me, too."

"But, Evie?"

"Yes?"

"I hate this. I really do. This sneaking around feels so stupid. It's not what I want."

Her heart went into overdrive, but in a good way this time. "It won't be long. Go get on the plane."

"Right. It could be worse. I get to see you soon." He laughed. "Maybe you can build a fire in that fireplace of yours."

She clasped the phone to her heart. Jake was coming home and they were going to be together. But there was no time to think about that now. Neva was alone and people were probably already lined up for coffee.

## Chapter Twenty-Three

Jake was tired. Three cities in five days, five games in six, and a home ice loss would do that to a man. But unlike some of his teammates, he wasn't upset. A three to two loss to the championship defenders in a preseason game wasn't the end of the world.

"See you later," Jake said to Robbie as he slung his backpack over his shoulder.

"Are you sure Evie is waiting for you?" Robbie asked as he straightened his tie.

"Yeah. I just texted with her." She was waiting at the south exit.

"See you two at Hammer Time, then," Robbie said.

Like hell. "No. I don't think so. I'm really tired."

"Okay," Robbie said cheerfully. "Want to work out tomorrow?"

"Probably should." They were off until Monday mid-morning, when they had stretch and practice. "If you rest, you rust. I'll check in with you."

"Not too early," Robbie said. "I want to sleep in."

"So do I," Jake said, though he dreaded sleeping alone. Evie wasn't ready and waiting was the right thing to do for where they were right now—but if being away from her had taught him anything it was that he wanted her to be his forever. He wasn't about to jeopardize that by pressing her to have sex before she was ready—no matter how much he wanted her. But at least he'd get to see her.

It couldn't be soon enough. He was tempted to avoid the autograph seekers. Dempsey, Bachet, and Bell were already working the crowd outside the locker room, so he could have slipped away. But it was hard to turn down a kid, impossible to disappoint one wearing his number. That led to a picture and more autographs and more pictures. After about fifteen minutes, he put up his hands.

"Thank you all for coming out. I've got to go now, but I have it on good authority that our goalie will be out any second." Wingo would stand there all night.

He bypassed the puck bunny line without a backward glance, though he heard his name called several times.

He had chosen to meet Evie at the exit he figured would have the least foot traffic and he was right. Even so, he walked quickly, eyes on the floor to avoid contact with anyone who might be hanging around.

The journey from the locker room seemed to be more miles than he'd traveled all week, but finally he arrived—and there she was. She waved from the driver's seat and he went to open the car door.

Locked.

She fumbled to unlock it, but rolled down the back window instead. She looked chagrined and tried again—and failed. She let out a little screech and they started to laugh. Despite the loss and that he was dead on his feet, it was easy to be happy. He'd gotten an assist. He wasn't on the road anymore. Fall had arrived in the South, chasing away the heat and humidity. Best of all, Evie was on the other side of this door...if she ever got it open.

Finally, she jerked the key out of the ignition, pointed the fob at the door with a determined look, and pressed the button. She looked adorable.

He was still laughing when he threw his backpack behind the seat and sat down.

"Sorry," she said.

"I thought for a minute there you had decided only winners get to ride in your car."

She vigorously shook her head and closed her eyes. "You're not—"

And though he didn't plan it, had thought he would wait until they were alone at her house, he jerked her into his arms and brought his mouth to hers. She smelled like apples, tasted like peppermint, and—just like before—there was no hesitation in returning his kiss.

It was almost his undoing when she snapped her seatbelt open so she could put her arms around him.

The desire that ripped through him was different. It wasn't pure lust with only one end in sight; it was sweet, hot longing that wanted more. He hadn't known until now that there were different ways to want.

Evie made a little *mmm* sound and reached up to stroke the sensitive place on his neck. She remembered.

Hellfire and brimstone! He'd always wondered what those people were thinking who got caught having sex in parks, on beaches, and in bedrooms at parties. Now he knew. They weren't thinking; they were feeling, wanting something more than quick release and see-you-later. That had to be it. His hand had a mind of its own and moved up her side toward her breast.

But then he stopped.

He broke the kiss, but took his time about it, caressing her tongue as he withdrew.

"I missed you." The words tumbled out of his mouth with no forethought. It was the raw simple truth.

"Me, too." She nestled her face into his neck.

He hugged her briefly to him before lifting his head to look at her. "Oh, yeah? You missed *yourself*? How does that even work?"

She blushed, so pretty. Had she always been this pretty? How had he missed it for so long? "You know what I mean."

"I hope I do," he teased her.

Then the arena door opened and they flew apart—probably much like those couples who got caught having sex in public places.

But it was only some arena staff.

"That could have been bad," she said.

Funny, he didn't care about that much right now. He probably should, but he didn't intend to keep this up long—a week or two, tops. Then he was going to have a talk with Killen and they were all going to get on with their lives on and off the ice.

"Humph."

She laughed. "You say that now…"

"I'm already tired of this. Robbie asked if we were going to Hammer Time. I don't want to go, but it makes me mad that we can't—at least not and keep our hands to ourselves."

"I think you're just tired, period," she said. "You look exhausted."

He took a deep breath and rubbed the back of his neck. "I am. We all are."

"Here." She reached behind his seat and handed him

a bag. "I got you a pulled pork sandwich and a bottle of water as I was leaving. It's probably cold."

"Thank you." He unwrapped the sandwich and took a bite. It wasn't very good, but that didn't matter. Evie had handed him food and that felt good. "I'm starving."

She buckled her seatbelt and started the car. "I thought it would hold you until we get home, and you can have pizza."

He liked that they were going to the same place and she called it *home.*

"What's the best place to order it from?" he asked.

"You don't have to order it." She pulled out of the parking lot. "I made you one. It's all ready to go in the oven."

He stopped short. "You *made* a pizza?"

"Technically, it is a pie."

He didn't have to ask to know it would be pepperoni and sausage. No mushrooms. And he was going to have beer, if she had one. He'd lived up to his vow to abstain during the preseason games, but the preseason games were over. He could hardly wait until he was finished with that other vow. December 13. Surely, she would be ready by then. He would think up a way to make it romantic, too.

"After you finish your sandwich, take a nap if you like," Evie said. "With this traffic we probably won't be home for a half hour."

Food, naps, and kisses from a woman who smelled like apples and was willing to drive him. Life was good.

"That was the best pizza I've ever had in my life." Jake finished his beer and set his plate and bottle on the coffee table. After eating two pieces, he'd had Mississippi mud pie, and then returned to the pizza to polish it off.

"In your *whole* life?" she said. "That's a lot of pizza."

He reached across the small space that separated them on the sofa and put an arm around her. "You've ruined me for all other pizzas. Same with chicken pot pies. I can't go back to Marie Callender." He let his blue eyes sparkle at her. They looked tired but they could still sparkle. Then he stage-whispered, "And Mississippi mud, but don't tell Louella."

"Then I guess we'd better get cracking on those cooking lessons and add pizza and Mississippi mud to the syllabus. Not my job to feed you." What a lie. She'd cook for him every day for the rest of her life, if he'd let her.

"Hey. I almost forgot." He stood up and crossed the room to where he'd left his backpack in front of the fire. He'd changed out of his suit into a Yellowhammer T-shirt and a pair of sweatpants. His feet were bare and his hair needed combing. He was delicious.

When he came back, he set a box beside her. "I promised you ice skates." He opened the package and pulled out a silver-and-pink skate. "They're comfort skates. The hockey blades are wider than figure skating blades and best for a beginner." He paused and pulled three pairs of socks out of the box. "Skate socks."

She reached for the pink ones. "Thank you. What's the difference between skate socks and regular socks?"

"They're tall and you skate in them." He yawned. "Do you want to try them on?" He held up a skate.

"Maybe later?"

"Good answer." He pushed the box aside and the next thing she knew she was lying in his arms on the sofa.

"How do you do that?"

"Do what?" He kissed her. She didn't care that he tasted like beer and pizza. In fact, she liked it.

"Get me in a reclining position before I know what's happened."

"It's my superpower." He kissed her again, deeper this time, and he took his time twining his tongue with hers. He came up for air and said, "Do you mind?"

"I might require it." She ran her hand up the back of his shirt and kissed him on the neck.

He let out a moan. "Your hand's cold."

"I'm sorry." She jerked it away.

"No, no." He hugged her to him. "It felt good. Do it again."

She did, but this time with both hands. It was heaven, the feel of his warm skin against her hands and his face pressed into her neck. This was going to happen. For a while there, she'd thought he might be too tired, but she knew—could feel—that wasn't true. He was hard against her, and she shifted to feel him better. Desire ripped through her. She wanted him. Of course she did. But even more, she longed for the intimacy and the bond that making love would bring.

"Mmm," he said against her ear. "This is nice—just being here together like this."

"Yes. So nice." *And I've waited for this so long.*

They kissed some more, for a good, long time. Then he buried his face in her neck, but he took things no further.

Should she? Was that what he was waiting for? For her to make the next move? What should it be? Guide his hand to her breast? Move her pelvis aggressively against his? Suggest they go to the bedroom? Jump up, rip off his clothes, and scream, "Take me now!"? That would be effective. Not that she would do any of that.

Before she could think of more things that she wouldn't do, he let out a little snore.

He had gone to sleep? *He had gone to sleep!* This never happened in books or movies. Now he was dead weight against her and was drooling on her neck—at least she hoped it was drool and he hadn't started to bleed from one of his orifices for some unknown reason. She reached up, rubbed her fingers against the little puddle of warm moisture, and looked at it. Not blood, so it had to be spit. Of all the fantasies she'd indulged in with Jake Champagne as the star, none had involved pools of spittle.

His falling asleep in what she'd considered at least a semi-erotic cuddle might not have been the best thing for her ego, but she wasn't going to let it ruin her night. Though sex wasn't happening.

"Jake," she said softly as she rolled away from him, and sat up. No response. "Jake." This time she said it a little louder. Nothing. If she brought in a mariachi band and got up and danced the tango, would he just keep sleeping?

"Jake!" She shook his shoulder. "You're asleep! Wake up!"

"What? Who…" He jerked his head up and then groaned. "I'm sorry, Evie." He moved into a sitting position and rubbed his eyes. "I don't know what happened." He laid a hand on her knee.

*Well, you were kissing me like you meant it, and the next thing I knew you were snoring.*

"I'm sorry," he repeated. "It's not the company."

He really did look regretful, and he *was* exhausted.

He'd also eaten a load of carbs and drank the first alcohol he'd had in a while.

"It doesn't matter. You need to go to bed. Come on. I'll take you home."

He nodded and started to get up, but then stopped. "Wait, Evie. No. Let me stay here with you tonight."

Had he said what she thought he had? She replayed it in her head. Yes. That's what he'd said. She wanted to shout, *Yes, yes, a million times yes!*—and she might have, if she could have found her voice.

He took her hand. "But before you say no, let me tell you something."

*I'm not going to say no, Jake. Ariel and Quentin are on pie duty. I am free, clear, and willing.*

"I promise I'll abide by what you asked," Jake went on.

*What did I ask?*

"I even agree with you. I think it's wise to wait—not have sex yet."

*What? When did I say that?* "I won't push you to do what you aren't ready for."

*What am I not ready for?*

"You were right Saturday night that it was the wrong time."

Oh, hell. He had misunderstood entirely, hadn't realized she'd meant she had her period. Should she tell him? Yes. She took a deep breath. How to put it? How to put it? Though his bodily fluid was still wet on her neck, she wasn't completely comfortable with talking about hers.

Before she could speak, he plowed on, "To be honest, though I didn't think so at the time, I'm not ready yet either."

Well, that changed things. At least she didn't have to figure out what to say.

"Please, just let me stay and sleep with you. I want to be close to you."

*Oh, Jake!* Her stomach turned over and she took a shallow breath.

And he widened his sleepy blue, blue eyes. Then he cocked his beautiful head to the side, smiled that sweet smile, and bit his bottom lip.

"I swear I won't cause you to be late for pie making."

She melted. How could she not? When he was sitting here so tired and so sweet, saying he just wanted to be with her?

Making love didn't matter. Well, it did. But not tonight. She would straighten that out later. Tonight, being with him was enough.

She smiled. "I don't have to make pies tomorrow. I don't have to go to Crust at all."

"Even better." He let his eyes drop to half-mast. "So?" He nodded toward the bedroom.

"Of course, Jake. And you didn't even have to bother with all that head-cocking and lip-biting."

He laughed and laid his cheek against hers. "But I'm *so* good at it. And I really wanted to wake up with you tomorrow."

"I want to wake up with you, too."

*And be with you tonight*—though she suspected he'd be asleep by the time she changed and brushed her teeth. Evie was right. By the time she crawled into bed beside him, he was out—but not so far gone that he didn't fold her against him. She didn't even care that he drooled all over her new nightgown.

# Chapter Twenty-Four

Jake was used to waking up and not knowing where he was. He supposed that came from all the random hotel beds he slept in.

But when he woke up this morning, he knew what bed he was in—Evie's. He smiled and reached for her, but came up empty. That was disappointing, but not devastating. The house smelled like coffee, so that meant she was here somewhere. He sat up and looked at his phone. Almost ten o'clock. No wonder she was up.

He went to the bathroom, found some toothpaste, and swished it around in his mouth with some water. He'd have to remember to bring a toothbrush over.

With all he knew about Evie, he had no idea what her mornings were like on her off days. Would she be busy doing laundry, sorting mail, and all the other things that got put on hold on workdays? Or did she sit around, drink coffee, and read the paper? If she read the paper, did she go online or old school? Did she work the cross-word puzzle?

Suddenly, he was overwhelmed with needing the answer. She was probably in the living room since that seemed to be the only real room in this house besides this bedroom.

Sure enough, that's where she was, but she wasn't doing any of the things he'd imagined.

What he found amused and delighted him, maybe unlike he'd ever been amused or delighted before.

She lay on her back on the couch, wearing a long flowy, white nightgown with her feet propped on the end of the sofa arm. She didn't see him at first, partly because he came up behind her and partly because she was contemplating her feet—and on her feet were the pink-and-silver skates he'd bought her. She was also wearing a pair of the knee-high skate socks—the purple-and-black-striped ones.

He paused to enjoy the sight. She picked up one of her feet, raised it toward the ceiling, and turned her ankle this way and that as she studied it.

Like the Grinch, his heart grew three sizes, and he couldn't stand not touching her another second. At first, she looked startled when he leaned over to give her an upside-down kiss. Then she smiled and set her mouth for what she knew was coming. As their lips met, she reached up and put a hand on either side of his cheeks.

Damn. How long until December?

When their mouths parted, he said, "Like what you see?"

"Yes, I do." He got the feeling she wasn't talking about the skates.

She started to sit up, but he stopped her. "No. Stay put." And he sat on the couch, swung her legs across his lap, and put his hand on her knee above the sock's edge. "Do they fit?"

"I think so. I haven't stood up in them. Adele is very proud of these hardwood floors. They're original to the

house, you know." She let her voice take on a mock re-
fined tone.

"Who's Adele?"

"Adele Landry Hampton. Future sister-in-law of Ava
Grace. Her family owns the houses on Bungalow Circle,
and she manages the property."

"I've already had enough of her and I don't even
know her." It was good talking about nothing.

"Oh, she's nice." She lifted her foot again. "Do you
think these look like witch socks?"

"That's what I thought when I bought them." He
hadn't really, but it was a good idea.

"Are you saying I'm a witch?"

"Hmm." He scratched his head. "No, but if I was one
of those guys in one of those movies where everything
turns out okay—"

"Romantic comedies?"

"Yeah, that. I might say you have bewitched me. But
I'm not that guy. I can't be that guy."

"No." She shook her head. "Never that guy. You're
a big famous hockey star."

"Yet…" When he kissed her, her tongue sought his
first. He wanted to pull her into his lap, strip off her
gown, and love her while she wore those skates. The
thought made him laugh against her mouth.

She pulled her face back. "What?"

"Nothing." He took her hand and laced their fingers
together. "I'm just happy. Am I allowed to be happy?"

She looked at him, all sweet and soft. "I've always
wanted you to be happy."

A burst of energy went through him. "Let's go out
for breakfast and take your new skates for a test run."

"Where?" she asked.

"I don't know. Who serves breakfast this late? There's a Cracker Barrel out by the interstate. Glaz swears by it. He even does his Christmas shopping there."

Evie rolled her eyes and shook her head. "I'm sure everyone looks forward to those presents. I meant where are we going skating? It's cooled off, but we're not going to find an isolated frozen pond around here. And the practice rink is out."

Fuck. Stupid Killjoy. He really was a Killjoy. But she was right. If they went to the iceplex, they would run into some of his teammates, there to work out. It was nice being here with Evie, but damn it all to hell, he wanted to go somewhere, have some food, have some fun. And it was impossible. Unless...

A thought began to form in his mind.

"You said you didn't have to go to Crust today? At all?"

Evie shook her head. "Barring disaster. But guess what we can do? It'll be a tight fit, but we can have that chicken pot pie lesson."

Damn. He'd all but forgotten that. Now that he didn't need an excuse to be with her, he definitely was never going to make pie of any kind.

"I've got a better idea," he said. "Let's go somewhere."

"I thought we were supposed to be on the down low."

"Let's get out of town."

She looked interested. "Where?"

"I don't know. We could go down to Orange Beach for the weekend. Or over to Atlanta. If the Braves or Falcons are in town, I can get tickets easy. Good tickets."

She nodded. "I'd rather see football than a baseball game."

"We could check and see if there's a concert we're interested in. I could probably get tickets to that, too, though it might be harder." Harder for Miles, though. Not him.

She laughed. "There's always Six Flags."

"I want to dance with you." It had been years since they'd danced. Maybe not since their cotillion days, but they'd always danced so well together. "I can't see that happening at Six Flags."

"Or a Falcons game—unless you want to be on the jumbotron."

Then, like lightning striking, he knew just the place. "I know. Let's go to New Orleans."

"New Orleans?" She frowned.

"Sure. You say it like it's in Australia. What is it? Five hours down there? Less if you're with me in a Lamborghini."

He wanted this, wanted to hold hands with her as they walked down Bourbon Street, dance with her in dive bars, buy her something expensive on Royal Street. He wanted to give her—and himself—the weekend they would have had in New Orleans for his fraternity formal if he hadn't been so stupid.

He just had to talk her into it. "It would be fun. You lived there so you know all the best places to eat. We could maybe go to a Saints game, if you really want to go to a football game."

"I don't. Not in particular." He could tell she was intrigued. "But that's a long way for a short time. I have to go to work Monday."

"So do I," he said. "If we left within the hour, we'd

be there in time for dinner. We'd have most of the day tomorrow. We could leave in the afternoon and still get back in time to rest up for Monday."

The more he talked, the happier she looked.

"This is crazy." But she was smiling.

"Not as crazy as hiding here and hoping Killjoy doesn't come to serenade you under your window."

"Jake! Be nice." She swatted at him.

"Sorry. The ride would even be fun. We can talk and listen to music. I'm not the type to deny you a bathroom stop."

She laughed. "Maybe we could stop at Cracker Barrel and do some early Christmas shopping."

"Right. Iron skillets for our mothers. Rocking chairs for our dads." He brought her hand to lay over his heart. "Am I detecting that you're possibly onboard?"

"You might be." She grinned. "Let's go casual. I know lots of great places to eat, no jacket required." She raised one eyebrow. "In fact, they might throw you out if you show up in one."

"Sounds good. So shorts and T-shirts. It'll be warmer there than here."

"Yes, quite a bit, but we're used to it."

"Okay." He stood up. "If you'll let me take your car, I'll go home to pack. I'll get online and get us a hotel. Where do you want to stay? Windsor Court? Ritz-Carlton?"

"I would like…that is… I've always wanted to stay at the Bourbon Orleans. I'm not sure how it compares in price, but I hear it's haunted." She said the last word in a whisper.

He laughed and gave her a brief kiss. "You've got it, sweetheart. If there's a room to be had, I'll get you a spook. I'll be back in an hour—in my car. I don't give a damn about what Hyacinth sees."

"She's at her shop. So don't…" She trailed off and went silent. The energy in the room changed. When he looked around, Evie was bent with her hands on her skate laces, but her eyes were trained on a stack of wrapped presents on a table across the room.

"What?" It was something, something not good.

"I can't go," she said quietly. "I have to go to Channing's baby shower tomorrow afternoon."

And just like that, he went from over-the-top excited to this-can't-be-fucking-happening faster than his car could go from zero to sixty.

## Chapter Twenty-Five

The day had started so well, but that was over.

"I'm not just sorry, Jake; I'm *really* sorry." She would never be able to communicate the depth of her sorrow. He'd been to New Orleans, sure, but you didn't get to know it by visiting now and then. She'd already mapped out in her mind the places she would take him in the French Quarter, the things she would show him. And he wanted to dance with her! The Quarter was made for dancing, made for romance.

He ran his hands through his hair and leaned his forearms on his knees. "Let me understand the situation here. You are going to a shower for my ex-wife, because she is having a baby with the man she left me for. That's what you want to do instead of going to New Orleans with me."

That sounded so much worse than it was. "I don't *want* to. Of course I don't *want* to."

"Then don't." He said it like it was just that simple.

"I have to. I said I would."

He shook his head. "Evie, you always do this—say yes, when you want to—*should*—say no."

"I know! I know I do that, but it wasn't like that this time. I'm trying to do better."

"Then do better," he said. "Call Channing and tell her you're not coming. Go to New Orleans with me like you want to—assuming that *is* what you want to do."

"It *is*. But my mother and sisters can't go. And I *did* say no at first, but then my daddy said he really wanted me to. It's not me. It's my parents."

He nodded. "It's always somebody, always has been—your parents, your sisters, your friends, Claire. Even me."

That hurt and she struck back. "Maybe *especially* you."

"Doesn't feel that way right now."

"I'd go with you if I could." Why couldn't he see that?

"You can."

"I have packages to deliver." She gestured to the gifts from her mother and sisters and the one she had bought.

"We can send them," he said.

This was maddening. Why was he being so unreasonable? "We can't. The party is tomorrow afternoon. The post office closes at noon on Saturday. That's less than an hour. Even if it didn't, they couldn't get there in time."

"Of course they could—can. I can hire somebody to take them."

"Who?"

He threw up his hands. "I don't know. Somebody. A courier service. Uber driver. The kid who cleans the rink. There are a million ways."

"The gifts aren't the point. I should go. She *is* my cousin."

"So what? She's never been very nice to you. She

didn't even have you in our wedding when she had every other female she'd ever run into at a beauty shop."

Not fair. And that *our* hurt more than she cared to admit. Which made her mean. "And why is that, Jake? Did you ever say, 'What about Evie? Why isn't my oldest friend, who happens to be your first cousin, a bridesmaid?' No, you did not. You told me you didn't even think about it. And why is that? Is it because you had ceased to ever think about me? Or talk to me. Do you think if you hadn't abandoned our friendship that maybe my participation or lack thereof in your wedding might have come up when we talked?"

His face was a mix of mad and sad. "You said you didn't care. You said you liked serving the cake."

"You brought it up." Evans crossed her arms in front of her.

"I did. But I guess all this is just one more thing you said *yes* to when you meant *no*—that you had forgiven me for 'abandoning our friendship,' as you put it. And clearly you're pissed about not being in that damned three-ring-circus of a wedding when you said you weren't. And you know what? I wish you *had* been in it and I had *not*."

His face went to neutral and his shoulders sagged. Then he leaned his head back against the sofa and closed his eyes. All the passion had gone out of him. He didn't seem angry anymore, but something worse. Defeated.

He was right, but she got the feeling if she said so, he would blast it back on her and say she was just being a yes girl. So she wouldn't go there, but it might still be possible to turn this around. "Look, maybe we can work this out."

He lifted his head and met her eyes. "Go on."

"It doesn't have to be New Orleans. When you first brought it up this was about going somewhere together to have some fun. We talked about other places. Why can't it be Nashville?"

His mouth dropped open and he put up a hand, all the while shaking his head.

"Wait! Hear me out. We could go up today. You could show me Nashville like I was going to show you New Orleans. You talked about a concert." She came across with what she hoped was a winning smile. "I have heard there's some music to be had in Nashville, here and there. I could put in an appearance at the shower—an hour tops. And then we could get on with our weekend. It's a lot closer than New Orleans and, truth be told, the weather will be better. Not so hot."

For one bare second, she thought he was going to at least consider it, but then his mouth went to a hard line. "That's not going to happen. I still want to go somewhere with you. I thought we'd decided on New Orleans, but I'm okay with anywhere except the one place where I was publicly humiliated and showed my ass because of it. I left a winning, top-notch team to get away from Nashville, and I am not going there today or any other day."

"Nashville is where I have to be at two o'clock tomorrow afternoon."

His face was not neutral anymore, or angry. It was a study in sad. He got up and laid a hand on her cheek. He withdrew his hand and looked at her for a long moment. "It was really nice while it lasted. I think it might have been nice for a long time."

He walked toward the door.

"Wait!" *Think, Evans, think!* There had to be a way to stop him, to fix this—but she came up empty.

He turned, and she thought she detected a little hope in his face.

"You don't have a car." Lame, but it was all she could think of. Maybe if she had to drive him home, that would buy time, and time could make this go away. "At least let me give you a ride."

"A ride? Really, Evie?" He closed his eyes and sighed. "I'm not seventeen and drunk on tequila, needing you to hide me from my mama. I'm a grown ass man, now. Grown-ups figure it out. Give it a try some time." And he was gone—leaving Evans sitting there in the nightgown that she had washed five times so it wouldn't look new and a pair of skates that always would because they would never see the ice.

## Chapter Twenty-Six

If ever there had been a finger sandwich and petit four hell, Evans was in it.

First of all, she'd been late, through no fault of her own. After a sleepless night and a silent phone, the day had dawned with a storm that matched the one in her heart. She'd left in plenty of time and had no trouble finding the address on the invitation. She figured she'd gotten the great parking spot in the driveway of the big Victorian house because she was a few minutes early. After all, didn't she deserve a little luck?

Apparently not. She was in the wrong place, also through no fault of her own. There was a sign on the door that had been printed out in a whimsical font:

Hello and sorry! Due to the storm we have had a change of venue! (After all, we don't want mom-to-be out in this rain, do we?) The shower will be held at Channing's lovely home! Sorry for the incon-venience, but you will get to see baby Grayson's new room. We can't wait to see you there!

Due to the hard-to-read font, Evans had to peruse the sign twice before she realized there was no address.

Apparently, everyone else knew where Channing lived. She'd trekked back through the rain with her stack of packages and called her mother. Straight to voice mail. No surprise. She would be at Cassandra's recital by now.

What to do, what to do? Maybe she'd call Jake. *Hi. I know you're upset with me, but would you mind giving me your previous address so I can go to a party honoring your ex?*

Yeah. That would go over well. He'd probably never speak to her again—not that he would anyway. At any rate, calling would be fruitless. He was about as likely to give her the address as he was to quit hockey to dance ballet.

For a moment, she'd considered turning around and driving straight back to Laurel Springs. Wouldn't that have been the irony of the century?

So she'd put on her big girl panties and scrolled through her phone until she found Aunt Cheryl, who was sure to be at the shower and probably wouldn't answer. But she did. Evans heard the party noise in the background before Channing's mother tersely demanded to know where she was and if she knew she was late.

Evans hadn't been so lucky with the parking at Chez Channing. Consequently, by the time she trudged to the massive doors with the stained-glass windows, the carefully wrapped packages were well and truly wet.

Now here she was at Channing's lovely home—if you liked chalkboard signs that shouted platitudes about love, Edison bulb chandeliers, and Mason jars full of wine corks. She'd arrived during the gift opening and no one had paid much attention to her. She'd just added her soggy packages to the pile and found a seat in the corner, where she'd watched Channing pronounce every little blanket and outfit *darling* or *precious* while her posse pandered to her. Did she need more sparkling water? Did she want to put this burlap pillow behind her back?

How did that woman do it? Attract a band of followers everywhere she went? Evans wouldn't know. She'd certainly never been part of it, hadn't wanted to be.

*Then what are you doing here?*

Good question. Daddy had asked her to go, sure—and she was a yes girl. God and Jake Champagne knew that. What if she had said no? Or canceled yesterday? No one, least of all Channing, would have cared. Her daddy certainly wouldn't have stopped loving her. No, she'd come because she wanted to get good girl points that she was never going to get. She didn't even know who she wanted them from.

Jake. She wanted them from Jake, and she had sure fixed that, hadn't she?

She ought to be in New Orleans with Jake right now. Was it raining there? It wouldn't have mattered. They would have splashed right through the puddles, or holed up in some French Quarter bar where the music was great and the beer was cold.

But it was too late for that, too late for Jake and her.

Or was it really?

Jake was mad at her, sure. Certainly disappointed. Maybe even a little disgusted. She'd felt all those things toward him on occasion, but she had still loved him through it all. The difference was he wasn't in love with her. *But the potential was there*, a voice whispered to her. And he was only angry and disappointed because he wanted to be with her. That had to count for something. If she went to see him and told him she was sorry—sorry in the way that she truly regretted what she'd done and would absolutely do differently given the chance—could they get past this? Or would he think it was easy to say you were sorry after you'd done what you wanted?

She didn't know, but there was only one way to find out.

"Evie? Dear?" Aunt Cheryl interrupted her thoughts.

Evie stood up to greet her, like she'd been taught, and her aunt kissed her cheek.

"It was so good of you to drive up in this terrible storm." She was probably trying to make up for being short before. "And those girls should have put the address on the note they left at Carrie's house."

"It's fine, Aunt Cheryl. I got here. That's all that matters." Except it didn't matter. Not at all.

"I appreciate that you came and I know Channing does, too. Have you had anything to eat?"

"Yes. It was all lovely." That wasn't really a lie. She had eaten in her lifetime, though not today, and she was sure the pretty little tidbits were the best money could buy from the hottest caterer in town.

Aunt Cheryl took her arm. "You must come and see the nursery. You won't believe how darling it is."

There was no way she was going to look at that baby's room. Though he would never know one way or the other, that seemed over-the-top disloyal to Jake.

"Actually, Aunt Cheryl, I think I'm going to slip out." She gestured toward the window. "The rain, you know." *And I am going to try to mend a fence, a very broken fence.*

"Oh, must you, darling?"

Evans almost laughed. She knew that tone and expression. It really meant: *I had to ask, but I'm not going to talk you out of it. I need to get on to the next person.*

"Won't you come say goodbye to Channing?"

Evans glanced across the room where Channing was surrounded by women holding crystal flutes and laughing as someone demonstrated how to use a breast pump on a teddy bear.

Evans patted her aunt's arm. "You tell her for me. I know she must be exhausted and ready for this to be over."

And she left without thanking her hostess—whoever that was. Miss Violet wouldn't have approved, but then, Miss Violet wouldn't have approved of any of this.

It was raining harder than before and lightning flashed, but she didn't care. Now that she'd made up her mind to try to fix things with Jake, nothing else mattered. The rain could soak her to her underwear for all she cared. The lightning could strike her—well, maybe not that.

She was laughing by the time she got in the car and turned on the heater. This was the first time she'd needed it since last winter. She didn't know exactly what she was going to say to Jake or when she would say it, but she'd figure that out on the drive home.

She was just about to leave when her phone rang.

She grabbed it. Maybe it was Jake. But no.

"Hey, Ava Grace," she said.

"Hey. Are you home?"

"No. I'm just about to leave Nashville. I've been to my cousin's baby shower. What's up?"

"Oh." Ava Grace sounded disappointed. "Mama wanted to talk to you about the pies for the gala. She just sprung it on me, and she wanted to ask if you could do it today."

"When? Obviously, I can't right now."

"She suggested that the three of us get together at Hammer Time for dinner, but that's probably not good for you."

Evans looked at the clock and calculated the time the drive would take. "I could make it by seven, I think." That settled the when she would talk to Jake. After dinner, she'd track him down—though she should probably go home and clean up first. She didn't mind seeing Ava Grace and Emma Frances with damp hair and crumpled clothes, but she needed to feel confident when she talked to Jake.

"That would be great," Ava Grace said. "It shouldn't take more than an hour."

"I'll meet you there," Evans said. "I'll call if I get delayed in traffic."

"Perfect," Ava Grace said.

And maybe it would be.

## Chapter Twenty-Seven

Jake swallowed four aspirin and chased them with half a bottle of water.

He hadn't been drunk since six months ago when the Sound lost in the playoffs, and he hadn't intended to get drunk last night, but his tolerance was down and one beer had led to another. The empty stomach hadn't helped. He'd ended up sleeping facedown on the couch in the same sweatpants and T-shirt he'd been wearing for twenty-four hours. Or more. Yeah, it was more.

He switched the TV from the Cowboys/Packers game to The Weather Channel. He couldn't concentrate on the game anyway. All he could think about was this damn storm and that Evie was out in it.

His doorbell rang. He couldn't even pretend that it was her. She didn't have the code to the elevator, and besides, about now she'd be doing whatever women did at showers. He was in no mood for company, but he was in no mood to be alone either, so he moved toward the door. Truth be told, he was in no mood for anything.

"You never called me to work out yesterday," Robbie said when Jake opened the door.

"No." Jake rubbed the back of his neck. "I did not. Sorry."

"You look bad, Sparks." Robbie followed him in and back to the den. "You don't smell too great either. Are you sick?"

Jake sat in the big easy chair and Robbie stretched out on the couch with his hands behind his head.

"I'm not sick," Jake said.

"Why do you have The Weather Channel on?" Robbie said with some alarm. "Is there a tornado coming?" As a rule, they didn't get tornadoes in Scotland, and Robbie had an irrational fear of them.

"No," Jake said. "Not that I know of. They haven't said anything about it."

"Then why are you watching The Weather Channel?"

Jake tried to think of a feasible answer, but was too tired to come up with anything but the truth.

"Because Evie's in Nashville. She'll be driving back in this if she's not already." He paused. "I'm worried about her."

"Nasty weather to be driving in for sure," Robbie said. "I wouldn't want my sisters out in this. Maybe it's not as bad where she is. What does she say?"

"She doesn't say anything—at least not to me," Jake said in a low voice. "We're not speaking."

Robbie narrowed his eyes. "What did you do?"

Jake bristled. "What makes you think it was me?"

Robbie shrugged. "Just a guess."

"Well…" Jake took a drink of his water.

"Jake," Robbie said.

"Yeah?"

"What's going on here?"

"What makes you think anything's going on?"

Robbie shook his head. "Because there is."

Jake took a deep breath. "Yeah."

And he told him—told him all of it, his attraction to Evie, that she seemed to return it, the hiding from Able, and the fight yesterday. He left nothing out, edited nothing to make himself look better.

When he was done, Robbie let out a low whistle. "Can't say I'm surprised. I could tell you were interested. I just wasn't sure you knew."

"I didn't. Not at first. But it's a moot point."

Robbie sat up on the couch. "Let me see if I've got this right."

"Okay," Jake said.

"This woman, who has been your friend since the cradle, talked to you every night while we were on the road, came to see you play, drove you home, made you a chocolate pie, made you a pizza—" That thought seemed to distract him. "A real pizza, with dough and everything?"

"Yeah," Jake said. "Pepperoni and sausage. No mushrooms."

"I didn't even know you could make pizza."

"Did you think it grows on a bush?"

"No. But I thought it was like jam. Or mayonnaise. You buy it. You don't make it."

Jake shrugged. "My grandmother makes mayonnaise. It's about the only thing she makes, but she says mayonnaise in a jar is an abomination. Some people make jam."

"How about that," Robbie said with some wonder. "But not the point."

"Is there a point?"

"Yes," Robbie continued. "This woman did all this for you. She let you stay over—"

"There was no sex," Jake said.

"None?"

"No. Some fooling around, sure, but no sex."

"Fair enough. Still not the point. She agreed to take off to New Orleans with you because that's what you wanted."

"But she didn't go," Jake reminded him.

"Because she had another obligation, one that it sounds like she momentarily forgot because her mind was on you—what with all the pizza making and hockey watching."

"But her obligation was to go to Channing's baby shower. She didn't even want to go. She always does that—says yes when she ought to say no."

"So what?" Robbie asked. "We all have to do things we don't want to, and Channing *is* her cousin."

"She was my friend first!" Then realizing how ridiculous that sounded, Jake added, "Not first, but *more*. She was more my friend."

"Doesn't matter," Robbie said. "Lots of people are pleasers. Better than being a displeaser. I bet you like it well enough when she tries to please you."

That struck a nerve. Hadn't Evie said something similar?

"She needs to stand up for herself," Jake said.

"As long as it's not to you."

"You're twisting this."

"That's what people say when they're not hearing what they want. Can't you be glad she wanted to live up to her obligation?"

Just then, the lights flickered and thunder shook the house.

Jake grabbed his phone and looked at the weather app where he'd been tracking the storm—not that it mattered. He had no idea where Evie was. He could call, but he didn't want her to answer if she was driving in this. He briefly considered calling Channing, but to what end? She might think she could control the weather, but that didn't make it true.

"I might add: if you had changed your little trip to Nashville like she asked, she wouldn't be in the storm alone."

He sighed. "Yeah." Which was what he should have done. In spite of what he'd said about the humiliation and showing his ass, there had been no good reason not to. He liked Nashville. They could have had fun there. He'd dug his heels in because he wasn't getting his way.

"I would like to point out that you're going to Nashville—and soon—unless you plan to sit it out when we play the Sound. I get that Channing is a sore spot for you, but she doesn't own Nashville."

That got his hackles up. "I do *not* have any baggage about Channing. I am over the whole thing."

"Don't get shirty with me. I didn't say you had baggage; I said you had a sore spot."

"And the difference is?" Though it didn't matter. He didn't have either.

"Baggage is like a broken ankle. It will keep you from playing. A sore spot is like a little muscle strain. It's annoying when you move just wrong, but it doesn't keep you from playing—or moving on. And before you start denying that, there'd be something wrong with you if you didn't have a sore spot. Hell, I have a sore spot and she didn't throw me out of the house on game day and get remarried before the ink on the divorce papers was dry."

*Or make you dinner and have sex with you, and*

*then get up early the next morning and pack your bags.* But Robbie didn't know that; nobody did. Maybe Robbie had a point. Maybe his fight with Evie was about more than digging his heels in because he wasn't getting his way.

"I wanted Evie to pick me over Channing." And that was the truth of it.

"Are you fourteen, man?" Robbie asked. "Better question: are you going to keep being fourteen? You had a spat—an argument, a disagreement. You're acting like she murdered your mum. And, Sparks, I've got to say—you're making too much of this. People argue. If arguing was a sign of the end, I—or any of my sisters—would have never been born because I am here to tell you my mum and dad can go at it. Apologize to her. End the argument. Then get on with this relationship."

Jake rubbed his forehead and sighed. "Maybe you're right. I guess I'm still a little stung. But apologize for what exactly?"

"The whole thing, but start with the melodrama. Did you really say to her that it had been good while it lasted and you thought it might have been good for a long time?"

"It's true," Jake said, but there wasn't much conviction in his voice. Out of somebody else's mouth, it did sound kind of like junior-high-speak.

"If only, if only"—Robbie raised a hand toward heaven—"she had done what you wanted, not carried through on what she'd promised, you maybe could have had life together." Robbie laughed. "I love you, mate. Love you like the brother one of my sisters should have been, but if you can't see what I'm talking about, you're probably never going to have a relationship."

"Yeah? You think you're better at relationships?"

"Me?" Robbie said. "No. But I don't want one. You do."

"I don't want just any relationship. I want one with Evie."

"That's the point," Robbie said like he was pleased with himself.

Maybe this was salvageable. Maybe he'd talk to her.

Thunder rumbled again. "Don't worry about the storm. I'm sure she's fine," Robbie said.

"Why are you sure of that?"

"If she'd so much as dented her fender, your mum would be on the phone with you. She's that sort, your mum."

"True." The Delta Queen grapevine was always on high alert. For once, it made him feel better.

"Here's something else that's true. You stink. Go shower and let's go get some food."

"All right." Surprisingly, that sounded like a good idea. By the time they finished eating, Evie ought to be back.

## Chapter Twenty-Eight

Hammer Time was emptier than Evans had ever seen it, probably because of the weather.

She sat in a booth across from Ava Grace and Emma Frances. They were talking pies, but not just any pies. Emma Frances needed pies that were common to the period when the first gala had been held in 1945 to celebrate the end of World War II. It wasn't until 1947, when sugar rationing came to an end, that the tradition of the dessert buffet began. No one knew what the menu was for the first two galas, and wasn't that a shame?

Evans had learned those little tidbits tonight and many, many other things. If this didn't end soon, it was going to be too late to talk to Jake.

"I think I have it all." Evans consulted her notes. "Would you mind if I read it back to you to be sure?"

"Please," Emma Frances said.

"Four pecan, three lemon chess, two vanilla chess, three cherry, two coconut, and two pumpkin."

"That's right," Emma Frances said. "I'm not sure we shouldn't have some apple, but I associate apple with Thanksgiving."

"You're having pumpkin," Ava Grace pointed out.

"That's Skip's favorite." Emma Frances gave her

daughter a little wink. "I think it's going to be a special night for him." Then she frowned. "Do you think we *should* have apple?"

Emma Frances had changed her mind so many times that Evans had spent the whole hour writing notes and had barely touched her grilled chicken sandwich.

"No," Ava Grace said. "I think you're having plenty. Remember all the cakes and candy, too."

"I keep thinking about pecan tassies," Emma Frances said. "They look pretty on a tiered pedestal and they are so Southern. Sometimes people just want a bite instead of a whole piece of pie. What do you think, Evans? Can you do those?"

"Sure, but if you want to do the tassies, you might want to cut out some of the pecan pies. They're basically miniature pecan pies."

"How many tassies would equal a pecan pie?"

Never in her existence had she been asked a question like that.

"Let me think." She did some calculations in her head. "One pie serves eight. I'd think about three tassies is a serving. I'd say about two dozen should equal a pie."

Emma Frances nodded. "Just to be safe, let's do five dozen tassies and cut out one pie. I want to have enough. Even though everyone knows it's just a dessert buffet, some people come without having dinner. I don't want anyone to leave hungry."

"I understand." Evans made the note.

"I'll bet Evans is hungry." Ava Grace gave her a knowing look. "You've hardly eaten a thing."

"And that's my fault," Emma Frances said. "You've spent the whole time writing." She checked her watch. "Oh, no. Ava Grace, we have to go." She looked at the check and put some cash in the folder. "I promised Evelyn I'd drop the minutes from the historical society meeting on our way home. She doesn't do email, you know. Evans, your food must be cold. Why don't you order something fresh to take with you?" She opened her wallet, ready to add more money to the check.

"No, no," Evans said. "This is fine." She didn't want to wait for that. She was hungry, but she just wanted to finish the rest of her sandwich, go home to freshen up, and—please, God—straighten out things with Jake. "I'm just going to sit a minute and finish this, but don't let me hold you two up."

"Are you sure?" Emma Frances asked.

"Absolutely." She held up her notes. "I'll price this out and email you tomorrow. If you think of anything you want to change, give me a call."

"Don't tell her that," Ava Grace said and ushered her mother out.

Evans pushed aside her notes and took a bite of her sandwich. Not as hot as it was two bites and forty minutes ago, but it filled the void in her stomach. She wondered idly if she could get away with not washing her hair. A ponytail wasn't the best look, but it would take thirty minutes to wash and dry it.

And she didn't want to wait another thirty minutes. In fact, she wanted to get on with it right now. She could eat on the way home.

She was wrapping her sandwich in a napkin when she heard Soup Carter's voice. "Is this okay for you, Mr. Champagne? Mr. McTavish?"

*Hell, hell, hell!* Her heart pounded. She wasn't ready, and they were going to walk by her any second.

But that second didn't come.

"Fine, Soup," Jake said. "And I've told you before. Call me Jake."

"Aye, lad," Robbie said. "You make me look around for my dad with all this Mr. stuff."

There was movement and settling in the booth right behind her.

"The soup tonight is creamy chicken and mushroom," Soup said.

"No thanks." That was from Jake and he was the one back to back with her. The booths were high enough that, even if he turned his head, he wouldn't know she was here. Theoretically, he or Robbie could have seen her before they sat down but, clearly, they had not.

"Tonight, our special is Memphis dry ribs, and our wings are half price."

"Great," Jake said. "Just what I want."

"Me, too," Robbie said. "Whole racks and two dozen wings."

Should she go?

Her raincoat hung on a hook right beside her head. She quickly grabbed it and, with some effort, got herself into it and put up the hood while still seated. Now all she had to do was get out the door. This was working out okay. She could be waiting for him at his building when they got home. It would take them a while to eat all those ribs and wings, so she had time. She could even do smoky eyes.

She started to rise.

"What would you like to drink, Mr. Champagne— I mean, Jake?"

Better wait until Soup left. He would almost certainly call her by name and say goodnight.

"Just water, Soup."

"I'll get this in and your server will be right over with some bread."

"No beer for you?" Robbie said. "I thought you'd want to drown your sorrows."

That was interesting. Was he still upset? Had he told Robbie? She'd been poised to jump up and move quickly, but she relaxed back into her seat.

"I already did that," Jake said. "Last night."

Maybe he had been as miserable as she was.

"There are better ways to deal with sorrow," Robbie said.

"None open to me," Jake said.

"I was talking about working a jigsaw puzzle," Robbie said. "Not chasing women."

Jake laughed. "I didn't happen to have one."

"Look, Jake," Robbie said seriously. "It's time we called off this stupid bet—especially in view of what you told me."

Bet? The two of them had a bet?

"No," Jake said firmly. "A bet is a bet. I'll see it through."

"If we call it off, you can get on with your life and you won't lose your lucky puck."

He still had that puck? She hadn't thought about it in years. They used to tease him about it. Once, when he was playing youth hockey, Christine had driven from Jackson all the way back to Cottonwood because he'd left it at home and insisted he had to have it. Blake had given it to him. If she remembered right, it was some sort of special commemorative souvenir. It had been important to him at the time and it must still be—doubly so now.

What had he been willing to risk it for?

"Not calling off the bet," Jake said. "There's no such thing. A bet ends in a win or a loss. You either see how it shakes out, or someone forfeits. I'm not forfeiting."

"Stop being so stubborn. Calling it off isn't forfeiting. We just say it never happened. I keep my St. Sebastian medal. You keep your puck."

St. Sebastian medal? Jake wouldn't care about that. The bet wasn't about him wanting something. It was just about winning. But what had they bet?

"No," Jake said. "I'll see it through."

"Okay. I forfeit. Here."

"Stop it," Jake said. "Put that back on."

"I'm trying to help you here," Robbie said. "The bet was stupid anyway."

*What, Robbie?* What *did the two of you bet?*

"You only bet because I said you couldn't do it," Robbie went on.

"Only partly. There was more to it than that. I told you at the time."

"It's unnatural for a man to go without sex for three months."

Robbie's words worked their way into her gut like termites burrowing into wood.

At first, she couldn't work out why, but she knew her universe had just shattered. She inclined her head to the side and waited to hear what Jake would say, but the next voice she heard was female.

"Hello, gentlemen! I'm Stacy and I've got some bread and drinks for you. Your food will be out soon."

Damn, damn, damn. Now there was only small talk and the sound of dishes and glasses being moved around. Maybe they would resume their conversation when Stacy left.

And they did, but not on the same subject. They moved on to talk about some goalie from some other team and how they thought he was washed-up. She didn't pay any attention to the details because her brain was too busy trying to put her universe back together again. This piece here, that piece there. When she'd finished it didn't look like it had before.

For reasons that weren't clear and didn't matter anyhow, Jake had bet Robbie he could go without sex for three months. She had begun to think that there was a chance they would be together forever, but he had never wanted her at all, except for a little distraction and a chicken pot pie. Despite his past antics, he would not have had sex with the girl from back home unless it meant something—maybe everything. That's why she'd been so eager; she'd needed assurance of a romance that wasn't going to happen.

The signs had been there when he'd said things like, *"I don't know what's happening here,"*

*"I can't know or promise where we'll end up,"*

*"I'm not asking for any promises."*

She had ignored it all, because she wanted his love so much. His motivation was obvious—at least to anyone who knew Jake. Jake had never done alone well. That's why they'd always spent the most time together when they were younger when he was between girls. And that's all it had been this time. He wanted someone to bide his time with until his lucky puck was safe and he'd won—someone who wouldn't tempt him. Sure, he might have been aroused, but that was just hormones and friction.

Wasn't winning the most important thing to Jake? Hadn't it always been?

She threw off her hood, picked up her bag, and rose—but not quickly or silently like she'd planned. Then she turned around and walked to the table behind her.

Robbie saw her first and broke into a big grin. "Hello, lass! Come join us. Have some wings."

Jake turned. In another time, in that universe that was hers before it shattered, she would have thought he looked pleased to see her. But she saw clearly now. That's what happened when you thought you were going to get everything you'd ever wanted, but it all turned out to be one big joke.

Jake started to stand up—like her daddy always did, like Miss Violet had taught him.

"Don't." She was never going to be the woman he needed to stand up for.

"Evie, I'm glad you're here. I wanted to talk to you."

"Yeah, you always did, didn't you? When you didn't have someone better to talk to." Cold calm settled over her. On another day, she might have been humiliated that she had been such a fool for wanting him and believing he wanted her, but that day was done.

Jake looked confused. "Not sure what you mean by that, but I needed to tell you—"

"Stop." She would not raise her voice or make a scene, but she was going to have her say. "You don't need to tell me anything, ever again."

Jake's expression went from confused to wary. He quickly glanced at Robbie and then right back at her. "Robbie, maybe you could—"

"Out of here." Robbie started to rise.

"No, Robbie," Evans said. "Sit." Though Evans kept her voice quiet, her tone was cutting—enough that it scared Robbie back into his seat. "I won't be here that long."

"Evie," Jake began.

She cut him off—something she could never remember doing before. She'd always been all too eager to hear what golden words would roll off his majestic tongue.

"I've been thinking about last Saturday night. You remember that, don't you? When you brought my phone back?" He opened his mouth to speak again, but she plowed on. "You got yourself into quite the little pickle, didn't you, Jake? Fixed it where you couldn't run off with Delilah, or Jolene, or whatever the hell her name was. So spending a little postgame time with good-old convenient, sitting-on-ready Evie was preferable to watching reruns of the *Golden Girls* and getting your pill organizer ready for the week. Hell, you didn't even plan it. You just stumbled into me because I dropped my phone. And if your mouth stumbled on to mine in the process, what the hell? You've survived better mouths than mine."

His eyes widened and his face went red. "It wasn't like that."

"It was exactly like that, Jake."

"Look, Evie, I was going to look for you. I was worried about you in the storm."

Not enough to slow down his wing eating, apparently. "No need. I weathered it." And she would weather this.

"I wanted to apologize for yesterday. If we can just go somewhere, if you'll just hear me out—" He took a deep breath. "I want to fix things between us. We were headed to a good place. I want to be there again."

"Great. Yes. I was hoping you'd say that."

He smiled and made to get out of his seat.

"Hold it there, Sparky." She clinched her fists in front of her. "I guess you didn't catch the sarcasm because that was exactly what you expected me to say."

"I don't understand."

"I'll explain it. I was always your go-to girl when you needed something—company, help with your algebra, or a ride because you'd had too much tequila. And I made it easy for you. Then Channing came along and you didn't need me anymore. Fine. I got used to it. Now, here you are again—wanting a distraction and chicken pot pie because you bet *him*"—she pointed to Robbie—"that you can go without sex for three months. Good old Evie. Always ready with plenty of free time and some baked goods. Well, no more. It's on me that I always made it easy for you, but that day is done. Call up Marie Callender."

"Evie, please!" His voice was a ragged whisper. Another time, that would have been enough to do her in. "Just hear me out."

"Not going to happen." She turned to go, but threw over her shoulder, "You can bet on *that*."

## Chapter Twenty-Nine

One good thing had come from Evans's brief almost-relationship—or was it more of an encounter?—with Jake. She had given Quentin and Ariel a chance, and all their lives were better for it. Or as good as hers could be right now.

"See what you think." Quentin handed Evans a small slice of butterscotch bacon pie.

She was skeptical, but that didn't last long. "Delicious," she pronounced. The salty candied bacon was a perfect contrast to the sweet butterscotch. "Is there some maple hanging around there somewhere?"

He looked pleased. "Maple sugar. I candied the bacon with it and put just a little in the leaf lard crust."

It was now eight days since she'd seen Jake. Her heart still hurt, but it got a little better every day.

She had no idea if he had tried to contact her. She'd blocked his number as soon as she'd gotten home that night. It was one of the hardest things she'd ever done, but necessary because she couldn't trust herself not to answer if he called.

After all, she hadn't been able to stop herself from checking the Yellowhammer schedule. They'd had two home games early last week and then road games Thursday, Saturday, and Sunday. She had not, however, kept up with the outcome of the games, let alone Jake's stats.

She was rather proud of herself for that.

And she was proud of herself for facing that she wasn't going to hear from him again. If there had been a tiny part of her that had hoped he would try to see her in person, that was history. If he hadn't shown up in person before leaving town, he wasn't going to do it now. And that was for the best.

"What do you think?" Quentin said, bringing her back to pie land. "Can we put it in the rotation? Give it a try?"

"Sure," Evans said.

Ariel drifted in. "I've been working on a way to decorate Quentin's new pie." She set down a sheet pan of dancing pigs made from pastry.

Stunned to silence, Evans jerked her head up and met Quentin's eyes.

"Pigs," Ariel said. "You know—for the bacon and the leaf lard."

"I told her not to do it," Quentin said. "I knew you'd think it was dumb. Or irreverent…offensive…or something…"

And just like that, for the first time in days, Evans began to laugh. "I would have thought maybe maple leaves, but pigs! I love it."

"You're all right with dancing pigs?" Quentin asked.

"Why not?" Evans took her apron off and handed it to Ariel. "Let's debut the pig pies Wednesday. I'm going home. You two can help Neva lock up."

They looked up in surprise. She was always the last one out the door.

"What's up with her?" Ariel said as Evans exited the back door.

A good question, and not one Evans was sure she had the answer for. She just knew she seemed to be evolving into a world where she didn't consider every angle or have to be in control of everything. There had been a time when she would have said no to those precious little pigs because: 1. They might make people expect a meat pie. 2. An artisan pie ought to be taken seriously and dancing pigs were anything but. 3. Someone from PETA might come in and take offense that a pig's image was being used.

To hell with all that. You couldn't plan away every mistake. You could prepare, anticipate, and work the angles, and life still slapped you in the face.

She needed more dancing pigs in her life, and she was going to have them.

As she stepped onto her street, she thought about how serious Ariel had been about those silly little pigs, while Quentin looked like he was expecting a meltdown of Biblical proportions—and she began to laugh.

She laughed and laughed—until she caught sight of the bugmobile. And there was Jake sitting on her porch steps.

For a second she felt nothing short of joy of the first degree, but that was just a heart muscle memory. When that passed she wasn't unhappy. There was a time when she would have hidden behind a tree until she had time to try to figure why he was here and all the ways she might respond.

But she was done with that.

She straightened her posture and quickened her steps. The sooner she got there, the sooner this would be over.

* * *

Jake had been sitting on Evie's steps for an hour before he saw her walking down the street. Even though he knew she wouldn't be home yet, he'd come as soon as he got back to town. It didn't make sense, but nothing about what had happened made sense.

He supposed he wanted to prove he'd sit here as long as he had to. After all, he hadn't come for a feeling of home, to salvage friendship, or even to see if she was okay. He was here for her heart.

He stood up as she approached. She didn't look mad.

"Hello, Jake." She spoke before he had a chance.

"I tried and tried to call you. I texted about forty times before I realized you'd blocked me." Actually, he hadn't realized on his own. Robbie had pointed out that none of the texts had been marked as delivered.

She half smiled and brushed past him to unlock the door. "Seems like blocking didn't keep you off my porch. I'll have to call Apple and see what they can do about that."

In spite of the half smile, he thought she might run him off but, after opening the door, she just turned around and looked at him. When he hesitated, she said, "Well, come on in. Let's get this done."

"Just so you know, I tried to follow you last Sunday night. Robbie said I shouldn't."

Evie sat down on the sofa and nodded toward the chair across her. Letting him sit was a good sign, even if she wasn't willing for him to sit beside her.

He sat down and leaned as far toward her as he could. "I would have been here before now, but Robbie said I should give you a couple of days to cool down. And then I had to go on the road. Robbie also said I shouldn't send you flowers, that it would just make you mad."

Evie crossed her legs and began to swing her foot. "Robbie did, did he? Robbie must be quite the expert."

"No." Jake looked from her bouncing foot to her eyes. "But I've done a piss poor job on my own, so I thought I'd try it his way. And you know, Robbie's family is in the wedding business. He's seen a lot of weddings. Couples. You know." As he spoke, he realized his words sounded just as dumb as his math grades had always indicated that he was.

"No, I can't say I knew that about Robbie." She sounded pleasant, but...detached. Like she was being polite to a stranger. He'd thought it was good that she wasn't mad anymore. Now, he wasn't so sure. It seemed like she didn't give a damn, one way or the other.

Might as well get started. He had a lot to say. "That night—the Sunday night at Hammer Time when—"

Evie nodded, in a get-on-with-it way. "I know the one, Jake. The day I went to Nashville."

"Yes. That. I wanted—still want—to apologize for the day before. It was inexcusable. I acted like a toddler who'd had his best toy taken away from him."

"I guess that's pretty much what happened, isn't it?" she said. "Though I wouldn't classify as *best*."

"I wouldn't call you a toy of any sort. That's not what I meant. I came to say you were right. You had an obligation. I was in a snit because I didn't get my way. I should have gone to Nashville with you. I wish to hell I had."

"Funny, that." She reached up and rubbed her temple. "It was my intention to apologize to you that night and tell you that I wished to hell I *hadn't* gone, that I had gone to New Orleans with you. I had a few realizations."

"I've had some of my own—one being that I still have a sore spot where Channing is concerned—not that I want her. Oh, hell no. But it was a tough time. Now that I know that, it won't cause me to act irrationally again. We can go to Nashville anytime you want."

She placed her hand on her forehead and closed her eyes. "Oh, Jake. Channing has left a lot of people sore—me included. It's her hobby. Of course you'd feel that way."

He felt some hope. "Then can we just agree that we've both had some realizations, that we both made mistakes? Can we just agree that it was a stupid argument that doesn't mean anything in the long run?"

"Absolutely, we can." She opened her eyes and met his. "Not that it matters."

For a second there, he had been elated, but then she zapped it like a ray gun in a video game.

"What do you mean?"

"Remember, I know about the bet now, Jake. I know you were just biding your time with me until you could go back to your glamorous blondes."

What kind of convoluted thinking was that? Didn't she know how much he wanted her? It might be best not to voice his opinion on her thought process, but he *could* deny it.

"No. That's not true. It was a stupid bet. It didn't mean anything. I had already decided to clean up my act when we made the bet. I told Robbie that. He said I couldn't do it and—well, one thing led to another."

"And it was easy with me, wasn't it? Good old Evie. Not much of temptress, but she sure can make a pie.

Always a good placeholder between better times." She let out a laugh totally devoid of humor.

That made him mad. But hadn't that been her intent? He'd hold it in check, be reasonable. He got up, went to stand in front of the fireplace, and turned to face her.

"No. That's not how it is. How can you say that about yourself, and how can you say I wasn't tempted? You were there with me. You make me feel things like never before."

"But not enough. Just so you know, when I said it wasn't the right time, I only meant right *then,* Jake. That night." She sighed and rolled her eyes at his undoubtedly blank expression.

He had no idea what she was saying.

"I had my period. If not for that, I would have slept with you right then."

"Oh." Why hadn't she said that, straight out? How was he supposed to have gotten that from what she'd said?

"*Oh*, is right." She got up and came to stand in front of him. "I guess you're surprised to find out that sleeping with me would have been so easy. Though you shouldn't be. Making things easy for you has been my life's work. And I wanted proof that I stood a chance with you. So you see, all that talk about how wise I was and how it was right to wait, that was really just relief that you wouldn't be expected to sleep with me for, what was it? Three months?"

"You've got this all wrong." He started to put his hands on her shoulders, but she gave him a look that let him know he'd better not, so he let his arms drop back to his side. "I was right there with you that night.

I wanted you, I would have made love to you, the puck be damned."

"I'm not sure about that, though I'll concede that you believe what you're saying. But, either way, in the light of day you were glad. You wanted to win that bet and keep that puck."

"It was never about the puck. I don't care about the damned puck. I want to make love to you right now. I want to make a relationship. Just give us a chance." This time he couldn't help himself, Jake reached out to lay his hands on her shoulders. "Please, Evie. Just say yes."

It was the hands that did it—made her hesitate. So far, she'd been strong and resolute, even when he was saying all the right words. She might still look cool and determined on the outside, but on the inside, she was a mess.

Her gave her a sad little smile, bringing attention to his mouth—the mouth she knew the taste of, that she wanted to taste right now. And, God help her, he let his hands slide down from her shoulders to the bare skin above her elbows.

Cold chills went over her. She could tell by the way he smiled that he noticed. Well, there wasn't anything she could do about that.

But she could do this: "No."

His smile died. "What?"

"You said I always say yes when I really want to say no. That it's my *problem*." Evie stepped back out of his reach and squared her shoulders. "And you're right. I do. This time I'm saying no when I want to say yes."

He opened his mouth, but she put up a hand and stopped him.

"You see, Jake, I'm saying no, because I *should* say

no. I wish it wasn't so, but I don't think I can ever trust you not to abandon me again the minute something gets inconvenient." She fought to keep her eyes from filling. "I've spent my life making myself convenient for you. That's on me. But I can't be your yes girl anymore and that's what you would always expect."

"I wouldn't," he said.

"You think that."

"I know it."

She leveled her gaze on him. "I have a question."

"Anything."

"This is probably an invitation for humiliation, but I have to know. That night at my parents' Christmas party, the night you met Channing—"

"Yes?" He set his jaw and dropped his eyelids.

"I got the sense—that is, before Channing came in— that something changed between us. I thought there was a spark."

"Yes. I was about to ask you to go to the Sigma Chi spring formal with me, and then—" He trailed off and looked at the floor.

She nodded. "And then Channing came in, sprinkling her fairy dust." There wasn't any malice in her voice.

"Fairy dust isn't real, Evie, and what we have is."

She shook her head. "We don't have anything, Jake."

"Is there anything I can do to prove to you that I wouldn't abandon you?"

"Nothing I can think of, but then if I had to be the one to think of it, what good would it be?"

He looked at her for a long moment and his sad eyes went straight to her heart. She looked away before she could start thinking that if he looked that sad, surely, surely it didn't have to end this way. But she knew it did.

"If that's your last word, I guess I'll go." His voice was ragged.

"Then you should go." She walked to the door and opened it.

She didn't want to cry. She wanted to be strong. But after saying no to the thing she had wanted so much for so long, holding back the tears until the bugmobile roared away was the best she could do.

## Chapter Thirty

Jake put bread in the toaster Evie had picked out for him and poured eggs into the copper skillet he'd bought to please her—not that it had, and she sure as hell wasn't pleased with him now.

He spread peanut butter on his toast and slid the eggs onto a plate. He'd forgotten to get bacon at the store.

Since he'd last seen Evie, he'd played some games—won some, lost some, played well, played mediocre, and—once, against Dallas—played outstanding, according to people who ought to know.

But Evie hadn't seen any of it.

He put his plate in the dishwasher and eyed the copper skillet. He'd wash it later. Or not. The cleaning service would be here tomorrow. Or maybe he could invite Killjoy over—though he might not do dishes anymore since he'd been named permanent captain. They could commiserate over what they didn't have.

When they were in New York last week, Robbie had practically begged him to go with him to take two women to dinner after the game. "Come on, man. It'll do you good. They aren't puck bunnies," Robbie had said. "They've never even been to a hockey game.

They're lawyers. I met them at the Starbucks around the corner from the hotel."

So he'd agreed. At the suggestion of the women, they'd gone to a small, quiet place with good food and white tablecloths, but a relaxed atmosphere, with live background music. His designated date was attractive and pleasant. It should have been a nice time, but he kept wondering why he was there. It wasn't for sex—that had been established—and it damn sure wasn't for a relationship. Even if he had been looking for a relationship, he wouldn't be looking in New York City.

Unless Evie was in New York. If she moved to New York and opened a pie shop, he'd tell Miles to do whatever it took to get him a contract with the Big Apples. Or the Minutes. He'd buy a heavier coat and a snow shovel and smile while he was doing it.

*If you'd be willing to do that, why aren't you doing anything now?*

That was a decent question, one he didn't have a decent answer for—or maybe he did. He wasn't doing anything because he didn't know what to do. Besides, she'd been perfectly clear. He'd screwed up and he wasn't going to get a do-over.

He needed some advice from someone other than Robbie—someone who might actually be helpful. He'd briefly thought about asking Hyacinth or Ava Grace, but decided that would be a trip to hell on a bad road.

*Addison.* He couldn't explain why he picked up his phone and called her. It was instinct, not unlike what he felt on the ice when he suddenly knew what he had to do.

She answered on the first ring. "Hello, brother of mine."

"Sorry to call you at work."

"No problem. I've been chasing my fanny for weeks, but things have settled down now."

"I guess rush has kept you busy there in Omega Beta Gamma land."

"Recruitment, Jake. We don't call it rush anymore."

"Whatever."

"Sorry we haven't talked lately. I've watched your games when I could. I know you've been busy, too."

"I have." He took a deep breath. "Addison, I want to ask you something."

"Sure. I'll tell you, if I know."

"Why didn't Channing ask Evie to be a bridesmaid in our wedding?" This could lead to something useful. He knew it just as surely as he sometimes knew that the puck was going to go in the second he touched his stick to it.

"Channing didn't tell you at the time?"

"I didn't question Channing on the details of the wedding. The less I talked about it, the better I liked it."

"Why are you wondering after all this time?"

"I just am."

She sighed. "I don't have a good answer for you. Channing mentioned in passing she was having her sorority sisters. I don't think she willfully excluded Evie; she just didn't think about her. Mama worried about it at the time, but Channing and her mother made it clear the wedding was their show and they were going to run it."

"At least you thought about it. That was more than I did."

"Don't give me too much credit. I didn't question Channing either. Like a lot of people, I was bowled over by her. She was good to me, always swore that I was her sister beyond Omega, beyond blood. And I bought it."

"I know." He had not called to talk about Channing, but his gut told him this was going somewhere. "She's charming. Miss Congeniality and all that."

"I've thought about it a lot, Jake. *Charm* means telling people what they want to hear, whether it's the truth or not. Channing was a master." She made a sound that was a mixture of a huff and a laugh. "People would line up to let that girl lie to them. At least when she was lying to you, she was talking to you. I've stood in that line. I'm not proud of it. And what she told me wasn't true. She did *not* love me. She was not my sister forever. Of course, all that was just a postscript to what she did to you."

"I had no idea this affected you so much," he said slowly.

"Well, you had problems of your own." She paused. "Evie never knew it, but I was a little mad at her right after the divorce."

"What? That makes no sense."

"I know. It didn't last long, but for a little while there, I blamed her."

"Why? Did you think she played matchmaker? She didn't do anything to encourage that relationship."

Addison laughed out loud. "No, Jake. I never imagined that she would have."

"Then what did any of it have to do with Evie?"

"Nothing. But you were so broken down and I kept thinking that I couldn't believe Evie had let you marry Channing. Channing was her cousin. Evie had to know how she was and should have warned you. How could she have let her come into our lives?"

Though he knew Addison couldn't see him, Jake shook his head. "Addison—"

"I know. Don't try to school me here. You couldn't have been stopped. Channing dangled her magic in front of you and you were gone."

*Fairy dust. Magic.* None of that was real. Even in stories where it was, there was always a price.

"It wasn't fair, but I kept thinking if Evie had just been more assertive, had tried harder, things might have worked out differently and none of us would have ever ended up in that mess to begin with."

Jake was completely lost. "Tried harder to what?"

"Oh, come on, Jake. You know what I'm talking about."

"I don't, Addison. I swear I do not."

"Evie's in love with you."

If only. "I can promise you she is *not*."

"Don't tell me you don't know it. She's always been in love with you. She probably heard your baby babble when she was in the womb and fell for you then. Probably came out looking around for you, hoping you'd be there to greet her."

His heart rate increased. "She told you this? That she loved me?"

Addison laughed. "Evie? With the way she plays things close to the vest? Of course she didn't tell me. I'd wager she's never told anybody, but everybody knew it. Well, apparently, everybody but you."

Could it be true?

"I'm amazed you're that dense," Addison said.

*Dense.* What was it his mother had said when she'd been telling him not to get involved with Evie? That surely he wasn't dense enough to think Evie would hurt him, that he would do the hurting?

"Well, hell." It was a lot to take in, but it made sense—sweet, eager to please Evie, who'd always had a smile and time for him. There had been no hesitation from her the first time he'd kissed her. No wonder she'd been ready to have sex—only it wouldn't have been just sex for her. It would have been making love. She'd been waiting for it. And he'd messed everything up. At that point, what would it have been for him? He didn't even have to ponder that. Sex. Maybe not *just* sex. Maybe sex on the way to something else, but sex nonetheless. But not now. He'd traveled a million emotional miles since then.

"You *really* didn't know?" Addison brought him back to the present.

"No." He took a deep breath. "I almost asked her out once. Later I thought it was just as well. Evie's so smart and focused. Like a million other guys, I just wanted to play pro hockey. I had no backup plan."

"Turns out you didn't need one," Addison pointed out.

"I was lucky, but it looks like I used all my luck up on hockey. As far as Evie goes, I'm hip deep in hell over here."

"How's that?"

"I have fallen in love with her." He'd never said it, even to himself, but there it was.

"Jake!" Addison sounded elated.

"And she won't have me."

"Oh." Her tone hit rock bottom. "That's no good."

"No. No good at all."

"Why won't she have you? Even with the way you've

been acting since the divorce, it's hard to imagine you doing something bad enough for that."

No way was he going to give Addison chapter and verse of what had gone on with him and Evie. Luckily, she was not as hungry for details as their mother.

"Let's just say I did something stupid."

"Then fix it. Do something smart—but only if you're sure. This can't be a 'let's see what happens' kind of thing."

Her words left him cold. Wasn't that exactly what he'd tried to do?

"I'm sure, Addison. I didn't know the meaning of the word until now. But maybe I shouldn't do anything." This went beyond what he wanted. It had to be what Evie needed.

"Why shouldn't you?" Addison asked.

"I've hurt Evie and, apparently, not just lately if what you say is true. I've hurt her with my stupidity, oblivion, and careless disregard for her feelings and our friendship." The truth of that went straight into his gut and sucked him dry. Maybe he should ask for a trade so she never had to see him again, maybe ask for a team in the coldest climate he could get. That's what he deserved. "Who's to say it wouldn't be best for her if I just left her alone?"

"Not you," Addison said. "You're not the one to say. And I think that asking the question says a lot. Don't make decisions for Evie."

"She's made her decision."

"Has she? Or was she hurt and mad?"

"What's the difference?"

Addison laughed. "Oh, brother. You have a lot to learn. You should try again. Give yourself another chance, and give her a chance to say yes. As I said, do something smart."

"What is this smart thing I need to do?"

"Jake, I don't know. Make a gesture—something big, grand, and wonderful. She's wanted you her whole life. Make her believe you really want her."

"Such as?" Addison might be on to something.

"I know! Go on the jumbotron at a game and tell her how you feel. She would love that."

"She would?" He didn't think so, but Addison had been spot on until now. Maybe she knew something he didn't.

"Of course. *I* would. Any woman would."

No, not any woman and most especially not Evie. She would be livid. "Evie isn't going to games," he said gently.

"Oh," Addison said. "How about a trip? Somewhere romantic."

Somehow he doubted that Evie was in any state of mind to go anywhere with him right now—even if he could go.

"I can't take a trip, Addison. I have games."

"Yeah, right." She hesitated, and then burst forth: "Then a hot air balloon ride! Have champagne. And chocolate." The more Addison talked the more excited she sounded, and why not? These were things she would like—not Evie. "Oh and, Jake? This is the best idea. Get her an engagement ring and make sure it's bigger than Channing's, if that's possible."

"Don't you think that would be a little presumptuous of me? Considering she doesn't even want to talk to me?"

"Since when do you care about being presumptuous?"

She had a point. That sounded like something he might have done at one time. That had been part of his problem.

"Addison, I don't think…"

"Okay, okay, okay. No engagement ring. Get some other kind of a ring. Emerald and diamond. Or a bracelet—something really nice. And put it in a Louis Vuitton bag. Give it to her in the balloon."

Despite the state of his heart, Jake had to smile. How many romantic comedies had Addison seen? Nonetheless, she'd been helpful. She was right about the gesture, just not the details of what it needed to be.

Jewelry was tempting because it was easy, but the gesture had to be something hard, something he couldn't buy.

"Thank you, Addison. You've helped me clear my head and given me some good ideas."

"Great. Just a second." There were voices in the background. "Jake? I need to go. Somebody needs me. But if you want any help picking a bag and some jewelry, call me."

"Sure thing, sister. Love you."

"Love you back, brother."

That was one consultation he wouldn't need. He could only imagine Evie's reaction if he tried to make her climb in a hot air balloon full of presents.

Inasmuch as he knew what *not* to do to win Evie, he didn't know what *to* do. Mindlessly, he moved to the stove, picked up his dirty egg skillet and ran water in it. Evie had said, in no uncertain terms, to never put it in the dishwasher.

He stopped and slowly looked down at the skillet.

And the wheels in his brain began to turn.

## Chapter Thirty-One

It had been two weeks since Evans had sent Jake away.

Now she was on Claire's doorstep with no idea why she'd been summoned. Not where she needed to be with twenty-four hours until fall fest.

She was fairly sure Claire didn't know about her confronting Jake in Hammer Time or she would have heard about it by now. Maybe she was going to be chastised for failing to attend hockey games. If so, that was just too damn bad. She could not sit in that arena right now and watch Jake play hockey. Possibly after the first of the year—or never.

"Come in, Evans," Claire said warmly. Maybe she wasn't going to chastise her. It could be a surprise catering job. Evans would rather be chastised.

Evans handed Claire the bakery box she carried. "We're doing a test run on the miniature pies for the fall festival Saturday. I brought you a little sample."

Claire opened the box, looked at the four tiny pies. "Evans, these are exquisite."

"There's cranberry pear, honey apple, chocolate chess, and pumpkin with candied ginger."

"They are almost too pretty to eat. You did a beautiful job, as always." They were decorated with scarecrows, pumpkins, leaves, and witches riding brooms.

"I can't take credit. Ariel decorated them. She has a real knack and she's fast."

"You're letting Quentin and Ariel make crusts?" Claire looked pleased—and surprised. "Are theirs as good as yours?"

Evans laughed. "I'm not going to give up my title as crust queen, but they're good. I should have done this a long time ago. They have great ideas. We've added slab pies and rustic tarts to our rotation, and Quentin is a genius at recipe development."

"That's great to hear." Clair held up the box. "Shall I brew some coffee to go with these?"

"None for me," Evans said. "I've sampled enough new recipes lately to put me off pie forever."

"Then I think I'll just save them for a treat later." She set the box on the foyer table. "Come on in."

As usual, a fire blazed in the living room. Claire wasn't above cranking up the air to offset the heat because she enjoyed the ambiance of a fire, but she didn't need it today. It was so beautiful and crisp out that no one would have guessed it was raining in Evans's soul.

"Can I get you anything?" Claire asked.

*Just the reason for being here when I have pies to make.* "No, thanks. I'm fine."

"All right." Claire sat in her usual chair and reached for her planner. Oh, hell. It was going to be a catering job. She knew it.

Evans sat across from her on the sofa.

"I'll get right to the point," Claire said. "I ran into John Hollingsworth at Rotary."

Claire paused a moment to let it sink in, but it was

a moment Evans didn't need. Frozen pie hell had come home to roost.

"I see," she said.

"He mentioned that his reps were having no luck in getting you to return their calls about a deal to mass produce a couple of your pie recipes. He wondered if you were being evasive, hoping for a more lucrative offer."

This was bad—worse than she could have imagined. Did the universe have to bludgeon her with everything at once?

"That must have been embarrassing for you. I'm sorry."

"No. Not embarrassing. I'm seldom embarrassed. Especially when it comes to money.

"I told him that, while I do know you well, I didn't know what your thinking was on this. Which I do not, of course, because I have been given to believe that no one from the company has tried to contact you."

Claire waited. Evans tried and failed to read her. That woman ought to be in Vegas playing poker.

Finally, Evans spoke, weighing her words as she went. "I shouldn't have been evasive with you, and I'm sorry. But it's not the money. This isn't something I feel good about. I don't want to do it for any amount."

Claire frowned. "I'm not sure I heard you right." But she carried on anyway. "Art for art's sake is one thing, but you make *pie*. Why would you not want to be all that you can be? You're not lazy. You work as hard as anybody I know. You deserve the payoff—and it's sitting right there for the taking."

Evans almost looked at the floor, wanted to cover her face with her hands. But something stopped her. It was now or never, and she was tired of not speaking her mind. She didn't have the energy to play dodge-ball anymore.

She met Claire's eyes head-on. "Yes, Claire, I do make pie—pie that you buy on a regular basis to serve your guests. And your standards are not what I'd consider low."

"My point exactly. Your pies are perfection."

"Yes. And that's what I want—to be the best. I don't need to be the biggest. I'm proud of what I do, of what I'm teaching my employees to do. If I put my name on some mass-produced product, I might get a big pay-check, but I won't be proud of it anymore since the quality won't be there. Because you can be damned sure they won't use European butter and locally grown fruit." If Claire withdrew her support, so be it. "And one more thing. I don't want to cater."

Claire was a hard one to surprise, but Evans had accomplished it. "And you've always felt this way?"

"Yes."

"Then, why? Every time I've suggested something, you've said yes or put me off, saying it was a great idea for the future."

*Yes.* There was that word again.

"I said no to the pastry press," Evans pointed out.

"And, if you'll recall, I accepted your decision without question."

Evans took a deep breath. "You did, and I should have given you more credit, but I know you want me to expand and I didn't want to disappoint you."

"It's immaterial to me whether you expand or not, Evans. You have led me to believe that's what you want—the catering, the deal with Hollingsworth. I have simply been trying to guide you in that direction."

"The irony is," Evans said slowly, letting the realization set in, "that I was too controlling in the Crust kitchen, thinking I had to do everything myself while, at the same time, I wasn't willing to step up and control any other aspect of my life." She sat up straighter. "But I've been working on that—less control in the kitchen, more control in my life."

Claire nodded, but said nothing.

"You gave me a chance and helped me do what I could have never done at my age without your backing. I wanted to repay you by being successful."

Claire shrugged. "And you think expanding equals success?"

"That's what you've done and you're the most successful woman I've ever known. You're always trying something new and making it work."

Claire shook her head. "Evans, what I wanted was a unique, top-quality bakeshop in Laurel Springs. I've got that. As long as you're making a living to keep yourself in the manner that meets your standards and are content and fulfilled in your work, isn't that success?"

"That's what I think," Evans admitted.

"Then I have to wonder why you want to please me so much? Why do you try to guess what pleases me?"

Yet again, the yes girl was trying to get good girl points.

"I'm sorry. I *am* content with my work. Would I like to earn more? Of course. And I expect to. But I'm no fool. I know I'm incredibly lucky to be turning the kind of profit I am after being in business for this length of time."

Claire smiled. "I think it has more to do with ability and hard work than luck, but that's a philosophical point and a topic for another time. Have you given any thought to what you might like to do to grow your business?"

"Some," Evans admitted, "but mostly rambling incomplete ideas about things that I end up deciding wouldn't work anyway. Unless I've got a rolling pin in my hand, it seems I've never been enough for myself."

Claire paused before she spoke again. "Most people have a hard time being honest with themselves about what they want, but I think you know exactly what you want, always have."

*You could preach a sermon on that, Sister Claire.*

"It's other people you need to be honest with. How can your expectations be met if you never voice them?"

Good advice.

If a little too late.

"So." Claire picked up her pen. "It's time for you to be honest with me about what you want and I'll be honest with you about whether I can help you get it."

"I do want to expand, but in my own way," Evans said.

"That's the only thing that will work," Claire agreed.

"I don't want my pies mass produced and sold in grocery stores. I want to make special, artisan pies of the best quality."

"That's what you're doing."

"While catering was too time-consuming and kept me from what I love to do, I *would* like to do more large special orders—like the Fairchilds' Christmas Gala. I might even want to provide pies for some restaurants down the line."

"Those are good ambitions." Claire wrote in her book. "I assume you feel better equipped to do those things since Quentin and Ariel have taken on some of the work."

"Yes. I'm even willing to think about delivering."

"Delivery would be essential if you want to supply restaurants. That's a good plan for us to work on." Claire closed her book. "I'll call John Hollingsworth and explain."

"No," Evans said. "I should do it. I need to apologize for dodging his reps."

Claire nodded and a ghost of a smile crept into her eyes. "Yes, Evans. You never want to burn a bridge."

Evans got the idea she'd passed a test.

They said their goodbyes and Evans stepped on to the porch feeling lighter. At least this aspect of her life had taken a turn for the better.

"Evans?"

When she looked back, there was a worried expression on Claire's face. "I hope you'll try to apply this lesson to other aspects of your life. Be enough for yourself and don't sit around wishing."

"I'll try," Evans said, but she knew trying wasn't always the answer.

# Chapter Thirty-Two

"The chocolate chess are going fast." Quentin handed off a tray of mini pies to Joy to replenish the tiered serving trays on the refreshment table.

Fall fest was in full swing and, thanks to Ava Grace, who had showed up at Crust to work some magic with her surplus pumpkins, leaves, and amber twinkle lights, the shop had never looked prettier.

*Magic.* A word Evans tended to throw around to describe things that others were good at, but she was not. Jake had said there was no such thing. He was right. In the end, it was a bit of talent and a lot of hard work. Maybe there were those who thought pie making was magic.

Evans couldn't quite stop herself from picturing Jake spinning his ghost stories against the backdrop of autumnal splendor at Heirloom. She took a deep breath. A dozen times she'd wanted to call him and take it all back, say that she was here, ready and waiting to be his yes girl—because anything was better than how she felt now.

But a dozen times, she'd resisted. It was getting easier, but she felt like Swiss cheese—still cheese, good, entirely edible cheese, but with holes.

"Here, Evans." Able Killen zoomed through the door and handed her a piece of paper. "It's the name and contact info for the winner of the first round of cornhole. I took his picture, tweeted it, and tagged Crust. I hope that's okay."

She should have thought of that. "Great, Able. Thank you."

"Sure thing." He winked and smiled, but in a friendly rather than flirtatious way. She'd wondered if he would change his volunteer job, but he was carrying through with his commitment without showing a trace of awkwardness. "I've got to get back. Time for the next round."

She watched through the window as Able and Miklos lined up people and handed out beanbags.

Ariel drifted up. "Why does that hockey player have a *C* on his hockey shirt? You called him *Able*. Shouldn't he have an *A*?"

Ariel, Ariel. God love her. Evans hid a smile. "He's team captain. That's what the C stands for. And the shirt is usually called a jersey or a sweater."

"Oh." Unless Evans missed her guess, Ariel was looking at Able with a little more interest than she usually showed in anyone. "But it's not a sweater."

"No. But they used to play in sweaters when they played outside." Just then, Able squatted and showed a little girl how to throw the beanbag. He patted her shoulder and she looked at him like he was the greatest guy in the world.

Maybe he was—not that Evans had any regrets. Just because she'd decided she couldn't be with Jake didn't mean she wasn't still in love with him. Maybe in time it would pass. Maybe not, but she'd learned her lesson about trying to distract herself with another man.

"Why do they call it cornhole?" Ariel leaned a little more toward the window.

"No idea," Evans said. "Ariel, could you do something?"

Ariel looked at Evans though her eyelashes. "What do you need?"

"I'd like you to make a nice tray of treats and take it out to our volunteers."

"Out there?" She pointed to Able and Miklos. "To him? I mean them?"

"Yes. They're our only volunteers."

"I can do that." And Ariel drifted away.

Evans had never done any matchmaking and she wasn't going to start now, but why not provide an opportunity for a little interaction?

For the next two hours, Evans moved through the shop, helping serve, selling pies from the case, replenishing platters, and making coffee.

Everything was going splendidly.

At last, the night was winding down. Able delivered the name of the last cornhole winner. Cleanup was well underway and Miklos and Able had put away the cornhole boards. Evans glanced out the window just in time to see Ariel go out to retrieve the tray she'd taken out to Able and Miklos earlier. Able finished signing an autograph and turned to talk to Ariel. They both smiled and that made Evans smile.

It was almost time to lock the door when Evans heard a voice behind her. "You look pleased with yourself."

She turned. "Hello, Claire. It *has* gone really well."

"I see that. The pie case is almost empty."

"Yes, and we took lots of orders for Thanksgiving. People seemed to like cornhole."

"Sorry I didn't get here sooner."

"Can I get you anything? There's still a few cranberry pear and ginger pumpkin."

"Oh, no," Claire said. "I'm stuffed. I had cake at Trousseau and a doughnut and cider at Heirloom. I can't remember the last time I ate a doughnut."

"Those Krispy Kremes are hard to resist." Jake had probably had a few. "How were things with Ava Grace and Hyacinth?"

Claire laughed and looked heavenward. "Hyacinth was about to come unglued. Robbie McTavish was over there playing piano, but he didn't pay a bit of attention to what she wanted played. When I was there, he was playing 'Werewolves of London.'"

"Uh-oh." Hyacinth had drawn up a playlist of wedding music and sent it to him over a week ago. Evans was sure she'd hear all about it at the after party the Chamber of Commerce was holding to thank the volunteers and merchants. She wondered, not for the first time, if Jake would go. If so, it would be the first time they saw each other since the night she'd sent him away, and it was bound to be uncomfortable. But seeing each other was going to happen and it might as well be tonight. "Hyacinth does not like to go off script."

"No, but her courtyard was full of people singing and dancing. The photo booth tweeting has been phenomenal. I'd call it a win."

Evans had to ask. "What about Ava Grace?" *And Jake? How did he do?*

Claire smiled. "You know, I was skeptical, but that Champagne boy was fabulous—so charming. He had everyone in the palm of his hand." Of course. "I kind of hate to admit it, but I stayed through two sessions to listen to him. That's why I was so late getting here."

"Maybe he can have a second career after he's done with hockey," Evans said breezily. "Good for Ava Grace. She needed a win."

Claire nodded. "You had a win here, too, Evans. I'm proud of you. I'll see you at the party?" she asked as she headed toward the door.

"For sure."

She had a win—a win on her own terms. No catering, no mass market pies, no pastry press. She ought to be happy. Maybe she was, somewhere deep in her broken heart and around all that Swiss cheese. But a broken heart didn't mean a broken life.

"I closed out the register," Neva said, bringing Evans back to Earth.

"I'm sorry," Evans said. "I meant to do that."

"It's fine. You were busy with Claire." She held up a bank bag. "Is it all right if I go ahead and take this to the bank?"

"Sure," Evans said. "Tell everyone else to go, too—to get to the party and enjoy themselves. I'll finish cleaning up."

Neva frowned. "I don't think there's much left to do, but are you sure?"

"Yes!" Evans clapped her hands together. "Everyone has worked really hard. I'll catch up."

Truth be told, she was in no hurry to get to that party.

Quentin was the last to leave and Evans began to straighten the chairs. She paused at the table where she and Jake had sat that first day. If she could call it back, she would do things differently. Or maybe not. Maybe it needed to play out exactly as it had for her to move on.

Suddenly, feeling weary, she sat pressing her back against the heart-shaped wrought iron of the chair. She'd just sit a minute before checking to make sure the kitchen was clean. Then, she supposed there was no escaping changing into her party clothes and heading out to Fairvale, Ava Grace's ancestral home, where the party was being held.

Then the hair on the back of her neck prickled, like it does when you're sure you're being watched. But she wasn't afraid. Call it intuition, call it witchcraft, call it a lifetime of longing, but she knew who it was before she looked out the door.

Jake leaned against the doorframe, his forehead against the glass—just waiting, it seemed. When she met his eyes, he lifted one corner of his mouth, though that couldn't be counted as a real smile. He silently tapped his index finger against the glass.

He had finally come. But why? It might be a mistake to let him in, but that was the only way to find out. And she had to find out, even if it crushed what little was left of her heart.

"I wasn't sure you'd open the door," he said after stepping inside, bringing with him the scent of soap and doughnuts. Her head hadn't let her heart know it wasn't supposed to speed up for him anymore.

She sighed. "I said we couldn't be in a relationship. I didn't say I'd never open the door for you again. Our lives are way too tangled up for that."

"Do you wish that wasn't so?"

Did she? Who knew? "If wishes were Lamborghinis, all teenagers would speed."

He smiled. "You *do* know what kind of car the bug-mobile is."

She shrugged and lifted her eyebrows.

He gestured to the dining area. "I know we have a party to get to, but can we sit? Just for a bit?"

She hesitated, but nodded. "Would you like pie?" Old habits died hard.

"No, thanks."

They went to the table where she'd been sitting, where they'd sat together before—only this time she sat in his chair and he sat in hers.

"Still no recliners. They have them in movie theaters now, you know." He set down the Yellowhammer bag he'd brought in with him.

"Could be the next big thing." *Pie and recline.*

"I've been thinking, Evie, and I'd like you to hear me out."

It was on the tip of her tongue to respond that they'd said all there was to say, but she was too curious to not hear him out. Even if he was just here to tell her she was right, that it would never have worked. She nodded.

"First, I need to tell you I forfeited the bet. I took the puck to Robbie and made him take it right after the last time I saw you."

"That's too bad. I know Blake gave you that puck."

"Robbie doesn't. He would never have asked me to bet it if he had. He's not that kind of friend." He closed his eyes for a second and shook his head. "Anyway. It doesn't matter. Having the puck won't bring Blake back, or change what we meant to each other. And it doesn't have any effect on how I play hockey."

Her heart hurt for him. "Be that as it may, I'm sorry. You've had it since you were a little boy."

"The bet was stupid and pointless. Like I told you before, I had already decided to 'straighten up and fly right,' as my nana would say."

They smiled together at the shared memory of the woman with fresh flowers on her hat, whom no one argued with.

"So…" It seemed he'd said what he came to say. Evans made to rise.

But Jake spoke again. "I've been telling ghost stories tonight—thinking about ghosts."

*Or not.* She settled back into her chair. "I hear you were a hit."

"Maybe. I wouldn't call it an MVP performance, but maybe a goal." He didn't widen his eyes and bite his lip, but he grinned.

"Did you scare anyone?" She smiled, though she wasn't feeling it. "Scare yourself?"

He shook his head, but he didn't laugh. "Ghosts aren't real—at least the kind that spook around in stories."

"There's another kind?"

He took a deep breath and closed his eyes for a second. "The ghosts of Jake and Evie past. We've spent a lot of time living with those ghosts."

"I'm not sure what that means."

"Ghosts. Mistakes. Good intentions, gone bad. Bad intentions, gone to hell."

"Jake, we've been through this…"

"You're right." He nodded emphatically. "We have— over and over. But the truth is you have never forgiven me for abandoning you." She would have protested then, but something in his face stopped her. "*And*—I couldn't forgive myself either. But now I have."

Those were such goodbye words. "That's good. You should."

"Yes, I should, but not because I deserve it. Because it's what has to happen to move forward."

This *was* it—the big goodbye. If she'd felt like Swiss cheese before, now—despite that she'd said it had to be this way—she felt hollow. But she had to respond, had to find her voice.

"I understand. Moving on from us is the right thing."

"No." He reached across the table and, for the first time tonight, he touched her. There was warmth in his fingers on the back of her hand—not hot, sizzling electricity, but something else. "You *don't* understand. I didn't say move *on*. I said move *forward*."

"There's a difference?"

"I'm not here to say goodbye, Evie. I'm here to ask for another chance."

Her heart hadn't gotten the message that it couldn't tap dance with joy—not when nothing had changed. Unless…unless, maybe it had. *Another chance.* Did she owe him that? He'd had a point when he'd said she hadn't really forgiven him. Still—wouldn't this be same song, second verse?

"Jake, I'm not sure—"

"Wait!" He reached into the bag at his feet. "I brought you something."

Well, hell. The tiny, sputtering flame of hope Evans had been harboring fizzled. If Jake Champagne thought he could buy his way back into her good graces, he had another think coming. She closed her eyes to delay seeing whatever frivolously expensive, completely thoughtless geegaw he'd picked up to bribe her with to get his yes girl back.

"There!" She heard the pride in his voice before she opened her eyes and saw it in his face. "See!"

Reluctantly, she let her eyes drop to the table, but there was no Tiffany blue box or anything that resembled a fancy gift at all. Instead, there was a round dish covered in aluminum foil.

"What? Did Ava Grace send me Krispy Kremes?"

"No." He smiled and pushed the dish toward her. "It's from me. I made it myself."

"Got to be scrambled eggs," she mumbled as she removed the foil. "That's the only thing you can make."

"Not true. I can make toast and bacon. And now I can make this."

She stared down at it in shock. "I didn't see this coming." Understatement of the century. What sat before her was a pie in the beautiful copper pan they'd bought ten thousand heartaches ago.

Nobody had ever made *her* a pie before.

"See how it's decorated? Just like you do."

"Yes, it is." With silhouettes of chickens and her name spelled out in perfectly symmetrical letters. "Chicken pot pie?"

"Obviously. That's why the little chickens." He pointed to the rim of the pie. "I did it with a cookie cutter. The letters for your name, too."

She covered her face. It was like she'd gone to sleep and woken up in an alternate universe.

"What's wrong?" Jake asked.

She met his eyes. "Nothing. Or, I don't know. It's just a lot to take in. I don't know what's more dumbfounding—that you baked a pie or bought cookie cutters."

His expression morphed to a mix of sorrow and sincerity. "I'd do anything, Evie. And just so you know, there are more chicken cookie cutters out there than you'd think."

She was torn between laughing and crying and she couldn't have said why she wanted to do either.

"I would be interested to know how you arrived at making chicken pot pie."

"It's a long story but, in the end, it was something you said that night at Hammer Time—that I just wanted you for a distraction and chicken pot pie."

"So now you don't need me for chicken pot pie." She didn't really like how that felt.

"Don't get mad, but I wasn't really interested in learning to make it when I asked you to teach me."

"You don't say."

"Well…"

"I got that, Jake. Eventually."

"I asked because I wanted to spend time with you. Anyway, I could have bought you something—really, anything. But I wanted to show you I was thinking about you. I needed to do something hard."

"And it was hard?" She picked up the pie and gave it a closer look. The crust wasn't quite brown enough, but it did look homemade. "You made the dough yourself? No one helped you?"

"No, ma'am." He sounded a little incensed. "Unless you count YouTube videos, and I do not. I bet I watched thirty."

She set the pie down. "Thirty? Really?"

He nodded. "For the insides, I had that recipe you left at my place. Only there wasn't a crust recipe."

She hid a smile and refrained from telling him the correct word for the "insides" was *filling*. "We were going to use refrigerated crusts."

"I know. But you didn't like it. So I watched all those videos and I kept trying. I had to go to the store for more flour three times. Cutting the fat in with two knives doesn't really work. You need a pastry blender. I think I figured that out after about the third time."

"Jake, how many times did you make this pie?"

He shook his head. "I don't even know. At first, I never even got to the insides, because I had to keep remaking the crust. But I knew I had to get it right. I tried different recipes until I found one that was sturdy enough to roll. And then I made it two more times."

A little joy shot through her. "You spent some time considering the crust."

"That's the foundation for the pie. That's what one of the videos said. And isn't the foundation everything?" He reached over tentatively and laid his hand on top of hers.

She got the feeling he wasn't talking just about pie anymore. "Yes," she whispered.

He nodded. "I considered other things, too. The ghosts. The forgiving. Turns out you have time to think when you're making pie."

"It's true," she agreed. "Maybe that's why I over-think everything."

"You do just the right amount of thinking." He squeezed her hand and she didn't pull away. "The insides part was easier, though I had to learn some new words. *Sauté. Béchamel.*" His eyes were huge. "Evie, I promise you I have been in chicken pot pie hell. I didn't know if it would be enough, if it would prove anything to you. But I had to try. I thought I was going to wear that poor pan out. And, as much as it cost, that ought not be easy to do."

"It's a little late to be complaining about how much that cookware cost. I tried to talk you out of it."

He nodded. "I couldn't be talked out of it. I bought it because it made you so happy that I wanted to see you cook with it."

The bottom fell out of her stomach. "You mean to say, all that talk that night about *someone* coming over to cook—you meant me?"

He nodded. "Well, yeah. I hadn't quite figured things out then, but I knew I wanted to be with you. What did you think?"

"Never mind. Let's just say I was jealous of ghosts."

"All I'm asking for is a chance. If you find you can't forgive me, can't trust me, I swear, all you have to do is say the word. I'll go and never come to you with this again. We'll be friends."

Was it possible? This chance he spoke of? Again, did she owe him? Or was a better question did she owe *herself*?

If it went bad, they would *not* be friends. There was no going backwards. She either had to give him a chance for more, or they would smile and exchange niceties when they ran across each other until one of them attended the other's funeral.

She laughed a little to herself over the melodrama in her head—but still. It was sad. So sad.

"I was afraid you were bringing me jewelry."

"It crossed my mind, but I decided it would take more than jewelry to impress you."

"And Miss Violet wouldn't have approved."

"I know that's a fact. 'Ladies!'" Jake tried and failed to imitate the woman. "'You must nevah—*nevah*—

accept a gift of expensive jewelry from a gentleman, unless you are engaged to marry him.'"

"Don't think we're anywhere close to that." She had to bring him and herself back to earth.

His face went serious. "I know that, Evie, but I can't help thinking—someday. I've spent a lot of time missing you and wondering why I've missed you so much. It's the liking. All my life I have taken for granted how much I like you. I like you with the kind of like that can grow into love. And it has. I like you more than anyone. And I love you more than anyone. And that's always going to be true."

*He loved her.* For so long, she'd wanted to hear those words, would have thought they would send her heart skyrocketing. That didn't happen. It felt like something better—like being cold and having someone cover you with a warm blanket.

"Oh, Jake." She rose and, though she never saw him move, they were suddenly in each other's arms. "I've loved you for so long."

And they kissed. And again. And again.

When they parted, he leaned his forehead against hers. "So how about it? Does this mean you're willing to, maybe, eat dinner with me sometimes? Watch me play hockey? Ride home with me for Thanksgiving?"

"Why, Jake Champagne, are you asking me to go steady with you?"

They both laughed at her use of the phrase from a bygone era.

"Yes, Evans Arlene, I believe I am."

"Only if you'll teach me to ice skate."

And they kissed again.

# Epilogue

*Thanksgiving afternoon*

"You cannot still be hungry," Evans said when Jake pulled his new Suburban into the parking lot of Fat Joe's. He'd said he wanted to "get away for a minute" since they'd barely had a second alone all day.

"Yeah, well." He parked, cut the engine, and turned to sparkle at her, but it wasn't his old sparkle—the kind he still used on everybody else. It was her own special sparkle. "I have to make the most of this quick trip. Hockey pays no mind to Thanksgiving."

They'd left Birmingham last night—with Robbie, Hyacinth, and eight pies in tow—and had to head back first thing in the morning because the Yellowhammers had an afternoon practice and a game on Saturday.

"Who knows when we'll have turkey day in the Delta again?" Jake reached across the space and took her hand. *We'll*, he said, like he believed they would always have Thanksgiving together. It had been a little more than a month now, and Evans had come to believe it, too.

"It's been a fun trip."

Jake let his mouth land in a pout. "One thing I did *not* like…"

"What?" Evans asked, but she knew.

"It was bad enough sleeping by myself last night, but you were in a whole different house. First night we've spent apart since the fall fest." They'd never made it to the party that night. They'd had unfinished business to take care of—glorious business they'd been taking care of ever since.

Evans laughed. "It is not. How many road games have you had?" They'd made a lot of pregame chicken pot pie, too. Sometimes he made it. Sometimes she made it. Sometimes they made it together.

"That doesn't count," he grumbled. "Those couldn't be helped."

"You knew it would be this way. Just because the Delta Queens are happy about us doesn't mean they were going to 'let us sleep together under their roof.'"

"I guess I just forgot there for a minute that I'm a grown-ass man."

Evans hid her smile. "Not in Christine's house, you're not. Are you saying you *wanted* to sit across the breakfast table from my daddy with bedhead?"

He shuddered a little. "Well, when you put it that way."

"They did go to some trouble to have a combined holiday meal, so we didn't have split up for that."

"That," Jake said emphatically, "*was* not going to happen." He looked at her, all soft. "You're a miracle."

"That's what I am!" She grinned at him.

"Well, my lady"—he opened the door—"your table awaits."

She opened her door, but he was there to help her down. "I don't know how you can eat tamales after all that turkey."

"I'm going to try." He led her to the picnic table they had sat at for so many hours, so many times.

"What's this?" There was already a sack of Fat Joe's red-hot tamales and two Abita beers on the table. "I've never known Joe to serve a table."

"I called ahead." This time—for the very first time— Jake sat down beside Evans instead of across from her. The spirit of her sixteen-year-old self appeared and whispered, *"You go, girl."*

"Joe's mellowed, making exceptions for big hockey stars."

"Are you kidding?" Jake slipped an arm around her. "What I want cuts no ice with Joe. He only did it because I told him I was bringing you here for a little reminiscing and romance. Said it was about time."

"I'm not having sex with you on this picnic table."

"That wasn't the kind of romance I was talking about." He looked heavenward. "Although…"

She laughed. "Just a couple more days."

"I guess," he grumbled. "I brought you a present." He laid a small box on the table.

"What's this?"

"Open it and see."

What was inside left her speechless. "Your puck?" The letters were almost worn away, but it was the Miracle on Ice puck.

He nodded. "After finding out Blake had given it to me, Robbie's been relentless—but so have I. I forfeited fair and square, and I wouldn't take it."

"Then how?" She held up the puck.

He rolled his eyes and shook his head. "He brought it to my mother for a hostess gift. Can you believe it?" Evans began to laugh. "And I am here to tell you, Robbie is one thing, but Christine is another. There's no telling her no."

"Why are you giving it to me?"

"I've sworn off magic and good luck charms, but I believe in miracles. You're my miracle, so I thought you should have the Miracle on Ice puck."

Her heart warmed like the late fall Delta sun on her face. "That's very sweet, but can't you just think of it as a memento from Blake?" She pushed the puck toward him.

He looked at the puck, then back at her. "Maybe it could be community property," he said in a whisper, with all the hope in the world in those blue eyes.

It took a beat for it to sink in. "But community property is—" she began.

He nodded. "Assets shared by a husband and wife."

She waited for the fear, the doubt, the panic to move in. But it didn't.

He put his hand over hers. "I don't mean to rush you. I didn't even come here to propose. I just wanted to sit at this table again with my friend, who is now also my whole heart. It just came out. Evie, I don't want to be without you—ever. Maybe you could just begin to consider…"

"Yes," she said.

His eyes were wide with confusion. "What? You'll consider? Or—"

"Or." That sixteen-year-old Evie was doing cartwheels. "I'm saying *yes*. Right now."

"Right now?" He pulled her closer.

"Let's go back and tell everybody," she said.

"Or not…" he whispered in her ear.

She pulled away. "What?"

"Or not." He smiled. "We could *not* go back to that place where we have to sleep in different houses. We could go back to Laurel Springs right now and be at the courthouse first thing in the morning. Saturday night, my wife could watch me play hockey."

His *wife*. It wasn't like she hadn't imagined it a million times, but the word had never come out of his mouth before. "That's crazy," she said, but everything inside her screamed *yes!*

"Is it?" he asked. "Do we need to know each other longer? When we come back here next month, do we want to wake up Christmas morning in different houses?"

It was sounding less and less crazy. "But how would Robbie and Hyacinth get home? Hyacinth only agreed to come because we promised she'd be back by midday on Black Friday."

Jake shrugged. "Somebody'll lend them a farm vehicle or broker a business company car. I think my old Pilot is still kicking around. Or Robbie can rent—" He stopped abruptly. "I'm sorry. I got carried away. It's probably too soon for you."

Was it? Was it too soon to have everything she'd ever wanted?

She rose. "Let's go."

"Where?"

"Home—home to Laurel Springs."

He got a faraway look in his eyes. "Yeah. Home."

"Don't forget the tamales." And she held out her hand to him.

"Not a chance."

And they ran back to the car, toward their new life, taking the smell of tamales with them.

\* \* \* \* \*

# *Acknowledgments*

Many thanks to super agent Tara Gelsomino, who has been with us through every phase of Evie and Jake's story from concept to fruition.

## *About the Author*

*USA TODAY* bestsellers Stephanie Jones and Jean Hovey write together as Alicia Hunter Pace.

Stephanie lives in Tuscaloosa, AL, where she teaches school. She is a native Alabamian who likes football, American history, and people who follow the rules. She is happy to provide a list of said rules to anyone who needs them.

Jean, a former public librarian, lives in Decatur, AL, with her husband in a hundred-year-old house that always wants something from her. She likes to cook but has discovered the joy of Mrs. Paul's fish fillets since becoming a writer.

Stephanie and Jean are both active members in the romance writing community. They write contemporary romance.

You can find them at:

AliciaHunterPace.com
Facebook.com/AliciaHunterPace
Twitter.com/AliciaHPace
Email: aliciahunterpace@gmail.com

*Keep reading for an excerpt from* Smooth as Silk,
*the second book in the Good Southern Women series
by* USA TODAY *bestselling author
Alicia Hunter Pace.*

*Thanksgiving Eve*

One of the best things about living in the American South was that you could eat ice cream in November. Not that it was banned in the Highlands of Scotland, in Switzerland, where Robbie had gone to prep school, or in New England, where he'd played junior and college hockey. You just wouldn't be as inclined.

"Best one yet." He raised his towering cone of mocha praline fudge and smiled at Constance, the owner of Double Scoop.

"That's what you say every day."

"Not *every* day." He licked his cone and headed for the door.

"Near enough." Constance laughed. "Not that I'm complaining."

He was probably eating too much ice cream, if there was any such thing. Double Scoop made their own and had new flavors every week. The cheery little bell chimed behind him as he stepped out onto Main Street. The Laurel Springs shopping district didn't look too different from his village in Scotland—pretty little storefronts with harvest decorations on the sidewalks.

The other thing he liked about the American South was Southern women. Really, he liked all women, but there was something intriguing about how Southern women wore pearls with blue jeans, drank straight bourbon, and put their initials on everything they owned.

And the sunglasses. Never had he known women who had sunglasses appear like magic in their hands the second they put foot to threshold. Maybe it wasn't magic. Maybe it was more like those claws that shot out of Wolverine's hands when he needed to fight, except these women were only fighting the sun.

He hadn't had much female company of late—at least not like he'd had when he was in Nashville. He'd left the Nashville Sound for the new Birmingham, Alabama, team when his best friend, Jake, had, figuring they'd continue on as they had before—keeping company with charming companions, exploring bars, and shutting down parties.

It hadn't turned out that way.

First off, Jake had, for reasons Robbie still wasn't all that clear about, decided he was tired of his partying ways. Then, before the season started, the head coach had been fired for sexual harassment, and Nickolai Glazov, the acting head coach, had threatened Robbie with benching if his bad boy ways showed up on the pro hockey gossip blog *The Face Off Grapevine*. Even if those things hadn't happened, nightlife wasn't exactly hopping here. The Yellowhammers' practice rink and offices had been built in this little outlying village rather than in the thick of downtown Birmingham, and most everyone connected with the Yellowhammer organization had settled here because it was more convenient.

And now Jake had started keeping steady company with his childhood pal Evans—and he was fair besotted, too, from the looks of things. Sure, Robbie could have scared up some excitement if he'd wanted to, but it was too much trouble. He'd lost his running buddy and, after skating and working out, he never felt inclined to drive all the way downtown to hunt a good time that was likely to get him in trouble anyway.

So he was bored.

Apart from some right fine victories on the ice, the most fun he'd had lately was playing piano at the bridal shop for the Laurel Springs Fall Festival last month right before Halloween—even if Hyacinth had gotten her dander up at him. Or maybe that had been part of the fun. He hadn't seen her since that night and wondered if she'd gotten over it yet.

Her shop was just up ahead. Maybe he'd pay her a little visit, see if she was still all wound up. He didn't have anything else to do. Tomorrow was Thanksgiving and Glaz had called practice off this afternoon to give a head start on the holiday, since they had to report back midday on Friday. Hockey didn't pay much mind to Thanksgiving and the Yellowhammers had a game Saturday afternoon.

He crossed the street right in the middle. You could jaywalk in Laurel Springs without getting run over.

The window of Trousseau could use a little work. There were two headless mannequins wearing wedding dresses, and that was the first problem. He hated headless bodies—they gave him the heebie-jeebies. The pumpkins and leaves were okay for this time of year, but Hyacinth needed something that would catch the eye, like blinking lights or an animated scarecrow. Maybe a turkey or two, though he could never understand why Americans decorated with the thing they were going to kill and eat. Santa Claus had better be on guard. Cannibalism might break out anytime.

Speaking of the right jolly old elf... If Robbie put his mind to it, he could think of some really good window decorations for Christmas—silver trees, twinkling stars, and maybe a snowman or some unicorns with flashing horns. People loved unicorns these days. His little nieces fancied them above all else.

Some motion beyond the display caught his eye. What on God's green earth was that and why was Hyacinth allowing it?

There was a woman on a little platform in front of a three-way mirror. Hyacinth and Brad—who'd kept Robbie in water the night of the festival—were hovering around. Hyacinth had a Professor McGonagall look going, all dressed in black, with a tight little bun—but that wasn't what horrified Robbie. It was the bride.

That dress absolutely did not belong on that woman.

Robbie knew everything about weddings that was worth knowing, and not only because he'd been involved in his sisters' weddings—six so far, and two to go. He'd seen hundreds, maybe thousands, of brides and he'd never encountered one in such a train wreck of a frock.

She was wearing a straight dress with a dropped waist that was meant for a tall, very thin woman with not much up top or in the bum area. This bride had a lovely hourglass figure with a small waist that was made for a ball gown. Now that he thought about it, her shape wasn't so different from Hyacinth's. Hyacinth had to know this dress was all wrong, so why had she allowed the bride to try it on? Hyacinth smoothed the skirt, smiled, and said something to the bride when she ought to be hauling her back to the dressing room and getting her out of that dress. If his granny were here, she'd march right in there and tell Hyacinth that she was about to ruin this poor woman's wedding day.

Holy Family and all the wise men! Just when he thought it couldn't get worse, Brad settled a jeweled band with feathers coming off it around the lass's head. It suited the dress but, given that the dress didn't suit the woman, they had no business encouraging her with that little bit of frippery. If somebody didn't put a stop to this, Hyacinth was going to run herself out of business.

He had to go in there. It was his duty as a wedding authority and citizen of the universe.

"Are you sure you wouldn't like to try a ball gown? Or an empire? Both would be so lovely on you," Hyacinth said to Daisy Dubois, who identified with Daisy Buchanan and was set on having a *Gatsby*-themed wedding but did not have the body for this dress. So far, Daisy had ignored Hyacinth's subtle suggestions.

Lois, mother of the bride, bit her lip and looked at the floor, probably wishing she'd never named her daughter Daisy. The four bridesmaids lined up on the sofa were no more enchanted with the dress than Lois. This had been going on so long that they had gone from sneaking peeks at their phones to blatantly scrolling and texting while they knocked back the cheap champagne that Hyacinth served.

There was no chance any of them were going to be honest with Daisy. Hyacinth had been down this road enough times to know that there were two kinds of bridal posses: the overly vocal and critical ones, and the ones who made the consultant be the bad guy. This bunch was firmly in the latter category. Hyacinth would be the bad guy if it came to that, but everyone would be happier if Daisy wised up on her own.

Daisy turned and pulled at the fabric around her hips. "Is it too small? It doesn't feel right."

Hyacinth pretended to study the dress and waited a few beats to say what she already knew. "Not too small. A larger size would swallow your shoulders and waist. This is just the nature of a column dress." Altering wouldn't fix the problem. "Let's try something with a flared skirt." She had already pulled a half-dozen dresses that would be a dream on Daisy. "Maybe a trumpet?"

"Would it have the *Gatsby* look?" Daisy asked.

Hyacinth exchanged looks with Brad. They both knew there was no way to sell that.

"To be honest, no," Hyacinth said, "but it would show off your beautiful small waist."

"And we could do some accessories that would give the feel of the period." You had to hand it to Brad. He always gave it the old college try.

Lois nodded and the bridesmaids looked up from their phones, hopeful.

"No," Daisy said stubbornly. "I don't want the *feel*. I want to look authentic. I want to try another drop waist."

They'd already been through this three times with three different dresses and there were only two more in the right price range. It wasn't going to get better. What Hyacinth needed was that Wonder Woman golden lasso. It would go a long way in getting people to do what they ought to. But she didn't have a magic rope and she was running out of options. Maybe it would be best to let Daisy try on the other two dresses and hope she saw the truth of the matter. If she didn't, Hyacinth would have to be blunt—and maybe confess that she couldn't help her.

"Of course. Let's get you back to the dressing room." Hyacinth held out a hand to help Daisy from the pedestal when the bell above the door jingled.

Hyacinth turned around, set to greet the newcomer, but she froze.

Robbie McTavish. That was the last thing this room needed right now, though it was her own fault he was here. He'd left his grubby kilt and shoes in the dressing room the night of the fall festival and she had procrastinated about calling him. If only she had, she could have directed him to pick his things up on her schedule. Now, not only was he here in the middle of a difficult bridal appointment wearing a faded I heart New York T-shirt with yet another worn-out kilt, he had a chocolate ice cream cone the size of the Statue of Liberty's torch.

The disastrous fall festival cake notwithstanding, Hyacinth did not allow food in her store beyond the champagne and cheese straws she served clients. She had a little whimsical sign outside over a trash can that said, "Check Your Coffee at the Door! Someone's Silk Dream Is Inside." Apparently she needed to add ice cream to that sign.

"Hey, Robbie," Brad said.

Robbie nodded. "Brad, my friend. You owe me a *Mortal Kombat* rematch."

"And you owe me a burger. I paid last time because you didn't have your wallet."

Brad had befriended this soup sandwich of a man? That was news to her, but none of her business. They were just an unlikely pair.

Robbie settled his eyes on Hyacinth. "And the lovely Hyacinth." He gave a nod to Daisy and then to her entourage. "Ladies."

"You must be here for your shoes and kilt," Hyacinth said. "I'll get them for you."

Robbie looked surprised. "I left them here? I wondered where they got off to. I had to get new gutties." He held up a glow-in-the-dark green running shoe. He had a scrape on his knee that needed some Neosporin and a bandage. It was when she was wondering idly how he'd hurt himself that she noticed his leg—and then the other one. They were chiseled, strong, and very attractive. How had she missed that before? "Do you like them?" She might have thought he was referring to his legs if he hadn't pressed a button on the shoe, causing the soles to burst into a light show. "Fancy, huh?"

"I didn't know they made those for adults." If he wasn't here for his belongings, *why* was he here? Not that it mattered. Good legs or no, she had to get rid of him. Bridal parties were notoriously protective of their time. But when Hyacinth turned to gauge the mood of the room, Daisy and Lois were smiling so bright you could practically see moonbeams swirling around them, and the bridesmaids sat a little straighter and had put down their phones. One crossed her legs and another pushed her hair off her face.

Okay, so he was hot. Annoying, but hot.

"Excuse me a moment," she said to the bridal party. "I'll be right back." She turned to Robbie. "Come with me. I'll get your things." Once they were out of earshot, she added with a hiss, "You need to take that ice cream and get out of here."

"What?" He licked the cone.

"The ice cream. I don't allow food in the store."

"What about the haunted house cake?" He continued following her as she turned the corner and advanced toward the counter—licking as he went.

"That was different." She turned around. "Stop right here. Stay clear of that dress display."

But she'd stopped too quickly and he'd been too hot on her heels. She knew what was going to happen by the look on his face before the huge scoop of chocolate sailed off the cone, over her shoulder, down the front of the new Rayna Kwan that she had put on display just this morning.

His mouth formed an O.

"Fuck," she said. (She never said fuck. Never thought it, it seemed, unless this man was around.) But nothing called for bad words like eight thousand dollars' worth of ruined beaded silk.

"Holy Family and all the wise men," he whispered, his brogue more pronounced.

They were both frozen in time.

He went into action first. "Sorry. I'll fix it." He removed the paper napkin from around his now empty cone and started to dab at the stain—and what a stain it was. There was a four-inch-wide band of chocolate from shoulder to waist—not unlike a royal sash—and splatters peppered down the front of the skirt.

"Stop! You can't fix it."

"I'll pay for it." He scooped up the ice cream from the floor and stood looking at it melting in his hand.

She grabbed the small trash can behind the counter and held it out to him. "Here," she said wearily.

He looked at the ice cream mournfully before he dropped it in. "I'll pay for it," he repeated as he wiped his hands on his kilt.

"I just put that out so it would be ready for an appointment I have on Black Friday." After numerous conversations with Connie Millwood about what she was looking for, and many hours of searching, Hyacinth had deemed this perfect for her. "The bride is coming from Georgia for the appointment."

"Did she ask for this dress?" He pointed at the ruined gown. "*This* particular one?"

"No…" she had to admit. But it had everything she wanted—the corset bodice, sweetheart neckline, mermaid skirt, crystal embellishments, and all the rest… Now it was a chocolate mess.

Robbie McTavish had the audacity to smile. "No problem, then. There can be another. And, as I said, I'll pay. I promise I can afford it."

"Not the point. Do you have any idea how much time and effort I put into finding a dress that fit this particular bride's body type, vision, and budget? How many hours I spend finding the perfect thing for every bride who walks through my door? You can't put a price on that."

"Well." He gave a backward glance to where Brad

was helping Daisy onto the platform in yet another un-flattering flapper dress. Robbie looked at her and raised an eyebrow. "That right there is indeed a product of genius."

The burning bush that was her head burned brighter—though to be fair, this might not have been the best time to point out her styling skills.

"You need to leave. Now. Out the back door. You've done enough here."

But did he do that? Of course not. He shrugged, threw a smile over his shoulder, and advanced on the bride. Hyacinth had to practically run to keep up with him.

"Lass, aren't you a vision. You're getting married. I fair love brides."

Daisy blushed. "I am. In eight months. It's going to be a *Gatsby*-themed wedding. I want it to be like the party in the movie—the one with Leo DiCaprio. I love that movie."

"Aye." Robbie nodded. "So do I."

Hyacinth would bet every inch of lace in the place that he'd never seen it.

"You want to look like Daisy? A flapper girl?" Robbie asked.

All right. Maybe she would have lost her lace, but she had trouble trusting haphazard people—and she knew haphazard—had cut her teeth on turned-off electricity, lost keys, and chronic, habitual tardiness. But no more. She'd fought to stay away from chaos all her life—fought hard—and now it had invaded her ordered little pristine world in the form of red hair, a faded kilt, and neon flashing shoes. And good legs.

Her heart raced.

The bride of the moment, however, had no sense that chaos was swirling about her. "My name is Daisy." She blushed some more.

"Ah, a beautiful name. Did you know it's sometimes a nickname for Margaret?"

"No. I'm just plain Daisy—named for my grand-mother."

"Never just plain. You could never be that."

He was getting more Scottish by the second and Daisy was eating it with a spoon. Hyacinth's heart raced even more. She'd lost control and had no idea how to recapture it. But she had to try.

"My name is Robbie, named for my grandda." His attention was fully on Daisy.

"You're from Scotland." Daisy stated the obvious.

"Aye. My family has a wedding business. Our an-cestral castle's the most popular spot for hitching in the whole of the country. We've had more weddings than Gretna Green." That was interesting, but was the mayor of Haphazard City telling the truth this time? He had no reason to lie, but neither had her dad had a reason to say he'd played guitar with Eric Clapton. "I've seen more brides than stars in the sky, but none more bonnie than you." He reached out like he was going to take Daisy's hands in his—hands he had not washed.

*Chocolate hands!* Fuck, fuck, fuck!

One ruined dress was one too many. She would be damned if there were going to be two. She grabbed the champagne bottle from the bucket on the table, tore off the damp cloth napkin, and slapped it in Robbie's hand.

"Ice cream," she said as if that explained everything.

She scrubbed first one hand and then the other. It was impossible to ignore that his hands were big, strong, and warm. But she didn't care about any of that. She only cared that they were clean before they touched another thing in her shop.

But then…but *then*…he circled her palm with his thumb. Slowly. And her body betrayed her by wanting him to do it again. And her body betrayed her again by raising her face to look at his. He dropped his eyelids to half-mast and smiled like he had a secret. Her stomach turned over. And no wonder. She hadn't had sex in nearly two years, hadn't been touched by a man except in passing in nearly as long.

And he squeezed her hand—but she would not let her body betray her again and squeeze back. Hell, no. She couldn't control everything—or really, maybe much of anything—but she could control this.

She jerked her hands away.

The silence in the room was deafening. Clearly they all thought she'd lost her mind. Well, let them think it. They weren't the guardians of thousands of dollars' worth of silk, satin, and lace.

"Thank you, lass." There was an edge of laughter in his voice. "It's been a while since I've needed someone to clean me up."

Before she could suggest that he run along now, he took right up where he'd left off with Daisy. This time, he succeeded in taking her hands, and he spread them wide as if to get a better look at her. Someone from the bridesmaid gallery sighed.

And all Hyacinth could do was stand there clutching a chocolate-stained napkin and watch it happen.

Daisy smiled at him like he'd been invented for her alone. Best case, he was going to convince her that dress had been made for her. Worst case, she was going to throw her engagement ring against the wall and follow him to the ends of the earth. And it would be preserved for posterity because one of the bridesmaids seemed to be videoing now. Hyacinth vaguely wondered how long that had been going on.

"There was a Scottish queen called Margaret— Margaret Tudor, wife of James IV of Scotland. She was Henry VIII's sister. Her marriage was a love match and James called her Daisy."

"Oh…" Daisy put her hand to her heart. More lies and Daisy was eating it up.

"She was a princess when she got married. Every girl ought to be a princess at her wedding, don't you think?"

Daisy nodded wide-eyed.

"I know you're going to get married in that flapper dress—and it looks wonderful. It truly does. But you know what I'd love? To see you in a real princess dress. Would you like to try one on, for fun?"

"Well…" Daisy cocked her head to the side and chewed on her bottom lip. It was all too obvious she wasn't going to tell him no. Hyacinth suspected that few did.

"Hyacinth won't mind, will you, Hyacinth?" Robbie gave her a crooked smile.

"Not at all." What else could she say? Besides, maybe this little development would turn things around. Here was the chance to get Daisy in the ivory A-line with a tiered skirt and portrait back. But she had to get rid of him, without sounding like a bitch in front of these people. She bit her lip and tried hard to channel her classy friend Ava Grace. "I know of just the thing. But I can take it from here, Robbie. I know you are a busy, busy man. Thank you oh-so-much for your assistance. Daisy, come with me." Hyacinth held out her hand. "Goodbye, Robbie."

"But Robbie wants to see me look like a princess."

Mother of pearl. This was the biggest nightmare in Nightmare City.

"Yes, Hyacinth. I never miss a chance for a princess sighting. I go to Disney World twice a year for that particular pleasure."

Every woman in the place burst into delighted laughter. And so did Brad. Traitor.

"Of course," Hyacinth acquiesced through gritted teeth. No getting rid of him yet. "Daisy?" She held out her hand again. "Let's see what we can find."

"Brilliant!" And before Hyacinth could stop him, Robbie went tearing around the showroom flipping through dresses. "I'll find something."

Lois and the bridesmaids chattered and giggled. Hyacinth picked up a word here and there—*charming, so funny, isn't he the sweetest?*

She stomped off after Robbie. "Stop it," she called. "That's the ball gown section. Daisy has made clear she will not have a ball gown. I've tried!"

By now she'd caught up with him and she was close enough for him to whisper. "Daisy doesn't know what she wants. She only thinks she does." And he continued to flip through the dresses.

"What do you know about wedding dresses?" she hissed at him.

"More than you think. Ah!" He didn't look at Hyacinth, but turned back to Daisy and her posse. "This! This! I've got it!" he called across the shop. And he presented Daisy with the biggest, blingiest ball gown in the shop—the Simone Donatella with the silver-beaded bodice and hem.

Daisy put her hands on her cheeks. "I could try it on—you know. Just for fun. But is it my size?"

"No." Hyacinth put her hands on her hips. This dress was a six and Daisy needed an eight.

"It'll fit," Robbie said. "Numbers don't matter. I have an eye for these things."

Brad took the dress from Robbie. "I'll take you back. Patty's waiting to help you."

The dress was two thousand dollars over Lois's budget, it wouldn't fit, and Daisy wouldn't go for it anyway. Yet this could be productive. Maybe Daisy had begun to think outside the box a little. While a ball gown was too far in the extreme from Daisy's vision, maybe they could get her in a romantic lacy empire or the ivory A-line.

Meanwhile, Robbie was leaving the minute he saw Daisy in this dress—and she intended to tell him that right now. Having collected herself, she walked back toward the seating area, where Robbie had made himself comfortable in the chair across from Lois.

"You have a real, live castle?" one of the bridesmaids asked as she handed him a glass of champagne—champagne meant for customers. "Does it have a name?"

"Aye. A wee one, as castles go. Thank you, lass." He accepted the glass and took a sip. "Wyndloch's the name, though my mum calls it Castle Crumble."

No way was he telling the truth. He'd happened on her shop, started wreaking havoc, and now his family was in the wedding business. That was all too convenient. Besides, wouldn't he have mentioned it when he was here for fall fest?

But apparently these people believed him. "And how did your family castle ever end up turning into a wedding venue?" Lois asked.

"Aye." Robbie nodded. "Came a time when keeping sheep didn't pay the bills. My great-grandma had the idea to let out the homestead for parties and weddings. Now Wyndloch is right popular."

Time to call his bluff. "Where might I have seen it advertised?" Hyacinth asked.

He shrugged. "Maybe you wouldn't have. We don't have to advertise."

"Mmmm. I see," Hyacinth said. "Waiting list?"

"Four years."

Despite herself, Hyacinth found herself buying into this—and she wasn't sure why she wanted so badly for him to be lying.

She could find out, here and now. She whipped out her phone and googled *Windlock Wedding Venue Scotland*. The site came up, despite her incorrect spelling. So he wasn't lying. She might have still doubted him had there not been a picture of the McTavish clan—including Robbie—standing in front of the "wee" castle—which had to be forty thousand square feet at the smallest. There were at least thirty McTavishes and they were all wearing tartan—the men in kilts, the women in skirts. She squinted. A small redheaded girl stood in front of Robbie, totally obscuring his legs. He had his hand on her head.

"Look at me, Mama!" Daisy swept into the show-room with Patty and Brad carrying her massive skirts.

Everyone—even Robbie—went silent as Brad helped Daisy onto the platform.

It was the perfect fit.

Daisy beamed at Robbie. "It feels…right." Lois and the bridesmaids gathered around her. "I could still have my *Gatsby* wedding, couldn't I? It wouldn't ruin it if I wore this dress, would it?"

"Of course not," Lois said, with the bridesmaids backing her up like a relieved Greek chorus.

"I think a princess does what she likes," Robbie said.

"But how much does it cost?" Daisy asked.

Now for the bad news. Maybe Robbie would buy it for her. It would serve him right to have to pay for this dress *and* the Rayna Kwan. He'd started this. Hyacinth never showed a bride a dress out of her price range.

"Your grandma Daisy said if you found *the* one she would pay the extra, up to four thousand dollars." Lois cast a questioning look at Hyacinth.

Relief settled over Hyacinth. It would probably take that. A veil to go with a dress like this was considerably more than a feathered headband.

"That will cover it," Hyacinth said. "How about we try some veils?"

"And a tiara?" Daisy asked breathlessly. "Could I have a tiara?"

"I'd be disappointed if you didn't want one," Hyacinth said.

"And I think a crystal-and-silver-beaded belt to accentuate your small waist," Brad said.

This was the best part of a bridal appointment—when the dress had been chosen and the bride was

truly delighted. The choosing of the veil and accessories and making appointments for fittings was all
high-spirited fun—sort of like picking up last-minute
stocking stuffers on Christmas Eve after the hard holiday things had already been done. Or at least that was
how Hyacinth imagined Christmas was for most people. Since her grandmother had died, she only had her
staff, Claire, Evans, and Ava Grace to buy for. That had
been done since August.

It was almost closing time when Lois slipped her
credit card to Hyacinth. "Tell Robbie thank you,"
she whispered. "I don't think we'd have a dress if he
hadn't charmed her into trying it on. It's almost as if
you planned it."

Hyacinth barked a little laugh as she ran the card. "I
can assure you that I did not plan for Robbie McTavish."

Where was he anyway? She'd all but forgotten him.
Evidently he had no opinions on veils because they
hadn't heard from him in a while. Her eyes cast quickly
about the store—he was nowhere to be found. Thank
goodness he'd left. She let out her first full breath in
a half hour.

But after she'd ushered Daisy and her posse out, Hyacinth caught sight of him sitting on the floor, leaning
against the accessories counter, eyes cast down, looking
as sad as she'd ever seen a man look. A chord of sympathy chimed inside her, though she had no idea what
she was sympathizing with. Maybe Trousseau made
him miss home. Maybe Daisy had reminded him of a
lost sweetheart.

"You're still here." She came up beside him.

He turned. "Hello, lass. All well with Daisy?"

"Yes." She was considering asking him why he seemed sad when she caught sight of where he'd been looking—the small trash can that contained the remains of his ice cream cone. The little sympathy chime turned into an iron clanging bell. "Please tell me you weren't considering eating ice cream out of a trash can."

He rubbed the back of his neck and squinted his eyes mostly shut. "Naw," he said around a yawn. "It's melted."

"It's melted? And that's the only reason you didn't consider eating out of a trash can?"

He shrugged. "How dirty could it be? It's not like you're butchering hogs in here. You're selling wedding dresses." He looked down at the can one last time and ambled to his feet. "It was excellent."

"If it was that excellent, why didn't you just go away and eat it instead of coming in here ruining dresses and causing chaos?"

"That girl needed help. *You* needed help." His green eyes bored into hers and he took a step closer.

Every hair on her body stood on end.

"*I* needed help? How do you figure that?"

"How do you figure that you didn't? The dress was all wrong for the girl. In the wedding business, your reputation is everything. And there is no repeat business—or at least not enough to count. What would people have thought if you had let Daisy go down the aisle wearing that dress?"

"If I had let her? *Let* her?" She wanted to scream. "For your information, I knew the dress was all wrong for her. I had done everything I could to steer her in a different direction. There was nothing else to do but hope she would figure it out for herself."

"She wasn't showing any signs of it."

"How do you know? You'd been in here all of fifteen seconds before you insinuated yourself in the situation."

"I was right, wasn't I?"

She would have rolled in mud wearing the most expensive dress in the shop before admitting that she'd been about to lead Daisy away to try on more of the same.

"She knew it wasn't right." That was true. "She was coming around." Debatable.

"Would you have sold it to her?" Robbie lifted his chin. "No matter how bad it looked?"

"Not without telling her point-blank that it wasn't flattering."

"Have you ever done that?" He took another step closer to her, all the while looking so smug, like he knew the answer.

"A few times. Most of the time the bride will see it on her own and I can guide her toward something suitable." He was close enough that she felt his body heat, but she would *not* step away. No way would she give him the satisfaction of thinking she had noticed.

"But if she hadn't?" He dropped his face closer to hers. Damn. He smelled like chocolate, probably tasted of it. "Would you have sold it to her?"

"You say that like you wouldn't have. In the end, it's not my decision."

"Reputation."

In truth, she'd never sold a dress that was truly hideously unflattering. But she wasn't going to tell Robbie that.

"You showed her a dress that was way out of her price range."

"Clearly not. They bought it." He narrowed his eyes and didn't quite close his mouth when he finished speaking.

"It's cruel to show someone something they can't have."

The moment froze. They locked gazes for what seemed like a long time.

Then the spell broke. "You're right." Robbie closed his eyes and stepped back out of her space. "It worked out."

"This time."

He came across with that damned cocky crooked grin again. "I have some other ideas for you. Your showcase window could use some livening up. I'm going away with a friend for Thanksgiving, but let me take you to dinner next week and I'll share my ideas."

Hyacinth stopped cold. He did *not* say that to her!

"This was kind of fun. The next time you have a difficult bride, call me. I'll be glad to come help you out." He frowned like he was trying to work something out, then brightened. "I know. I'll get you some game tickets. You can come see me play. Then we'll have dinner."

There weren't enough deep breaths or golden lassos in the universe to bring her back from this.

"I don't like hockey. I don't have time for it." Never mind that Claire had given her a whole set of season tickets.

"You don't like hockey?" He said that as if she'd said she didn't like breathing. "Well, just dinner, then. I can still help you out with your window and I might change your mind about hockey."

"Tell you what, Robbie, let's *not* have dinner. I can

tend to my own window and my own brides. You tend to your hockey and leave me out of it."

"I can tend to more than one thing."

"Here, tend to this." She reached under the counter and got a bag that contained the kilt and shoes he'd left. "I mended the hem." She had not been able to help herself. She'd washed it, too.

"That was good of you." He looked inside the bag. "It looks like it's been ironed."

She gave a half nod. "Only sloppy seamstresses don't press their work." Memaw had taught her that.

"Then I *do* owe you dinner." He held out his hand. "What do you say?"

"I say no, thank you."

"Have it your own way," he said.

"Believe me, I try, but that seems nigh on impossible when you're around."

He laughed. "Goodbye, lass, I'll be going now. Need to pack for a little trip I'm taking. You have yourself a fine Turkey Day." He gave a little salute as he left.

She locked the door after him and sighed with relief. Never had she known a human who wore her out like Robbie McTavish.

Why was she not surprised that he wasn't packed for wherever it was he was going? She was taking a little trip, too—to the Delta for a quick turnaround Thanksgiving. Her suitcase was not only packed, but sitting by her front door at home, where Jake and Evans were going to pick her up.

Her stomach did a happy little flip-flop, like it did every time she remembered, since the fall fest, that Evans had been hip deep in what seemed like the romance of the century with one of those Yellowhammers. This was her best chance yet for getting on *All Dressed in White*.

Also, her first chance. Her only chance so far. If only they would get engaged.

*Don't miss* Smooth as Silk *by*
USA TODAY *bestselling author Alicia Hunter Pace,*
*available wherever Carina Press books are sold.*

*www.CarinaPress.com*

*Also available from Alicia Hunter Pace*
Sweet Gone South

Welcome to Merritt, Alabama, where summers are lazy, tea is sweet, and guests are always welcome…

Luke Avery needs a wife to help raise his motherless three-year-old. Candy shop owner Lanie Heaven desires a child but can never have her own. When Luke moves into the apartment above Lanie's shop, she can't help falling for the sexy single dad and his sweet little girl.

Luke's not planning to fall in love ever again—but easing the ache of loneliness with pretty Lanie isn't falling in love. Still, proposing to her could solve all his problems and give his child what she needs.

Lanie believes her dreams of love and family are finally coming true. Until she's faced with evidence that Luke's heart is locked away tight. Can Luke learn to slay his demons and put the past to rest? Or will he lose Lanie—and any hope he might've had for a sweet life—forever?